*She pledged to be his wife,
but can she capture his heart?*

A CONVENIENT
Marriage

Three classic stories from
beloved authors
Betty Neels,
Liz Fielding
& Lindsay Armstrong

Betty Neels sadly passed away in 2001. As one of our best-loved authors, Betty will be greatly missed, both by her friends at Mills & Boon and by her legions of loyal readers around the world. Betty was a prolific writer who has left a lasting legacy through her heart-warming novels, and she will always be remembered as a truly delightful person who brought great happiness to many.

Liz Fielding was born with itchy feet. She made it to Zambia before her twenty-first birthday and, gathering her own special hero and a couple of children on the way, lived in Botswana, Kenya and Bahrain – with pauses for sightseeing pretty much everywhere in between. She finally came to a full stop in a tiny Welsh village cradled by misty hills and these days, mostly, leaves her pen to do the travelling.

When she's not sorting out the lives and loves of her characters, she potters in the garden, reads her favourite authors and spends a lot of time wondering "What if..." For news of upcoming books – and to sign up for her occasional news-letter – visit Liz's website at www.lizfielding.com

Don't miss Liz Fielding's exciting new novel, *Secret Baby, Surprise Parents,* available this month from Mills & Boon® Romance.

Lindsay Armstrong was born in South Africa but now lives in Australia with her New Zealand-born husband and their five children. They have lived in nearly every state of Australia and have tried their hand at some unusual – for them – occupations, such as farming and horse-training – all grist to the mill for a writer! Lindsay started writing romances when their youngest child began school and she was left feeling at a loose end. She is still doing it and loving it.

A CONVENIENT
Marriage

Betty Neels
Liz Fielding
Lindsay Armstrong

M&B™ and M&B™ with the Rose Device
are trademarks of the publisher.
Harlequin Mills & Boon Limited, Eton House,
18-24 Paradise Road, Richmond, Surrey TW9 1SR

A CONVENIENT MARRIAGE
© by Harlequin Books S.A. 2009

The Hasty Marriage © Betty Neels 1977
A Wife on Paper © Liz Fielding 2004
When Enemies Marry... © Lindsay Armstrong 1995

ISBN: 978 0 263 87512 6

024-0409

Printed and bound in Spain
by Litografía Rosés S.A., Barcelona

THE HASTY MARRIAGE

Betty Neels

CHAPTER ONE

LAURA heard the car draw up outside the house while she was still in the kitchen cutting bread and butter for tea, but she didn't stop what she was doing. Her father and Joyce would be in the sitting room waiting for their visitors, and there would be a small delay while they were greeted and ushered indoors; she would be able to slip in at the last minute.

She started to arrange the slices on a plate, reflecting that it would be pleasant to see her godfather again; he had always come to England at least twice a year, but now, since his illness, he lived semi-retired from his medical practice and no longer drove a car. It was fortunate that there had been this old friend who had been coming to England anyway and had suggested that they might travel together. She laid the last slice in its place, washed her hands

and went from the nice old-fashioned kitchen, down
the back hall and into the sitting room. Old Doctor
van Doorn de Pette was there, sitting in one of the
large, rather shabby armchairs by the window,
talking to her father, and she went straight to him
and gave him an affectionate hug.

'Lovely to see you, Godfather,' she exclaimed in
her pretty voice. 'You must be tired—tea's all
ready.'

He studied her, smiling. 'Dear Laura—not
changed, and glad I am of it. Tea will be delightful,
but first you must meet my friend, Reilof van
Meerum.'

She had been aware of him, of course, talking to
Joyce at the other end of the long, low-ceilinged
room, but she hadn't looked at him. And now,
crossing the polished floor to shake his hand, she
hardly heard her godfather saying: 'My goddaugh-
ter, Reilof—Laura,' for she was fighting bewilder-
ment and delight and surprise all rolled into one,
because at last here was the man she had been
waiting for—standing in front of her, all six feet
three inches of him, rather heavily built and no
longer young—but then she was twenty-nine herself,
wasn't she?—and so incredibly good-looking, with
his dark hair silvered at the temples and dark eyes
under heavy brows. With the greatest effort in the

world she composed her ordinary features into a conventional smile of greeting, said 'How do you do?' with a calm she didn't feel and made some remark about his journey. He answered her politely, and when Joyce chimed in, turned back to her with every sign of interest—and not to be wondered at, conceded Laura, as she went back to her father to tell him that she would be bringing in the tea tray in a few minutes, Joyce was worth anyone's interest; pretty—very pretty and fair, with large baby blue eyes, and nine years her junior to boot.

She thought it without envy; from the moment that Joyce had been born, she had been the focal point of the household, and later, of their circle of friends, and although she had been spoilt by her parents, very few had ever discovered the fact. As for Laura, she had quickly come to take it for granted, for when her sister was born she had been a disappointingly gawky child of nine, with light brown hair, straight and fine and worn, for convenience's sake, in two pigtails, and her small face, its childish chubbiness lost, was already settling into its unexciting mould. Only her hazel eyes were fine, large and richly lashed, but even they stood no chance against Joyce's gorgeous blue ones.

It was natural enough that her mother and father should have been delighted to have such a pretty little girl, and she herself had been overjoyed to have a small sister; Laura had spoilt her too, and after their mother had died she had done her best to take her place, but somehow, by the time Joyce was twelve years old, she was already making it plain that she no longer needed Laura for a companion, and it had been a relief to them both when Laura went away to London to train as a nurse. Now, although she came home fairly frequently, she had grown used to Joyce's casual treatment and her assumption that when Laura was home she would take over the burden of the household so that Joyce might be free to go where and when she wanted.

She went back to the kitchen and picked up the loaded tray, and was faintly surprised when Doctor van Meerum crossed the room to take it from her, and caught Joyce's quick frown as he did so—so silly of her to be annoyed, thought Laura, when he was only being polite; surely his quick, impersonal smile made that clear.

The conversation became general during tea, but that didn't disguise the fact that Joyce had captivated their visitor, and indeed she was behaving charmingly. Laura, watching her, thought how nice it must be to attract people—men, she amended honestly—without any effort at all. She took very little part in the talk, but occupied herself with filling the teacups and passing plates of cake and sandwiches, replying to any remarks made to her in her unassuming way, and when tea was finished, sitting quietly beside her godfather, listening to him discussing the finer points of an article he had just had published.

While she listened she glanced from time to time at Joyce and Doctor van Meerum, sitting a little apart, deep in a talk of their own. They made a striking pair; Joyce, her cheeks faintly pink with excitement, her eyes wide, had the big, rather silent man beside her already ensnared. Laura told herself that if they were mutually attracted, there was nothing to do about it; he might be the man she had dreamed about for so long, but that didn't mean that she could expect him to fall for her; in any case, while Joyce was around that was so unlikely as to be laughable.

She started to put the tea things back on the tray very quietly, so as not to disturb the conversation, wondering if it might not have been better never to have met Reilof van Meerum than to have found him now only to see him bowled over by Joyce's lovely little face. She went into the kitchen again and washed up, fed Mittens the cat and started to get the supper ready. Presumably the doctor would stay, and anyway one more would make no difference.

She put the soup she had made that morning on to heat, for the April evening was chilly, and started on a cheese soufflé. She had made a trifle that afternoon and there was plenty of cheese, and now she poked round in the old-fashioned larder for ingredients with which to make a salad; apples and a tomato or two, a lettuce and a providential head of celery—she mixed a dressing for it, put the soufflé into the oven and went to lay the table.

The dining room looked cosy, for she had had the forethought to light a small fire there; its rather shabby old-fashioned furniture looked pleasant in the light of the shaded lamp over the big mahogany table, the silver shone in it too, and when she had finished she looked at it with satisfaction and then ran upstairs to her room to tidy herself before putting out the drinks. Her room was at the back of the house, square and airy and furnished with the white-painted furniture of her childhood. She sat down before her dressing-table glass, making no attempt to do her face or hair, but staring at her reflection with a critical eye. She wasn't exactly plain, but she wasn't pretty either. Her mouse-brown hair was fine and silky and very long, but as she usually wore it piled on top of her head, its beauty was scarcely seen, and although her eyes were nice they weren't in the least spectacular. Her nose and mouth were just ordinary, and although her figure was pretty she was barely of middle height, and as she tended to dress in an unassuming manner it was seldom that anyone took a second glance at her.

But her mouselike appearance was deceptive; she was a clever girl and a splendid nurse, holding a Ward Sister's post at St Anne's hospital in London, highly prized by the people she worked with and for. Besides, she was a good housewife and cook, got on well with animals and children and was liked by everyone. But she also had a fine temper when roused to anger, which wasn't often, and could be, on occasion, extremely pig-headed. She had long ago come to terms with herself and accepted life as it came, and if it wasn't quite what she had hoped it would be, no one heard her say so. She spoke to her reflection now:

'It's a good thing that you're going back to St Anne's in the morning, my girl, before you start getting silly ideas into your head—out of sight, out of mind, and don't you forget it.' She nodded sternly at herself, smoothed her hair, powdered her undistinguished nose and went back downstairs, where she was greeted with the news that Doctor van Meerum had accepted Joyce's invitation to stay the night and go on to London in the morning. It vexed her very much to hear her sister declare: 'You can

give Laura a lift,' with the certainty of one accus-
tomed to having her every wish granted; she wasn't
in the least deceived by his polite agreement to do
this—he wanted to please Joyce…

Laura had plenty of opportunity to observe
Doctor van Meerum during supper. His manners
were nice and he had undoubted charm; he main-
tained a steady flow of small talk without monopo-
lising the conversation, said very little about
himself, gave his full attention to any remarks addressed to him and showed a sense of humour which
delighted her. All the same he was unable to prevent
his dark eyes dwelling upon Joyce whenever the
opportunity occurred, and his smile, when their eyes
met, would have set any girl's heart beating faster.
It annoyed Laura that she had no control over that
organ and was forced to suffer its thumping and
jumping. It almost stopped altogether when they
had finished their meal at last and she began to clear
the table as the company dispersed to the sitting
room, for he turned round at the door to look at her
and then walked back into the room, saying, 'You
must let me help you…'

She had no chance to say yes or no, for Joyce had
turned round too and cried with careless affection,
'Darling, I'll wash up, you've had all the chores to

do—Reilof will help me.' She turned a laughing face to his. 'You will, won't you? Although I don't think you do it at home.'

He laughed with her. 'No, I can't say I do, but I see no reason why I shouldn't try my hand at it.' He added, with a quick kindly glance at Laura: 'You must be wanting a chance to talk to your godfather.'

She pinned a cheerful, pleased expression on to her features and agreed untruthfully that there was nothing she wanted more, and slipped away to run upstairs and make up the bed in one of the spare rooms.

The house, although not large, rambled a good deal, with several rather poky passages, unnecessary steps and a variety of windows. The room she went into had a square bay overlooking the flat Essex countryside, flooded in moonlight, and she stood for a minute or two to admire it before she pulled the curtains and began to make the bed. That done, and the room ready for their unexpected guest, she went along to her own room once more to pack her over-night bag; she had had a long weekend and it was a pity that her godfather had arrived only a few hours before she would have to leave. Still, she would be able to come home again at the end of the week, she had Friday evening and a free day on Saturday and it was only thirty or so miles from London. Perhaps Joyce would be free to drive in to Chelmsford and meet her train; if not she could always get old Bates, who ran a taxi service in Rodwell, to fetch her.

She went downstairs again and found the two older gentlemen happily deep in medical matters and no sign of the other two. She fetched the petit-point she was stitching and settled down at a small work table, a lamp at her shoulder, and began to work on it. It was almost two hours later when Joyce and the doctor came in and her sister explained, 'It was such a heavenly moonlit evening, we went for a walk—I hope you didn't miss us?'

Her father paused momentarily to look at her fondly. 'I can't say that we have, my dear, and Laura has been so engrossed in that embroidery of hers that I don't suppose she has either.'

Laura looked up and smiled in the general direction of everyone. 'Such a nice peaceful occupation,' she murmured.

'Oh, Laura,' Joyce laughed, 'you sound just like an old maid, and you're not—at least, not just yet.'

There was general laughter at her joke and Laura joined in, although it wasn't a joke really—Doctor van Meerum would know, if he hadn't realised it already, that she was getting a little long in the tooth. But it wasn't that which hurt, it was knowing that her sister considered her past the age to attract a man's interest and found it amusing.

They set out after breakfast the following morning, she and Doctor van Meerum, in his Aston Martin, and although she had spent a more or less sleepless night, she perked up at the sight of the elegant car—she hadn't seen it the previous evening and she had imagined that he would drive something far more staid; he hadn't struck her as being the type of man to like fast cars.

She couldn't have been more mistaken; he was a superb driver, fast and careful and relaxed. She sat back and enjoyed it all, keeping quiet because she sensed that he didn't want to talk much. They were halfway there and hadn't exchanged more than a few words when he asked suddenly: 'Joyce—she tells me that she has just left her job. Does she intend to become a nurse too?'

Joyce had left several jobs if the truth were to be told; she became bored easily, or the office was too small, the people she worked with not to her liking or she wasn't paid enough... But Laura was a loyal sister.

'No, I don't think so,' she told him carefully, 'it upsets her to see people who are ill—she's young and it's difficult to decide what one wants to do sometimes. I expect she'll stay at home...'

'You didn't, you decided,' he persisted.

'Yes, but nursing was something I wanted to do.'

She didn't tell him that she had wanted to be a doctor, but somehow it had all fallen through because Joyce had to be educated at the best schools. It had taken her a long time to get over the disappointment. But that had been ten years ago and in that time she had become content enough, but always cherishing the hope that she would meet the man she would want to marry and who would want to marry her—and now she had, and a lot of good it had done her. She roused herself from her thoughts to hear her companion say, 'Joyce is a very lovely girl, she must have any number of men friends.'

'Oh, rather, but not one special one.'

'And you?' he asked, to surprise her.

She told him no rather shortly and briskly changed the conversation. 'Are you going to be in England long?'

They were driving more slowly now, with London's outskirts creeping upon them from all sides. 'A week or so—I have to go to Birmingham in a few days and then to Edinburgh. I hope I may have the opportunity of seeing you again before I go back.'

'But you'll be driving Godfather home, won't you?'

'Certainly.'

'Oh, you mean to come and see us before then,' she stated forthrightly. 'I'm sure Father and Joyce will love to see you—don't wait to be invited...'

'Joyce has asked me to stay the night on my way to Birmingham if I could arrange it—perhaps I could give you a lift home? Let me see, it would be on a Friday or Saturday—next weekend.'

'What a pity,' said Laura instantly, longing to accept and perversely determined to do no such thing, 'I've already promised my staff nurse the weekend and I couldn't possibly disappoint her, but thank you for asking.' She would have to remember to give Pat Emery, her right hand on the ward, a long weekend and invent some excuse for not taking her own usual weekend. 'If you would drop me off somewhere along Stratford Broadway, I can pick up a bus. I've heaps of time.'

'I'm going to St Anne's—I have to meet Mr Burnett there.'

She would be seeing Mr Burnett herself in a few hours' time; he was the senior consulting surgeon on Men's Surgical. She said: 'Oh,' rather blankly and added, 'Do you know the way?'

'Yes, thanks.' He demonstrated his knowledge by taking a short cut through the rather dingy streets around them. 'Do you go to Holland to visit your godfather?'

'No, but I'd like to. He's always come to us, you see. He and Father are such old friends—they talk and talk…' She broke off as there was a sudden commotion in front of them; a squealing of brakes, shouting and a dog's yelp. The car in front of them turned off the road, giving them a view of a group of people standing to stare at a little dog lying in the road. It tried to crawl away, yelped again, and lay still.

'Stop!' commanded Laura, and without waiting to see if her companion would do so, undid her seat belt and put an urgent hand on the door. Doctor van Meerum drew up smoothly, put out a restraining hand to stop her and said calmly, 'Stay where you are—I'll go and look.'

'Don't you dare leave him there!' she urged him fiercely. 'They drove on, the brutes—and look at all those miserable people, staring…'

He didn't answer her, but got out of the car and crossed the street to where the dog lay, squatting on his heels to examine it and then picking it up carefully and carrying it back to the car, quite unheeding of the warning voices telling him that he would get bitten for his pains. The unhappy creature he held didn't look capable of biting anything or anyone; Laura whisked the scarf from her neck and spread it on her knees, and opened the door to receive the stricken creature on to her lap.

'Hind legs broken,' said the doctor. 'Do you suppose there's a chance of patching him up in Casualty?'

Laura gave him a grateful look. 'Yes—the Sister in charge is a great friend of mine, she could hide us away somewhere…could we hurry?' She put a gentle hand on the whimpering little creature. 'He must be in frightful pain. If only I'd seen who ran him down.' Her voice was wobbly with her rage and the doctor gave her a long look, although he said nothing as he got back into the car and drove with what speed he could to the hospital, where he drove round to Casualty entrance, told Laura to sit still and went inside, to return almost immediately with Sylvia Matthews. She greeted Laura with a cheerful: 'Hi there, ducky, what's all this about a casualty?' She cast an eye over the bedraggled little beast and grinned at the doctor beside her. 'A hushed-up job, I gather? Do you want to do it, sir, or shall I get the CO?'

'Oh, I'll do it, I think, Sister, then if there's any trouble I can deal with it. But we shall need someone to give the dope. Are you busy?'

'Not at the moment. There's an end cubicle you can have; whoever does the round hardly ever goes there, and if they do…'

'I'll take the blame,' said the doctor easily, and

opened the car door. 'Laura, it would be less painful for that little beast if you could manage to get out and hold him at the same time.'

She nodded and slid carefully out of the car and into Casualty, where, obedient to the doctor's advice, she sat down carefully again in the poky little cubicle at the end of the passage while one of the anaesthetists was fetched. He stared rather when he saw the patient and began an indignant: 'I say, Laura old girl, I can't…' before he caught sight of Doctor van Meerum and stopped. 'Sorry, sir— you're the old man's—I should say, Mr Burnett's Dutch colleague, aren't you? We were told that you would be here.'

'Splendid,' murmured the doctor, and stripped off his jacket. 'If I could have an apron, and if you could knock this little chap out for long enough for us to set him to rights, I should be greatly obliged.' He smiled with great charm. 'I don't know your name…'

'Clark, sir, Jeremy Clark. I'm with Mr Burnett for six months. I'll get the dope.'

To save the dog more pain, he rather gingerly put him under with Laura still holding him on her lap, but the moment the small creature had been trans-ferred to the table she stood up, rolled up her sleeves and professed herself ready to help. 'I'm not on duty until eleven o'clock,' she explained, 'and if anyone comes, you can head them off, Sylvia.'

Her friend nodded. 'And there'll be coffee when you're through—in my office.' She whisked away with a wave of the hand and a conspirator's wink.

The dog's legs were miraculously clean breaks. Doctor van Meerum set them, put them into plaster and set about checking for other injuries. When finally he straightened his massive frame, he remarked: 'Nothing else, bar some bad bruising. What are we going to do with him?'

Jeremy spoke first. 'What about a dogs' home?'

'Certainly not!' exploded Laura. 'And he must surely belong to someone—ought we to advertise or tell the police, and I'll keep him in my room until…'

The doctor interrupted her. 'I doubt if he belongs to anyone,' he observed, 'he's half starved and he hasn't a collar. I think, if you would agree, Laura, that he should come with me.'

The relief flooded over her face like a burst of sunshine. 'Oh, could he? But where will you keep him?' She frowned uncertainly. 'You can't have him with you, he'd be dreadfully in the way.'

'I'm staying with someone who I have no doubt will be glad to keep an eye on him if I have to leave him, and he should be well enough to travel to Birmingham with me.'

'Yes, but what will happen to him when you return to Holland?'

The doctor was washing his hands at the sink. 'I'll take him with me. I have an elderly sheepdog who will be delighted to have company.'

Laura heaved a sigh. 'Oh, won't that be nice for him,' she declared. 'But would you like me to have him now? He won't come round for a little while, will he?'

'Quite soon, I should think. Would it not be better if someone were to find me a box or basket, and I'll keep him with me.'

'Aren't you addressing a post-graduate class, sir?' asked Jeremy doubtfully.

'Certainly I am, but I hardly think that this animal will disturb us.' He had put on his jacket and was standing placidly, waiting for someone to do as he had suggested. It was Laura who found a suitable box, lined it with old papers and a layer of tow and watched while the dog was laid gently into it. They had coffee then, although she didn't stay more than a few minutes, excusing herself on the grounds of getting into uniform after thanking the doctor for her lift and Sylvia for the coffee. She made no mention of seeing him again as she wished him goodbye and nor did he suggest it, but as she stooped to stroke the animal's matted head she said earnestly, 'Thank you for stopping and making him well again.'

He eyed her gravely. 'If I remember rightly, you ordered me to stop in no uncertain terms, although I can promise you that I would have done so even if you hadn't said a word.'

She smiled at him; she had a sweet smile, which just for a moment made her fleetingly pretty, although she was unaware of that. 'I shall hear how he goes on from Joyce,' she told him guilelessly.

Someone had brought her case in from the car and she picked it up as she went through Casualty, already filling up with minor cuts and burns, occasional fractures and dislocations; all the day-to-day cases. She glanced round her as she went; she wasn't likely to get anything sent up to the ward as far as she could see, although probably the Accident Room would keep her busy. She hoped so, for there was nothing like work for blotting out one's own thoughts and worries, and her head was full of both.

She climbed the stairs to her room in the Nurses' Home feeling alone and sad and sorry for herself, and cross too that she had allowed herself to give way to self-pity. As she unlocked the door and went into the pleasant little room she had made home for some years now, she bade herself stop behaving like a fool; she wasn't likely to see the doctor again and she would start, as from that very moment, to forget him.

CHAPTER TWO

SHE saw him exactly two hours later, for he accompanied Mr Burnett on his bi-weekly round, towering head and shoulders over everyone else. He wished her good morning with cool affability, remarked that they seemed to be seeing a good deal of each other that morning and added, 'The little dog is doing very nicely.'

'Oh, good.' Laura spoke warmly and then became a well-trained Sister again, leading the way to the first bed, very neat in her blue uniform with the quaint muslin cap perched on top of her neat head.

She handed Mr Burnett the first set of notes and advised him in her clear, pleasant voice: 'Mr Arthur True, facial injuries, concussion and severe lacerations of the upper right arm—admitted at eleven o'clock last night.'

Mr Burnett rumbled and mumbled to himself as he always did, cleared his throat and said, 'Ah, yes,' and turned to his registrar. 'You saw him, George? Anything out of the way?'

George White was earnest, painstaking and thoroughly reliable, both as a person and as a surgeon, and he was quite unexciting too. He gave his report with maddening slowness despite Mr Burnett's obvious desire for him to get on with it, so that Laura, aware of her chief's irritation, wasted no time in getting the patient ready for examination; no easy matter, for he was still semi-conscious and belligerent with it. But she coped with him quietly with a student nurse to help, and presently, when Mr Burnett had had a good look and muttered to Doctor van Meerum, his registrar and Laura, they moved on.

'Mr Alfred Trim,' Laura enlightened her audience, 'double inguinal hernia, stitches out yesterday.' She lifted the bedclothes and Mr Burnett stood studying his handiwork, apparently lost in admiration of it until he said finally: 'Well, we'll think about getting him home, Sister, shall we?' and swept on his way.

The next bed's occupant looked ill. 'Penetrating wound of chest,' stated Laura. 'I took the drain out an hour ago…' She added a few concise and rather bloodthirsty details and Mr Burnett frowned and said, 'Is that so?—we'll have a look.' He invited Doctor van Meerum to have a look too and they poked and prodded gently and murmured together with George agreeing earnestly with everything they said until Mr Burnett announced, 'We'll have him in theatre, Sister—five o'clock this afternoon.'

His gaze swept those around him, gathering agreement.

Five o'clock was a wretched time to send a case to theatre; Laura exchanged a speaking glance with her right hand. She was due off duty at that hour herself, and now it would be a good deal later than that, for Pat wouldn't be back from her afternoon until then and there would be a lengthy report to give. She checked a sigh and looking up, found Doctor van Meerum's dark eyes on her. He looked so severe that she felt guilty although she had no reason to be, and this made her frown quite fiercely, and when he smiled faintly, just as though he had know exactly what she had been thinking, she frowned even harder.

A tiresome man, she told herself strongly, walking into her life and turning it topsy-turvy, and whoever had made that silly remark about it being better to have loved and lost than never to have loved at all needed his head examined. She had been jogging along, not quite content, it was true, but at least resigned, and now she felt as though she had been hit by a hurricane which was blowing her somewhere she didn't want to go…

She swept past the next bed, empty for the moment, and raised an eyebrow at the hovering nurse to draw the curtains around the next one in line. Old Mr Tyler, who had had a laparotomy two days previously—Mr Burnett had found what he had expected and worse besides, and Mr Tyler wasn't going to do. Laura looked at the tired old face with compassion and hoped, as she always did in like cases, that he would die in his sleep, and waited quietly while the surgeon chatted quietly with a convincing but quite false optimism. He drew Doctor van Meerum into the conversation too, and she listened to the big man saying just the right thing in his faultless English and liked him for it. She supposed she would have loved him whatever he was or did, but liking him was an extra bonus.

The next three patients were quickly dealt with; young men with appendices which had needed prompt removal and who, the moment they were fully conscious, set up a game of poker. Laura had obliged them with playing cards, extracted a promise from them not to gamble with anything more valuable than matches and propped them up in their chairs the moment they were pronounced fit to leave their beds. And here they sat for the greater part of their day, a little wan, but nicely diverted from worrying about their insides.

They greeted Mr Burnett in a cheerful chorus, assured him that they had never felt better, that Sister was an angel, and that they couldn't wait for the pleasure of having her remove their stitches. All of which remarks Laura took with motherly good nature, merely begging them to refrain from tiring themselves out before steering her party forward to the neighbouring bed. Its occupant, Mr Blake, was thin and middle-aged, and although his operation had been a minor one, a continuous string of complaints passed his lips all day and far into the night.

Mr Burnett, his entourage ranged behind him, stood by the bed and listened with an impassive face to details of uneatable porridge for breakfast, the callous behaviour of the house doctors and nurses, and Sister's cruelty in insisting that he should actually get up and walk to the bathroom. He shot her a look of great dislike as he spoke and Mr Burnett said quite sharply that since he was making such excellent progress he would do better to convalesce at home, where he would doubtless find nothing to grumble about. 'Though I doubt if you will find a better nurse or kinder person than Sister Standish,' he concluded severely.

He stalked away, muttering to himself, and Laura hastened to soothe him by pointing out the excellent progress the next patient was making.

'I don't know how you put up with it, Laura,' said Mr Burnett, half an hour later, when they were all squashed into her office drinking their coffee. 'For heaven's sake get married, girl, before you lose your wits. That Blake—I'll have him home tomorrow; he's fit enough, and besides taking up a bed he must be driving you all mad.'

'Well, that would be nice,' conceded Laura mildly, 'for he does wear one down, you know. But they're not all like that, you know, sir.'

He passed his cup for more coffee and snorted: 'If I wasn't a married man and old enough to be your father, I'd marry you myself just to get you out of this ward,' he assured her, and they all laughed, because Laura was considered to be one of the Sisters in the hospital whom no one could ever imagine leaving. Young but settled, the principal nursing officer had once described her, and Laura, who had heard of it through the hospital grapevine, had considered that it amounted to an insult.

They all got up to go presently, and Doctor van Meerum, who had said very little anyway, merely murmured vague thanks in her general direction as he went through the door. She went and sat at her desk again when they had gone, doing absolutely nothing until Pat came to remind her that she had expressed a wish to inspect the previous day's operation cases.

She managed to forget the Dutch doctor more or less during the next few days; she had plenty of friends, she was popular in a quiet way and there was no reason for her to be lonely. And yet she was, and the loneliness was made worse when Joyce telephoned at the weekend and told her gleefully that Reilof van Meerum was spending it with them. 'We're going out to dinner,' she bubbled over the wire. 'I shall wear that blue dress—and on Sunday we're going out for the day in that super car of his. Laura, do you think he's rich?'

'I really don't know. Did he say anything about a dog?'

'Yes—rather a bind, really; he has to bring the creature with him, he says, because it's broken its legs. Still, I daresay we can dump it on someone.'

Laura didn't answer. Somehow the doctor hadn't struck her as being a man to opt out of something he had undertaken to do, and he had promised her... She said mistakenly, 'It's only a very little dog.'

'How do you know?' asked Joyce after a tiny pause, and Laura, sighing for her unguarded tongue, told her, 'It was knocked down by a car just as we reached the hospital—we took it into Cas...'

'Have you seen Reilof?'

'He did a round earlier in the week with Mr Burnett. I didn't talk to him at all—or rather, he didn't talk to me.'

She knew exactly what her young sister was thinking; that no man, no young, attractive man at any rate, would bother very much about a young woman who was looking thirty in the face. Thirty, to Joyce, was the absolute end.

Laura went home again at the end of the following week without having seen the doctor again, although she had found a note on her desk one morning to tell her that he had gone back to Holland, and that he had the little dog, now in excellent health albeit hating his plasters, with him. He was hers, RvM. She put the note away carefully and told herself once again to forget him.

Easier said than done, as it turned out, for when she did get home he was Joyce's main topic of conversation; they had had a super weekend and he was coming again just as soon as he could manage it. 'I've got him hooked,' declared Joyce happily. 'He's a bit old, but he's very distinguished, isn't he? and

Uncle Wim says he's carved himself an excellent career—he's got a big practice somewhere near Hilversum. I imagine that the people who live round there are mostly well-off.' She added dreamily, 'I expect he's rich.' She smiled beguilingly at Laura. 'Look, be a darling—I don't dare to ask Uncle Wim any more questions, but you could, he dotes on you, and I do want to know.'

Laura shook her head; her godfather might dote on her, but he was the last person in the world to gossip about anyone. 'Why do you want to know so badly?' she asked.

Joyce grinned wickedly. 'I wouldn't mind being a doctor's wife, as long as he was very successful and had masses of money and I wouldn't have to do the housework or answer the door, like Doctor Wall's wife does in the village.'

Laura kept her voice matter-of-fact; Joyce fell in and out of love every few weeks, maybe her feeling for Doctor van Meerum was genuine, but on the other hand someone else might come along. 'Chance is a fine thing,' she remarked lightly, and wished with all her heart that she might have that chance.

'Like to bet on it?' Joyce looked like a charming kitten who'd got at the cream. 'I've bowled him over, you know; he's thirty-eight and he had a wife years ago, only she died, and now he's met me and discovered what he's been missing.'

Laura had been sitting in the window, perched on the open window sill, but she got up now, shivering a little; it was still a little chilly in the April sun, but that wasn't why she shivered. 'I must go and get tea,' she said. 'Are Father and Uncle Wim still playing chess?'

Joyce shrugged and yawned. 'How should I know? Why don't you go and see for yourself?'

In a way it was a relief to be back at work again, although Laura loved being at home, but on the ward there was little time to bother with her own affairs. It was take-in week and the empty beds were filling fast, so that there was more than enough to do. She went her calm, sensible way, checking drips, seeing that the cases went on time to theatre and when they returned, were dealt with with all the skill available; and all the while being disturbed times out of number by housemen, George at his slowest, the Path Lab people, the lady social worker, and Mr Burnett, never at his sunniest during take-in week.

Moreover when she did escape to her office to catch up on her paper work, it was to be interrupted again by nurses wanting their days off changed, evenings when they had mornings, mornings when

they had afternoons free...she did her best to accommodate them, for she could remember her own
student days and the agonising uncertainty of days
off not fitting in with one's own private life. Staff
was going to have a long weekend, which meant that
Laura would be on call for a good deal of that
period, something which she didn't mind about, for
to go home and listen to Joyce eulogising about
Reilof van Meerum was more than she could bear.
It would be better, she reflected, when he had either
gone for good or he and Joyce...she tried not to
think any more about that, but Joyce could be
ruthless when she wanted something or someone.

It was a pity that her father had told her that she
need not look for another job, she could stay home
and do the housekeeping; he engaged a daily housekeeper at the same time, for as he was at pains to
tell Laura, Joyce wouldn't be strong enough to cope
with running the house on her own. And that meant
that she would idle away her days, cooking up
schemes with which to ensnare the doctor yet more
deeply.

Laura went home the following weekend, and
although her father had told her on the telephone
that either he or Joyce would bring the car in to
Chelmsford to meet her train, there was no one
waiting, for her when she arrived. She waited for

a little while and then telephoned home. Mrs Whittaker, the new housekeeper, answered. She sounded a dear soul but a little deaf and not at her best with the instrument, for she wasted a good deal of time saying 'Hullo', until Laura, getting in a word edgeways at last, asked for her father or Joyce. She had to repeat her question and when Mrs Whittaker finally grasped what she was saying, it was disappointing to be told that there was no one home.

Well, it had happened before. Laura left a message to say that she would get old Mr Bates to fetch her in his taxi from the village, and rang off. It took her a little while to get hold of him, and then she had had to wait half an hour for him to reach her, and she was tired and peevish by the time she opened the house door and went inside.

The hall was cool and dim, but the sitting room had a great many windows, allowing the spring sunshine to pour into the room. There was no one there, though; she went through the house then, and found the kitchen empty too, with a note on the table 'Soup in saucepan', presumably meant for her. She went upstairs to her room next, unpacked her overnight bag, got into a rather elderly tweed skirt and a thin sweater and went downstairs again.

It was almost one o'clock by now and there was no sign of lunch or anyone to eat it; possibly her father and godfather had gone off on some expedition of their own and forgotten all about her arrival, but Joyce knew that she was coming. Laura hunted round the sitting room once more, looking for a note, and found none. She wandered into the kitchen, served herself some of the soup and sat down on the kitchen table, supping it from a bowl while she decided what she should do with her afternoon, for it looked as though she would have nothing but her own company for the next few hours.

But in this she was wrong; she had finished her soup and was sitting doing absolutely nothing, her head full of Reilof van Meerum, when the front door opened and she heard Joyce's voice, high and gay. She heard her father's voice too and then his rumbling laugh, and a moment later the kitchen door opened and her sister and the Dutch doctor came in.

Laura didn't get up, indeed she was too surprised to do so—Joyce hadn't mentioned that he would be there and just for a moment she could think of nothing at all to say. It was Joyce who spoke.

'Laura—oh, darling, I quite forgot that you were coming home.' She bit her lip and went on quickly: 'Daddy and Uncle Wim wanted to go to some fusty old bookshop and Reilof turned up—wasn't it lucky?—and took them in the car, and then we went for a drive—we've just had lunch at the Wise Man…' Her eyes fell on the empty bowl and she gave a charming little laugh. 'Oh, poor you—I told Mrs Whittaker not to bother because you'd probably not come…'

The man beside her gave her a thoughtful glance and Laura saw it and said at once: 'My fault, I usually telephone, don't I—I changed my mind at the last minute and got Bates to fetch me from the station.' She smiled at her sister. 'I wasn't hungry, anyway.' She turned the smile on the doctor. 'Hullo—how's the little dog?'

He answered her gravely: 'He's fine. I had to leave him at home, of course, but my housekeeper is his slave and will take good care of him.' He paused for a moment. 'If I had known that you were coming home this weekend I would have given you a lift.'

Very civil, thought Laura, even though he was dying to get Joyce to himself; he could hardly keep his eyes off her, and indeed her sister looked delightful in a new suit and those frightfully expensive shoes she had wheedled out of her father. 'And my new Gucci scarf,' thought Laura indignantly, suddenly aware that her own clothes did nothing to enhance her appearance.

She got down from the table then, saying in a bright voice: 'I'm going along to see Father and Uncle Wim—what happened to Mrs Whittaker?'

Joyce's blue eyes were like a child's, wide and innocent. 'I told her to take the rest of the day off. Laura darling, I do feel awful…' and Laura thought without anger: 'If she weren't my sister, I would believe her, too.'

'You see,' Joyce went on, 'Daddy and Uncle Wim are going to Doctor Wall's for dinner—his wife will be at the WI meeting and Reilof is taking me to that gorgeous place at Great Waltham…'

'And we shall be delighted if you would join us,' the doctor interrupted her gently.

He was kind, thought Laura; he might have dozens of faults, but lack of kindness wasn't one of them. 'That's sweet of you,' she replied hastily, allowing her voice to show just sufficient regret, 'but actually I've reams of things to do and I was looking forward to an evening on my own.' For good measure she added, 'We've had a pretty hectic time on the ward.'

'Poor old Laura,' Joyce spoke with facile sympathy, 'but if that's what you want to do…'

Laura considered for one wild moment telling Joyce what she really wanted to do, and then looking up she found the doctor's dark, questioning gaze upon her, so that she hastily rearranged her features into a vague smile and said enthusiastically, 'Oh, rather. There's nothing like a quiet evening, you know.' She prolonged the smile until she reached the door, said ''bye' to no one in particular and left them together.

The house was very quiet when everyone had gone out that evening; her father had pressed her to go with them to the doctor's, but if she had done so the three old friends would have felt bound to exert themselves to entertain her, whereas she knew well enough that they wanted nothing better than to mull over the latest medical matters. So she repeated her intention of staying at home, saw the two elder gentlemen out of the front door and a few minutes later did the same for her sister and Doctor van Meerum. Joyce looked radiant and the doctor looked like a man who had just won the pools. She went back indoors, shutting the door firmly behind her, and wandered into the kitchen to get herself some supper. Scrambled eggs, rather watery because she cried all over them.

But no one would have known that a few hours later; she sat, composed and restful, in the sitting room, her newly washed hair hanging in a shining mousy cloud down her back, the coffee tray and sandwiches set ready, the local paper on her lap. The older gentlemen got back first, as was to be expected;

they had drunk most of the coffee and made great inroads upon the sandwiches before they were joined by Joyce and Reilof van Meerum. Joyce glowed, looking quite breathtakingly lovely— enough to turn any man's head, and it was obvious that that was what had happened to the doctor—he wasn't a man to show his feelings, but some feelings couldn't be concealed. Laura went away to get more coffee and when she returned he took the tray from her, asked her kindly if she had enjoyed her evening, and expressed the hope that she would be free to join them on the following day.

Laura, aware of Joyce's anxious wordless appeal to say no, said with genuine regret and a complete absence of truth that she had promised to go back early as she was spending the afternoon with friends. The doctor's polite regret sounded genuine enough but hardly heartfelt, and later, when they had parted for the night, she wasn't surprised when Joyce came to her room.

'Thank heaven I caught your eye,' she observed. 'Heavens, suppose you'd said yes!' She smiled sunnily. 'He was only being polite, you know. We're going out for the day—to Cambridge—he was there, simply ages ago.' She settled herself on the end of the bed. 'Laura, isn't it super—I'm sure he's going to ask me to marry him.'

Laura was plaiting her hair at the dressing table and didn't turn round; although she had been expecting Joyce to tell her just that, now that she heard the actual words she didn't want to believe them. She finished the plait with fingers which trembled and said carefully: 'Is he? However do you know?'

Joyce laughed, 'Silly—of course I do,' and she added with unconscious cruelty: 'But you wouldn't know…'

Laura smiled ruefully. 'No, I wouldn't. And are you going to say yes?'

'Of course—lord, Laura, I'd be a fool if I didn't— he's very good-looking and he adores me and I'm sure he's got plenty of money although he hasn't exactly said so—but he's got that marvellous car and his clothes are right.'

Laura stared unseeingly at her reflection in the looking-glass. Her face, she was thankful to see, looked just the same, although inside she was shaking with indignation and rage and a hopeless grief. 'Do you love him?' she asked.

Joyce got off the bed and strolled to the door. 'Darling, I'm prepared to love anyone who can give me all the pretty things I want.' She paused before she closed the door behind her. 'I suppose he turns me on, if that'll satisfy you.'

Laura got up early the next morning. She had

slept badly and the urge to get out of the house before anyone else got downstairs was strong. She got into slacks and a blouse and went, quiet as a mouse, downstairs. Breakfast was already laid in the dining room, but she went straight to the kitchen, made tea, cut a slice of bread and butter to go with it and fetched a jacket from behind the kitchen door. It was a splendid morning as only an early May morning can be and she went through the village and then turned off down the narrow lane which was the back way to the neighbouring village. It had high banks on either side of it and the birds were already there, singing. There were catkins and lambs-tails too, and the hedges were thick with bread and cheese, green and fresh, and tucked away here and there were clumps of primroses and patches of violets.

The lane wound a good deal, so that it took twice as long as it needed to to reach Masham, but she had time and to spare; Joyce and Reilof van Meerum weren't likely to leave the house much before ten o'clock, and Laura had just heard the church bells, still quite a way away, ringing for eight o'clock service. She reached the first few cottages as a handful of people came out of the church with the rector on their heels. He saw her at once and greeted her with pleasure, for they had known each other all her life.

'Laura—you've strayed into the wrong parish, but how nice. It's early, though.' He gave her a questioning look.

'I've got a weekend,' she told him, 'and it's such a lovely morning, I simply couldn't waste it in bed. I love the walk through the lane.'

He nodded. 'Peaceful and quiet, designed for thinking one's own thoughts.' He gave her a quick glance, taking in the pallor of a sleepless night and her unhappy eyes. 'Come and have breakfast with Martha and me,' he begged her, 'the house is so quiet now that Guy's up at Cambridge.'

He led the way down the village street and across to the white house at the end of it. A charming house, built in the days when the village parson had half a dozen children and needed the rooms. Now, as Laura knew, it was almost empty and a well-loved millstone round the rector's neck. They went in through the kitchen door and found Mrs Lamb frying bacon at the old-fashioned stove, and presently they all sat down to a leisurely meal before Mr Lamb got on to his bicycle and went off to a hamlet nearby to take morning service, leaving Laura to help with the washing up, peel the potatoes for lunch and set the table.

It was almost eleven o'clock by the time she got home, and time to get a meal for her father and godfather. She found them walking in the garden, deep in some conversation or other. They greeted her absentmindedly, asked vaguely if she was going to make them some coffee, and resumed their perambulations, leaving her to go to her room, change into a suit, do her hair and return to the kitchen. She gave them their coffee presently and then set about getting lunch, and it was over this meal that her father mentioned that Joyce and the doctor had left directly after breakfast and didn't expect to get back until after tea. 'They seem to be greatly interested in each other,' he observed, 'although I think myself that Reilof is too old for my little Joyce—still, if the child wants him, I'll not say no—he's obviously greatly taken with her.' He glanced at Laura across the table. 'I daresay you've noticed, my dear?'

She said yes, she had, her voice placid, and went on to remind him that she would be going back on the three o'clock train, whereupon he offered to drive her to the station. 'It will be a nice little run for your godfather, too,' he said with satisfaction, and added a little anxiously: 'How about our tea, my dear—and supper?'

'Tea's all ready on a tray on the kitchen table, Father, you only have to boil a kettle. It's cold supper, on the top shelf of the fridge, but I should think Joyce would be back by then. I'll lay up another tray after I've washed up, though, just in case she isn't.'

The matter being settled, she got on with the chores, repacking her bag once more before going in search of her father to remind him that he was taking her into Chelmsford. She sat with her godfather on the back seat because he complained mildly that he had seen almost nothing of her, and presently she wished she had insisted on him sitting with her father, because the questions he put to her were a little disconcerting and far too searching. Was she happy at the hospital? Had she any plans for the future, had she a young man?—an old-fashioned term which hardly fitted the circumstances, she considered, half amused. And what did she think of Reilof van Meerum?

She hedged round the last question. She didn't know him well—he seemed very nice, but how could she know…?

'You don't need to know anything about anybody,' stated her godfather, 'either you like them or you don't.' He gave her a sidelong glance. 'You do, Laura?'

'Well, yes, Uncle Wim.' She hastened to give the conversation another turn. 'You'll be here when I come home again—I'm not sure when…?'

'I'll be here—I shall go back with Reilof, but he

comes so frequently I have no plans at present but shall fit in with him.'

'Then I shall see you again.' She checked, just in time, a sigh of relief as her father came to a halt before the station entrance, then she bent to kiss her companion and bade him stay where he was as she got out. She retrieved her bag, kissed her father too, and hurried away to catch her train. She spent the journey wondering what Joyce and Reilof were doing; Joyce had been very sure of him—any time now, thought Laura unhappily, I shall get a message to say that they're going to get married. She gazed out of the window, seeing nothing of the rather dreary fringe of London and wishing she could be miles away, so that she couldn't be telephoned, then she would never know—no, that would be far worse. The sooner she knew the better. Then she could start to forget Reilof as the man she had fallen in love with, and think of him as a future brother-in-law. The idea appalled her.

CHAPTER THREE

LAURA was sitting in Ann Matthew's room, drinking tea and joining in, in an absent manner, the end-of-day talk. Ann had Women's Surgical and had been on duty for the weekend, as had several other of Laura's friends, and she had been greeted with the news that there had been a minor train accident that morning with a large number of light injuries to be dealt with as well as several cases to be warded.

'Sunday morning,' protested Audrey Crewe, who ran the Accident Room with the efficient nonchalance of an expert and was the envy of every student nurse who worked for her. 'The one time in the week when I can really get down to the wretched off-duty and have two cups of coffee in a row—they poured in, ducky, and so dirty, poor souls—though most of them only had cuts and bruises and shock. I had to send four up to you, though, Laura—they'll keep you busy for a day or two; two have had surgery, the others won't be done until tomorrow, they're not fit enough.'

'It's news like that that brings me rushing back,' remarked Laura tartly, and was instantly sorry she had said it, because someone asked, 'Why did you come back this afternoon, Laura? You usually sneak in at the last possible moment.'

'Well, Joyce was out for the day, and the earlier train fitted in with Father's plans...'

'Go on with you,' said a voice from the door. 'You've quarrelled with the boy-friend. You're wanted on the telephone, love—I expect he wants to make it up.'

There was a little outburst of laughter as Laura went out of the door, and she laughed with them while her insides went cold. It would be Joyce, to tell her that she was going to marry Reilof van Meerum, and she was so certain of it that when she heard her sister's excited voice telling her just that, it wasn't a shock at all, just a numbness which gripped her brain and her tongue so that Joyce asked sharply:

'Laura? Are you still there? Why don't you say something?'

'It's marvellous news,' she managed then, her voice calm and pleasantly surprised, 'and I hope you'll both be very happy. Does Father know?'

'Yes,' bubbled Joyce, 'and so does Uncle Wim, but you know what old people are, they hum and ha and sound so doubtful…'

'Well, as long as neither of you is doubtful, I shouldn't think there was anything to worry about, darling.'

'We've opened a bottle of champagne—isn't it all wildly exciting? Reilof's here—he wants to speak to you.'

Laura drew a long breath and thanked heaven silently that she didn't have to meet him face to face. At least by the time they did meet again she would have her feelings well in hand. All the same, when she heard his quiet 'Laura?' in her ear, she had to wait a second before she could get out a matter-of-fact 'hullo'.

'Aren't you going to congratulate me?' he asked.

'Of course, with all my heart.'

'That's nice to hear. I'm sure you're going to be a delightful sister-in-law. A pity that you aren't here to celebrate with us. You must be sure and have a free weekend next time I come over.'

'Oh, rather.' Laura was aware that she sounded far too hearty, she would be babbling if she wasn't careful, any minute now her tongue would run away with her. 'Such a pity I had to come back early,' she chattered brightly, 'but I'd promised ages ago…'

His 'Oh, yes?' sounded faintly amused and a little bored; she was wasting his time, time he could be spending with Joyce. She held the mouthpiece a little way from her and called: 'Okay, I'm coming now,' and then spoke into it again. 'So sorry, someone's waiting for me—have a glass of champagne for me, won't you? See you soon. 'Bye!'

She hung up and went slowly back up the stone staircase, not going back to Ann's room but into her own. But that wouldn't do, sooner or later someone would come looking for her. She snatched up a towel and sponge and went into one of the bathrooms and turned on the taps, and presently when a voice asked her if she was in there, she was able to answer quite cheerfully that the telephone call had taken so long that it hadn't seemed worthwhile going back to them all.

'Not bad news, I hope?' asked the voice anxiously.

She forced her voice into just the right tones of pleased excitement: 'Lord, no. Marvellous, actually—Joyce has got engaged. I'll tell you all about it later.'

Later was breakfast, a blessedly hurried meal, so that she barely had the time to repeat the news baldly, listen to the excited babble of talk when someone realised that Reilof was the dishy doctor who had been seen with Mr Burnett, admit that he had been visiting her home quite regularly for the past week or so, and gobble her toast before the hurried race to the wards.

The four new cases kept her busy all day; none of them was very well and the two who were to go to theatre had to be prepped and doped and reassured, and once they had been wheeled away on their trolleys, there was everything to set in readiness for their return to the ward. Their wives came too, hurrying in from their suburban homes, leaving heaven alone knew what chaos behind them, to be sat in Laura's office, given tea and sympathy and reassured in their turn. Presently, when they had calmed down, she took them along to the visitors' room where they could sit in some comfort, with magazines to read and coffee and sandwiches served from time to time, although in Laura's experience the magazines were rarely opened and the sandwiches and coffee were returned untouched.

And this time it was worse than usual, for one of the men died only a short time after he had been returned to the ward from the Recovery Room; a sudden collapse which all their skills couldn't cure. Laura, instead of going off duty, stayed with the bereaved wife until relations came to take her home, and then went over to the home, to her own room, so tired that she no longer had any very clear thoughts left in her head. Ann gave her a mug of tea after she had had her bath and she barely gave herself time to drink it before falling into bed and sleeping at once.

But the rest of the week was better than that. The other three men improved rapidly, the poker players, their stitches out, went home, sheepishly offering her a large bunch of flowers as they went, and Mr Bates, to her great astonishment, gone home a week or more, returned one morning to offer his grudging thanks for the care he had received while he had been in the ward. Laura was so surprised that she could only stare at him and then, realising what an effort it must have been for him to have made such a gesture, she took him into the ward to see one or two of the patients he had known. They weren't all that pleased to see him, for he had been unpopular with his fellow sufferers, but as one of them pointed out to Laura afterwards, his visit relieved the tedium of the long hospital morning.

She was on duty that weekend, and towards the end of the week following it she telephoned Joyce and invented a mythical friend who had invited her out, for her sister had telephoned her earlier in the week to tell her that Reilof van Meerum would be coming once more, and made it clear that if Laura were to go home it would spoil their outings together, for he would be sure to invite her along too, out of politeness.

'And I don't see much of him, darling, do I?' Joyce's voice sounded vaguely discontented, and it was then that Laura had determined to make some excuse to stay in London, and on the Friday she telephoned to say that the girl from Physiotherapy who had got married a few months previously had asked her to spend the weekend...

Joyce wasn't really interested. 'Oh, lovely for you,' she observed carelessly. 'Reilof's coming next weekend too—flying over—but of course you won't be free, will you?'

Laura said no and what a pity, knowing that Joyce would have been furious if it had been otherwise. 'But I'm coming home the weekend after that,' she warned, 'because I want some summer clothes from my room.'

It was after she had rung off that she decided to see what could be done about changing her days for that particular weekend—she could have Friday instead of Saturday; Reilof usually arrived on a Friday evening, but she could be gone by then. Really it would be a relief when they were married and living in Holland and she could settle down to her usual home visits.

She sighed. They wouldn't be the same any more, a reflection which did nothing to lighten her heavy heart. She turned her attention to the papers on her desk and resolutely closed her mind to her own affairs.

She hated staying in London over the weekend, it seemed such a dreadful waste of her free days, for of course the girl from Physiotherapy had been nothing but an invention…still, she made the best of it by going to see a collection of pictures she had been told were well worth a visit, doing a little shopping and going in the evening to the cinema with George, who, although dull and a thought pompous, was at least company. He took her to an intense film she couldn't understand because it was Italian and she suspected that the dubbing wasn't anything like the original script. Besides, he kept up a low-voiced monologue in her ear, describing just how he had removed a very nasty cyst from a man's shoulder—it was more of a mutter, actually, and too soft for anyone else to hear, but all the same she felt acutely uncomfortable about it. He took her to supper afterwards, too, and over their sausages and chips gave her a lecture on antibiotics.

She considered that, on the whole, she had earned both film and supper; probably George would make some girl a kind husband one day, but it was such a pity that he had no sense of humour. Probably Reilof van Meerum had none, either; she didn't know him well enough to discover that, but she was quite certain that George wouldn't have stopped in the middle of a busy street to pick up a little mongrel dog which had been run over, and certainly he would never have dreamed of taking it to Cas. To a vet, yes, where he would, give him his due, have paid any fees necessary and then, his duty done, washed his hands off it.

The week went slowly and when she telephoned home it was her godfather who answered, assuring her that he intended to stay another week or so and asking if she would be home for the weekend. 'For we see little enough of you,' he reminded her gently.

Laura told him that yes, she would be coming, but forbore from saying that her visit would be for a few hours only on Friday. She would be able to think of some excuse when the time came, she decided hopefully, as she made some vague reply to his invitation to visit him later on in the year. She would have to wait and see about that; Uncle Wim lived close to Reilof van Meerum, although she wasn't sure just how often they saw each other, but there was the ever-present risk of meeting Joyce and Reilof and she didn't think she would be able to bear that. Later on perhaps, when she had learned to school her feelings.

She caught an early morning train on Friday without telling anyone she was coming and she didn't phone Bates till she got to Chelmsford, because he was quite capable of telling her father, who would probably tell Joyce to upset all her plans and make her furious. But Bates, when he arrived, showed no curiosity as to her movements; he had a wedding on his hands that afternoon, and his talk was all of that.

It was beginning to rain as she went up the garden path, and the house, with its door closed, looked forlorn. It was barely eleven o'clock; she had plenty of time to get her things, but she would first find her father. His study was empty, so was the sitting room, and there was no Mrs Whittaker in the kitchen. Rather puzzled, Laura went upstairs and was relieved to hear the radio playing in Joyce's room. She hurried her steps a little and opened the door and stopped short.

Joyce was standing in the middle of the room, the contents of her wardrobe spread out around her on the bed, the chairs and open drawers. Her case, the expensive one her father had given her for her last birthday, was open on the bed, half packed.

She looked up quickly as Laura opened the door,

her pretty mouth open in surprise, her eyes wide. She said: 'It's only Friday—you never come home on Friday.'

'No,' said Laura, 'I don't—but now I'm here, although no one else is. Where is everyone, Joyce?'

'Father and Uncle Wim have gone to those gardens—you know, they're open now—I suggested it,' Joyce spoke defiantly, 'and Mrs Whittaker wanted to go to a wedding.'

'You're going away?' Laura made her voice casual, feeling her way cautiously—perhaps Joyce had quarrelled with Reilof. It struck her suddenly that it wasn't that at all, she was going to him...

Her sister folded a skirt, her pretty mouth sulky. 'Yes, I am, and since you're here, poking your nose into my affairs, you can jolly well help.'

Laura pushed some clothes on one side and sat down on the bed. 'Look, love, what's the matter? Don't you want a village wedding? I know Father is keen on you having one, but you only have to say so—Are you going off with Reilof somewhere quiet to get married? You only had to say so, you know.' She shook out a crumpled blouse and folded it carefully. 'If you'd explained what you wanted...'

Joyce laughed. 'You're so silly, Laura, I suppose that's because you're getting on a bit. I'm going away all right, but not with Reilof. Oh, he's all right,

I suppose, he would have given me everything I asked for, and I would have turned into a good little housewife with a string of noisy kids.' She gave a little laugh. 'He likes children, did you know?' She flung a dressing gown on top of everything else and closed the case. 'I'm going to America with someone I met a couple of weeks ago—he's got a special licence and we're getting married at the Registrar's Office in Bishop's Stortford.' She glanced at her watch. 'In about an hour's time. He's fabulously rich and he likes a good time and he loves me madly.'

Laura had listened to this astonishing speech with a sense of unreality so strong that she pinched her arm to make sure that she wasn't dreaming. 'Reilof...' she managed. 'But you said you loved him—he thinks you're going to marry him—he's coming here this evening—you can't...'

'Who says I can't? I'm going to do what I like with my life, Laura, and get the most out of it, too. Reilof's almost middle-aged, and I'd have settled for him because there wasn't any one else around with his kind of money, but now Larry has turned up, it's different.' Joyce was putting on her coat now. 'You can tell him, Laura—I've written him a letter, of course, and you can give it to him and explain it at the same time. You can tell Daddy too.'

'I won't.' Laura was surprised to find herself shaking with rage.

'All right, don't—I don't care; let them find out for themselves.'

'Joyce, you can't do it; Father will be so upset, and what about Reilof?'

'Father won't be upset for long, you know he always lets me do what I like, and Reilof...' She shrugged her shoulders. 'There are plenty more girls.' She picked up her case and crossed the room to give Laura a perfunctory kiss. 'There's the taxi. Wish me luck.'

Laura suppressed a wish to burst into tears. She said gently, 'I hope you'll be very happy, darling, even though you've made Reilof very unhappy. You'll write or telephone, won't you? Father won't be happy until he hears from you. And what about Reilof?'

'He can take care of himself—really, Laura, he's not a baby, you know. I daresay I'll telephone later. 'Bye for now.'

She had gone, leaving the room in complete disorder.

Laura started to tidy up, her movements automatic as she put discarded clothing neatly back into drawers and cupboards, trying to make her mind tackle the situation. Presently, with everything neat and tidy again, she sat down on the bed, the better to think.

It was no good giving way to concern for Reilof, it was important that she should tackle the deplorable affair as impersonally as possible. She remembered that Reilof never arrived before the evening and there was no reason to suppose that he would do anything different now; she would be able to tell her father and leave him to explain when the doctor got to the house. 'Man to man,' she told herself out loud, 'that should be much easier—I'll give Father the letter too, then if Reilof wants to he can go back home at once.' The home he had expected to share with Joyce, her heart reminded her; his plans shattered, heaven only knew what plans he had made. He had given Joyce a ring too— Laura hadn't seen it, but her sister had telephoned her in order to describe it at great length. A solitaire diamond in a modern setting; she had been jubilant about it, especially as Reilof had wanted her to wear what she described as some dreary old ruby thing which just everyone in his family had worn at some time or other. But she had twisted him round her thumb easily enough, she had added gleefully, and Laura would be able to see it next time she came home.

'Well, I am home,' said Laura worriedly, talking

to herself again, 'and a pretty kettle of fish it is. I wish Father would come home.' She heaved a sigh as the front door opened and shut. She snatched up Joyce's letter and raced down the stairs, to stop two-thirds of the way down, because it wasn't her father but Reilof standing there, looking up at her.

He smiled, 'Hullo, I didn't expect to see you, Laura,' but when she just went on standing there, her earnest, ordinary face the picture of surprised woe, the smile disappeared and his dark brows drew together in a questioning frown. 'Something is the matter? Joyce?'

Laura nodded; it was a funny thing, she reflected; on the ward she was capable of dealing with any situation, however sticky, which might crop up, but now she hadn't a clue how to begin. She went on gaping at him, feeling a slow resentment that she should have been forced into such a wretched situation. If it had been anyone else—a man she didn't know well—but Reilof, whom she loved and was powerless to help—it was past bearing.

'Well, supposing you tell me?' Reilof had taken off his car coat and flung it into a chair, now he lounged against the door, his hands in his pockets, no expression at all upon his handsome face.

She swallowed. 'Joyce asked me to give you this.' She watched his face anxiously as he walked over to her and took the envelope from her hand. It hadn't changed at all, it looked calm, even placid, and remained so as he opened the envelope and took out the letter within. When he had finished reading it, he folded it neatly and put it back.

'Did you know about this?' he inquired, and his voice was very even.

'Not until I came home about an hour ago—less than that. Joyce was—was just leaving. You see, she didn't expect me.'

'And your father?' He sounded politely interested, no more.

'He and Uncle Wim—well, Joyce suggested that they went to those botanical gardens—she didn't want them to know...I hoped they would be back...I didn't expect you'd be here until this evening.'

His smile held a faint sneer. 'Poor big sister Laura, left with the task of breaking the news.' His voice held bitterness now. 'You didn't do it very well.'

This annoyed her, and she said with some spirit, 'Well, if you must know, I was going to explain to Father and he would have told you.' She added idiotically, 'Man to man.'

The smile became a short derisive laugh. 'Oh, but I much prefer woman to man—sympathy, the tender touch and all the rest of it.'

My goodness, thought Laura, he's in a rage for

all that calm face. She asked doubtfully, 'Are you going to go after her? I don't expect they've…'

'Got married yet? You silly girl, of course I'm not going after Joyce.' He looked away for a minute. 'It's hardly my intention to drag her back by the hair of her lovely head—and she's quite right, of course, I am too old for her.'

Laura gasped. 'She didn't say that? But it isn't true—you're thirty-eight, aren't you? That's not old.'

'Perhaps not to you, Laura, but Joyce is only twenty.'

She went a little pale at his unthinking unkindness, but she said steadily: 'Age doesn't have anything to do with it.'

He raised his eyebrows. 'Oh, how would you know about that?'

'That's twice you've been abominably rude,' she pointed out. 'It's all right, though—I know you're angry and shocked and unhappy. I—I think I understand a little of how you feel; you'd like to knock someone down, I expect, but there's no one here, only me, and I shouldn't let you.'

The sneer was there once more. 'Indeed? And how could you prevent me from doing so?'

'Never you mind.' She came down off the stairs at last and said carefully, 'Reilof, there are a great many other girls—pretty girls—in the world. I know that seems a dreadful thing to say, but it's true. Once you've got over this...'

His dark eyes, so hard that she winced, swept over her. 'My dear good girl,' and his voice was almost a drawl, 'she wouldn't need to be pretty; anyone will do after Joyce, there couldn't be another girl like her.' He laughed without humour. 'Good God, girl, if it comes to that, I might just as well marry you.'

'Then why don't you?' asked Laura, very much to her own astonishment. She hadn't meant to say that at all, the words had popped out, and now there was no way of getting them back again. She lifted her firm little chin and met his dark look.

If he was astonished too, he didn't show it. 'Indeed, and why not?' he echoed smoothly, 'since I'm obviously too—er—mature for Joyce, then I must learn my lesson from her, mustn't I, and take someone nearer my own age.' His eyes narrowed. 'And you, Laura, are reaching thirty, are you not?'

He was being deliberately cruel now, but she could understand that; he wanted to hit back and she was the nearest thing to hit. She agreed in a quiet voice but made no other comment, and presently he went on:

'We're both old enough not to expect romance,

I imagine. At least I am cured of that illusion, although I must admit that having made up my mind to marry again, the prospect of remaining single for the rest of my life doesn't appeal to me any more.' He took his hands from his pockets and came towards her, his voice quite kind now.

'A marriage of friends, Laura, nothing more—I want no more of romance; companionship, someone to run my home and entertain my guests and friends, that will suffice for me. And what about you? Is that enough for you too? Or do you want to go on waiting patiently for the man of your dreams to come along?'

She shook her head. 'I can promise you I shan't do that,' she assured him seriously. 'You only have to take a good look at me—nudging thirty and what my mother always described as homely. And even if my dream man came along, he would hardly take a second glance at me, would he?'

He nodded in agreement and she thought what a preposterous conversation they were having.

'Then you would marry me?'

'Yes,' said Laura baldly.

He studied her at length. 'You're very certain. Why?'

It would have been nice to have been able to answer him truthfully, instead she said soberly: 'Mr

Burnett was quite right, you know; the prospect of being a Ward Sister for the rest of my working life quite appalls me. I've been nursing for ten years now and I love it, make no mistake about that, but it's a narrow life and an exacting one, and there are so many things I want to do and so far I've never had enough time to do much of any of them.'

'For instance?'

She was aware that he was only giving her his polite attention while the rest of his mind was given over to the shattering news she had just given him, but she went on talking, knowing that the only way to treat an abnormal situation was to be as normal as possible. A pretended normality, but at least it kept one from an outburst of rage which one might regret later. Children were lucky, she thought inconsequently, they could express their feelings exactly as they wished, whereas here was Reilof, and for that matter, herself too, both shocked and unhappy though for different reasons, and all they could do was have this ridiculous conversation.

'Petit-point,' she murmured, and when he smiled faintly, 'reading all the books I've ever wanted to, having a garden and tending it and picking the flowers and arranging them—taking hours over it—and meeting people—oh, I meet people every day; doctors and nurses and patients, and we all talk about the same thing, each from our own point of view. I want to meet people who know things—like Uncle Wim…'

She thought that he hadn't been listening, but now he gave her a considering look and she wondered if, just for a moment, he had forgotten Joyce. 'And if we were to marry you would be content with such simple pleasures as these? No holidays abroad, no theatres and dances and dinner parties—you wouldn't expect me to change my selfish bachelor ways to suit you?'

'Would you have changed them for Joyce?'

His face was bleak. 'Of course—it's different when one loves someone. One wants to please them, to make them happy.'

Rather a poor outlook for me, thought Laura, and said calmly, 'No, I'd not bother you—I'd be there if you wanted me, though.'

His mouth twisted and she went on quickly, 'It's not what you'd hoped for, but it might be better than being lonely for the rest of your life.' She went on in a matter-of-fact tone, 'But there, I daresay you don't mean a word of it—one says things when one is angry or upset.'

He interrupted her brusquely. 'I mean every word, Laura. I'm not at all sure of my reasons, but I do mean what I've said. But you—you must have time to think it over; I stand to gain a hostess for my friends, someone to run my home, bear me company, but you gain very little—a disgruntled man, disappointed in love and used until recently to leading a solitary life. There may be days when you'll hate me and wish that you'd never married me.'

He paused to look at her and she said placidly, 'Very likely,' while her heart cried silently, 'Never that,' and presently he went on: 'Would you consider giving in your notice at St Anne's—that would give you a month or so to make up your mind.'

'Very well.' It was time this extraordinary conversation was brought to a close, and she asked politely: 'Would you like a cup of tea? You must be tired after your journey.'

He let out a bellow of laughter. 'Not tired, Laura, but I'll have your cup of tea. Is it not supposed to be the panacea of all ills?'

CHAPTER FOUR

BACK in St Anne's that Saturday night, Laura, so late in that all her friends were in bed and asleep, made no attempt to go to bed herself, but sat in the small easy chair provided for each Sister's comfort, by her window. There was nothing to see; it was pitch dark and even in daylight the view was nothing but chimneypots and rather shabby slate roofs, and anyway, she wasn't looking at anything. Her brain was busy going over the events of her stay at home. Because of course she had stayed—she hadn't intended to, but there was no point in rushing off again now that Joyce's departure was a known fact, and it might have looked as though she was chickening out of an unpleasant situation. So she stayed and cooked supper for them all while her father and Reilof had gone to the study and Uncle Wim had kept her company in the kitchen, getting dreadfully in the way and talking about everything under the sun except the one topic uppermost in her mind, until at length she had asked: 'Godfather, what do you think? I mean about Joyce and Reilof—he must be broken-hearted.'

Her elderly companion had settled himself more comfortably in the shabby old chair by the Aga, Mittens on his knee. 'For the moment, my dear—only for the moment. You see, love and infatuation are rather alike to begin with.'

Laura stirred her soup. 'You mean he didn't—doesn't love her?'

'Shall we say that he thought he did, and still thinks so, and what man would not? Such a pretty girl with all that lovely golden hair and those eyes—but of course it isn't eyes and hair which count in the long run, Laura, and after a while a man comes to his senses and realizes that.'

'Oh, does he? And how does one tell the difference?'

'My dear child, you ask me that when you already know the answer.'

'Me?'

'Have you not known the difference between your love for Reilof and Joyce's infatuation for him, or rather for the things he could give her—striking good looks, the assurance of an older man, money—although she wasn't quite certain about that, was she?—and the satisfaction of being adored by a man of the world?'

Laura hardly heard the last bit of his remark. 'My love for Reilof,' she uttered. 'Godfather...'

'Oh, don't worry, Laura, no one else even guesses, and certainly not Reilof. You have no need to look so alarmed.'

She was at the table preparing bread for croutons, and paused, knife in hand, to ask, 'But you knew?'

'Well, yes, but then you and I have always been close, have we not? I think of you as my own daughter, and perhaps I know a good deal more about you than you do yourself.'

She popped her bread cubes into the pan and watched them crisp. 'Uncle Wim, this may sound crazy to you, but he's asked me to marry him. We were talking and he was so angry, although he didn't look angry, if you know what I mean, and he said he might as well marry anyone if he couldn't marry Joyce, so I said, well, why not me? And—and he agreed in a nasty smooth voice and we talked about that for a bit too, and then I said I supposed he'd been talking wildly, but he said no, he hadn't, and I might as well give a month's notice at St Anne's and think about it and let him know... He only wants a companion and someone to run his home, he says he's done with romance.'

She had dished the croutons and lifted her saucepan lids and peered inside, prodding their contents with a fork.

'Of course he has, we all say that at such times, it's a very natural reaction,' her godparent had observed comfortably. 'It happens time and time again. You will of course accept.'

Laura remembered how quickly she had said yes, she would.

She undressed then and got into bed, her brain still busy. Joyce had telephoned late on Friday evening and had contrived, as only she could, to wring forgiveness out of her father, even a reluctant acceptance of her actions; she was deliriously happy, she had said. Larry was super and although they would be flying to America in a few days she would bring him home before they went, and anyway, he was so rich that she would be able to come home and see them all just whenever she wanted to.

She didn't mention Reilof at all, and Laura, who had whisked him off to the kitchen when the telephone rang, kept him at the sink washing the supper things until she judged that Joyce would be finished. And Reilof, wiping his hands at the end of his unaccustomed task, had said in that bland voice she was beginning to hate because it hid his feelings so effectively: 'That was thoughtful of you, Laura—do you intend to smooth my path as diligently when we're married?'

She had resented his cool assumption that she would accept him, even though she had more or less done so, but all she had said had been:

'No—I imagine you're perfectly able to do that for yourself. I thought it might have been awkward for Father.'

And he had laughed and murmured: 'Cut down to size for the second time today! And don't look so stricken, Laura, I dislike sympathy.'

'Wretch,' Laura reflected, 'ill-tempered, arrogant wretch—just let him wait until we're married!' Upon which satisfying resolution, not taking into account resentment or uncertainty or anything else, she fell sound asleep.

The astonishment on the Principal Nursing Officer's face when Laura presented herself at the office and gave in her notice was quite ludicrous. Laura had seemed to her to be a safe bet for the rest of her working life, but she swallowed her surprise and asked in a coy voice which went ill with her stern visage, 'And who is the lucky man, Sister?'

'Doctor van Meerum, Miss Moore.'

It was difficult to know whether to be flattered

or insulted by her superior's look of sheer disbelief. Her, 'You'll be living in Holland, then? Well, I must wish you every happiness and accept your resignation as from today, Sister Standish,' was uttered in a tone which implied that she considered the happiness rather doubtful. Laura conceded that she was probably right; any happiness which came her way she would have to fight for—excellent tooth and pretty pink nail.

There seemed little point in keeping her departure a secret, as the grapevine would get hold of it anyway, and rather than allow its sometimes inaccurate gossip to spread through the hospital, Laura told Ann while they were having their morning coffee together. The news spread like wildfire, and if its hearers were mystified by it, only the more indiscreet of them made reference to the fact that they had understood that it was Joyce who had become engaged to Doctor van Meerum. Those who did were hushed at once, for Laura was liked throughout the hospital and the good wishes she received were sincere. But in reply to the numerous questions as to when and where she would marry, where she would live, and most important of all, what she intended wearing for the wedding, she was forced to prevaricate, for she had only the haziest of ideas herself. Indeed, when she considered the matter, she wasn't sure if she had actually said that she would marry Reilof, and supposing, just supposing he had changed his mind?

He hadn't; she had taken it for granted that they would see each other again when she went home, but towards the end of the week he came to see her at St Anne's. The moment was hardly an auspicious one, for she was busily engaged in restraining one of the patients from removing the cannula from his arm; he had taken exception to the flask of blood hanging beside his bed and had made several attempts to tug the tubing free, each time restrained by Laura, who was outwardly composed but wishing heartily that her nurses would come back from their supper so that she could telephone George. The man was written up for more sedatives, but the difficulty was getting them...she heard the step behind her with relief and said at once, still calmly, so that the other patients shouldn't be disturbed, 'George, do come and hang on to this arm while I get his injection.'

But the arm in its well-tailored sleeve which reached from behind her didn't belong to George; she would know that large well-kept hand anywhere. 'It's you!' she exclaimed idiotically.

'In person, and on this occasion arriving at the right time, I think.' He was beside her now and gave her a brief smile. 'Run along and get whatever it is he needs while I hold him—what is he?'

'A bad laceration of scalp with concussion—he really needs a special for a bit, but there's no one to spare until the night staff come on.'

She sped away, unpinning the DDA key from her uniform as she went. It took only a few minutes to unlock the cupboard in her office, find the drug, check it and draw it up and then go quick-footed down the ward once more. Doctor van Meerum was standing just as she had left him, a firm hand on the patient, and he kept it there until she had given the injection and it had taken effect. Only when the man quietened and sank into unconsciousness once more did he relinquish his hold.

'No nurses?' he inquired.

'At supper—they'll be back any minute.'

'Surely a little rash to send everyone but yourself with such a patient on the ward?' His tone was mild, but she flushed.

'I have two first-year nurses on duty with me; it would have been most unfair to keep one back and then leave the other one by herself to cope while I gave the report.'

He said gravely, 'I stand corrected. Here they are now. Shall I stay for the moment? Just until you've given the report to the night nurses, that would allow your two to keep an eye on the other patients.'

She gave him a relieved glance. 'Oh, would you? It would be very kind—they're both very good, but it's their first ward and everything's strange. I'll be about ten minutes.'

She was as good as her word, and leaving the night staff nurse and her junior as well as a third-year male student nurse to sit with the concussion case, she went down the ward once more, murmuring her goodnights to the patients as she went. Reilof had relinquished his post to the male nurse and was standing idly waiting for her, and turned without a word as she reached him. They left the ward together and started down the stone staircase.

'Supper?' he suggested.

Laura stopped to look up at him. 'That would be nice—are you staying here?'

'In London? Yes. There's a meeting I have to attend tomorrow. I flew over.'

She nodded. 'I see.' She searched his impassive face with anxious eyes. 'Have you heard from Joyce?'

There was no expression on his face at all, but his voice was bland. 'Should I have? No—what would be the point?'

Laura resumed her brisk trot down the stairs.

'Well—none, I suppose. I just thought...well, that she might have explained...'

'I think she gave all the explanation necessary in her letter. She's married now, Laura,' he gave her a mocking smile. 'Don't tell me that you're having ideas about her discovering that she has made a mistake and rushing back to me—you're wasting your time.'

They had reached the long corridor which would lead eventually to the back entrance of the Nurses' Home and Laura stopped. 'I go down here.'

'I'll wait for you at the front entrance. How long will you be? Ten minutes?'

She almost smiled, imagining what Joyce would have said if he had put that same question to her. Apparently her own appearance didn't matter all that much; it was a sobering reflection. All the same she used her ten minutes to good effect, showering and making up her face nicely and re-doing her hair into its neat topknot before putting on what Joyce called her middle-of-the-road Jaeger shirt-waister. Its soft silvery grey was kind to her mousiness and set off her charming figure to advantage. She caught up the grey flannel coat which matched it so exactly, tucked a rose-pink scarf into the dress's neck and sped towards the entrance, pleased that however sober her dress was, her shoes and handbag were high fashion, bought in a burst of extravagance only a few weeks previously.

Reilof was waiting, leaning against a wall talking to Mr Burnett. They both looked up as Laura crossed the vast expanse of floor, and came to meet her. Mr Burnett stayed talking for a few minutes before he wandered away and Reilof said briskly, 'Delightfully punctual—we'll get a taxi.'

They crossed the forecourt to the street and a passing taxi wheeled out of the traffic and stopped. 'The Baron of Beef,' instructed the doctor, and Laura, pleased that she knew what he was talking about, said: 'Oh, yes—Gutter Lane.'

'You've been there?' Reilof sounded very faintly bored and she wished suddenly that she hadn't come.

'No—but one of the chef's assistants was in the ward with a severed tendon.' She couldn't think of anything else to say after that and was thankful that their ride was a short one, and even more thankful to find that the restaurant was almost full of chattering people; at least the atmosphere was cheerful and would create the illusion of a pleasant meal ...*á deux*. She sat down with her usual composure, her busy mind mulling over topics of conversation which might serve to divert her companion.

She need not have bothered; once he had ordered

their drinks and suggested that she might like to try the *pâté maison* and follow it with sole *au gratin*, while he himself decided on steak and kidney pudding with oysters to precede it, he sat back in his chair and said matter-of-factly: 'Now, let's discuss things in a businesslike fashion, shall we?'

Laura gave him a bleak look. Would they spend the rest of their lives being businesslike? she wondered unhappily. Perhaps with time, when he had got over Joyce, he would talk to her with the same warmth he had shown towards her sister and his eyes would smile instead of looking like black stone.

'By all means,' she agreed, and took a good sip of sherry to give her heart. It was an excellent sherry; she took another sip and felt a little better, relaxing in her chair, waiting for him to say whatever it was he wanted to be businesslike about. She had to wait a few minutes, for he said nothing at all, only looked at her in a thoughtful way as though he expected her to say something first. Well, she wasn't going to; she took a third sip of sherry and eyed him with faint belligerence.

He said surprisingly, 'You look nice—you always seem to wear slacks and blouses…'

'Only because when I'm home I have the house to see to and do the cooking,' she pointed out tartly, and was instantly mollified by his,

'Well, you won't need to do that. I have an excellent housekeeper who will be only too glad to relieve you of both housework and cooking,' and then, as though he sensed that he hadn't said quite enough: 'Your cooking is excellent.'

'Thanks, but not on a par with this.' She indicated the pâté which had been set before her, and went on deliberately: 'Joyce didn't like cooking—how were you going to manage?'

His eyes were like black ice. 'I have just told you—I have an excellent housekeeper. Laura, will you oblige me by not talking about Joyce? There seems no point in doing so.'

She buttered a finger of toast and popped it into her mouth. 'Well, I won't if you don't want me to, but you can't just cut her out of your life like that.' She hesitated. 'Perhaps you can, though.'

He didn't answer her. 'Have you resigned your job?'

'Yes, I leave...' she calculated quickly, 'in three weeks and a day.'

He nodded. 'Early July, that should suit us very well. We can have a quiet wedding and a short holiday before we return to Holland.'

She gave him a straight look. 'Aren't you being a little high-handed?' and had to wait for his answer while he sampled the wine the waiter had poured.

When their glasses had been filled, he said: 'I beg your pardon, you've scarcely had time to make up your mind, have you?'

She replied with disarming honesty. 'Yes, I have, only you—you're taking everything for granted. If we're to make a success of it we have to start off with everything understood, don't we? I think,' she went on a little shyly, 'that we must be honest with each other, mustn't we? Like good friends.'

'I hope we shall be that, and you're quite right, of course. We must also undertake not to interfere in each other's lives.' He saw her bewildered look. 'That's to say, while we will, I hope, live together comfortably enough, there must be no question of encroaching upon each other's privacy.'

Just for a moment Laura quailed; the wish to put down her knife and fork and walk out of the restaurant was strong, but only for a moment. She loved this withdrawn, proud man sitting opposite her. Perhaps he would never love her, she strongly doubted it, but she might, in the course of time, win his affection. Anyway, what did life hold for her if she decided not to marry him after all? Nothing.

'A very good idea,' she agreed pleasantly. 'You will, of course, have to put me right as we go along. You were saying about the wedding…is it to be from my home?'

'Why not?' he wanted to know coolly. 'I'll bring the car over and we can go somewhere quiet—the West Country perhaps.'

'That would be nice. Just exactly where do you live, Reilof?'

'Between Hilversum and Baarn in a very pleasant part of the country. There are woods around and villages tucked well away from the roads. My home is almost exactly between the two towns, very convenient, as I have beds in Hilversum hospital and consulting rooms in both places. Patients occasionally come to the house, too. I have a partner, a good deal younger than myself—Jan van Nijhof.'

Laura sat silent while the waiter served her sole, and only when they had started to eat again did she ask him: 'And family?'

'A married sister in den Haag, two younger brothers—one has a practice in Toronto, the other is working for his fellowship at Leiden. My mother is dead and my father lives in Loenen, a small place quite close to Hilversum. He retired several years ago, although he occasionally does some lecturing.'

'All doctors,' commented Laura, very much struck.

'Every man jack of us, and my sister is married to an orthopaedic surgeon.' He smiled so nicely at her that she was emboldened to ask, 'Did they know that you were going to get married?'

'I mentioned the possibility, no more.'

She heaved a sigh of relief. 'Oh, good.' She added in a muddled fashion, 'I mean they won't know it's me instead of Joyce.'

Presumably he understood her, for he agreed blandly before asking her what she would like for a sweet; quite obviously he wasn't going to discuss his feelings on the subject. She ate the delicious sorbet set before her with no more pleasure than if it had been the prunes and custard so often offered in the hospital canteen, while she talked with determined cheerfulness about the weather, the prospect of a warm summer, the little dog he had rescued and other safe but rather dull topics. Her companion, replying to her remarks with unfailing politeness, demonstrated to her quite clearly that he was thinking about other things. They got up to go finally, still exchanging platitudes, and at the hospital entrance she broke off her muddled thanks for her dinner to say: 'It won't do, you know—you're bored stiff with me, aren't you, and hating every minute. We'd better stop now before it's too late…'

His sudden grip on her arm made her wince. 'Laura, I'm sorry. If I have appeared bored, believe me that wasn't the case; if I've been a poor companion, I apologise, but I have to make a fresh start and you can help me—you're helping me already, just by being you; quiet and undemanding, allowing me my ill humour and lack of interest. If you will have patience just for a little while…' He half smiled. 'I'm a poor bargain, aren't I? But you see, it's rather like waking up from a beautiful dream and getting used to reality again. Very likely I shall find reality far better than the dream, but I have to forget the dream first.' He loosed his hold on her arm and took her hands in his. 'Do you know, I don't believe that I could have said that to anyone else?'

He bent suddenly and kissed her gently, and she stood looking up at him, smiling uncertainly. She didn't know whether to laugh or cry, and when he observed, 'I have always thought of you as a plain girl, but I was mistaken. When you smile you're quite pretty,' she had no words with which to meet his remark, so she wished him goodnight and went up to her room, to sit before her dressing-table mirror and stare at her face.

Presently she got up and started to get ready for bed. 'He must have been looking at me in a poor light,' she remarked to the room at large.

He came, to her surprise, the following day, and put his head round the office door while she was sitting at her desk writing up the charts.

'You're off at five o'clock?' he wanted to know;

a rhetorical question, since he already knew, but Laura said cheerfully that yes, she was, and why?

'If you're not too tired, would it be a good idea to go to your home and have a word with the local parson?'

'Of course, why not?' Her placid face showed nothing of the excitement tearing around inside her. She added prosaically: 'I shall probably be a little late—ops day, you know.'

Reilof went away after a few minutes, leaving her to jumble up the charts in a hopeless manner while she tried to look into her future. A quiet wedding, he had said, and then a brief holiday—could one call it a honeymoon? She thought not—she would have to think about clothes, it was a cheering thought to brighten her other, gloomier ones.

It said much for her good sense that she gave her usual careful report to Pat when she came on duty, personal thoughts damped down.

She wore the Jaeger dress again, for the evening, though bright, was cool, and by dint of hurrying she managed to reach the hospital entrance as it was striking six o'clock. It was as she was hurrying down the corridors that she recollected that Reilof hadn't got the car with him—they would have to go by train and at this time of the day it would be packed. But as she reached the door she saw Reilof leaning against the bonnet of an old Morris which she recognized as belonging to George.

When she reached it she exclaimed, 'Hullo, how on earth did you get George to lend you his car? He never lends it…'

'There's an exception to every rule,' he remarked easily. 'He swears it goes like a bomb, but I'm not so sure—as long as it gets us there and back again.' He opened the door for her and then went round to sit beside her. 'This will teach me not to come over without a car.'

'Then why did you?'

They were edging into the evening traffic. 'I hadn't a great deal of time and I wanted to see you, Laura.'

She couldn't think of anything else to say but 'Oh,' and then sat silent until at length the traffic thinned a little as they reached London's outskirts. Only then she asked, 'Why?'

It was surprising what speed he was getting out of the elderly car. 'I wanted to be certain— not of myself, but of you; to know that you really meant what you had said; to get our plans made and settled.'

Laura could understand that; he had to forget Joyce, hadn't he? as quickly as he could, and he was going the right way about it, although it must be a painful experience. She suspected that he was a man of determination when it was needed and she was sure that once they were married he would treat her with consideration, albeit perhaps with indifference. But he certainly wouldn't throw Joyce in her teeth, and would never let her feel that she was second choice. She paused in her reflections to say: 'If you turn off left at the next crossroads there's a short cut…'

Presently he began to talk—about nothing in particular it was true, but it was agreeable to find that they had quite a lot in common, and even though he hardly noticed her as a girl they were getting on far better than she had imagined. By the time they reached her home she was beginning to feel completely at home with him, and fancied that he too felt the same. All to the good, she told herself as she got out of the car, since they'd chosen to share their life together.

The evening passed satisfactorily; her father seemed to have accepted the situation without much trouble, and Uncle Wim behaved as though the pair of them had intended to marry all along. They talked for a bit, the four of them, and then Laura took Reilof down the road to the rectory, where the Rector, a dear, dreamy man with a frightful memory, discussed their wedding with evident pleasure, digressing a good deal to inquire after Joyce, and even breaking off in the middle of a sentence to say: 'I rather thought that our little Joyce had been thinking of marrying you, Doctor van Meerum, which just shows how mistaken one can be. She showed me a magnificent ring one day, I remember, but she refused to tell me who had given it to her—now I realise that it was this rich young man from America. I hope the dear child is very happy—such a pity that they were unable to marry here. I daresay that you've heard from her?'

The doctor said gravely that no, he hadn't, and reminded the Rector that he hadn't told them if ten o'clock in the morning would be too early an hour at which to be married.

'Certainly not—and it's to be a quiet wedding, that seems to me to be an excellent choice. Of course Laura is well known in the village and popular, too, but she would hardly want to wear white satin and orange blossom.' He smiled with kindly tactlessness at her. 'I remember when you were christened, my dear—almost thirty years ago.'

Laura choked and caught Reilof's eye and saw the gleam in it before managing to say, 'I've not had time to think what I shall wear, but I'm sure it won't be white satin. May we settle for ten o'clock then, Mr Lamb? And now we really must go; I'm on duty in the morning, you know.'

As they walked back Reilof observed: 'It would serve everyone right if you were to turn up in bridal finery and a dozen bridesmaids behind you.' He looked down at her thoughtfully, and she thought that he was really seeing her. 'You don't look as old as you are,' he told her kindly, a remark which left her seething, although she thanked him in a colourless voice and bit back the retort ready on her tongue, while a resolve, a little vague as yet, took shape in the back of her head that one day he should eat his words.

The rest of the evening passed pleasantly enough. No one, meeting the doctor for the first time, would have guessed, even remotely, that he was suffering from a broken heart. His manners were delightful, he entered into the conversation readily, and gave no indication of his true feelings, and only when Uncle Wim deliberately introduced Joyce into their talk did Laura see the little muscle twitching at the corner of his mouth and his face assume the bland expression she so much disliked.

All the same, their return journey was cheerful enough, although she would have been happier if he had shown more interest in their wedding. He saw her to the Nurses' Home, assured her that he would be seeing her again before long and wished her goodnight, adding: 'I have a ring for you, I must remember to give it to you the next time we meet.'

A more casual way of becoming engaged she had yet to discover. She fumed her way to bed, alternately positive that she wouldn't marry such a wretchedly unfeeling man, and just as sure that she would make him such a good wife that he would forget Joyce completely.

CHAPTER FIVE

THE next three weeks passed quickly. Laura embarked on a shopping expedition, using up a good deal of the money she had saved during the last few years; refusing the good-natured help of her friends, she spent her free time combing the shops for exactly what she wanted, pretty clothes which would detract from the plainness of her face. She chose a beautifully cut dress and jacket for her wedding in a rich clotted cream crêpe with a little turban hat of the same colour patterned with green and turquoise and ruby red; this last as a concession to the ring Reilof had given her—the ring Joyce had refused to wear because it was old-fashioned. Laura loved it; its three rubies were set in an oblong of diamonds and mounted on gold, and it had fitted her finger exactly. Childishly she had taken that as a good omen.

She had bought shoes and handbag to go with her

wedding outfit too, and then laid out the rest of her money on a dress or two, more shoes and sandals and all the undies she could afford. It was after she had spent all her money that she recollected that her evening dresses were out of date and few in number; perhaps Reilof didn't go out much in the evening, but it would be awful to find that he did and she had nothing to wear. She was pondering the problem when it was solved for her by the unexpected cheque which her father sent her, and she spent the whole of it on two long dresses, one a pale pink chiffon with a tiny bodice and a floating cape and the other brown, the colour of her eyes, with little cape sleeves trimmed with lace, its low neckline trimmed with lace too.

Satisfied at last with her purchases, she invited her friends to view her new wardrobe and was delighted when they presented her with a gift—a suitcase, not leather, it was true, but smart and good-looking all the same. She packed her new finery into it feeling that at least she wouldn't put Reilof to shame with shabby possessions, and left St Anne's for the last time.

Most of the odds and ends and her other clothes had already been sent home, and Reilof was to pick her up on his way from Holland. He was waiting for her as she went through the main door, a handful of her closest friends with her. And this time there was no Aston Martin but a silver-grey Rolls-Royce drawn up in the forecourt. Laura hesitated for a moment, feeling suddenly uncertain, but he came to meet her and in the burst of talk from her companions she forgot the uncertainty and felt only excitement. All the same she had lost her tongue, and it was only when she had said her final goodbyes and had been ushered into the car and Reilof was beside her that she said: 'How super being met by a Rolls…'

He smiled a little. 'It seemed a more suitable car to the occasion than the Aston Martin.'

'Well, yes—I suppose so, but aren't you a bit nervous of driving it?'

He sounded amused. 'Er—no, not in the least. I've been driving one for some years now.'

She turned a surprised face to him. 'It's not yours?'

'Yes, it is. You sound disapproving, Laura.'

'Well, I don't mean to be.' She hesitated, watching him steer the big car through the traffic. 'I know it's not my business and I don't mean to pry, but are you very successful?'

'If by that carefully wrapped up question you want to know if I can afford to run a Rolls, yes, I can. And it is your business.'

Laura frowned. 'I didn't wrap up the question,' she pointed out rather coldly, 'how very horrid of

you to say so. I'm sure I don't wish to know anything you don't choose to tell me.' She glared out of
the window, feeling remarkably put out, and then
looked at him as his hand covered hers for a
moment.

'It's quite my fault,' he observed mildly. 'I've
never discussed anything with you, have I? We've
not had much time, but I'll tell you anything you
want to know while we're on holiday. And there's
a letter from my father in the pocket beside you—
take it out and read it.'

She did as she was told, carefully scrutinising the
writing on the envelope before she opened it; it was
large and flowing and somehow it reassured her. The
letter within wasn't all that long, but it warmed her
heart. Reilof's father must be a dear. She didn't know
if he had known about Joyce, but even if he had, there
was no sign of it in his letter. It welcomed her into the
family with a warmth she hadn't expected, and the
writer expressed the hope that they would meet and
become friends very soon: 'For I am sure that Reilof's
wife will be as dear to me as to him,' it ended. She
folded it carefully and put it back in its envelope,
feeling almost physical hurt at the words, because of
course Reilof's father would imagine her to be a much
loved bride. He couldn't know about Joyce…

Reilof's voice cut across her reflections. 'Father

knows about Joyce. I've explained the whole to him, for of course I had described her to him and he would have been surprised…'

Laura flushed brightly, went pale and then to her horror felt the tears welling up into her throat. Nothing she could do would stop them, they trickled down her cheeks and she didn't dare wipe them away, for he might turn and see what she was doing. Better to sit quite still.

Too still, though, for he glanced briefly at her, made a small sound which could have meant anything, and pulled the car into the side of the suburban road along which they were driving.

He stared at her wet cheeks for a few seconds. 'Something I've said?' he asked gently. 'You don't feel well?'

Her charming bosom heaved as she found her voice, rather watery but almost steady. 'I feel very well. Of course your father would be surprised; he expected a lovely golden-haired young girl, didn't he? And all he'll get is me, nudging thirty and as p-plain as a p-pikestaff. But you needn't have told me—do you really think I don't know?'

She felt his arm across her shoulders, pulling her comfortably close.

'Oh, my dear girl, what a clumsy wretch I am, and I had no thought of hurting you—and Father won't be surprised. I told him about you, but I mentioned neither your looks nor your age, although why that should matter I can't imagine.'

'It matters very much,' she assured him rather peevishly, 'and if you were a woman you'd understand.' She sat up straight and blew her nose and managed to smile. 'Oh dear, I don't know why I had to behave like a fool. I'm sorry.'

'Wedding nerves,' he observed comfortably. 'I believe all brides are supposed to have them.'

Joyce hadn't. Perhaps if you were going to marry a man you loved so much that you were prepared to throw over another man with no compunction at all, you were beyond nerves. Laura said with a certainty she didn't feel: 'Yes, I expect that's it, for I'm not usually so silly. I'll not do it again.'

His smile was kind. 'Then you will be a very exceptional wife. Esme—we married when she was eighteen—was very nervous at our wedding. It was rather a grand one—she had that sort of mother.'

'What was she like? Or would you rather not talk about her?'

'I was twenty-four when we married and she died eleven years ago of leukaemia.'

'Reilof, I'm sorry, how terrible for you. Perhaps you'd rather not tell me…'

He had started the car again and they were ap-

proaching the more open Essex countryside. He said
slowly: 'It's a long time ago now, and months before
she died I knew that I'd married the wrong girl. She
hated my work—hospitals, going out at all hours of
the day and night, coming home late and leaving
early—poor Esme, she was very young. I believe
that she had no idea of the life she would lead as a
doctor's wife.'

He was silent for a few moments and then went
on quietly: 'I suppose we were happy for about six
months, and then in a year or less I began to suspect
that she was ill—she never knew. I took a partner and
cut my work to a minimum so that she could enjoy
the kind of life she wanted; dining out, dancing,
theatres, holidays in the south of France. Shortly
after she died my partner went abroad and I was on
my own for a few years, but the practice got large and
I began to lecture as well. I took a partner last year,
Jan van Mijhof, he's younger than I, a very good sort
too and a first-rate doctor. He's not married and lives
close by. I should warn you that I am a busy man,
Laura.'

'Well, I shall have plenty to occupy me—I shall
have to learn Dutch, shan't I?' She thought for a
moment. 'There's the little dog, too—I can take him
for walks. What do you call him?'

'Lucky. Oh, yes, he likes his exercise and so does

Hovis, my other dog. The country round about the house is very pretty, I think you'll like it.' He glanced at her. 'Do you ride?'

'I haven't done for years. I daresay I'd be all right on a very staid kind of horse.'

He laughed. 'Well, we'll have to see about that.'

She asked rather wistfully, 'I suppose you don't want any help in the surgery?'

'Er—no. Later on perhaps. I have a surgery nurse and a secretary, and if either of them should be ill I might be glad of your offer.'

His voice sounded friendly enough, but she could hear a note of reserve; he didn't want her to have anything to do with his work; she would have to remember that. She started to talk about something else and kept the conversation to trivialities until they reached her home.

An hour later, in the kitchen getting supper, Laura found it difficult to believe that she was actually getting married the next day; her father and Uncle Wim had been delighted to see her, but their interest in the forthcoming wedding was only mild. Of course they were delighted that she was to be the bride, but she suspected that they were equally delighted that it was to be such a very quiet affair, necessitating no unnecessary dressing up and no fuss and bother with guests, wedding breakfasts, and the

like. And as for Reilof, once he had taken their
things up to their rooms, he had settled down with
the two older men, to an absorbing discussion of
some medical matter. Even Mrs Whittaker, who
would have been an interested and highly satisfac-
tory audience, was at home nursing her brood of
children through the measles.

It was left to Mittens to be Laura's confidante,
and she only pretended interest while she waited for
her supper. Laura, longing to discuss the most important event in her life so far, sighed, and then
chided herself for giving way to self-pity. She had
made her bed and she was going to lie in it, she
assured Mittens as she offered the little cat her
evening saucer of milk.

'And what exactly do you mean by that?' asked
Reilof from the door, and when she turned to look
at him he wasn't smiling.

'Nothing,' she told him swiftly. 'Have you come
to see if supper's ready?'

He seemed content to let his question go unan-
swered. 'Your father has opened a bottle of champagne and he wants you to join us.' He glanced round
the kitchen in a vague way. 'Is there anything I can
do?'

She told him no and went with him to her father's
study and smiled at the gentlemen when they toasted

her, laughed obligingly at Uncle Wim's gentle little jokes about weddings in general and hers in particular, and then went back to the kitchen to dish up.

As the evening progressed she found that she had no feelings at all about the next morning's ceremony, only a kind of hazy acceptance of it; the haziness was probably due to the champagne. Just after ten o'clock she wished the three men good night and went up to her room, where she laid her wedding clothes ready, washed her hair, did her nails and jumped into bed, to fall immediately, contrary to her expectations, into a refreshing sleep disturbed only by her alarm clock sounding off seven o'clock the next morning.

Not quite five hours later she was in her bedroom again, making ready to leave with Reilof. The wedding had been a surprisingly cheerful affair, for despite the lack of guests the church had been filled to capacity by those people in the village who had known her for most of her life. Indeed, she had been astonished when she and her father, after walking the short distance from her home to the church, had been greeted by so many smiling expectant faces, all staring over their shoulders to get a first glimpse of her. She faltered a little, but then she saw Reilof waiting for her, the only person in the church not looking at her. He could have least shown a little interest, she fumed silently as she and her father started down the aisle, and then her ill-feeling vanished, because as she reached his side he looked down at her, not smiling but kind and reassuring, and she felt absurdly happy despite the doubtful future.

She got out of her wedding outfit and packed it carefully before getting into the cotton shirtwaister—a pretty garment patterned in summer flowers on a silvery grey ground—did her face and hair and stood wondering what to do with the elegant little spray of orange-blossom, roses and orchids which Reilof had given her before he had left for the church that morning. It seemed pointless to keep it, for it had been given with a casually friendly, 'Brides always have flowers—I don't see why you should be the exception,' which had robbed the gift of any sentiment, but all the same she wrapped it tenderly in a scrap of tissue paper and slipped it into her overnight bag before going downstairs to inform her three companions that she was ready.

They were sitting around in the study, talking easily just as though the day were the same as any other. Reilof, she saw at once, had changed the beautifully-cut grey suit he had worn in church for an equally well-cut tweed jacket and cavalry twill trousers; the ring she had given him during the ceremony caught her eye, and without knowing that she did it, she touched her own wedding ring beneath the rubies of her engagement ring.

Reilof looked up then and saw her standing in the doorway and got to his feet, saying easily: 'Ah, here she is—I'll go and get the car and fetch the bags, shall I, while you say goodbye.'

It was a splendid summer's day and the Rolls ate up the miles. For the first few of them Laura had nothing to say, but presently, anxious to break the silence, she asked: 'You don't think Uncle Wim will mind staying another week with Father? I believe he meant to go back to Holland several weeks ago…'

Reilof swung the car away from Chelmsford, taking a country road which would bring them out on to the London road beyond Ongar. 'I'm sure he doesn't mind at all, and probably when we go back for him in a week's time he'll find some excuse for staying even longer.' He added to surprise her, 'You looked very nice this morning, Laura, and that's a pretty dress you're wearing.'

She could think of nothing to say but a murmured thank-you, and presently, to fill the silence, inquired which way they would go.

'The ring road—we can pick up the motorway at Chertsey, it will take us as far as Cadnam Corner.'

'Oh—exactly where are we going?'

'Heavens, did I not tell you? I've booked rooms at Corfe Castle. Do you know it?'

'I've been there once or twice, but never to stay. I liked it.'

'It won't be very quiet at this time of year, I'm afraid, but I thought we might drive out each day and go where inclination takes us. But if you don't like the idea, do say so and we'll try something else.'

'But I do like it,' she said positively, 'and I love exploring.'

The journey passed pleasantly enough, indeed, Laura was hard put to it to remember that she was actually married to the man beside her. It seemed more as though they were two friends out for the day, bent on entertaining each other. Only when they reached Corfe Castle and entered the picturesque old hotel in its little square was the fact of her married status brought home to her when she was addressed as Madam and heard Reilof saying that Mrs van Meerum would like to go to her room as soon as someone could be found to carry up her luggage.

She followed the porter upstairs to the first landing, where she discovered that they were to have two adjoining rooms at the back of the hotel. Very comfortable they were too, each with a bathroom and furnished with old-fashioned comfort. There was no sign of Reilof, so she unpacked her case, tidied her hair, saw to her face and wandered out on to the small balcony, where he presently joined her. It might have been the balcony scene from *Private Lives*; only their conversation held no hint of romance, for he asked at once if she was hungry and if so, would it not be a good idea for them to dine early and then take a stroll through the little town. 'I'll be back in fifteen minutes,' he suggested as he strolled away to his own room.

She changed her dress, more to please herself than for any other reason; since she had some pretty clothes she might as well wear them, and the round-necked, short-sleeved silk jersey dress in a pleasing shade of honey was certainly pretty. But if Reilof noticed it, he forbore from saying so, merely commending her on her promptitude as they went downstairs to the dining room where they had a leisurely meal at a small table in the window, a circumstance which Laura considered fortunate, for there was plenty to see in the square and it made a happy source of conversation. The dining room was almost full, but no one, she decided, would have any idea that they were newly married.

Indeed, their manner was more that of a couple who had been man and wife for some years, who, while enjoying each other's company, weren't excited by it. It was on the tip of her tongue to make some joking remark about it, but perhaps it would be as well to wait until they were on their own, for he might not find it amusing. It was disconcerting when he remarked: 'We must be the most untypical newly married couple ever heard of.' He smiled with sudden charm. 'Perhaps we should have gone to one of those enormous anonymous hotels where they hold dinner dances every night and you're known by your room number.'

She doubted very much if he had ever been to such a place, but she had followed his train of thought easily enough. 'No,' she declared firmly, 'it's quiet here and we have to get to know each other—I mean, you never really get to know anyone if you just go out to dinners and dances and theatres with them, do you?'

He agreed gravely and asked quietly, 'You're not regretting our marriage, Laura?'

She shook her head. 'No, but then I haven't got used to it yet, though I can't think of any reason why I should regret it, you know. I had a month in which to think about it and I'm not an impulsive girl.'

He raised his brows. 'Not in general, I think, but surely you were a little impulsive when you agreed to marry me?'

She went pink, although she poured his coffee with a steady hand and handed him the cup. 'You were impulsive to suggest it,' she pointed out. 'I daresay it's a good thing to do something on the spur of the moment now and again.' She sugared her coffee. 'There are a great many questions I should like to ask you during the next few days, so I hope you won't mind answering them.'

'I'll do my best, but shall we leave them until tomorrow? It's a delightful evening, we might walk round the town if you would like that.'

And it had been very pleasant, Laura decided as she got ready for bed. Strolling along, peering into the small shop windows, discussing where they should go, wandering round the church, reading the memorial tablets on its walls and then back to the hotel for a drink before bed. She yawned hugely, deliberately dwelling on the trivialities of the day; it hadn't been like a wedding day at all, but she hadn't expected that it would be, and she had promised herself that she wouldn't dwell on her love for Reilof but be thankful for what she had got. Not much, she decided sleepily, but the thin end of the wedge, perhaps? Or did she mean half a loaf was better than no bread at all? She wasn't sure, and she was too sleepy to decide.

* * *

Life seemed normal again after a sound night's sleep, and nothing could have been more prosaic than Reilof's manner at breakfast. They spent their day in Salisbury because Laura had expressed a wish to see the cathedral again, lunched at the Rose and Crown and then made their way back to Corfe Castle, keeping to the country roads and stopping for tea at a little cottage run by an old lady, very spry despite her grey hair, who served them with strong tea in a brown pot, scones of her own baking and a great dish of clotted cream and strawberry jam besides. Laura made a good tea, quite at ease now with Reilof after a day's undemanding conversation with him. They hadn't talked much of his home, although he had given her snippets of information about Holland and the way of life there. Very much the same as in England, she had considered, and wished that he would tell her more about himself and his family—still, there would be all the time in the world to do that when they got back. She polished off the last of the scones, bade the old lady a cheerful goodbye and accompanied Reilof back to the car, where he invited her to get into the driving seat and try her hand.

'I don't dare,' she protested vigorously. 'Supposing I should smash it up—it's a Rolls...'

'You haven't smashed a car up yet, have you?'

he wanted to know calmly. 'I can see no reason why you should do so now. Besides, I shan't let you.'

She was nervous at first, but presently she forgot she was driving a wildly expensive car which wasn't hers and began to enjoy herself. Only when they rejoined the main road once more did Reilof take over again, assuring her that she drove very well and that once they were back in Holland she should have a car of her own. 'Nothing too large, though.'

'But you've got two cars already,' she pointed out.

'It will be best for you to have your own, all the same,' he told her reasonably, and began to talk about something else.

They went out each day, sometimes merely pottering through the lanes around the town, sometimes going farther afield, and although Laura still felt a slight constraint between them, she was content that they enjoyed each other's company well enough, and as she pointed out to herself in the privacy of her room, they were all day and every day together now, and once they were in Holland they would see far less of each other. If they could get through the week without falling out or getting on each other's nerves, she felt that it augured well for the future.

It was the day before they were due to return that they visited the Blue Pool. They had been recommended to visit it by several people at the hotel, but somehow there had always been other places to see and other things to do, but now, after spending the morning at Lulworth Cove, already over-full of holidaymakers, they decided to find it on their way back to the hotel. They took the narrow road over the hills that wound its way in and out of hamlets, apparently going nowhere. The day had been fine and now in the afternoon it was pleasantly cool as they drove slowly down the narrow lane for the last mile or so of their journey, and even then they weren't quite there, for there was a narrow, half-hidden track to negotiate before they found themselves in a large clearing with the entrance to the Blue Pool at one side of it.

They parked the car and went through the gates into the grounds surrounding the pool, and at first Laura thought it all a bit overrated; there were some splendid trees and shrubs, true enough, but there was no sign of a pool…they saw it unexpectedly, lying below them, a deep circle of bright blue ringed by a narrow strip of sand and dense shrubs, intersected by a great many narrow paths.

'How absolutely super,' exclaimed Laura, craning her neck to see through the bushes, 'and what a heavenly blue!'

'The special clay bed,' Reilof informed her, 'but don't ask me more than that, because I don't know.

It is rather splendid.' He took her hand and her heart, taken unawares, turned over. 'There's a path, shall we explore a little?'

They wandered slowly round the water, catching glimpses of it below them, and as they went they discovered a bench perched high on a bank, and sat down. For some reason there were very few people about, and from where they sat they could hear the distant laughter and cries of some children on the other side of the pool, and all around them the birds singing. It was peaceful as well as beautiful.

'If ever I wanted to run away from anything,' mused Laura out loud, 'and hide, I think I should come here.'

Reilof looked at her sharply. 'Why do you say that?'

'No reason really, just a feeling. I don't usually run away from anything and I can't imagine having a reason—it would have to be something quite dreadful.' She smiled at him. 'We go back tomorrow, you know, and I still don't know very much about your home.'

'It will be *our* home now,' he observed, and she heard the bitterness in his voice and winced at it. She had tried very hard during the last few days to get to know him better and she believed that they had become friends, but she didn't know his deepest feelings. He would still be in love with Joyce, she was sure of that, but that was to be expected. She would have to have patience and in the meantime play the colourless part he had offered her.

She sighed soundlessly and then said cheerfully: 'I'd love a cup of tea—could we try that tea-room we passed as we came in, do you think?'

Forty-eight hours later, sitting beside Reilof once more and with Uncle Wim in the back seat as they drove up to Harwich to catch the ferry to Holland, she decided that on the whole their first week together had gone well. At least they were quite at ease with each other now, and when her godfather had asked her, 'Are you happy, Laura?' she had been able to say yes and mean it. She had reservations about the future, of course, but they could be faced later on.

CHAPTER SIX

IT WAS most unfortunate that by the time they reached Harwich, the weather had changed very much for the worse; clouds which had been hovering on the horizon all day suddenly massed themselves together, blown by a freak gale, bringing not only rain with it, but thunder and lightning as well. Laura didn't like storms, and she paled a little with each flash and moved, almost without knowing it, nearer Reilof, so that when they went on board she sighed with relief and went straight to her cabin before joining her companions in the bar.

'Tonic water?' suggested Reilof with a sidelong glance at her pale face, and when they had finished their drinks and Uncle Wim had voiced his intention to go to his cabin without delay, Reilof suggested that they might go on deck for a little while. The rain had ceased by now and the storm was a mere muttering in the distance, and only the wind howled and sighed around them. Laura, her hair in a splendid tangle, clung to a nice solid rail and looked with loathing at the heaving water below.

'It's going to be rough,' she observed in a hollow voice, and was irritated by her companion's cheerful, 'Oh, I imagine so—there's a gale force wind.' He dismissed this disquieting news carelessly and went on, 'Take a look behind you, Laura; you won't be seeing England again for a little while.'

She didn't care if she never saw it again. She said in a carefully controlled voice, 'I'm going to be sick,' and Reilof, who had never been sick in his life, gave her a startled look, said: 'My God, so you are,' and proceeded to deal with the situation with a calm matter-of-factness which, if she hadn't been feeling quite so ghastly, would have earned Laura's approbation. As it was, she was only too thankful to have someone there to hold her head, and presently, when the worst was over, to help her down to her cabin. Here she made a great effort to pull herself together, but Reilof took no notice at all of her rather half-hearted protestations that she was feeling fine, but laid her out on her bunk, took off her shoes, covered her with a blanket, wiped her face with a damp towel and rang for the stewardess. Laura didn't see him go, for the cabin was revolving and dipping in a most alarming manner and she had shut her eyes;

when she opened them again it was the kindly face of the stewardess which she saw hovering above her.

'Yer 'usband says yer ter 'ave this, Mrs van Meerum,' she said in a cheerful cockney voice, 'a nice drop o' brandy.'

'Ugh,' said Laura, drank it obediently and mumbled that she would be sick again at any moment, then went soundly to sleep.

She slept until shortly before they landed and woke to a still tossing ship which miraculously didn't matter any more, although she felt very hollow. But fortified by the tea and toast the stewardess had brought, she made shift to make herself presentable, so that when Reilof came to fetch her she looked much as usual, although still wan, in sharp contrast to his own elegant appearance, for he had the look of a man who had slept all night and who had, moreover, the time to spare in which to make a leisurely toilet.

That he had remained awake for the greater part of the night and had visited her half a dozen times at least during it was something she didn't even guess at. During the whole of her life she had never been cosseted by her parents even though they had loved her; the cosseting had all been for Joyce and she had long ago become used to it, so that now it never entered her head that anyone, and certainly not Reilof, should concern themselves about her. She wished him good morning in a composed manner, begged his pardon for making a nuisance of herself on the previous evening, and accompanied him on deck where her godfather was waiting. He, it turned out, had slept like a log and had never felt better. The two men, thought Laura, standing between them, looked quite disgustingly healthy, which put her at a disadvantage, although neither of them mentioned her seasickness, merely hoping that she felt well before they embarked on a discussion as to the best road to take when they disembarked.

The boat was full and most of the passengers were already crowding into the saloon, anxious to rejoin their cars on the car deck, but Reilof seemed unaware of this; he leaned against the ship's rail, one arm flung carelessly across Laura's shoulders while he argued lazily with Uncle Wim, and pausing now and then to point out something of interest to her as the ferry crept to its berth at the quayside. Only then, when the first rush of passengers had subsided, did he usher his companions back to the car.

One of the last off, once they had cleared the little town he shot the Rolls ahead, and when they joined the motorway a few miles further on he outstripped everything ahead of them. 'It will be a dull trip,' he warned Laura, 'motorway all the way, but it's quick and your godfather is anxious to get home—he lives quite close to us. We'll drop him off first.' He glanced at her. 'Once we're through Rotterdam we'll stop for coffee.' He added with a faint smile, 'I daresay you're feeling a little empty.'

Laura admitted to hunger. 'But don't stop on my account,' she begged him, 'if Uncle Wim wants to get home…' She added, 'Is it far?'

'About sixty miles—no distance. We shall be home in time for a very late breakfast. All the same, we'll stop.'

He drew up before a pleasant-looking road house just off the motorway very shortly after, and although it was still early the coffee when it came was hot and fragrant and creamy. Laura had two cups and a *kaas broodje* besides and got back into the car feeling almost her own self again, so that she was able to obey her godfather's gentle demands to look at first one landmark, then another. The motorway might be dull, but the flat country around them made it possible to get a wide view of it, as well as getting a distant glimpse of the various towns and villages they skirted. They bypassed Utrecht, the doctor barely slackening speed, and took a side road to Baarn; the country was prettier here and wooded, and there were large villas tucked away almost out of sight of the road. Laura craned her neck in her efforts to see everything, and when her godfather warned her that they would be passing the royal palace in only a few moments, she begged Reilof to slow down just a little. 'Only for a moment,' she pleaded, 'just so that I can see it.'

He laughed and did as she asked, pointing out at the same time that as they lived quite close by, she would be able to see it as often as she wished in the future.

'Oh, are we almost there?' she wanted to know, and felt a small thrill of excitement and apprehension. Supposing the house was awful—it might even be a flat; she had never thought of asking and now it was too late. And supposing the housekeeper he had told her about didn't like her, or she didn't like the housekeeper? What if none of his friends liked her—worse still, his family? Her gloomy thoughts were brought to a halt by Reilof's quiet: 'There's the palace.'

He had slowed the car's splendid rush only momentarily, and a moment later he had put on speed again and presently, at a busy crossroads, had taken the left-hand fork to stop within a minute or two to slide the car gently into a tree-lined avenue of pleasant houses, each standing in its own garden. Halfway down he turned again, this time through a white-painted gateway, and drew up before a white-walled villa with a thatched roof: Doctor van Pette's house. Its door was instantly opened by an elderly, gaunt woman, who bustled out, bursting into speech as she came. The two men greeted her like an old friend, and Reilof said: 'This is Miekje, your god-father's housekeeper—she rules him with a rod of iron and he loves it. We have been asked to go in, but I think we should go straight home now. Wait there while I take the luggage in.'

Laura bade her godfather goodbye, promised to see him at the first opportunity, and sat quietly while his bags were taken indoors and Reilof made his own goodbyes before getting in beside her once more.

'He's tired,' he said abruptly. 'I've sent him straight to bed—a day's rest won't do him any harm.'

'He's not ill?' she asked sharply.

'No—but he's had a couple of coronaries, you know, and he's well into his seventies.' He smiled at her. 'I have the greatest dislike of my patients taking risks.'

'Oh, he's your patient—I should have guessed that, shouldn't I?'

They were back on the main road again; a magnificent one, lined with great trees backed by woods through which she caught an occasional glimpse of a house. 'Where are we now?' she wanted to know.

'Halfway between Baarn and Hilversum.' He slowed to cross the road and go through an open gateway between tall brick pillars, and she said: 'Is this it?' in such a scared voice that he said instantly, 'There's no need for you to worry, Laura.'

The drive was short, bordered by shrubs and ornamental trees, and beyond its curve the house came into view.

'Well, I never!' exclaimed Laura with a surprise which brought the doctor to an abrupt halt.

'You don't like it?' he asked quietly.

She turned to stare up at him. 'Like it?' she whispered. 'Like it? It's magnificent. I don't know what I expected and you didn't tell me…it's a bit scaring, actually.'

'Oh, never that, my dear girl—it's old and rambling at the back, and I suppose it's a little on the large side, but it's never scared anyone in its long life.'

He spoke lightly, laughing at her, and she made haste to explain: 'Not the house—it's just that I'm going to live in it, and it's rather grand.' She added with faint annoyance, 'You could have told me!'

'I never thought about it,' he answered her suavely, and she knew, just as though he had told her in so many words, that he hadn't wanted to; probably he had planned to tell Joyce, describing to her every stick and stone lovingly…

For something to say, she asked: 'It's old—eighteenth century?'

'Yes—the first half. Anyone who had any money at all then built their houses in some pleasant country spot not too far from Amsterdam—twenty miles or so—even in those days it wasn't a great distance.'

He had stopped the car on the wide gravel sweep before the great door, and while he was getting out she had another good look. The house was large, with a flat face, a stone balustrade and a large wrought-iron balcony above the front porch. Its windows were enormous, shining in the morning sun, set in precise rows across its face. She suspected that the rambling bit he had mentioned was at the back because she could just see a half-hidden wing to one side with much smaller windows set haphazard into its wall. And all around were green lawns and vast flower beds, so that she asked him, 'However many gardeners do you keep?'

He looked surprised. 'Two—oh, and a boy, I believe.'

'Don't you know?'

'I'm ashamed to say that there are several things

I don't know about my own home—you see, of late
I have been away a good deal; I leave things to Piet.'

Laura was beside him now, at the foot of the
steps leading to the door. 'Piet?'

As if in answer to her question, the door opened
and a portly man, no longer young, with white hair
and very blue eyes, appeared on the top step. He
beamed a welcome at Reilof, who shook him by the
hand and exchanged some laughing greeting with
him before saying, 'Well, Laura, you wanted to
know who Piet was—this is he. He has been with
my father and mother all their married life, and now
he looks after me. I'm sure he will do the same for
you.' He added reassuringly, 'He speaks English.'

Laura let out a little breath of relief and extended
a hand. 'Oh, how very nice,' she exclaimed. 'How
do you do, Piet.' She smiled at him and received a
fatherly beam in return as he shook her hand.

'And if you are wondering why he isn't looking
after my father instead of being here, I should tell
you that his son performs that office.'

As he spoke Reilof had ushered her inside,
leaving Piet to close the great door behind them, and
she found herself in a square hall with doors on
either side and a carved staircase at the back, flanked
by arched doors presumably leading to the back of

the house. It was a handsome and lofty apartment, its walls panelled in white-painted wood, picked out with gilt and lighted by delicate crystal wall sconces. A magnificent grandfather clock in a tulip-wood case stood between two double doors on one side, and against the opposite wall was a side table in carved and gilded wood, flanked by two arm-chairs upholstered in needlework tapestry.

But she had little time to study these treasures, for Reilof took her arm and opened one of the double doors, urging her into a room, just as lofty and with two enormous windows draped in a rich terracotta velvet. The same colour was predominant in the Anatolian carpet and the comfortable chairs scattered about its vast floor; it was a pleasant contrast to the silvery wood with which the walls were panelled and the golden satinwood of the large rent table set between the windows. The same wood was used for the bow-fronted wall cabinets on either side of the marble fireplace, the silver and porcelain they displayed winking and glowing through their glass doors. There were a number of small tables, too, and another great wall cabinet of superb mar-quetry. A beautiful room, and Laura, pausing to take it all in on its threshold, was aware that all this mag-nificence was hers to live in now. It was a daunting thought, and she looked at Reilof with a touch of uncertainty.

'I hope you'll love it as much as I do,' he said gently, just as though he knew what she was thinking. 'This is the drawing room; we'll have our coffee and something to eat in the small sitting room, through here.'

He led her across to a narrow door by the fireplace which opened into a much smaller apartment, with Regency furniture and remarkably cosy, with its French windows opening on to a wide expanse of lawn, and chintz curtains blowing in the light breeze. The circular table in the centre of the room was laid with a snowy cloth and rose-patterned china, and two chairs had been drawn up to it most invitingly.

They were greeted here by Lucky, free of his plasters and a little stiff in his hind legs and his coat glossy and sleek, who got out of his basket and came to sniff delightedly at them, closely followed by an elderly sheepdog, stiff in the hind legs too, but from age. Laura made much of them both, and looked up to ask: 'Why Hovis?'

'He adores brown bread,' said Reilof. He put a hand on the old dog's head. 'The pair of them get on splendidly.'

The door opened then and a small, thin woman

darted in, said something to Reilof and set a tray of coffee on the table. He answered her with a laugh and turned to Laura. 'This is Truus, Piet's wife—she looks after the house and does the cooking. I'm afraid she doesn't speak any English, but you will quickly learn some Dutch.'

Laura offered her hand once more and smiled and said how do you do, which she realised was rather silly, but what else was one to say?

Truus smiled and broke into speech again, and Reilof said: 'Truus says that she can see that you will be a good housewife and she welcomes a mistress to the house; she will be happy to work for you and to show you anything you may wish to see.'

Laura went a pretty pink. 'How kind! Please will you tell Truus that I shall value her friendship and help. It's generous of her to be so friendly—after all, I'm a complete stranger.'

'You are my wife.' Reilof spoke coolly and she wondered if she had annoyed him in some way. Perhaps he was reminding himself of the lovely bride he had expected to bring with him. Laura turned away to tickle Hovis's chin, for his woolly head was comforting under her hand and she needed comfort. There would be many more such moments before her, and the quicker she faced up to them without self-pity the better. Reilof, with Truus gone, asked her to pour their coffee and the face she turned to him was serene again; she had no intention of ever letting him see it otherwise.

They had their early lunch together, talking casually about nothing in particular, and when they had finished Reilof said shortly, 'You won't mind if I leave you? I have a good deal of work to attend to, I doubt if I shall be finished before the evening. I'll tell Truus to take you round the house. Piet will give you tea whenever you want it, and I daresay you want to unpack and have a rest. I have always had dinner at half-past seven, but if you would like to alter that time, please do as you think fit.'

Laura eyed him with surprise; he could have been addressing the new home help, but she forgave him. After all, he wasn't yet used to having a wife, if one could call her that. 'I don't expect I shall want to change anything,' she told him in a sensible voice, 'and if I did, I shouldn't dream of doing so until I consulted you and Truus.' She smiled a little. 'How wretched for you, having to plunge straight back into your work, though I daresay you don't mind at all. I'll see you this evening, then.'

He looked slightly taken aback as though he had expected her to complain at his going, although all he said was: 'I'll send Piet in as I go.'

Piet proved a mountain of helpfulness and common sense, and Laura found her afternoon gently organised for her. She should be taken at once to her room where she would find her clothes unpacked, and perhaps she would like an hour or so to herself, then perhaps Truus might come to her room at three o'clock and take her round the house. He would accompany them if *mevrouw* had no objection, so that any questions she might wish to ask could be answered.

Laura smiled at the cheerful little man. 'That sounds perfect, Piet,' she told him. 'I'll go to my room now if Truus will take me there.'

She followed the housekeeper up the thickly-carpeted staircase and along a gallery which ran round three sides of the hall, and found her room to be at the front of the house, a large, light apartment with wide windows opening on to the wrought-iron balcony. A wide four poster bed was hung with the same pink and blue chintz as curtained the windows, and a delicate bow-fronted chest of satin-wood with painted panels stood against one wall. There was a sofa-table too between the windows, with a shield-back mirror upon it and elegant satin-wood chairs upholstered in pink striped silk, and on the bedside tables were exquisite china groups serving as lamps. Laura stood trying to take it all in. 'It's beautiful,' she said at length. 'I've never seen such a lovely room.' Her eyes roamed everywhere; it certainly lacked nothing, from its silk-striped pearly pink walls to the thick carpet under her feet, it was perfection itself.

'*De badkamer.*' Truus had opened a door cut into a wall to reveal a bathroom as modern and luxurious as any woman could wish for. Pink again, its shelves stocked with every soap and powder and lotion one could think of. Reilof would have bought these, Laura guessed, ready for Joyce's use. She wondered if Piet and Truus were surprised to find that his new wife was such a homely-looking girl with none of the sparkle attributed to a new bride, but when she thanked the housekeeper there was nothing in Truus's face to suggest it. It smiled back at her with genuine goodwill and a desire to please while the housekeeper got herself to the door with a few cheerful, unintelligible words. When she had gone, Laura had a leisurely bath, put on another dress and disdaining the desire for a nap, did her face and hair, this time allowing her mousy tresses to hang down her back, tied back with a chiffon scarf, and by the time she had done that there was a discreet knock on the door and Truus came in. Piet's voice from behind her said: 'If you are ready, *mevrouw*, we shall be most happy to show you the house.'

Perhaps they found it a little odd, mused Laura as she walked beside Truus along the gallery, that the doctor's new wife should be shown her new home by the housekeeper and not her husband. A vivid picture of Joyce arm-in-arm with Reilof, waltzing in and out of the rooms, discussing their furnishings, making him laugh, wheedling him to alter this and buy that, imprinted itself on her brain, but she frowned it away; Joyce mustn't be allowed to spoil any chance of happiness there might be for Reilof and herself, although perhaps contentment was the word she needed.

They inspected the rooms downstairs first; the drawing room, which she now went round at her leisure, the smaller sitting room behind it, the elegant dining room with its Hepplewhite chairs and table and massive side table. Twenty persons could sit down to dinner, Piet informed her with pride, and the dinner service used for such occasions was almost two hundred years old. Across the hall was the doctor's study; Laura didn't go in, but stood at the door, looking at the kneehole desk with its big, solid chair behind it, the shelves of books and the two leather armchairs drawn up to the hooded fireplace before going on to a small panelled room which Piet called the parlour, and much used, she fancied, for there was a small oval table in its centre with a magazine or two on it, a couple of books and a bowl of fresh flowers. The dogs' baskets were here too, as well as a charming little work-table with a button-backed balloon chair beside it.

Piet saw her looking at it and said at once, 'The doctor's mother used this room, *mevrouw*. She liked to have her tea here and sit quietly—he would come here each evening when she was alive...'

Which raised a problem. Would Reilof like her to use it too, or was it to be out of bounds? She would have to find out.

The kitchen premises last, said Piet firmly, leading the way upstairs again, past her own room, to open a neighbouring door with the words: 'The doctor's room, *mevrouw*.' A very masculine apartment it was, too, its mahogany furniture set off by a honey-coloured carpet and amber curtains and bedspread. Laura, feeling an intruder, glanced round, murmured appreciatively and turned her back on it to be shown the adjoining bathroom before passing on to the second side of the gallery. There were three rooms here, a good deal smaller than her own but large enough by her own standards, each furnished with great good taste, and along the third side there was a larger room again, with a narrow passage beside it running towards the back of the house. She had been right, the back wing rambled; the passage had corners, steps and unexpected windows and a great many rooms, some small, all exquisitely furnished, leading from it. She rather lost count of their number and the bathrooms which adjoined them, but there seemed a great number.

'The work!' she declared, round-eyed.

Truus understood her and smiled, but it was Piet who answered. 'These rooms are used only for guests,' he explained. 'At New Year and Christmas and when there is a family gathering. We have sufficient help in the house, *mevrouw*, and every modern aid to make the work light.'

Laura nodded. Reilof must have a great deal of money to live in a house of this size. Presumably, when he saw fit, he would tell her such details—after all, she was his wife, she had a right to know. She frowned; there were more and more problems cropping up to which she had given no thought at all.

The passage took a sharp turn and Truus opened the door which confronted them. '*Kinderkamer*,' she pronounced happily, and Piet said: 'Truus is very fond of children, *mevrouw*. This is the nursery—here is the day nursery, and here the sleeping rooms, three

for the children, and one for the nursemaid. The
doctor's nanny lives here still—perhaps you knew
that? She is old now but very sound in the head. She
is at present in Scotland with her niece.'

He beamed at Laura and when she looked at
Truus, Truus was smiling too. Presumably her arrival
to them meant a nicely-filled nursery. The thought
gave her a heartache; a number of little van Meerums
romping around in the homely room would be
exactly what the old house needed. She managed a
smile, going a little pink in the face because she was,
in a way, deceiving them. The pinkness made it
worse; they exchanged happy, conspiratorial glances
and shut the door with a satisfied click before escort-
ing her up a narrow staircase to the floor above—
more bedrooms and a small sitting room, cosily
furnished.

'Annie and Els, the two housemaids,' explained
Piet, 'they have their rooms here, and there are also
attics and store rooms and a bathroom. If you are not
tired, *mevrouw*, we will go to the glass house.'

He meant the sunroom, a vast one, running the
width of the house at the back and entered from the
small sitting room where they had had their lunch
as well as a narrow door in the hall. It housed a
variety of plants and flowers, and a white-painted
table and chairs as well as comfortable loungers. It

opened on to a wide lawn behind the house, sur-
rounded by a herbaceous border, flowering shrubs
and ornamental trees and there was a square pool in
its centre with a little fountain playing. Laura gazed
about her, taking in its beauty, conscious of a feeling
of resentment that Reilof hadn't told her about it.
Perhaps he had thought that she wouldn't be interested, perhaps he couldn't bear the thought of her
enjoying something which Joyce would have
revelled in. 'Luxury,' muttered Laura, and turned to
listen to Piet explaining about the paths leading
away from the lawn and into the shrubbery.

'There is a swimming pool on that side,' he
waved an explanatory arm, 'and on this side there
are the garages and outbuildings, and at the end of
the garden there is a pretty summer house, very
quiet. You like it, *mevrouw*?'

'Oh, I do,' declared Laura fervently, 'it's pure
heaven.'

He gave her a kindly look. 'There is time enough
for you to inspect the kitchens, *mevrouw*—you
shall sit here and I will bring you the English afternoon tea. There is a pleasant seat near the
fountain and a little table...'

She was pouring her first cup of Earl Grey from
the gadrooned silver teapot when Piet came across
the lawn once more, this time with a visitor. A

thickset young man of middle height, with lint-fair hair and blue eyes in an open face. He smiled but didn't speak until Piet announced: 'Doctor Jan van Mijhof, the doctor's partner, *mevrouw*.' He added, 'I will bring another cup and saucer.'

Laura was on her feet, holding out a hand. 'Oh, how nice,' she exclaimed, 'I was feeling just a little lonely. Reilof told me about you, of course, but I didn't expect to meet you so soon.'

His smile broadened. 'For that I am guilty, Mevrouw van Meerum, I knew that Reilof would be back today. I am just returned from Amsterdam and I thought that I would call in on my way home. I expected that he would be here. Did some emergency make it necessary for him to work today?'

'I—I don't think so. He said that he had a great deal of work and wouldn't be back until this evening. I'm delighted that you called, though. Now I can have tea with someone…'

Piet had brought another cup and saucer and she bade her guest sit down while she poured his tea and offered him one of the little macaroons Truus had put on the tea tray. She had liked the young man at once; here, at least, was someone she would be able to talk to. He was about her own age, perhaps a little younger, and he had an open face which invited friendship.

'I've dozens of questions,' she said happily. 'You

don't live here? Close by, I suppose? Do you share Reilof's consulting rooms, and do you have beds at the hospital too? And are you married...?'

Her companion laughed, although the look he gave her was thoughtful; it seemed that Reilof hadn't told her much, which seemed strange, surely he would have told her these things long ago? All the same, he answered obligingly: 'I live in Baarn, and yes, I have a room at Reilof's consulting rooms, although he has by far the greater number of patients—he's well-known, you see, and much sought after. I'm lucky to be his partner, for I've only had a few years' post-graduate work, but when he offered me the partner-ship I jumped at it. I'm only a junior partner, of course, but I'm learning his ways and methods as quickly as I can.' He added reverently, 'He really is a splendid doctor and a fine man, *mevrouw*.' He refreshed himself with a macaroon and continued, 'I'm not married—at least, I should like to be...' He looked suddenly shy and Laura said kindly:

'Will you tell me about it when you know me better?'

'I should like to—I don't want to bother Reilof—in fact, I haven't told anyone, only you.'

'Then I'll keep the secret,' she promised. 'Have some more tea and tell me how and where I can get someone to teach me Dutch.'

He gave her another thoughtful look. 'I expect Reilof knows of someone,' he suggested hesitantly, and when she just smiled, added boyishly: 'I say, Mevrouw van Meerum, I am very glad that Reilof has married. He is a marvellous man, you know, although it's silly for me to say that to you, isn't it?'

Laura said soberly: 'He's a very good man, and by the way, since you and he are on Christian name terms, could you call me Laura? I feel a hundred when you say Mevrouw van Meerum.'

They laughed together and were still laughing as Reilof came out of the house towards them. He was quite close before Laura looked up and saw him, and she called gaily, 'Oh, how nice, you're home for tea after all—I'll get another cup. Jan called to see you and stayed to keep me company.'

Reilof gave her a bland look which concealed she knew not what. 'So I see—don't bother about another cup, I had coffee at the hospital.' He took a handful of Truus's macaroons and sat down to eat them. 'How are you, Jan?' His voice was friendly, but the bland look was still there; he was annoyed about something and she didn't know what. Of course, she could be imagining that; she would have to be a little less sensitive, and indeed, there was nothing in his manner to bear out her suspicion.

He stayed talking to Jan about their holiday for

ten minutes or so and then suggested that they went to his study so that they might discuss some patient's treatment. His, 'I'll be back shortly, my dear,' was exactly the remark any wife might expect from a husband. She watched their retreating backs, relaxing in the sunshine. Jan was nice. His 'goodbye, Laura,' had been friendly and just a shade differential, which amused her very much; of course she was his partner's wife… She mused gently about nothing in particular, and presently closed her eyes and slept.

She was surprised to find that she had been asleep for almost an hour. The tea tray had gone and the two dogs, who had been sitting with her, were nowhere to be seen. Perhaps Reilof had come back, decided not to disturb her, and gone back to the house. But when she went indoors there was no sign of him; she went in search of Piet finally, and he told her in some surprise that the doctor was in his study and that Doctor van Mijhof had been gone for half an hour or more. His look registered polite surprise that she hadn't been to see for herself, and she said hastily: 'I'll not disturb him, he's bound to be busy,' very conscious that a newly-married man, however busy he might be, might be expected to welcome a visit from his bride, and went to her room. There was more than an hour to dinner, so she occupied it in changing her dress for the honey-coloured jersey and sweeping her hair up into its tidy bun once more.

There was no one in the drawing room when she went down, nor in the little sitting room behind it, and she sat down by the open window and leafed through a Dutch newspaper to no purpose at all and feeling lonely. Reilof's quiet, 'Hullo, so there you are,' from the open door took her by surprise, so that she dropped the paper all over the floor and uttered a feeble, 'I wasn't sure where to go…'

He raised his eyebrows. 'Anywhere you wish, Laura. I usually work in my study for an hour before dinner and again afterwards. I'm afraid I keep late hours, but that shouldn't bother you.' He added surprisingly, 'You've put your hair up.'

She decided to ignore that. 'It won't bother me in the least,' she assured him cheerfully as she accepted a glass of sherry. 'At what time do you have breakfast?'

'Half-past seven. If that is too early for you, one of the maids will bring it to your room, or you can come down later.'

She felt like an unwelcome guest being treated with the minimum of good manners. 'I shouldn't dream of putting anyone to the trouble,' she told him, a thought snappish. 'Breakfast at half-past seven suits me very well. You won't need to talk to me, you know.'

He looked surprised and then laughed. 'I'm sorry, I didn't mean to be so ill-humoured. I suppose I'm not used to being married again.'

'I know exactly what you mean,' she told him kindly. 'I feel a bit the same myself. But don't imagine that I shall interfere with your life or your habits—I told you that I wouldn't and I won't, only you must tell me when I get in the way or do something to vex you, otherwise I shan't know.'

He put down his glass and came to stand before her. 'Laura, you're a nice girl and an understanding one. Give me a little time, will you? And I promise you that I'll tell you when you vex me, and you must do the same. Shall we go in to dinner?'

He pulled her to her feet and tucked an arm into hers so that her heart bounced against her ribs. 'Tell me, what did you think of the house?'

Getting ready for bed later that evening, she decided that the evening had been a success; they had enjoyed their meal together and Reilof had told her something of his work at the hospital and a little, but not much, about his private practice. And later he had telephoned his father and arranged for them to drive over to see him the following evening, so that she was able to see him go to his study and wish him a placid goodnight without too much disappointment. After all, he had warned her that he worked each evening, and she had their visit to his father to look forward to. 'Count your blessings, my girl,' she admonished her reflection, and jumped into her enormous bed, to sleep at once and dream of Reilof.

CHAPTER SEVEN

REILOF was already at the breakfast table when Laura got down the following morning, deep in his letters and with a newspaper spread out before him as well. Evidently not a chatty meal—she wished him a quiet good morning and sat down opposite him, accepting the English newspapers laid neatly beside her plate as a strong hint to maintain silence. She poured herself some coffee; Reilof, who got to his feet as she went in, had returned to his mail once more, sparing a few seconds to hope that she had slept well and inviting her to help herself to anything she wanted and ring for anything she wished. She rather fancied that he didn't hear her polite 'Thank you,' and he didn't speak again until he had finished his letters, when he swallowed his coffee and rose to his feet once more.

'I expect to be home about six,' he told her, and

halfway to the door remembered to wish her a pleasant day.

'Doing what?' asked Laura silently to his disappearing back, and then remembered that he had asked her to have patience. As it turned out there was plenty to occupy her time; the kitchens to inspect— a roomy complex with a separate scullery and laundry, and what she supposed was the Dutch equivalent of a butler's pantry. She met the two maids, too, Annie and Els, strapping young girls who smiled widely as they greeted her and then the gardener, an old man with a weatherbeaten face and a fringe of white hair, and when she had had her coffee in the sunroom she was borne away to inspect linen cupboards, kitchen equipment and the housekeeping books. The latter made almost no sense at all, but she felt it was incumbent on her to make a start. The amount of money spent on food rather staggered her, but presumably Reilof could afford it, although when she changed the guldens into pounds the total made her open her eyes.

And after her solitary lunch she went to the swimming pool and spent a lazy hour. She swam well and the pool was a good size and the water warm, then she dressed and had tea in the garden, then went up to her room to change her dress, ready for Reilof's return.

They were to dine with his father, he had told her, and she put on one of her new dresses, a silk print in shades of green, sleeveless and nicely cut, adding the Charles Jourdan sandals which she hadn't really been able to afford because she wanted to make a good impression. But they made no impression on Reilof when he came home; he put his head round the sitting room door, said, 'Hullo—shan't keep you long,' and went straight upstairs to reappear presently in a pale grey checked suit and a rather splendid tie. She doubted very much if he had any idea at all of what she was wearing, and he barely glanced at her as he suggested briskly that they should leave immediately.

Laura got to her feet at once, wished the dogs goodbye and accompanied Reilof out to the car— the Aston Martin this time—and he didn't speak at all until they were through Hilversum and almost at Loenen. 'You don't have much to say for yourself,' he observed a little impatiently.

'I have plenty to say for myself,' declared Laura with asperity, 'but only when people want to listen to me. If you wish me to greet you,' she went on with some heat, 'with a flow of small talk of an evening, you have only to say so. I didn't get that impression when you came home just now.'

'My dear good girl, you don't have to fly at me

like a wildcat! You are free to say what you want and when you want to say it, you know.'

'That isn't what you said, you told me that you didn't want your present way of living changed.' She stared out of the window at the pretty country they were passing through and added without looking at him, 'I haven't taken umbrage, only made myself clear.'

His voice was silky. 'Very clear, Laura. You sound exactly like a wife.'

She nipped back the answer to that just in time and held her tongue with an effort, until in a silence grown too long she observed sweetly:

'How pretty it is here.'

'Delightful.'

They were on a narrow road running alongside a lake of some size. There were boats of all shapes and sizes moored at its edge, and on the other side of the road were handsome villas, each standing in its own spacious grounds, screened from the road by shrubs and trees and well-clipped hedges.

It was through the gate of one of these houses that Reilof drove the car, to stop before the already open door of a fair-sized house with a thatched roof with a patio, screened by climbing roses, at one side.

'Oh, very pretty,' exclaimed Laura, refusing to be damped by Reilof's silence, and jumped out before he could get round to open her door, but he caught her by the arm as they went up the path so that at a distance at least they must have looked like a devoted pair. And so it must have seemed to the man waiting for them at the door—Piet's son, looking just like a younger version of his father—for he smiled in a pleased way as Reilof introduced him to her and said in rather quaint English: 'It is a great delight that you enter the van Meerum family, *mevrouw*,' before leading them across the dim, cool hall to a room at the back of the house which over-looked a formal garden, its doors wide to the summer evening.

Its only occupant got to his feet as they went in and came to meet them; an elderly man with iron-grey hair and dark eyes, as tall as his son and as broad too, but unlike his son he was smiling. He said: 'Reilof...and your Laura,' and then turned to put his hands on her shoulders and kiss her cheek. 'My dear girl, I am so happy to welcome you into the family.' He held her away a little and studied her face while she stayed quiet under his look. 'I have always wanted another daughter,' he told her kindly, 'and now I have a charming one. I am glad that Reilof brought you here to meet me before he shows you off to the rest of the family.'

He took her arm and led her to an enormous sofa.

'Come and sit down and tell me about yourself. Reilof, will you get us all a drink? Dinner will be in about half an hour.'

The evening was a huge success; Laura, completely at ease with the elder of her two companions, wondered why it was that Reilof didn't allow himself to show the charm which his father demonstrated so easily. That he had charm she was well aware, and on one or two occasions during the evening he did relax, so that they were all talking and laughing like old friends with no hint of restraint, but the barrier he had put between them was there again once they were on their way home again. He refused to be drawn into more than polite, brief comments on their evening, despite her efforts, so that by the time they had arrived home once more she could find nothing more to do than wish him goodnight.

They were to go again to his father's house later in the week, and the rest of the family would be there too—a celebration dinner, old Doctor van Meerum had told Laura. She was to wear her prettiest dress and perhaps they would clear the drawing room of its furniture and dance afterwards. It had all sounded fun, but thinking about it the next morning she wasn't so sure; supposing none of them liked her?

She went down to her breakfast feeling subdued, and was made more so by Reilof's announcement that he would be going to Maastricht for a seminar and would be away for two days. 'I believe that I did mention that I go away frequently for a day or two at a time,' he observed, 'but I'm sure that you'll find plenty to do—get Piet to drive you if you want to do any shopping in den Haag or Amsterdam. You have enough money?'

'Yes, thank you, Reilof.' She tried to make her voice cheerful. Of course she had plenty of money, he had been more than generous with her allowance; she had never had so much money to spend on herself in her life before—only she would have forgone the lot in exchange for just one gift from him, something he had bought himself. Not even a wedding present, she told herself forlornly, and re-membered the gold cufflinks she had bought for him and had hidden away in a drawer when she realised that he had no thought of giving her anything.

'I don't think I shall need to bother Piet; there's heaps for me to see in Hilversum and Baarn, and the bus service is awfully good.'

He looked surprised. 'Oh, is it? I don't have occasion to use it.' He got up and came round the table to her chair and surprisingly bent to kiss her cheek. 'Piet will look after you,' he told her. '*Tot ziens.*'

He left her sitting there while the two dogs bustled along at his heels to see him off. Given the slightest encouragement Laura would have seen him off too, but she wasn't given any.

She filled the two days somehow, writing letters, exploring Baarn and Hilversum, shopping a little, spending long hours in the garden with her head bent over the embroidery she had bought to keep her occupied. There were the dogs to take for walks too, and Truus to consult about meals, but all the same she thought about Reilof almost all the time, wondering what he was doing and who he was with. It was strange to love a man so much and know so little about him.

He came back very late on the evening of the second day; she had been in bed for an hour or more and it had struck midnight before she heard the car turn into the drive and stop. Laura skipped out of bed at once and peeped from her window to see Reilof enter the house, and presently she heard him come upstairs and go to his room. She shivered a little by the open window and got back into bed; it would have been nice to have gone downstairs and made him a drink or sandwiches, but he might not have liked that. All the same, it was lovely to have him home again—she would ask him about Dutch lessons in the morning. She had half expected him to mention them, but perhaps he had been too busy… She drifted off into a daydream in which she learned to speak Dutch with a faultless accent and surprised and delighted him with her brilliance, and presently she went to sleep.

She brought the matter up at breakfast and was agreeably surprised when he said instantly: 'Yes, of course you shall have lessons—I know just the man to teach you, too. I'll telephone him this morning and arrange it. At what time of the day would you like him to come?'

Laura considered: she spent an agreeably pleasant hour in the kitchen with Truus after breakfast and then another hour walking the dogs. 'Eleven o'clock?' she wondered out loud. 'I should like to learn Dutch as quickly as possible. I did ask Jan about lessons, but he said you would be bound to arrange something…'

'You asked Jan…?' There was no mistaking the annoyance in his voice, although he looked placid enough.

'Well, yes—you see, I don't see you very often, really, do I? And you're busy.'

He let that pass and gathered up his letters. 'I'll arrange for eleven o'clock each day except Saturday and Sunday. Mijnheer de Wal can come here.'

'Does he have far to come? If he lives in Baarn or Hilversum I could easily catch a bus...'

Reilof was ready to go. 'I prefer him to come to the house,' he said briefly. 'I shall be home just before tea.'

So she began lessons with Mijnheer de Wal, a nice old gentleman with a luxurious moustache and beard, a benign expression and a firm determination to teach her to speak correct Dutch if it was the last thing he should do. After the first lesson she rather enjoyed herself, took his stern corrections meekly and made peculiar mistakes which she longed to laugh about with Reilof. But he, beyond asking her if she had started her lessons, made no further inquiries as to her progress, so that at the end of the week, when they were bidden to his father's house, she was able to surprise him by uttering a handful of painstakingly correct phrases, learned especially for the occasion.

And it had been an occasion, a red-letter day to be looked back on with pleasure. Reilof had asked her to wear her wedding dress, and, rather mystified, she had done so, and when she had gone downstairs he had been waiting for her in the drawing room, very elegant in his dinner jacket. He had stared at her rather as though he had never seen her before, before opening a leather case on the table beside him.

'I asked you to wear that dress because it would provide a suitable background for these,' he said. 'Stand still a moment.'

He had hung a necklace round her neck, a magnificent affair of rubies set around with diamonds, and then turned her round to see her reflection in the big Chippendale mirror on one wall. She was gasping with surprise when he lifted her hand and clasped a matching bracelet round her wrist.

She looked at that too, her eyes round with excitement and delight.

'They're gorgeous!' she managed. 'I suppose…'

'These too, but you'll have to put them on for yourself.'

The earrings were pear-shaped drops of rubies and diamonds in a heavy gold setting, and she poked the hooks into her ears and swung her head from side to side, admiring them. Her eyes met his in the mirror and she smiled widely and then turned towards him. 'Thank you, Reilof—I've never had…'

His matter-of-fact, 'The eldest son's wife inherits them. I can hardly take the credit for giving them to you,' damped her delight as effectively as a bucket of water would have done. She said bleakly, 'Oh, I see—and of course I have to wear them this evening…'

'Just so. Are we ready?'

But despite that unhappy little episode, the evening had been a success. Her father-in-law liked her and Margriet, Reilof's sister, had been charming and kind and friendly too. She was a pretty girl in her thirties, with his dark eyes, and her husband, a tall, bony man, good-looking in a rangy way, treated her with a casual warmth which she had found very reassuring. As for Laurent, the youngest of the family, he made no bones about liking her on sight; they had got on famously and were instant friends, so that the evening which she had been dreading had proved to be the greatest fun.

There had been uncles and aunts too, and half a dozen cousins, all making much of her, and after the family dinner party, friends had come in for drinks and to offer congratulations. Laura stood beside Reilof, shaking dozens of friendly hands, very conscious of him and the hand he had tucked under her arm from time to time. She had done her best; presumably his family, though perhaps not his father, thought that Reilof had married her for love and not just on an impulse, and she had behaved, she hoped, just as she ought, unaware that each time she had looked at him her love showed so clearly that all the members of the van Meerum family had gone home delighted that Reilof had fallen in love with a girl who so obviously adored him.

And Reilof—his behaviour couldn't be faulted.

He had said and done exactly the right things, smiling pleasantly as they had talked with first one and then the other of the family, and he had smiled at her too, his eyes dark and expressionless, so that she had felt cold inside. But when they were home again he observed pleasantly enough that everyone had liked her and she had been a great success with the family. She had thanked him quietly, wishing that he could like her and more than that, and then went upstairs in her magnificent jewels, sparkling in the light from the chandelier, and cried herself to sleep.

But there was no point in wishing for the moon; she was Reilof's wife and sooner or later she was determined to win his regard and even his love. She was beginning to fit nicely into his life now; she got on well with Truus, and Piet was her devoted slave; she had taken over a number of small chores about the house, gone shopping, and armed with the necessary basic Dutch Mijnheer de Wal dinned into her, coped with the telephone, callers, and the wives of Reilof's colleagues, who came to see what she was like. Because she was friendly and unassuming and a little shy they liked her, a fact which Reilof remarked upon one evening at dinner.

'Quite a success,' he told her blandly. 'You have slipped into your new role very easily, Laura.'

She wasn't sure if he was being deliberately

nasty. 'Your family have been more than kind to me. I have a lot to thank them for—your friends too. And Mijnheer de Wal is a wonderful teacher, and Jan gives me lots of tips…'

'Jan?' Reilof was on his way to his study.

She had got up from the table with him. 'Well, yes—I see him from time to time, you know.'

His eyebrows lifted. 'Indeed? You like him?'

'Oh, very much…' She noticed then that his dark eyes were studying her closely. She added lamely, 'He makes me laugh.'

He crossed the hall without a word and went into his study, closing the door very quietly behind him.

It was a couple of days later that he came home in the afternoon. Laura had been sitting in the garden, lounging on the grass with the two dogs and learning Dutch verbs, and was quite unprepared for his unexpected appearance, strolling across the grass with his hands in his pockets. She got to her feet at once, exclaiming happily, 'How lovely, you're early!'

He bent to fondle the dogs. 'Yes—if you're not busy doing anything special, I should like to show you something.'

She cast her books on one side. 'Grammar,' she told him, 'and I'm sick of it—it's a frightful language. Of course I'll come.'

They went round the side of the house where the

garages were; a converted coach-house with a broad sweep before it. All three garage doors were open. The Rolls and the Aston Martin were snugly stowed away, and outside the third was a small Fiat, new and shining and bright blue. 'Yours,' said Reilof.

'Mine?' Laura choked a little with excitement. 'Reilof, what an absolutely super present! Thank you...'

He glanced at her briefly. 'Hardly a present, more a necessity, I should have said.'

All her lovely excitement faded, and if it had been physically possible she would have picked up the little car and flung it at him. Instead she contented herself with an airy, 'How kind—I shall enjoy going around on my own.' She almost added, 'As usual.' but thought better of it. She was wandering round the bonnet as she spoke and didn't see the look of faint surprise on his face as he suggested:

'Why not try her out now?'

'Now? But the traffic's on the wrong side of the road...I shall have to get used to it.'

'So you will,' he agreed mildly, although there was a glimmer of laughter in his eyes. 'Why not run her down to the gate and get the feel of her?'

He was holding the door open for her to get in and it seemed a good idea. With him beside her, she started the engine and rather gingerly drove to the gate, and

when she reached it he said in a no-nonsense voice:
'We might as well go to Hilversum—take your time
and get across to the other lane.'

She was speechless; a little scared and cross at the
trick he had played on her, but she did as she was told
because pride wouldn't let her do anything else. His,
'Good girl, nicely done,' mollified her a little, but as
he followed it with: 'Don't strangle the wheel, let it
run through your hands, otherwise when you get to
a corner you won't have a hand left,' a criticism
which made her say tartly, 'I can drive, you know,'
and then because it was rather fun driving her very
own car with Reilof beside her, she laughed. 'It's
super!'

'That's better—you're doing very well. We'll call
on Father, he thinks you're a girl in a million and
here's your chance to prove it.'

She changed gear with a clash. What was the use
of her father-in-law prizing her so highly when his
son did not? She put her foot down and the car shot
forward too fast, and Reilof said on an unperturbed
chuckle, 'He'd like to see you in one piece, though.'

She drove the rest of the way with exaggerated
care and no further comments from Reilof, and the
old gentleman's delighted welcome should have
soothed her ruffled feelings, but Reilof, charming as
ever, remained aloof from the small jokes and con-

gratulations, just as though it didn't matter to him whether she could drive or not. When they got home his, 'You did quite well, Laura, but don't go out on your own yet,' did nothing to make her feel better.

'You're almost never home,' she pointed out waspishly, 'and when you are you're too busy to bother…'

He stared at her for a long moment. 'Ah—I neglect you, Laura?' he asked silkily.

'I didn't say that. I'm stating a fact, that's all—you told me you'd have very little time for me,' she reminded him.

They were standing outside the front door and she felt at a disadvantage because she had to look up at him. She said quickly, 'Well, it doesn't matter, you know, I'm not throwing it in your teeth or anything like that.'

His smile enchanted her, for it was unexpected and just for a moment he looked different, almost as though he liked her very much. She said breathlessly to fill the silence between them, 'I'm sorry if I was beastly.'

His arm caught her round the waist and clamped her tight. 'Never that,' he said softly, 'long-suffering, patient, understanding, but never beastly.' He kissed her suddenly and hard and then released her, opened the door, ushered her inside, then said: 'I've a patient to see—I'll see you at dinner.'

But at dinner there was a message to say that he had been called to the hospital and she wasn't to wait. Laura went to bed early and lay awake for a long time thinking about his kiss; it hadn't been like the routine peck he occasionally gave her. Perhaps there was the very beginnings of a chance…

It was going to be a remote one, she realised the next morning, for Reilof wished her a good day with his usual cool pleasantness and told her at once that he would be away lecturing in Brussels, for three days this time. The salute he bestowed on her cheek as he went was as impersonal and brief as the conventional salute one would give an aunt whom one disliked, so that when he said curtly, 'Don't go out in the Fiat alone, Laura,' her mood was ripe to ask him huffily why not.

'Because I ask you not to,' he said, making it worse. He had closed the door behind him before she had an answer ready.

She went about her quiet life as usual after he had gone while she allowed the idea that he had no right to order her about to fester in the back of her mind. She was, after all, a fairly good driver and no head-strong teenager. By the third day she had convinced herself that he had told her not to drive the Fiat because he was bossy and arrogant, and by the time lunch was finished she was so convinced of this that she went to the garage, took the car out and drove it out of the gate and on to the main road. She was a little vague as to where she would go; she was in the lane to Hilversum, so she might as well go shopping. She still had almost all of the allowance Reilof had given her and some new clothes might make her feel better, she told herself, and put her foot down hard on the accelerator.

Plans for this buoyed her up through the intricacies of getting herself to the heart of the town, and she was almost there when her eye caught a sign to Amsterdam—and why not? she asked herself, turning the Fiat into the side street it indicated. It was quieter here and led to a still quieter street, with narrow houses and a canal running through its centre; she guessed that it would bring her sooner or later to the main Amsterdam road and slackened her pace, ignoring the faint feeling of guilt she hadn't quite got rid of, pleased with herself and almost happy.

Reilof, just back unexpectedly a day early from his lectures and standing idly at the window of his consulting room, was watching the street below while he waited for the first patient of the afternoon, and seeing the Fiat going past he felt neither of these sensations, however. He stared at the little blue car, with Laura's profile and mousy head of hair just visible, and then exploded into forceful Dutch as he strode from the room. His secretary was alone in the reception room and gaped in surprise when he told her harshly that he was called away urgently.

'The patients?' she wanted to know.

'Make new appointments—telephone, do anything you think fit—I leave them in your capable hands, Willa. I'll telephone you later. Go home as usual if I'm not back.'

Willa, middle-aged, cosy and highly efficient, persisted doggedly, 'But where are you going, doctor?'

He was halfway through the door. 'I haven't the faintest idea.'

Laura was on the motorway, Hilversum behind her, heading for Amsterdam, and by now she rather regretted her impulse. The traffic was heavy and very fast; she crept to the slow lane and stayed in it while huge juggernauts, speed fiends and long-distance transports sped past her. But she kept a steady pace, not allowing them to upset her, so that when there was a splintering crash a hundred yards ahead of her and a car somersaulted across the fast lane and cannoned across it to the shoulder of the motorway, she had ample time to drive on to the shoulder too, and stop. Miraculously, there didn't seem to be any other car involved, indeed the traffic was streaming ahead as though nothing had happened, so that she was the only person to reach the upside-down car. There was only occupant, suspended upside down too from his seat by his safety belt, and fully conscious.

She couldn't understand a word he said, of course. She made haste to say in her careful, slow Dutch, 'I'm English—speak slowly, I don't understand Dutch very well.' It was a great relief when he said in tolerable English: 'My legs are held...'

They were indeed, and it would take more than her strength to help him. She looked over her shoulder in some desperation and saw that several cars had stopped now and men were running towards the wreck. Nice, strong men, she saw with relief; they would need all their strength to roll the car back on to its wheels without hurting the man trapped inside. 'For heaven's sake, take care,' she begged them, heedless of the fact that they might not understand what she was saying, and peered in once at the unfortunate driver. 'Hold on to the seat,' she warned him. 'They'll be as careful as they can, but you're bound to bounce a bit.'

He bounced a lot before they were finished, and

was unconscious as the men hauled him carefully out on to the grass verge. Laura looked at his pale, sweaty face and felt a feeble pulse before asking for a penknife from her willing helpers and slitting a trouser leg, urging someone to do the same with the second one. She did it slowly and with great patience, presently exposing a badly crushed limb, so engrossed in her task that she neither saw nor heard the Rolls pull up silently within yards of her.

'My God, I'll talk to you later,' said Reilof with soft fury in her ear, adding in an impersonal, professional voice: 'Hold that foot steady and I'll do what I can,' and after one look at his white, set face, she did as she was told without a word. He had his bag with him and began to work on the leg, giving brief orders to the other men as he did so, and ignoring Laura except to give her even briefer instructions from time to time. The ambulance and police had arrived by the time both legs had been dealt with and Laura, no longer needed, stood on one side watching them load the victim into the ambulance and drive away while the police went from one to the other of the men, taking statements. They knew Reilof, something she was thankful for when it came to her turn, for she told her part in the episode to him and he repeated it in his own language. When she had finished he took her arm and said, 'Will you get into the car? I'll be with you in a moment, I must get someone to drive the Fiat back.'

'I can…' she began, caught his dark gaze and got meekly into the Rolls. His expression had been inscrutable, but that cold stare had warned her that he was in a very nasty temper. She braced herself for a forceful outburst—quite unnecessarily, for he drove all the way home without saying a word. Only as they went into the house he said at his silkiest: 'A moment of your time, Laura.'

She went past him into the study and took the bull by the horns.

'You came back a day early…'

He ignored this obvious remark. 'I asked you not to drive the Fiat on your own, Laura.' He drew a chair forward. 'Will you not sit down?'

'No,' said Laura, 'I'd rather stand, and you didn't ask me, you know, you ordered me in the most arrogant way.'

'My apologies. Is that why you did it?'

She said honestly, 'Yes, I think it was. You see, I'm not a bad driver and I'm not a silly young girl.'

'No, just a silly one,' he observed icily. 'When I saw you drive past my consulting rooms just now, I…' He paused. 'Well, never mind that now—perhaps you can imagine my feelings when I saw the Fiat on the shoulder and you nowhere in sight.'

Laura was still recovering from being called a silly girl so scathingly. She said furiously, 'No, I can't imagine your feelings—you haven't any for me, anyway. And now if you've quite finished lecturing me, I'll go to my room. I have a headache.'

He took a step towards her. 'Laura, you weren't hurt?'

She turned her back and made for the door, longing to have a nice long cry in peace and quiet. 'No, but it would have served me right if I had been, wouldn't it?' She slammed the door after her and raced upstairs and banged her bedroom door too, and when Els came to see if she would like a tray of tea she refused it and moreover told her to let the doctor know that she wouldn't be coming down to dinner—a high-handed decision she regretted later when her normally healthy appetite made itself felt. There was a tin of biscuits beside her bed, so she ate the lot and washed them down with water from the bathroom while she thought with longing of the carefully-chosen menu she and Truus had decided upon that morning. She took a long time over her bath, washed her hair and experimented with her make-up, and it was still only a little after nine o'clock. Presently she got into bed, to lie awake listening for Reilof to go to his room. He still hadn't come when it struck midnight, and worn out with hunger and the reaction from the afternoon's adventure, she fell asleep.

Dressing the next morning, she had the vague idea of apologising over breakfast; she didn't see why she should, but on the other hand, someone would have to offer the olive branch. But when she sat down opposite him to face his cold politeness and hard eyes, she quailed. They ate in silence and it was a relief when Reilof got to his feet with the remark that he would be in for lunch, and strode from the room. Laura did her small morning chores, gave only half her attention to Mijnheer de Wal and the subtleties of the past tense, and went into the garden with the dogs.

It was here that Jan found her; he had called to leave a patient's case notes for Reilof to advise on, and stayed to pass the time of day with her. It was almost lunchtime by now, but Piet brought more coffee and they sat together by the swimming pool, talking easily about nothing much until Jan said, 'I haven't liked to ask you before, Mevrouw van Meerum, but I think perhaps you could help me...'

Laura turned to look at him. His face was earnest and worried and she said warmly, 'Of course I will, but only if you call me Laura. What's the matter?'

'Well, I wish very much to marry and I would like to tell Reilof about it. You see, when he took me as his partner, he allowed me to live in a small flat he has in Baarn—just right for me, for the surgery is close by—and he told me that if I should want to marry, he would let me have a house which he owns, also in Baarn. Now that is splendid, is it not? But Ella, the girl I wish to marry, is refusing to do this. She says that I must buy a house of my own, not live in one which Reilof has given me. She will not marry me unless I have a home of my own, for she says that he will expect me to work harder and do more for him, and that he will take advantage of me. I know that this is nonsense; we are great friends although Reilof is so much older than I, but I cannot make her see…it would be between friends, you understand. I would do the same for him if I were in his place. I wonder if you would talk to her, make her see that he would never do a mean thing to anyone. And perhaps you could suggest to Reilof that I might buy the house from him—it would take me years, of course, and he will not like it, for he has a great deal of money and knows that I have only my income. You think that I should see him about this, but he is absorbed in his work, and besides, now he has you to absorb his thoughts and days.'

Laura smiled wryly. 'So he has. Of course I'll help. Where does your Ella live?'

'In Utrecht. I have to go there tomorrow and I wondered if you would come with me—and talk to her?'

'A splendid idea. In the morning? I'll go to work on her and then perhaps you could talk to Reilof. I know just how your Ella feels, but if you could persuade him to let you buy the house—and you'll have years in which to do that, won't you?—that should solve the problem. But first we have to make Ella see. Now, what time...?'

They had their heads together as Reilof came across the garden towards them, so engrossed in times and meeting places that they didn't know he was there until Hovis and Lucky came out of the shrubbery to rush barking towards him. They turned slightly guilty faces towards him in consequence, the effect made worse by Jan jumping up, declaring that he had to be off at once and that he had left his patient's notes in Reilof's study and would see his partner later on in the day.

Reilof saw him off the premises with his usual friendliness, and rather to Laura's surprise didn't mention him at all during lunch. Instead he kept up a steady flow of nothings, as though he was determined to be pleasant at all costs however difficult it might be, and presently left Laura to go back to his consulting rooms, leaving her puzzled; he had been annoyed when he had found her and Jan in the garden and even though he had been at his pleasantest during lunch, he had looked at her searchingly once or twice and the annoyance was still there, although well concealed.

It was a hot and airless morning when Laura got up the next day, and over breakfast Reilof told her that he would certainly be late home, information which couldn't have pleased her better, for she had agreed to meet Jan at ten o'clock in Baarn. She caught the local bus without hindrance, met him at the arranged spot and was soon being driven to Utrecht, sitting beside him in his Citroën as she listened with a sympathetic ear to the ups and downs of his courtship of Ella.

That young lady proved to be quite charming; small and fair and blue-eyed and, Laura suspected, with an iron will of her own which Jan quite rightly didn't intend to give in to. Now she could see why he had asked her help; he wanted to marry his Ella on his own terms and not on hers. He had left them together over coffee in one of the big cafés with the promise that he would return and take them out to lunch at half-past twelve, and the coffee pot empty,

Laura suggested that they might go somewhere quiet where they could talk. It hadn't occurred to her that Ella might not speak English, but now she thanked heaven that her knowledge of the language was so good, for it would make it much easier to explain about the house and Jan's wishes.

It made her feel rather old, giving advice about husbands to this pretty creature, especially as she knew so little about them herself, but she put the case clearly and in such a matter-of-fact way that before long Ella was at least prepared to rearrange her ideas. Over lunch, Laura was happy to see that Jan, if he was tactful and in no hurry, would get his own way. He seemed to think so too, for he was in great good spirits on their way back, and when he dropped her off outside her own front door, he got out of the car with her, and although he refused an invitation to come inside, he gave her a hug and kiss and told her she was a fairy godmother to them both.

'Good,' laughed Laura. 'Now all you have to do is to make quite sure of Ella and then go and see Reilof.'

He nodded. 'You won't say anything to him yet?'

'No, I won't—Ella still needs a little coaxing; you want her on your side before you do anything more.'

He was about to kiss her again when the house

door opened and Reilof strolled out and Laura, utterly taken aback, said with an aplomb which amazed her, 'Oh, hullo—Jan has just brought me back from Utrecht. He was going there and I wanted to do some shopping.'

He smiled without saying anything, a very nasty smile, and she added hastily as he allowed his eyes to roam over the car, 'But I didn't buy anything.' She turned to Jan. 'Thanks for the lift—I expect I'll see you some time.'

'I'll see you at the hospital this evening,' cut in Reilof, at his pleasantest, 'that meeting at nine o'clock,' and Jan said hastily, 'Oh, yes—I hadn't forgotten. *Tot ziens*.' He got into his car and drove off, waving as he went.

Laura went indoors with Reilof and as he shut the door, he asked: 'You had a pleasant day?'

'Very nice, thank you.'

'You didn't expect me back until the evening?'

'No—you said you would be late.'

'I hope I haven't disturbed any plans you may have made with Jan?'

'Plans? Me? With Jan?' She choked on surprise. 'What plans could I possibly have with him?'

'Certainly not shopping in Utrecht,' he commented silkily. 'That was a lie, wasn't it, Laura?' He was standing in the centre of the hall, watching her.

'Yes,' she said steadily, 'it was, and I can't explain it. Why are you so angry and suspicious, Reilof?'

He smiled then. 'You would be surprised if I told you why; I'm surprised myself.' He came nearer. 'Laura, is it too late for us to try and regain the friendship we first had? It has been my fault; I've treated you badly, anyone other than you would have washed their hands of me long ago, instead of which you've run my home to perfection, charmed my family and friends, made devoted slaves of my servants and struggled to learn my language.' He paused. 'Do you regret marrying me?'

She longed to tell him just how little she regretted it, but she kept her voice level and friendly. 'No, I don't regret that, Reilof, and I can't see why we shouldn't be friends. You—your life has been upset and I realise that it made you difficult sometimes.' She smiled at him. 'Let's try again. You know, just now, when you came out of the house I thought you were blazing with rage...'

His dark eyes glinted. 'Now I wonder why you should have thought that? Have you had tea, or shall we have it in the garden?'

Sometimes the gods were kind, thought Laura. She must seize her chances of happiness whenever she could—this was one of them.

'I'm famished,' she told him happily. 'We'll go by the pool, shall we? Truus made one of her gorgeous cakes this morning and I could eat it all!'

CHAPTER EIGHT

A WEEK went by, and at its end Laura, reflecting upon it, nodded her head with satisfaction; at least she and Reilof hadn't fallen out once, or worse than that, ignored each other. He had found time to sit beside her while she drove the Fiat to the Hague to visit his sister, and taken time off to arrange for her to take a driving test; he had even taken her to his consulting rooms to meet the faithful Willa, shown her his surgery and the hospital where he had beds and explained about his lecture tours. It was as though he intended to admit her to part of his life at least, although he wore an air of thoughtful reserve which had prevented her from being anything but pleasantly friendly. She had contented herself in responding readily but without eagerness to any suggestions he had made for their mutual entertainment, and had done a little quiet shopping for a new dress or two, had her mousy hair becomingly dressed and indulged in a whole new stock of make-up. She had applied herself to her lessons too, and taken care not to say anything which might give Reilof cause to think that she wasn't perfectly content and happy with her life, and although he still spent most of his evenings in his study and avoided being alone with her for any length of time, she told herself that she must persevere and not mind too much.

It was halfway through the following week, while she was sitting in the drawing room, working away at the petit-point she had always hankered after, when Piet came to tell her that there was a lady to see her. He spoke in Dutch to her nowadays, very slowly and simply, but she recognised it as a compliment of the highest order and she replied in that language, asking him to usher in the visitor. It would be Ella, perhaps, or Barones van Deille ter Appel, a formidable old lady who had known Reilof since he was a small boy and was embarrassingly inquisitive on occasion; she had taken a fancy to Laura and had a habit of calling at all odd hours. Laura put down her needlework and prepared to receive her visitor, but she was neither Ella nor the Barones.

Joyce stood in the doorway, looking lovelier than ever, dressed with an elegance which betokened money and plenty of it. She had, Laura considered, rather too much jewellery on her person, but she dismissed that thought as a spiteful one as she got up from her chair and went to meet her sister, thanking heaven silently that she was wearing the new blue denim dress, very simple, beautifully cut and obviously not off the peg. 'Joyce, my dear, what a surprise! We had no idea…'

'I didn't mean you to—we've been spending a few days with Father and Larry said we could come for a quick visit, he's got business with someone at the Hague anyway.' Joyce pecked Laura's cheek and sank into a chair and looked around her. 'Well, well, Laura, you haven't done so badly for yourself, have you? You could have knocked me down with a feather when Father told me—did you catch Reilof on the rebound? You live in style too—I had no idea it was like this. Reilof told me about it, but I didn't pay much attention, I imagined it to be some hideous Victorian villa. He must have a great deal of money.'

Laura didn't answer. 'Tell me all about yourself,' she begged, 'and Larry, of course. Have you a lovely home, and do you like America? You don't write often, you know, and then you don't say much…'

'There's so much to do, I haven't time to write letters. I always hated it anyway, and we've three homes—two houses and an apartment. Larry is rich, you know, he gives me everything I want.' Joyce's blue eyes studied Laura's calm face. 'And **Reilof**? Does he hang you round with jewels and buy you more clothes than you can ever wear?'

Laura was saved the problem of answering this, for at that moment Reilof came in. He was early—hours early, and just for a moment she wondered if he had known about Joyce coming, and then dismissed the idea. She gripped the silver teapot with a hand which shook a little, and watched his face with anxious eyes. He had paused in the doorway, staring across the room at Joyce, who was smiling her lovely smile at him, but he wasn't smiling, his eyes narrowed for a moment and then his expression became bland, giving nothing of his feelings away.

After the tiniest pause, he said: 'Joyce...' and crossed the room towards her, but before he reached her she had jumped up to meet him halfway to throw her arms around his neck and kiss him. Not a sisterly kiss; Laura looked away because she couldn't bear to watch them.

'I'll get some fresh tea,' she said brightly to no one in particular, and clutching the teapot, went blindly out of the room. Reilof hadn't said a word to her—indeed, he hadn't appeared to have noticed her, and she fought back tears as she rushed across the hall to encounter Piet halfway. He took the teapot from her and said with gentle reproof: 'You should have rung, *mevrouw*,' and went off to the kitchen with it, leaving her with nothing to do but go back to the drawing room.

Joyce was back in her chair and Reilof was standing near her and they were laughing together; they looked round as she went in and he said easily: 'Larry and Joyce have asked us to dinner this evening, Laura. They're at the Hotel Hooge Vuursche—will eight o'clock suit you?'

Laura agreed pleasantly that it would and busied herself pouring the tea which Piet had brought in, aware that Joyce had taken the conversation into her own hands and had no intention of including her in it, although Reilof drew her into their talk whenever possible. And Joyce was at her best, wistful and gay by turns, grumbling prettily that Larry had to spend so much time away on business: 'All the way to the Hague,' she pouted at Reilof, 'and here's poor little me on my own…'

'Could you not go with him?'

She made a charming face. 'And what should I do with myself while he's with his dreary business friends?' She smiled enchantingly at him. 'Reilof, couldn't you spare a day—two days, and take me out? It's such a pity not to see something of Holland while I'm here.'

He had gone to sit in his great winged chair by the window. 'My dear girl, I'm a working man.'

'Home at half-past three in the afternoon?' she interpolated quickly.

His eyes rested momentarily on Laura. 'That was for a special reason—besides, why shouldn't Larry take you? Surely he can spare a day?' He glanced again at Laura, sitting so quietly, her face a pleasant mask that felt as though it would crack any moment now. 'Laura has a car—I'm sure she would drive you around.'

Joyce's face clouded for a moment, and then broke into smiles. 'But it's you I want to go with, Reilof—there's so much to talk about.'

He got up and went over to Laura with his cup and saucer. 'We shall have this evening,' he reminded her, 'and now you must excuse me, I've a patient to see and a good deal of work to do. Until this evening, then.'

He smiled at her and then spoke to Laura. 'I'm expecting Jan. Will you tell Piet?' His dark eyes searched her face unsmilingly and she answered lightly,

'Of course—is he to go straight to your study?'

He nodded briefly, 'Please,' and was almost at the door when Joyce cried:

'Oh, Reilof, you must take me out tomorrow! I'm so lonely—and I thought... I've been looking forward to spending a day with you, there's so much I want to explain…' She had never looked prettier, but all he did was shake his head and laugh a little and go away without saying anything.

He had scarcely closed the door behind him when Joyce spoke. 'Well, you may have caught him, Laura, but I doubt if you'll keep him—for one thing, he's still in love with me, though I don't suppose you would know that—and you don't exactly sparkle, do you? He must find you dull… Why on earth did you marry each other?' She didn't wait for an answer but went on: 'Oh, I've no doubt that he was in the mood to marry anyone when he discovered that he couldn't marry me.' She saw the tell-tale colour creep into Laura's cheeks and declared triumphantly, 'That's it, isn't it? Oh, don't bother to answer, I see by your face—and you? I suppose you saw the chance to marry well and took it.' Her laugh was unkind. 'I can't say that I blame you; I'm quite sorry that I didn't marry him myself.' She looked round the beautiful room. 'All this, and some of it's priceless, I should imagine—but he didn't tell me, I thought it was just an ordinary house. He told me the furniture was old, but I never thought… He's clever too, isn't he? Father was telling me—a professor of something or other and one of the best-known, too, with a marvellous future—probably he'll get a knighthood.'

'They don't give titles in Holland, at least not in the same way as they do in England.' Laura was aware as she spoke that it was a pointless remark to make; Joyce wasn't listening. She had curled her legs under her and sat, chin in hand, deep in plans which were nonsense but which somehow she managed to make horribly possible.

'Who knows,' she said thoughtfully, 'divorce is easy.' She smiled widely across at Laura. 'You may have him for a month or two, ducky, just while I divorce Larry, then all you'll have to do is to leave him, then he can divorce you—he'll see that you're provided for. You'll be able to live where you like. Yes, I think I should enjoy living here—it's got something…'

Laura had listened to this amazing speech with growing horror and rage. 'You're mad,' she said slowly, 'and you don't mean a word of it—you're happily married to Larry.'

Joyce gave her a contemptuous look. 'Larry?' she shrugged. 'He's all right for the moment. And I'm not mad, Laura, didn't you see Reilof kiss me just now? Under your nose, though I daresay you're prissy enough to look the other way. He couldn't help himself.' She smiled. 'You never imagined that he'd look at you again if he could have me?'

Laura felt as though a leaden weight filled her chest. It was like being in a hideous nightmare, only she wouldn't be able to wake up from it. True, she hadn't seen Reilof kiss Joyce, but then, just as her sister had said, she hadn't looked. With a great effort she kept her voice quiet and steady. 'No, I've never imagined that, but isn't this whole conversation getting a little ridiculous?'

Joyce got up and wandered across to the little walnut cabinet against the wall. 'You've always been a fool,' she observed. 'Do you really suppose that you can pretend that everything's just as you want it to be? I meant every word. You'll see, Reilof will take me out tomorrow because he wants to—then perhaps you'll believe me.'

Laura's voice was sharp. 'However much he wanted to do so, his work is more important to him than anything else. He would never neglect it for anything other than some emergency.'

'Pooh—there you go again; that's what you want to think.' Joyce opened the cabinet door and took out an exquisite soft paste Sèvres *trembleuse* cup and saucer. 'What's this pretty thing?'

Laura told her. By now she knew and loved everything in the old house; to give it up would break her heart for a second time. Not that she intended to give Reilof up without a fight; only if he really loved Joyce enough to go through all the dreary business of a divorce would she do that. She wanted him to be happy above everything else, and if to part from him was the answer then she would have to do it, but first she would have to be very sure that that was what he wanted.

'I must just go and speak to Piet,' she said. It was a respite; she gave him instructions about Jan, told him that they would be out for dinner and went back to the drawing room, pausing on the way through the hall to peer at herself in the great gilded mirror hanging there. The face which stared back at her looked exactly the same as usual; which considering that her heart was breaking and the little world which she had been building so precariously was in ruins around her, seemed extraordinary.

Joyce went presently, borne away by a taxi Laura had asked Piet to get for her. Her farewells were gay and lighthearted and Laura wondered if she had forgotten all the dreadful things she had said—perhaps she had been teasing. She went upstairs and spent half an hour deciding what to wear, and another hour bathing and doing her face and hair before getting into the pearl-grey chiffon dress she hadn't yet worn.

It had a high bodice and a low neckline, with long tight sleeves and tiny pearl buttons to fasten it. She put on the diamond and ruby earrings, added the ring Reilof had given her, and with a last look in the pier-glass, went downstairs. There was still an hour before they needed to leave for the hotel; she went to the little sitting room and sat in an upright armchair, spreading her gossamer skirts carefully round her before she picked up a book to read.

She didn't read of course, for a conglomeration of thoughts, all of them unhappy, chased themselves round and round her head. None of them were either sensible or constructive, and presently she discovered that she had given herself a headache. But she thrust this on one side, willing her brain to think lucidly. As far as she could see, she had two alternatives; to ignore the whole thing and continue to run Reilof's home, welcome his friends, arrange pleasant little dinner parties for them, accompany him to those same friends' houses, deal with all the petty interruptions which might threaten him or interfere with his work, and wave a cheerful goodbye when he went on a lecture tour. She viewed these tasks without much enthusiasm, but she had been engaged upon them since they had married and she was prepared to go on doing them for as long as he wanted her to—which might not be long, not if Joyce had her way.

And the alternative—to tell him that she loved him. An impossibility, and supposing—just supposing she was fool enough to do that, how would it help the situation? Not at all, as far as she could judge. She would force Reilof's hand and he would hate her for it, for whatever his feelings were for Joyce, he would consider himself in honour bound to remain her husband; he was that kind of a man. She would merely make all three of them unhappy. It would have to be the first course, at least it gave Reilof and Joyce the chance to be happy together if they loved each other so dearly. Larry might have something to say, of course, but she couldn't be bothered with him at the moment; she had enough on her own plate and he was a grown man, capable of charming Joyce away from Reilof in the first place. He couldn't be such a fool.

Reilof came in just then, and she sat up straighter than ever and smiled brightly at him. He looked elegant and remote and thoughtful, although he apologised for keeping her waiting. 'And that's a new dress, isn't it?' he remarked surprisingly. 'And very charming too, a splendid background for the earrings.'

It was a warm evening and Laura didn't need a wrap as she accompanied him out to the Rolls and got in, arranging her dress carefully once more, and during the short journey she made small talk about nothing much, pretending not to notice how brief and absent-minded his replies were.

The hotel was imposing, its wide drive and fountains clearly visible from the road, its elaborate towers and balconies looming behind them. It was a little sad, reflected Laura, that the first occasion upon which they were visiting it should be to dine with Joyce and Larry, for she remembered very clearly Reilof telling her about it, and adding at the same time that he would take her there when they were living in Holland.

But that had been when they had been on holiday in Dorset—they had been friends then. They had become friends again, or so she had begun to think, and now Joyce had appeared out of the blue to rekindle Reilof's love. Godfather had called it infatuation, but she didn't believe that any more. She got out of the car without looking at him and sailed into the hotel, her head high, and for all her ordinary little face and mousy hair, several people turned to look at her.

In bed, hours later, she reviewed the evening minute by minute. On the surface at least, it had been a delightful evening. Larry had turned out to be a youngish man, short and inclined to plumpness and wearing heavy glasses. That he was a man of substance was obvious from the diamond in his ring and the pearl studs in his shirt front, and as if these were not enough he made a point of telling them the value of his houses, the number of cars he owned and the many details of the steam yacht he used each autumn. Laura showed the appropriate interest, and listened to Reilof saying all the right things to Joyce while she studied her sister. She looked stunning in a blue dress the colour of her eyes; it showed off to advantage the diamonds she was wearing and made her hair more golden than ever. A man would have to be made of stone not to admire her; a reflection which hadn't helped at all because Reilof was flesh and blood like anyone else, and when she stole a look at him, it was to see his dark gaze riveted on Joyce.

The meal had been long and elaborate and Larry had fussed over the wine. He fussed over Joyce too, asking Laura's opinion of the diamond ring he had brought back with him from the Hague. He harped too much on his wealth, and yet she had the suspicion that Reilof had a good deal more money than Larry. She dismissed this as unimportant, for Reilof would have been just the same man without a cent in his pocket. For her at least. Inevitably her thoughts returned to him. He had behaved with his usual charm and courtesy, the perfect guest, ready with small talk, a good listener, attentive to Joyce and herself. There was no fault to find.

Laura punched her pillows into comfort for the tenth time. Whatever his feelings were for Joyce—and hadn't Joyce told her?—he had concealed them admirably. She slept at last, haunted by dreams in which he and Joyce wove their way through a series of improbable events, always leaving her desolate and alone, watching them from a distance.

But with the morning her common sense reasserted itself. Silly dreams weren't going to deter her from her usual calm manner; she went downstairs to breakfast, wished Reilof a cheerful good morning, commented suitably upon the weather, poured his coffee, gave Lucky and Hovis each a piece of toast and immersed herself in her post when she saw that the doctor was frowning over his own letters. But presently he laid them aside and remarked with the air of a man who felt inclined for a pleasant chat, 'A delightful evening, wasn't it? I've always liked that hotel. I thought Joyce was looking quite lovely—if it were possible one might say that marriage had improved her looks.'

Laura looked up from a letter from her father; apparently her own marriage hadn't done much for her own appearance. 'Oh, yes—she did look super, didn't she? I'm so glad she's happy.' She paused, for it was delicate conversational ground; she wondered how he could bear to talk about Joyce at all.

His dark eyes rested on her thoughtfully. 'You believe that she's quite content? She gave me to understand that she had some regrets—Larry goes away a good deal, I believe, two or three days at a time…'

'So do you,' Laura reminded him with some asperity. She hadn't meant to say that, but the words had popped out before she could stop them, and it was an effort to meet his eyes across the table. He looked neither surprised nor angry, indeed there was the beginnings of a smile lifting the corner of his mouth.

'That's true,' he observed mildly, 'but hardly a fair comparison.' He gathered up his letters and got to his feet. 'I shall be at my consulting rooms for most of the day,' he told her. 'Will you be in for lunch?'

'Yes.' She tried hard not to sound too pleased.

'Good—I shall try and come home. I've a number of patients this afternoon, but I'll be home about teatime. Uncle Wim's coming to dinner, isn't he?'

'Yes, and Barones van Dielle te Appel.'

'Oh, lord, I'd forgotten.' He was on his way to the door when he turned back to stand beside her chair. 'Laura, are you happy?'

The question was as sudden as it was unexpected, and she could only gape at him. 'Happy?' she repeated stupidly. 'I—I…yes, at least I…yes, thank you, Reilof.' She was aware that it was a poor reply, anyone quicker-witted would have seized the opportunity…but her wits were addled. She heard her voice, wooden and polite and quite unconvincing. He stood looking down at her, saying nothing, waiting for her to say something else, and when she didn't he said, 'Laura…' thought better of it, and went out of the room, leaving her to sit there thinking of all the clever replies she could have made and hadn't.

Presently she got up and went along to the kitchen to discuss lunch with Truus—a salad, because Reilof liked them, and some of the little chicken patties which Truus made so well, and to follow a bowl of fruit—there were nectarines and peaches and grapes in the hothouse at the bottom of the garden, but she would have to go out and get pears and apples.

The little errand did her good; it was so normal to set out with her shopping basket over her arm, and drive herself into Baarn and practise her bad Dutch on the obliging tradespeople. It was a lovely morning too, and still early, and she didn't hurry. Her purchases made, she drove back home, wondering if she should telephone Joyce. She had said during dinner the previous evening that she might go with Larry after all, but Laura hadn't been too sure of that; she could have changed her mind—they might go round the shops together and she could take Joyce back home for lunch. Would Reilof be pleased? she wondered. But wasn't that the modern civilised way of dealing with the situation?

She was still trying to decide what to do when she arrived back, and leaving the car at the door she let herself into the cool, dim hall. She was almost at the door leading to the kitchen when the telephone rang. She put down her basket, called to Piet that she would answer it, and went along to the sitting room.

It was Reilof, and although her heart had rushed into her throat at the sound of his voice she made herself answer his hullo calmly. But he didn't speak for several moments and she rushed into speech. 'Have you left something behind? Do you want me…?'

He cut her short then, and said curtly, 'Something has turned up, Laura—I shan't be home for lunch, probably not for tea either. I'll do my best to get home for dinner.' He sounded hurried and preoccupied.

'What's happened? Where are you going?' she asked urgently.

'Not now, Laura.' He hung up and she replaced the receiver slowly.

'He could have said goodbye,' she muttered, fighting disappointment and a faint apprehension; surely he could have told her and set her mind at rest. She had been a fool not to ask from where he was telephoning. She frowned, remembering a background of voices while she talked. Not a hospital ward and not his consulting rooms—more like a hotel…

She had been on her way out of the room, now she flew back to the telephone. When the clerk at the reception desk at the Hoog Vuursche Hotel answered she asked for her sister. There was no reply from her rooms, she was told, and who was calling?

'Her sister, Mevrouw van Meerum,' stated Laura, and added mendaciously: 'I was expecting her. I wondered why she hadn't arrived.'

The voice was eager to oblige. 'Her sister? In that case I can tell you, Mevrouw, that Mrs Eldridge went out about ten minutes ago.'

'Not by herself?' queried Laura, and waited with miserable certainty for the answer.

'You have no need to worry, *mevrouw*, she was fetched by Doctor van Meerum. I spoke to him myself.'

Laura drew a steadying breath. 'Oh, good,' she managed in a quite normal voice, 'they should be here at any moment. Thank you.'

She put the receiver back and went slowly upstairs, where she walked about, going from room to room in an aimless fashion and then wandering downstairs again. Presently, she told herself, she would be able to sit still and think sensibly, but in the meantime she couldn't stay still. She whistled to Lucky and Hovis, snoozing in their baskets, and went into the garden, where she would probably have stayed for the rest of the morning, mooning around, if Piet hadn't come to tell her that Jan de Mijhof had called and might he join her in the garden?

She hadn't seen Jan for some days, for she had been careful to avoid his company, something which she told herself was ridiculous. But Reilof had seemed strangely annoyed about her outing with Jan, and although she hadn't felt free to tell him her reasons for going she saw no reason in vexing him still further. But now she didn't think about that; here was a friend, someone with whom she could while away half an hour while she pulled herself together. She crossed the lawn to meet him, forgetful of her pinched, unhappy face, smiling her pleasure.

'Jan—how nice, now you can have coffee with me. I don't seem to have seen you for a few days.'

He took her hand and shook it, smiling at her although his kind eyes missed nothing of her wan looks. 'I'd love some coffee, although I really came to see if Reilof was here. His secretary told me that he has cancelled everything for today; she passed on some of his patients to me...I thought he might be here, playing truant in your company.'

She shook her head and pinned a smile on to a mouth which shook a little despite her best efforts. 'He's not here. He telephoned a little while ago to say that he didn't expect to be home for lunch or tea...'

'Gone off with a girl-friend,' said Jan laughingly, and stopped short at the look on her face. 'Sorry,' he said quickly, 'I make these silly jokes—I need a wife to make me toe the line.' He didn't look at her again but tucked an arm in hers and strolled back to the house. 'Actually, I hadn't intended to tell you yet, although you would have been the first to know for you were so kind and understanding. Ella has promised to marry me—on my terms.'

Laura stood still. 'How super—Jan, what splendid news! I am glad. I know you'll both be very happy, she's such a dear girl and so gay and pretty. When do you plan to marry?'

'Just as soon as it can be arranged.' They were in the little sitting room by now and she saw that Piet had already brought in the coffee tray. She busied herself pouring it, waving him to a chair opposite her own and handed him his cup.

He took it from her, hesitated and said diffidently: 'I haven't mentioned it before, Laura, but I had the idea that Reilof was annoyed because you went to Utrecht with me. He said nothing to me, but I hope he wasn't vexed with you? Did you tell him about Ella?' He smiled broadly at her. 'He would be amused that you should play the part of fairy godmother, I think.'

She ignored most of this and said lightly, 'You asked me to say nothing, so I didn't—it didn't matter in the least,' and as if she knew that wasn't quite enough explanation: 'He's been frightfully busy.'

Her companion gave her a quick glance. 'Yes. Yes, of course.' He set down his coffee cup. 'Ella and I would like you both to come out to dinner with us, but before that I should like to talk to Reilof about this house he offered me.' He stood up. 'You will forgive me if I go? I have quite a number of patients to visit after lunch and work to do first. I'll telephone Reilof later.'

Laura said all the right things, went with him to the door and watched him drive away; Jan was a dear and a good friend to them both, which made it impossible to confide in him and ask his advice, but at least she could tell Reilof now why she had gone to Utrecht… She remembered suddenly that it really didn't matter now; what hope had she of improving their relationship now that Joyce had come dancing back into his life? She sighed, went to tell Truus that she wouldn't be in to lunch as the doctor was prevented from coming home, and with Lucky and Hovis at her heels, she set off for a walk in the woods.

The day crawled by and there was no message. By tea time she was both furiously angry and frightened too. That Reilof was spending the day with Joyce she had no doubt; had she not had proof of that from the hotel? But surely he would come back. Whatever his feelings towards her were, he would, for the time being at least, present an unruffled front to his friends and especially his guests that evening.

But it seemed she was wrong. She went up to change her dress and returned to the drawing room to wait for him. Their guests had been bidden for eight o'clock; at five minutes to the hour she poured herself a glass of sherry, drank it very fast and went to warn Truus that they might have to start dinner without the doctor. And at eight o'clock exactly Uncle Wim and Barones van Dielle ter Appel arrived. Laura greeted them with composure, explained that Reilof had been detained and sent his excuses, and fortified by a second glass of sherry with her guests, made bright conversation until Piet came to tell her that dinner was served. They had reached the sweet and Laura was ready to drop from her efforts to keep the Barones suitably amused and her godfather from making awkward observations, when Reilof came in.

He was wearing the dark grey suit he had been wearing when he left the house that morning, and although he was immaculate as he always was, he looked preoccupied, but he greeted his guests with his usual charm and good manners, made his apologies for being late and dropped a brief kiss on her cheek before going to his own chair opposite her. He refused her offer to ask Truus to send up his dinner, saying that he had very little appetite and would eat whatever they were having. So she served him some of Truus's trifle which he hardly touched, and then suggested in her pleasant voice that they should all go to the drawing room for their coffee. But although she appeared composed now that Reilof was home again, she found that she was so angry with him that she could barely contain her rage. The moment their guests had gone, she would say her say, she promised herself as she embarked in her ramshackle Dutch on the recipe for trifle which the Barones had asked for.

At any other time she would have been delighted to receive such a signal honour from the fierce old lady, but now she didn't care in the least. She was all the more astonished, therefore, that the Barones should sweep her on one side as she was on the point of leaving and murmur, 'You are worried, child, although you conceal it well—one day you will be as good a hostess as I am, and that is saying a great deal. It is a pity that I do not know you well enough for you to confide in me; let us hope that by the time we are on such a friendly footing as that, there will be no need for you to wish to do so.'

She bent her stately head, and Laura, very surprised, kissed the elderly cheek.

Reilof shut the house door behind him and she stood irresolute, not sure whether to speak to him now or wait until he had gone to his study as he always did each evening. The urge to burst into speech was great, but she was sure that she would lose her temper and maybe shout at him, too. Piet and Truus were in the kitchen and weren't likely to hear, but one of the maids might come into the hall for some reason or other. She decided to compromise and ask him to go with her into the small sitting room, and was on the point of suggesting this when he said quietly: 'And what did you do with your day, Laura?'

She was so annoyed of being stymied at the last moment that she snapped, 'Nothing,' before she had stopped to think.

'Jan was here?' His voice had become very silky.

'Oh, yes—I quite forgot...'

'How convenient. I had thought, although I had said nothing to you on the subject, that you had understood how I felt about you spending the day with Jan.'

Her voice spiralled. The entire household could have come into the hall as audience and she wouldn't have cared. 'Perhaps you would explain?'

'Certainly,' the silkiness was still there. 'You are my wife and as such I expect you to conform to certain standards. Jan is my junior partner and a friend of some years' standing, and he is also younger than yourself and he seems to find you attractive.' Laura watched his mouth curve downwards, as though he found this quite beyond his understanding. 'I have always considered you a sensible woman, but it seems as though you have allowed his admiration to go to your head. We are, I should remind you, recently married...'

His words bit into her mind like acid into silk; she wanted to explain about Jan and Ella, but why should she if that was what he thought, and how dared he... She said in a shaky voice, 'Don't be pompous! And where have you been all day, and who with?' She drew a difficult breath. 'I telephoned the hotel this morning—I wanted to speak to Joyce. They—they told me that she had gone out with you…' She gulped another breath, her anger nicely alight. 'And since you mention it, you don't seem above being attracted yourself, do you? Of all the nonsense…talk about the pot calling the kettle black…!' She raised her voice and said very clearly: 'If I had a pot I'd throw it at you this very minute!' Having delivered this muddled speech she flung round and raced upstairs, banged her door shut and fell on to the bed. She never wanted to see Reilof again, she told herself, and after a good burst of tears, she spent the next hour wondering just what she would say to him when she saw him in the morning.

As it turned out, she need not have spent the best part of the night cudgelling her brain, for she fell asleep as it began to grow light and woke late. By the time she got down to breakfast, Reilof had gone, leaving a brief note for her; he would probably be away for several days, it told her; anything urgent was to be passed on to his secretary. He hoped that on his return they might have a talk, as there were several matters to be cleared up between them.

Laura read the brief message several times, trying

to extract comfort from it, although she was finally forced to admit that it contained none. He could have told her he was going away, although on second thoughts it wasn't very likely that he would have done so, especially after her outburst. And where had he gone? She ignored her breakfast and flew to the telephone. The reception clerk at the hotel was polite and positive. Mrs Eldridge had not yet returned since she had left the hotel on the previous day; it was understood that she would be back to collect her luggage, as she had taken only a small case with her. Would Mevrouw care to leave a message?

Mevrouw declined the offer, replaced the receiver, drank a cup of black coffee, gave the dogs their toast and went up to her room. There seemed to be only one thing left to do. Joyce had got her own way once more, only much more quickly than Laura had expected. She wondered what her sister could have said to Reilof to cause him to turn his back on his well-ordered, busy life, his lovely home—he must love her to distraction. Laura, too sad for tears, opened her clothes closet.

She packed carefully, discarding anything she didn't absolutely need and taking only a small suitcase, then she changed into a blue shirtwaister and sensible shoes, put all her jewellery into the jewel box in the bow-fronted chest—even her engagement ring, although it hurt her to do so—and left with only her wedding ring, sat down to compose a letter to Reilof. It took a little time to write, for it had to be brief, sensible and friendly and giving no clue as to where she was going, only the address of her father's lawyer. 'So that you can contact me through him when your plans are made,' she wrote, 'and I hope that you will be very happy.'

She had cried over it a little and made a splodge, so that she had to write it all over again. As she put it into its envelope and sealed it down, it seemed to her that was what she had done with the brief chapter of her life with him—pushed it out of sight and closed it.

CHAPTER NINE

TRUUS and Piet would be having their coffee in the kitchen and the two girls and old Mevrouw Blok, who came in to do the washing and ironing, would be with them. Laura checked that she had her passport and enough money with her, picked up her case and went softly downstairs. She put her letter to Reilof on the desk in his study, left a note on the hall table telling Piet that she had taken the car and reminding him to feed Lucky and Hovis, and went to say goodbye to the dogs. That was the hardest thing she had to do, for Hovis whined softly and Lucky looked at her with his soft boot-button eyes, puzzled that he wasn't going with her.

She bade them return to their baskets, kissed their anxious faces and hugged them fondly before she went through the garden door and round the side of the house to the garage. The Fiat was cleaned and ready for the road, a job Piet did with pride. Laura slung her case on to the back seat and without looking back, drove out of the gate to join the stream of traffic going in the direction of Amsterdam.

She drove mechanically, not allowing herself to think about Reilof or the life she had left behind her. At Schiphol she left the car in the park and bought a ticket for the next flight to London. She didn't have long to wait, and once she was on board she didn't look out of the porthole to watch Holland slide away beneath her, but buried herself in the newspapers she had been provided with, reading the same few sentences over and over again without seeing them at all.

She still hadn't made up her mind where she would go when the plane landed at Heathrow. She was making her way rather aimlessly through the reception hall when she saw Joyce, looking elegant and cool and pleased with herself, and carrying a big dress box. Her sudden appearance crowned the personal nightmare Laura was in, and she stood still, not quite believing her own eyes. But Joyce had seen her too and came hurrying towards her. 'Laura,' she said breathlessly, 'what on earth are you doing here?' Her lovely eyes widened. 'Have you come to look for me? Is Larry worse?'

'Worse?' echoed Laura slowly, and Joyce said impatiently: 'Oh, surely Reilof told you—he had a coronary soon after he left the hotel the morning after our dinner party. He was in the car and had the sense to stop. What a piece of luck that Reilof was actually passing when it happened and stopped to see what was the matter! He saved his life, I suppose, for he took him to hospital and saw to everything and then came back to the hotel to fetch me.' She pouted. 'You can keep your Reilof, ordering me around, telling me what to do…he's furious with me because I simply had to fly over this morning and fetch this simply gorgeous dress I'd ordered. What use am I at the hospital, anyway? And Larry looks awful, all tubes and bottles and nurses and doctors fussing round—I hate people being ill, I told Reilof so—he looked at me as though…' She paused. 'He says Larry will get over it.'

Laura asked faintly, her mind at sixes and sevens, 'Did Reilof stay with him all day?'

'Yes—until the evening when he started to recover.' She looked curiously at Laura. 'But he must have told you…?'

'We had guests and he had to leave very early today.'

Joyce wasn't very interested. 'I know—some doctor or other told me—Reilof was off to Antwerp to do something or other vital for some old man— not a penny to bless himself with, so I was told;

Reilof won't make a penny out of it. I'd no idea he was like that—wrapped up in his profession.' Her pretty mouth sneered. 'I bet he comes home late and misses parties and forgets to bring you flowers. I'll stick to Larry.'

Laura said quietly: 'Yes, I think I should. That's your flight being called. I hope Larry is better soon…'

Joyce had gone with a casual wave and Laura stood, jostled by the hurrying people around her. What a fool she had been, and now she had burnt her boats, Reilof wouldn't want her back; if he had loved her perhaps he would have come to look for her and taken her back home again, but he didn't love her. He didn't love Joyce either. Uncle Wim had been quite right, he had been infatuated and got over it like a child with the measles, and all he would want to do would be to forget her and go back to his busy, well-ordered life.

She wandered on to where the air terminal bus was waiting and got in, still thinking about him, not giving a thought as to where she would go. It was as she was getting out of the bus that she knew; she found a taxi and at Waterloo Station took a ticket to Wareham and went to join the queue for the next train.

The journey seemed endless and she was tired when the train stopped in the small station, but it

was easy enough to get a taxi to take her to Corfe
Castle. It was early evening by now with not much
traffic about, and for the first time she wondered if
there would be a room for her at the hotel, but her
fears were unfounded; the holiday season was
almost over and there were few guests, so she
handed her case to the porter and for the first time
since she had begun her journey, relaxed in the wel-
coming atmosphere of the old hotel. There was a
room for her too, low-ceilinged and furnished with
an enormous bed, an old-fashioned chest of drawers
and a ponderous dressing table, but it was very
clean and comfortable and there was a bathroom
next door. She unpacked her few things and went
down to the dining room for her dinner, conscious
that she was hungry, for she had eaten nothing all
day. Presently, nicely full and sleepy from the glass
of wine she had had with her meal, she went
upstairs again; bed would be delightful, even if she
didn't sleep.

But she did, for the first part of the night at least,
to wake in the early hours and worry about the
tangle she was in. It would be a simple matter to
telephone Reilof, she reflected, but supposing he felt
himself to be well rid of her, she had been stupid
enough...although any girl might have done the
same. And he should have told her about Larry; all

he had done had been to attack her about Jan—of all the nonsense…

If she had seen him at breakfast perhaps he would have told her then, and she would have explained about Jan and Ella—it could have led to a better understanding between them at the very least. She tossed and turned in the wide bed, her thoughts getting more and more muddled. She had imagined, just once or twice, that he had begun to like her. She dropped off into a restless doze on the thought, and woke to the early morning sounds of the little town and thankfully got up and got dressed, her mind already busy once more. If Joyce saw Reilof, and surely she would, would she tell him that she had met her at Heathrow? Knowing Joyce, she thought it unlikely, and supposing Larry died after all, would Joyce turn to Reilof again? She had seemed disenchanted with him at the airport, but he was rich and successful and if he had loved her once he might well do so again.

Laura tied back her hair, suddenly impatient of it, and went down to make a pretence of eating her breakfast.

She spent the morning wandering round the small shops and although she wasn't hungry, lunch whiled away an hour. She had been given the same table she and Reilof had shared, for the landlord had remembered her, forcing her to think up a tale about Reilof not being able to come at the last minute, and when she had sat long enough she climbed up to the castle, wandering about the steep slopes until it was long past tea time.

She felt calmer now, although she still could think what to do. She had money enough for a few weeks and she could always go home to her father, and surely she would hear before very long...it all rather depended on poor Larry. She shut her mind off from the various possibilities of the situation and went back to the hotel to change her dress and eat her solitary dinner after having a drink with some of the guests staying there. They were pleasant and friendly and she shared a coffee tray with them afterwards, but when they invited her to make a fourth at bridge she declined on the excuse that she had letters to write and was a poor hand at the game, anyway. And indeed, she did have one letter—a rough draft of what she would write to her father's solicitor, but not yet—she must give Reilof time; she would send it in four or five days' time.

The letter composed to her liking, she brushed her hair and got into bed, and because she was really tired now, she slept at once and until morning.

The next day she hired a bicycle and went to the Blue Pool. The morning was fresh and the narrow roads almost empty and she enjoyed the exercise, and the moment she had parked her bike and saw the first glimpse of blue water below her, she knew that this was where she had wanted to come. There were very few people there, and she climbed the narrow paths to the place where she and Reilof had sat together, and perched herself on the rustic bench. The pool gleamed bluely beneath her, not a ripple on its smooth surface, the trees and shrubs already yellowing a little with the approach of summer's end. It was very quiet; someone had told her that the birds only sang on one side of the pool and where she was there was nothing but the rustle of the trees as the wind stirred them.

The peace of it wrapped itself around Laura and gradually stilled her busy mind; it had been peaceful when she had been there with Reilof; he had enjoyed being there too, and she…her head had been full of half-made plans and high hopes.

She sat on, oblivious of time, until hunger sent her down to the little tea-house for a pot of tea and toast before she cycled back to the hotel to eat her dinner with more appetite and go to bed early.

She went again the next day, not bothering to take a book with her, but just sitting and dreaming and thinking about Reilof and the lovely old house; she missed it all—the dogs, Piet and Truus, old Mijnheer de Wal, but she supposed that in a little while she would get over her longing to see them all again.

One more day, she told herself the following morning, and then she would pull herself together, write to the solicitor and make some sensible plans. It was almost a week now, at least she was used to the idea of being on her own again and had conquered a desire to burst into tears each time she thought of Reilof. She had no appetite for her breakfast; she made short work of it and set off for the Blue Pool once more, wearing the shirtwaister and a cardigan, both of which she was heartily sick of. Her hair she had tied back with a scarf and she hadn't bothered overmuch with make-up. She parked her bike and wandered round the now familiar paths, finding her way at last to the rustic seat above the pool. She sat there for a long time, lulled by the quiet, and presently she closed her eyes. She was on the edge of sleep when she heard footsteps on the rough path which led up from the water, but she didn't bother to open her eyes at once. When she did, Reilof was standing there, very close to her.

Laura sat staring at him, her heart pounding so hard that she had no breath to speak, and only when he sat down beside her did she make a small sound, half sob, half sigh. At least he was flesh and blood and not a ghost made from her longing; dressed with his usual elegance, too, although his face was weary and showed lines she had never noticed before. He took her hand in his and turned to look down at her. 'My darling girl…' he said softly, and smiled, so that the weariness and lines disappeared completely.

She tugged at her fast-held hand and his grip became rocklike, although still gentle. 'You went away!' she burst out furiously, but he took no notice, only picked up her hand and slipped the ruby ring back into its place above her wedding ring, and then kissed it so that she almost wailed, 'Oh, you'll have to explain…'

He let her hand go then, and pulled her close and kissed her, and she, so suddenly transported from nightmare to dearest dream, kissed him back, so that Reilof kissed her again with most satisfying thoroughness. All the same, she said into his shoulder: 'I don't understand—at least, I'm not sure that I do. I met Joyce at Heathrow and she told me about Larry and that you'd saved his life…' She thumped his great chest with a furious fist. 'Oh, why didn't you tell me…'

'My dear love, wait a minute—you met Joyce? But why didn't she tell me?'

'Then how did you know I was here?' demanded Laura.

'The car at Schiphol—no, let me begin at the beginning, my darling. I telephoned Piet and he told me that you had gone out hours earlier and hadn't come back—you had left him a note about the dogs, and he was worried, so I cancelled my lectures, went back home and found your note. I looked for you, my dear heart, I searched high and low. I telephoned your father and went to Uncle Wim and went to see Joyce, but she said nothing about seeing you. And then they telephoned about the car at Schiphol and I knew at last where you had gone. You see, I remembered the day we sat here together and what you said: That if ever you wanted to hide from anything or anyone, you would want to come here.'

Laura tilted her head, the better to look into his face. 'But why? I thought that you loved Joyce. And she—she told me that she intended to divorce Larry and marry you—that I could have you until she was ready...'

His laugh was full of genuine amusement. 'She said that? But not to me, my darling Laura. Perhaps she knew when we met again that I hadn't even a flicker of interest in her any more. You see, I had been in love with you for quite some time, dear heart, although I didn't choose to admit it to myself and certainly not to you, for I didn't think that you loved me. Only on that day when I looked out of my consulting-room window and saw you driving past, looking so defiant and so small, did I admit it—I couldn't go after you fast enough, and when I saw the Fiat on the side of the motorway…I could have boxed your ears, my little love.'

Laura said indignantly: 'You were beastly, and you were beastly about Jan, and I only went to persuade his girl-friend to marry him and live in your house, and you thought a whole load of rubbish—I could have thrown something at you!'

There was a gleam in his eye as he studied her face, taking so long about it that she cried quite crossly, 'Oh, don't look at me, I know I look a complete hag.'

He shook his head. 'No—you're the most beautiful girl in the world, and when I came home and found that Jan had been to see you I could have wrung your lovely neck.'

Laura sat up, the better to look at him once more. She might not be the most beautiful girl in the world, but she certainly felt as though she was. She said, a little breathless, 'Well, well—I never did! I thought you didn't care a button for me—I have no looks, you know, and not much conversation.'

'You are a stubborn girl, for I have just told you that you are beautiful and I find your conversation quite delightful.' Reilof tightened his hold a little and kissed her again, and presently she settled down against his shoulder once more.

'Oh, do you,' she asked, 'do you really? But there's a lot that's not quite clear.' After a moment she said, 'I think I'd like a cup of tea.'

He kissed the top of her head and said fiercely, 'You're too pale and thin, and it's my fault. You shall have all the tea you can drink, dear love, and tomorrow I'll take you home.'

She said a little shyly: 'I'm staying at the hotel.'

'Yes. I know. I called in on the way here. The manager remembered me; he was disappointed that we should be leaving in the morning. I told him that we should come again and bring the children.'

Laura jerked upright. 'Children? But we haven't any…'

'These things take time, my darling, but we mustn't disappoint the man, must we?'

'Lucky and Hovis will be marvellous…' Suddenly she was crying. 'Oh, Reilof darling, I've been so homesick!'

His arms wrapped her close in the most comforting manner. 'Never again, dear love, I promise you.'

She sniffed. 'Oh, dear, I'm so happy, I think I'm going to cry…'

Reilof put a finger under her chin and kissed her very gently. 'You may have ten minutes, dearest, before we go and have our tea,' and when she gave a little watery snort and said, 'I haven't got a hanky,' offered his.

She blew her red nose and mopped her eyes and asked, 'Do I look awful, Reilof?'

His dark eyes were tender, although he was laughing a little. 'Must I tell you again that you're the most beautiful girl in the world?'

Laura smiled from a tear-stained face. 'Yes, please, dear Reilof.'

A WIFE ON PAPER

Liz Fielding

CHAPTER ONE

His brother was late, the restaurant was crowded, noisy, the kind of fashionable look-at-me-I've-arrived place he loathed, and Guy wished he'd made an excuse, stuck to his original plan to have a sandwich at his desk as he worked through the evening.

A rush of cold air as the door opened behind him gave him hope that his ordeal would soon be over, but as he turned he saw that it wasn't Steve but a young woman rushing to get in out of the rain.

She paused momentarily, framed in the entrance, spotlit by the bright lights of the cocktail bar against the darkness outside.

Time stretched like elastic. The earth stopped turning. Everything slowed down. He felt as if he could count every one of the raindrops sparkling in her corn gold hair.

It was tousled, as if it had been caught by the gusting wind that she seemed to have brought into the restaurant with her, stirring everyone so that they turned to look. Kept on looking. Maybe it was because she was laughing, as if running through the rain was something she did for fun. Because she *was* a breath of fresh air…

She lifted her arms to comb her fingers through her hair, shake it back into place, and the dress she was wearing rode up to expose half a yard of thigh. When she dropped her hands and the hem descended, the scooped neckline of her dress fell too, offering a

5

glimpse of what the clinging fabric so enticingly suggested.

Nothing about her was flat; everything about her seemed an open invitation to his hands to describe her, to stroke the sinuous lines of her body. She wasn't beautiful exactly. Her nose lacked classical perfection. Her mouth was too big, but her silver-fox eyes sparkled as if she was lit up from within and the glow that emanated from her eclipsed every other woman in the room.

And, as time caught up with them, his body reacted as if she'd touched his personal blue touch-paper.

Pulse, heart rate, all the physical responses leapt into overdrive, but it was more than a lustful response to the kind of stimuli that probably had half the men in the room in the same condition.

It was like coming face to face with destiny. Coming face to face with the reason for your existence.

As he rose slowly to his feet she saw him, their gazes locked, and for a split second the laughter froze on her lips, and he thought that she felt it too. Then his brother was there, closing the door, cutting off the rush of cold air, breaking the connection between them as he put his arm around the girl's waist, pulled her close against him.

Something hot, possessive, swept through him and he wanted to grab Steve, pull him away, demand to know what the hell he thought he was doing. Except, of course, it was obvious. He was saying to the world—saying to him—this woman is mine. And, as if the gesture wasn't enough, he grinned and said, 'Guy, I'm glad you could make it. I really want you to meet Francesca.' He looked down at her with the look of a man who'd won the Lottery. 'She's moving in with me. She's having my baby…' Make that a man who'd won the Lottery twice.

'Mr Dymoke…' He started at a touch to his shoulder, opened his eyes to see the stewardess smiling down at him. 'We're about to land.'

He dragged his hands over his face in an effort to dispel the lingering wisps of a dream that, even after three years, continued to haunt him.

He straightened his chair, fastened his seat belt, checked the time. He should just make it.

Guy Dymoke was the first person she saw as she stepped from the car. That wasn't what surprised her. He was the kind of man who would stand out in any crowd. Tall, broad-shouldered, deeply tanned, his thick dark hair lightened by the sun, he made everyone else look as if they were two-dimensional figures in a black and white photograph.

The effect was mesmerising. She saw it in the effect he had on the people around him. Had to steel herself against it, even now.

She wasn't even surprised that he had taken the time from his busy life to fly in from whatever distant part of the world he currently called home to attend his half-brother's funeral.

He was a man who took the formalities very seriously. He believed that every t should be properly crossed, every i firmly dotted. He'd made no secret of his disapproval of her and Steven's decision not to do the 'decent' thing and get married. Demonstrated it by his absence from their lives.

As if it was any of his business.

No, what truly astonished her was that he had the

nerve to show up at all after three years in which they hadn't seen or heard from him. She hadn't cared for herself, but for Steven...

Poor Steven...

Thankfully, she didn't have to make an effort to hide her feelings as their gazes briefly met over the heads of the gathered mourners. Her face was frozen into a white mask. Nothing showed. There was nothing to show. Just a gaping hollow, an emptiness yawning in front of her. She knew if she allowed herself to think, to feel, she'd never get through this, but as she walked past him, looking neither to left nor right, he said her name, very softly.

'Francesca...'

Softly. Almost tenderly. As if he cared. And the ache in her throat intensified. The mask threatened to crack...

Anger saved her. Hot, shocking, like a charge of lightning.

How dared he come here today? How dared he make a show of offering her sympathy when he hadn't bothered to so much as lift a telephone when Steven was alive and it would have actually meant something?

Did he expect her to stop? Listen to his empty condolences? Allow him to take her arm, sit beside her in church as if he gave a damn...?

Just for appearances.

'Hypocrite,' she replied as, looking neither to left nor right, she swept past him.

She looked brittle. Insubstantial. Like spun glass. Altered out of all recognition from the vital young woman who'd changed his life in a moment with just one look.

Thin watery sunlight filtered through the October sky to light up her pale hair, emphasise the translucence of her skin, as she stood by the church doorway, shaking hands with those who'd taken the time to come and pay their respects. Inviting them back to the house. Cool, composed, apparently in control. The only moment when she'd seemed real, herself, had been that quick angry flush to her cheeks when he'd spoken her name. The rest was all just a role she was playing, he thought, a performance to get her through the nightmare.

One tap and she'd shatter...

He hung back, waiting until the others had moved off, before he stepped out of the shadows of the porch. She knew he was there, but he'd given her the chance to walk away, ignore him. But she was waiting for him to say his piece. Maybe she hoped he'd explain, but what could he say?

The words for what he was feeling hadn't yet been invented. The loss, the pain, the regret that the last time he'd seen his brother, Steve had been at his worst. It had been deliberate, of course. A ploy to make him angry. And he'd risen self-righteously to the bait...

Neither of them had come out of it with any glory.

But she'd lost the man she loved. The father of her child. How much worse must it be for her...

He stepped forward. 'I'm sorry I couldn't get here sooner, Francesca.'

'Ten days. Time enough to have got from almost anywhere, I would have thought.'

He wanted to ask her why she'd left it so late. Too late.

'I wish I could have relieved you of the burden of organising this.' His voice seemed to belong to someone else. Someone cold, distant...

'Oh, please. Don't apologise. Your secretary rang, offering to help— I imagine Steven's lawyer must have called your office—but a funeral is a family thing. Not something for strangers.'

He wasn't talking about the funeral, but the months before that, when Steve had been dying and he'd been on the other side of the world, unaware of the tragedy about to overtake them all. By the time the message that his brother was running out of time had reached him, it was too late.

'It took me days to get to any kind of landing strip when the message came through about Steve.' He sounded, even to himself, as if he were making excuses. 'I've come straight from the airport.'

Finally she turned to look at him. Acknowledge him.

'You really needn't have bothered. We've managed perfectly well without you for the last three years. The last six months changed nothing.'

Her voice was cold, too. Every word an ice dagger striking at his heart. But this wasn't about him. His feelings.

Right now all he cared about was her. He wanted to say that she was all he'd cared about for the last three years. Instead he said, 'Are you going to be all right?'

'All right?' She repeated the words carefully, as if testing them. Trying to divine his meaning. 'In what way could I possibly be "all right"? Steven is dead. Toby's daddy is dead...'

'Financially,' he said, pressing on, even though he knew that he was making things immeasurably worse. Or perhaps not. How could they possibly be worse?

Her silver-grey eyes regarded him with utter disdain. 'I should have known your only concern would be for the practicalities. Ensuring that I did it by the book. It isn't feelings that matter with you, is it, Guy? It's appearances.'

Which answered that question.

Smothering the pain, he pressed on. 'Practicalities have to be addressed, Francesca.'

Listen to him! He should be putting his arms around her, offering her comfort, taking a little for himself, but since that was denied him he was talking like a lawyer. If he'd been a lawyer there would be some excuse...

'Please don't concern yourself about us, Guy. By your standards I'm about as "all right" as it's possible to be. The house. Life insurance... That is what you mean, isn't it?' With that, she turned and crossed to the waiting limousine. The driver held the door for her, but she didn't get in, just stood there for a moment, head bowed, as if gathering herself for the ordeal ahead. After a moment or two she straightened, glanced back at him, then with a lift of her shoulders she said, 'I suppose you'd better come back to the house. For appearances.'

Then she climbed into the car and waited for him to follow her.

He didn't mistake her invitation for a thaw but he abandoned the car that had been waiting for him at the airport without hesitation.

'Thank you,' he said as he joined her.

'I don't want your thanks. He was your brother. I haven't forgotten that, even if you did.' And she shifted to the farthest end of the seat, putting the maximum distance between them, not that he had any intention of crowding her. Offering comfort that she clearly didn't want—at least, not from him. But he had to say something.

'I'm sorry I wasn't here.'

That earned him another look to freeze his heart. 'That's just guilt talking, Guy. If you'd cared about him you wouldn't have stayed away. Why did you do that?' For a long moment she challenged him. Then, in the shadowy interior of the limousine, he saw a faint colour smudge her pale cheeks before, with the smallest lift of her shoulders, she let it go. 'The cancer was virulent. Faster than anyone anticipated. I asked him if he wanted me to call you, but he said there was plenty of time.'

Instinctively he reached to hold her, comfort her as he'd hold anyone in distress, but her eyes flashed a warning. It was like hitting a force field at speed. Shocking. Painful.

He'd intended only to reassure her but realised that anything he did or said would simply fuel her resentment that he was alive, while the man she loved was dead. She clearly thought him capable of feeling nothing but guilt. And that only at a stretch.

'He was so sure that you'd come,' she said.

'I'm not clairvoyant.'

'No. Just absent.'

He bit back the need to defend himself. She needed to strike out at someone and he was a handy target.

If he could do nothing else for her, he could take the blame.

When he didn't say anything—and he didn't believe she expected or wanted him to respond—she looked away, staring out of the windows at the passing urban landscape as if anything was better than looking at him. Talking to him. Only a tiny betraying sigh escaped her lips as they turned into the elegant city street with its tall white stuccoed houses, where she and Steve had made their home.

The sound cut deeper than any words—no matter how much they were intended to wound.

The car drew up at the kerb and he climbed out, hesitating between offering his hand and the certainty that she would ignore it. But as she stepped on to the pavement her legs buckled momentarily beneath her and neither of them had much choice in the matter. He caught her elbow beneath his hand. She felt insubstantial, fragile, weightless as, briefly, she allowed him to support her.

'Why don't you give this a miss?' he said. 'I can handle it.'

Maybe, if he had been someone else, she might have surrendered control, leaned against him, allowed him to take the strain. But she gathered herself, shook off his support and said, 'Steven managed without you, so can I.' Then she walked quickly up the steps to her front door to join the subdued gathering.

Francesca paused on the threshold of her drawing room to catch her breath. She had never felt so alone in her life and, unable to help herself, she glanced back to where Guy was shedding his coat. For a moment their eyes met and she glimpsed his pain. But she buried her guilt. She'd meant to hurt him, wound him for staying away, and not just for Steven. Then someone said her name, put an arm around her, and she allowed herself to be wrapped up in this show of care from virtual strangers, no matter how shallow their sentiments, how empty their words of support.

But the imprint of his fingers still burned into her and she rubbed at her arm, shook her head as if to loosen the image. Forced herself to concentrate. This wasn't just her tragedy. There were other people here, people who needed reassurance about their jobs, the future of Steven's business. She'd left it to tick over in the hands of the staff for the last few months. Now she would have to take control, make decisions. But not today.

Today she had to lay Steven to rest in style, ensure that everyone had something to drink. Something to eat. Give his friends time to talk about him.

And avoid Guy Dymoke.

'Fran?'

She jumped as a voice at her elbow brought her back to the present. This minute. This dreadful hour that she had to get through.

'Did everything go smoothly?'

She looked down, made an effort to pull herself together. Put on a reassuring smile for her cousin. 'Yes. It was a beautiful service. Thank you, Matty.'

'You should have let me come with you.'

'No. No, really, I needed to know that Toby was with someone he loves and I didn't want Connie distracted while she was making sandwiches.' Then, with a little jab of panic, 'Where is Toby? Is he okay?'

'He was a bit fractious so Connie took him upstairs

and put him down for a nap. With a bit of luck he'll sleep through this.'

'I hope so.' Another hour and it would be over. Just one more hour. She could do it. She'd held herself together for so long. She could manage one more hour. She wasn't going to break down now. Not in front of Guy Dymoke.

Guy watched her as she took on the role of comforter, taking the hand of a thin young woman confined to a wheelchair as they exchanged a few words, hugging people, allowing them to grieve. She was the perfect hostess, ensuring that everyone had something to eat and drink, all the while managing to keep her distance from him without so much as a glance in his direction. As if she had some sixth sense that warned her when he was getting too close.

He decided to make it easy for her, seeking out those friends of his brother's that he remembered, catching up with their news. Introducing himself to those he did not. Checking the arrangements for the reading of the will with Tom Palmer, the family lawyer. As executor he would have to be there, welcome or not. More than that, he wanted reassurance that Francesca and her son were indeed 'all right'.

'You're not eating.'

He turned around and found himself confronted by the woman in the wheelchair, offering him a plate of sandwiches.

'Thank you, but I'm not hungry.'

'That's no excuse. It's part of the ritual,' she said. 'Man's natural reaction to his own mortality. An affirmation that life goes on. You know...eat, drink and

be grateful it was someone else who fell under the
bus. Metaphorically speaking.'

'In my case,' he replied, 'I suspect it would have
caused a great deal less bother all round if it had been
me. Falling under the metaphorical bus.'

'Is that a fact?' Her eyebrows rose to match her
interest. 'Then you must be Guy Dymoke, the rich,
successful older brother who no one ever talks about.
You don't look like Steven,' she added, without waiting for confirmation.

'We're half-brothers. Same father, different mothers. Steve favours—favoured—his. Mother.'

'Should one speak ill of the dead at his own funeral?' she enquired, with a refreshing lack of senti-
mentality. Then, clearly not expecting an answer, 'I'm
Matty Lang,' she said, offering her hand. 'Francesca's
cousin. So what's the mystery? Why haven't we
met?'

'There's no mystery. I'm a geologist. I spend a lot
of time overseas in remote places.' Then, because he
didn't want to elaborate on why he didn't include
family visits when he was in London, he said, 'Francesca must be glad to have you here. Her parents live
overseas, I understand.'

'They do. In separate hemispheres to avoid blood-
shed. As for the rest of them, they're all too busy to
waste time at a funeral that won't benefit them in any
way.' She looked around, rather pointedly, then at
him and said, 'It was one of the things Fran and
Steven had in common, apparently.'

'I'm surprised his mother isn't here.' A B-list ac-
tress who had been through half a dozen husbands
and lovers since his father had paid through the nose

to be rid of her, she rarely missed a photo opportunity. 'She looks good in black.'

'She sent flowers and her excuses. Apparently she's filming some lust-in-the-dust mini-series in North Africa. She was sure Fran would understand. Call me cynical, but with Francesca getting top billing I suspect she decided there wasn't any PR mileage in admitting to having a son old enough to have made her a grandmother.'

'Not good for the image,' he agreed, doing his best to keep the bitterness from his voice. 'She was never cut out for grandmotherhood. Or motherhood, come to that.' Every time that Steve had got himself into trouble, every time he had sworn that this was the last time he'd dig him out, he had found himself re-running a long distant memory of his stepmother screaming at his father, furious that she'd had to surrender some film part because she was pregnant. Had found himself remembering the miserable little boy sobbing his heart out when he had finally realised his mother wasn't coming back.

And he was no better. He'd walked away, too. He'd told himself that Steve didn't need him any more now he had a family of his own. But that had just been an excuse.

'I'm glad Francesca had you to give her some support today,' he said.

'She was there for me when I had my own close call with death-by-transport.' Her smile was slightly wry. 'Not a bus, in my case, but a combination of speed, black ice and a close encounter with a brick wall.' The sympathetic response that came to his lips on automatic was neatly deflected as she went on, 'Of course, since I live in the basement I didn't have to make much of an effort to be here.'

'The basement?'

She clearly misread his expression. 'I believe that Lower Ground Floor is the correct "estate agent" term. It's not as bad as it sounds, I promise you. It's a basement at the front, where I have my kitchen and bedroom and a front door for visitors who can handle steps, but the land slopes away at the rear. My sitting room and studio is on ground level so that I have direct access to the rear garden, the garage and my car. I can't walk now, but I can still drive.'

'I'm familiar with the layout,' he said, although her reference to a studio puzzled him. 'My maternal grandmother used to live here,' he explained when she looked surprised.

'Did she? I didn't know that it was a family house. I thought Steven had paid...' She clearly decided that she was getting into something that was none of her business. 'What I meant to say is that I'm not dependent. I'm totally self-contained and go for days without seeing either of them.' She stopped, clearly realising that 'either' was no longer a possibility. 'Fran managed to convince Steven that the conversion was a good idea. That a self-contained granny-stroke-staff flat would increase the value of the house.'

'I'm sure she's right.'

'She's more than just a pretty face. Of course I paid for the extension work.'

'Of course.'

'Are you sure I can't tempt you to one of Connie's sandwich surprises?'

'Who is Connie?'

'Another of Fran's lame ducks. She has a bit of

trouble with English and can't seem to tell her lemon curd from her mayonnaise, which tends to make her cooking a bit of a gamble.'

'In that case I'm quite sure,' he replied.

Matty grinned. 'Where's your spirit of adventure?'

'I left it behind in a steaming swamp. It needs a rest.'

'Fair enough.' Then, looking at the crowded room, 'Oh, good grief, this lot look as if they've taken root. I'd better go and circulate. There's nothing like a wheelchair to make people thoroughly uncomfortable, make them remember that they have to be somewhere else. And, if that doesn't shift them, I'll fall back on my pathetic-relative-from-the-basement act and dribble a little. I don't think Fran can take much more of this.'

For a moment they both looked in her direction.

'How's she doing?' he asked.

'What do you think?'

Francesca's smile was fixed, her eyes glassy with fatigue and the effort of listening to the two men who seemed to have her pinned in the corner.

'Actually, I think she needs rescuing.' He also knew that she'd endure anything rather than accept help from him. 'Who are those people? Can't they see she's at the end of her tether?'

Matty shrugged. 'I've no idea. Probably people Steven was doing business with. Obviously things have been let go a bit in the last few months.'

'Obviously,' he muttered, heading in their direction, furious with Steven, furious with himself, but most of all furious with them for bothering Francesca at a time like this. She might not want his help, but she was getting it anyway. 'We haven't met,' he said, offering his hand to one of the men and, as he took it, he turned him away from her, stepping between them. It wasn't subtle. It wasn't intended to be. 'Guy Dymoke, Steven's brother. I've been out of the country for a while. You're friends of his?'

'We're business acquaintances.' They introduced themselves, but he cut them off as they launched into an explanation of their precise connection with his brother.

'It's very good of you to give up your valuable time in this way.'

'No trouble. I was just asking Miss Lang—'

'This really isn't a good time. Why don't you give me a call?' he said, handing the man his card and mentally willing Francesca to take advantage of the opportunity to escape, but she seemed fixed to the spot. Beyond help.

'As I was just saying to Miss Lang,' the man continued, stubbornly refusing to take the hint, 'it's really a matter of some urgency and no one at the office seems to know—'

This time he was cut off mid-sentence as Matty caught him behind the ankle with her wheelchair. 'Oops, sorry. I can't seem to get the hang of this thing.' she said. Then, 'Fran, sweetheart…' It needed a second prompt before she responded. 'Fran, you're needed in the kitchen.'

'Oh, right.' She snapped out of whatever memory she was lost in and saw him. That seemed to do the trick. 'If you'll excuse me…'

'But Miss Lang, I really need—'

'Not now.' Guy softened the words with a smile,

all the while urging them firmly towards the door. 'I know Francesca appreciates your sympathy, but it's a difficult time for her. Bring your problems to me.'

Realising that they were not going to get any further, they took the hint and left.

'Jerks,' Matty said as she watched them leave, one favouring his left ankle.

'I don't think you're a very nice person, Matty Lang.'

'Really?' She grinned. 'That's the nicest thing anyone has said to me in ages. For some reason, because I'm confined to a wheelchair, people seem to think I should have suddenly been transformed into a saint.' Then, 'Can I leave you to mop up the stragglers while I go and rustle up a pot of tea?'

No one needed her in the kitchen, although she was just in time to prevent Connie from loading crystal glasses into the dishwasher. Matty had simply been giving her a chance to escape, Fran realised belatedly. Guy, too, although it hurt to acknowledge that he might have even one kind bone in his body.

She should go back. People would be leaving, but she couldn't face the drawing room again. The polite condolences which, for the most part, simply masked the unasked questions she could see in everyone's eyes. They were sorry Steven was dead, sympathetic, but their concerns were with the future. Would the company go on? Would they have their jobs at the end of the month? Survival was the name of the game. For them, just as much as those two tactless imbeciles who undoubtedly wanted to know when their bills would be paid.

Questions to which she had no answers.

It occurred to her that she was now the owner of a business that she knew next to nothing about. She'd talked about going back to work once she'd had Toby, but Steven had insisted that she had enough to do running their home, being Toby's mother. That it was his job to take care of them.

Even while he was dying he'd insisted that he'd got it sorted…that he was going to take care of them all.

She choked back a sob as she sank on to the saggy old sofa that filled one corner of the kitchen, curling up into it for comfort. For endless days she'd been holding on, knowing that once the funeral was over she would have to confront the future. But not now. Not today.

Guy shut the door on the last of the mourners, then went through to the kitchen to find Francesca. He had no illusions about his reception, but he had to convince her that she must call him if she had any problems. That he'd be there for her. He doubted that she'd ask him for help, but he'd leave his number with Matty anyway. She was sharp enough to call him if…

A ball bounced at his feet and he turned to confront a small boy who was standing on the half-landing. There was no mistaking who he was. He had something of Steve about him, a nose that was a gift from his grandfather, his mother's corn-gold hair.

The wrench at his heartstrings was so unexpected, so painful, that for a moment he clutched his fist to his chest as if to hold his heart in place. When he'd read that Francesca and Steve had a son he had been bombarded with such a mixture of emotions that he hadn't known what to do with himself. The truth was that there was nothing to do. Only endure.

He bent to pick up the ball but for a moment couldn't speak, just stood there, holding it.

The child bounced down the stairs one step at a time, then, suddenly shy, stopped about halfway. Guy swallowed, tried to form the words, finally managed, 'Hello, Toby.'

'Who are you?' he said, hanging on to the banister rail as he hopped down another step. 'How do you know my name?'

He'd read it in a newspaper clipping sent to him by his secretary.

Francesca Lang and Steven Dymoke are pleased to announce the birth of their son Tobias Lang Dymoke.

He'd sent the antique silver rattle, a family heirloom that should have been passed to his own first-born. A gesture that was meant to say to Steve that he was valued. That they were equals. He'd hoped that with a woman like Francesca at his side, with the birth of his son, Steve might have discovered an inner strength, self-confidence to finally realise that. Maybe he had, but his gift had been returned. The message was clear. Keep away.

'I'm your Uncle Guy.' He offered the child the ball

and he descended another couple of steps until they were at the same eye level. Then, as he made a grab for the ball, he lost his balance and Guy found himself with an armful of small boy.

'What are you doing?'

Francesca's anxious voice startled Toby and he began to cry.

'Give him to me!' She didn't wait, but wrenched the child from his arms, making things worse as she hugged him tight, frightening him. 'What is it with you? You think just because Steven's dead you can walk into his home as if you own the place, pick up his son—'

'The boy overbalanced, Francesca. I caught him before he fell.' About to add that he was fine until she'd shouted, he thought better of it. She'd just suffered one terrible loss and it was only natural that she'd be protective. 'I was looking for you to let you know I'm leaving.'

'You've said it. Now will you please just go.'

Distraught, grieving, she wasn't about to listen to him and he wasn't about to try and justify his absence from their lives. 'I simply wanted to let you know that you don't have to worry about the paperwork, Steve's business. I'll handle it, and if there's anything you need—'

'You won't,' she declared, lifting her chin a little. 'It's my concern, not yours. And I don't. Need anything.'

Her rejection felt as physical as a slap. He took a breath. 'All you have to do is call my office. Speak to my secretary—'

'Your *secretary*? Well, thanks. It's good to know where I stand in your priorities.'

'I thought…' He'd thought that dealing through an intermediary would be easier for her, but the truth was that in the face of her complete refusal to see him as anything other than her enemy he felt utterly helpless.

Matty appeared in the kitchen doorway. 'I've made a pot of tea if anyone fancies a cup,' she said, then glanced from him to Francesca and back again. 'I can make that Scotch if you'd prefer?'

'Another time. I have to go.' He crossed to her, bent to take her hand, then taking the opportunity to slip her the card with his mobile number on it, the one he'd been planning to give Francesca. 'It was a pleasure to meet you, Matty.'

'Well, don't say it as if was the first and last time.'

'I'm sure Guy has more pressing demands on his time, Matty. A potential oil field or three needing his expertise.'

'I'll be staying in London for a week or two.'

'That long?' The scorn in Francesca's voice would have withered crab grass. 'Oh, well, then we've got absolutely nothing to worry about, have we…?'

She was near the edge of hysteria, he thought, and his presence wasn't helping. Maybe Matty realised that too because she caught his eye and said, 'I'll see you out.'

'It's all right. He knows the way. This used to be his house until he sold it to Steven at the top of the property boom.' He looked up and, seeing the shock on his face, she said, 'What's the matter? Did you think I didn't know how much he paid you?'

What could he say? Tell her that she was wrong? That the man she loved, nursed, cared for, had lied to her?

'He adored you, Guy,' she said, as he turned to leave. 'Worshipped you. He was always making excuses for you. In his eyes you could do no wrong...'

How he wished that was true, but wishing helped no one. Instead, he smiled at the child who had stopped crying and was peering up at him from beneath long wet lashes.

'Goodbye, Toby,' he said, through what felt like a rock in his throat, and the child thrust the ball he was still holding towards him.

He didn't know what was expected of him and he got no help from Francesca. Feeling helpless was becoming repetitive. He wasn't used to it. He didn't like it. Choosing action, he took the ball and said, 'Thank you, Toby.' The child buried his head in his mother's shoulder.

'I'll call you tomorrow, Francesca.'

'Don't bother.' She didn't wait to see how he reacted. She swept from the hall, taking Toby with her, and he forced his unwilling feet towards the door.

'Shall I leave this with you?' he asked, offering the ball to Matty.

'Toby gave it to you because he wants you to come back,' she said.

'His mother doesn't feel the same way.'

'Possibly not, but I don't see anyone else crossing continents and oceans to be at her side—'

'Steve was my brother,' he said.

'—or leaping to her rescue when she was being

hounded by men anxious about their invoices,' she continued as if he hadn't interrupted. Her face, thin, plainly marked with everything she'd suffered, was bright with intelligence and he sensed an ally.

'Have they reason to be?' he asked. 'Anxious?'

'Steven didn't confide in me but he hasn't been in any state to run the business himself for the last six months.'

'I wish she'd let me know.'

'He wouldn't let her. At the end she called your office anyway, but it was too late. All you can do now, Mr Knight Errant, is stick around and help her pick up the pieces.'

CHAPTER TWO

FRANCESCA was shaking so badly that she had to sit down before her legs gave way. Toby struggled to free himself, but she clutched at him as if he was the only thing standing between her and some dark chasm that yawned in front of her.

She'd been so sure that Guy wouldn't come today. It had been pure relief when his secretary rang to tell her that although she'd finally managed to get the news to him he was unlikely to make it home in time, even for the funeral. Easy enough to assure the woman that she understood, decline all offers of assistance.

She should have known he would move heaven and earth. Steven had once told her that his brother was a man who simply refused to contemplate the impossible, that only once had he backed down, retreated from the challenge to get what he wanted. Guy Dymoke was a dark, unseen shadow that had seemed to haunt Steven. She should have, could have, done something to change that, she thought guiltily. Made an effort to bridge the gulf that had opened up between them, but an uneasy sense of self-preservation had warned her to leave well alone.

'Why don't you go and put your feet up, Fran? You look done in.'

Grateful to Matty for distracting her, she finally allowed Toby to escape. The one thing she mustn't become was a clinging mother, weeping over her child. 'I'm fine, really. Where's Connie?'

'She's tidying up the drawing room.'

'You've both been wonderful. I don't know what I'd have done without you.'

'I wish I could say that the worst is over.'

'It is. I just have to see the solicitor tomorrow. Sort out the will.' She didn't anticipate any difficulty. Steven had told her that he'd made sure she and Toby were taken care of; he must have known he was dying then, despite the fact that neither of them had ever acknowledged it and she had to believe he meant it.

Her real problem was his business. What was going to happen to that?

'Just remember that you're not alone,' Matty continued, distracting her. 'I'm here, and Connie will hold the fort with Toby—'

'It's not necessary, really.' She'd been forcing her mouth into a smile, her voice into soothing tones of reassurance for so long that it did it on automatic. But she was determined not to worry Matty. She'd made an amazing recovery but she was still far from strong.

'She wants to help, Fran. To be honest I think she's terrified you'll move away and won't take her with you.'

'No! I couldn't... I wouldn't...' Even as she said it she realised that Matty was appealing for reassurance too. 'She's family,' she said.

'Of course she is. That's what I told her. And Guy Dymoke looks like the kind of man a woman in trouble could lean on.' Then, while she was still trying to get her head around the idea of leaning on Guy, 'Is there going to be trouble?'

Francesca was drained, exhausted, tired to the

bone, but it wasn't over yet and she forced the smile into a grin. 'Are you kidding? I've got a company to run and the most challenging thing I've had to think about for the last three years is the menu for the next dinner party. That sounds like enough trouble for anyone.'

'Don't undersell yourself, Fran.' Matty reached out, took her hand, held it for a moment. Then, 'I need to know. Is there going to be *trouble*?'

She wanted to say no. Absolutely not. The way she had to Guy. But she'd encouraged her cousin to come and share the house after her accident. Steven hadn't been wildly keen, but the house was huge, far too big for the three of them. Matty had needed to be in London for treatment, needed to have someone close she could call on in an emergency, and there was no one else. Nowhere else. And it wasn't a one way bargain. She was company during Steven's absences abroad seeking out the merchandise he imported.

The truth was, she just didn't know. Steven had never talked about the business. Had always brushed aside her interest, her questions, as something she needn't bother her head about, until she'd stopped bothering to ask. She wished she hadn't allowed herself to be so easily distracted, but he obviously hadn't wanted her involved, and she had Toby and Matty...

'I don't want to think about it,' she said. 'Not today. Let's have that Scotch.'

'But what about the house?'

She heard the fear and knew it was a fair question. Matty had an investment in the house. She'd spent her own money on the conversion of the lower ground floor into a self-contained flat suitable for her wheelchair. A talented illustrator, she'd extended it to make a studio so that she could work there.

'He always promised me that the house was safe.' Always promised that he would never use their home to raise finance. She wanted to believe that he had meant that, but if the company was in any kind of trouble—and what company wasn't these days?—and the bank wanted its pound of flesh…

She and Toby could live anywhere, but Matty would never be able to find another home in London. Not like the one she had with them, especially converted to her needs. With the space. Room for her drawing board…

'I'm sorry. Of course he did. It was your palace—he said so often enough, and you were his princess.' Matty looked around. 'I wonder how he raised enough cash to buy it at the top of the property boom?'

'He didn't have to. His father left him some money. Nothing like the fortune Guy had in trust from his mother, of course—especially after some City fraud put a major dent in the family finances—but there was enough for this house. He just wanted everything to be perfect for me.'

As if he had something to prove. There had only ever been one person he needed to prove himself to—and, torn between relief and fury that Guy had never bothered to show up and be impressed by his success, she declared, 'And it was. Perfect.'

But she couldn't quite meet Matty's eye as she said it.

Guy paid the cab driver, peeled off the parking ticket stuck to his windscreen, tossed it into the glove box and headed for the echoing space of the Thames-side loft apartment that he'd lavished time and money on, but which only served to remind him of the emptiness at the heart of his life.

He poured Scotch into a glass, sank into the comfort of a soft leather armchair and stared out across the river. He wasn't seeing the boats, didn't notice the lights that were coming on as dusk settled over the city, blurring the familiar skyline. All he could see was Francesca Lang. Not sombre in black with her hair coiled up off her neck, but the way she'd looked the first time he'd set eyes on her.

He sipped the whisky, but its heat didn't warm him. There was nothing in the world that could warm him other than the arms of a woman who was forbidden him in every code he lived by. A woman who today had looked at him as if he was something that had crawled out from under a stone. He'd anticipated a frosty reception, but he hadn't anticipated this level of animosity. Every single word she'd uttered had felt like a blow. He'd been taking them from her all afternoon and he felt bruised to the bone.

He abandoned the whisky—there was no help for what ailed him in a bottle—got up and walked restlessly across to the window, seeking distraction. Finding none.

He leaned his forehead against the cool glass, closed his eyes. Running the endless loop of memory that was all he had of her.

If he'd had any idea what was coming he'd have been on his guard, but the moment Francesca had appeared in the doorway of that restaurant she'd stolen his wits as well as what passed for his heart, blindsiding him, so that he'd been exposed, vulnerable, and

Steve—clever Steve—had instantly picked up the signals and positively revelled in the fact that, for the
first time in his life, he had something that his half-
brother wanted, something he could never have.

He hadn't blamed him for that. He had just wanted
to be somewhere else, a million miles from the restaurant, but there had been no escape. There had been
an entire evening to get through first and all he could
do was pull down the mental shutters, shake Steve's
hand, brush Francesca's cheek with his lips as he welcomed her into the family, congratulated her. It had
been a quiet torture then and the slow drip of it had
never left him.

His mind, stuck in an endless re-run that he
couldn't escape—didn't want to escape—continued to
play that moment over and over every time he
stopped concentrating on something else. Every time
he closed his eyes.

The peachy softness of her cheek. A subtle scent
that hadn't come from any bottle but was a fusion of
her hair, the warmth of her body, her clothes, the fresh
air she'd brought in with her, all enhanced by a touch
of something exotic and rich. He'd had three years to
analyse it, reduce it to its constituent parts.

All he had been able to do was wish them well, be
glad that Steve had finally found what he'd always
been searching for. Someone who loved him.
Someone who would always be there. A family of his
own.

And live with it.

Attempt to carry on a normal conversation.

'Where are you planning to live?' he'd asked.
'Steve's flat isn't big enough for two, let alone a
baby.' It was like prodding himself with a hot needle.

'We're looking around for just the right place...'
Then, with a casual shrug, Steve added, 'Fran and I
looked at the Elton Street house yesterday.'

His heart missed a beat as he forced himself to turn
to Francesca, include her in the conversation. 'Did
you like it?'

'It's a beautiful house,' she said, not quite meeting
his eyes.

'Fran fell head over heels in love with it,' Steve
said emphatically. 'I'd like to come and see you tomorrow. Talk about it.'

He ignored the opening his brother had left him.

Maybe he was the one avoiding eye contact.
Avoiding a repeat of that moment when, with one
look, the entire world seemed to slide into place and
lock with an almost audible click; the kick-in-the-
stomach pain that went with the loss of something
precious.

He forced himself to look directly at her.

'You would like to live there?' he asked.

For a moment something shimmered between them
as, very quietly, she said, 'It felt like home.'

He dragged himself back from the edge. From stepping off. From saying, *Come with me and I will give
you everything your heart desires. The house, my
heart, my life...*

'Then I'm sure Steve will find a way to give it to
you.'

'It depends on the price. Unlike you, brother, I
don't have unlimited means at my disposal.'

'No one has unlimited means.' But he'd got the
picture. The reason for the invitation to dinner. The
last time he'd had a call from his half-brother—make
that every time he'd had a call from him—it had been

to 'borrow' money, on the last occasion to ask for start-up funds for his latest business venture. He'd assumed tonight was going to be more of the same, but clearly it wasn't to help with some half-baked business plan he wanted this time.

'Have you set a wedding date?' he asked, evading a direct answer and Steve didn't push. He clearly didn't want Francesca to know that he was asking for help with finance. But then why would he push? In the past all he'd had to do was lay out his desires and wait for guilt to do the rest.

'Wedding? Who said anything about getting married?'

'Isn't that the obvious next step?' He looked at Steve. A youthful marriage was the one mistake he hadn't been called to bail him out of, but anything was possible. 'Unless there's some good reason why you shouldn't?' He managed a grin of sorts. 'Is there something you haven't told me?'

Steve grinned right back. 'Relax, Guy. I don't have a secret wife or three tucked away. Fran's the only woman I've ever wanted to settle down with.'

'Then what's your problem?' If Francesca Lang had been his, nothing on earth would have stopped him from swearing his undying love in front of as many witnesses as he could cram into one room. Making that public vow to love and honour and keep her, in sickness and in health, for as long as they both should live... 'If you're setting up home together, having a baby...'

It was like poking a sore tooth. Something he knew he'd regret, but he couldn't stop himself.

'For heaven's sake, listen to yourself. Marriage is meaningless in this day and age. An anachronism.

Outdated. Just a way of keeping lawyers fat when it all goes wrong.'

He glanced at Francesca to see how she was taking that 'when', but she was looking down at her plate.

With no clue as to her feelings, he shrugged and said, 'I believe you'll find that even in the twenty-first century it offers some benefits.' What they were, beyond the special bond that swearing till-death-us-do-part vows to one another, he couldn't immediately summon to mind. But then that would be enough for him.

'The chance to dress up and have a party? I don't think we need to go to church first, do you?' Then, 'Look, you know the kind of nasty divorce Dad went through with my mother. Fran's been through much the same thing with her parents.' Steve leaned across and took her hand, grasping it in his, emphasising their relationship. 'We're allergic, okay?'

Guy fastened his gaze on some point in the distance. 'If you believe that not getting married will protect you from the fallout of a disintegrating relationship, think again. Once property and children are involved…'

'Guy, I hear what you're saying, but that stuff is just for rich people.' He didn't add …*like you.* He didn't have to.

'It's your decision, of course,' he said, wondering if Francesca felt quite as strongly on the subject— she'd remained silent—but he didn't dare look at her again. He didn't want to see the love shining out of her eyes. Not when she was looking at another man. 'Just don't discount it without real thought.'

'We have thought about it.' He lifted Francesca's hand to his lips and kissed it. Then, with a smile, he said, 'But if you want to play the big brother you can pay for the champagne.'

The message came over loud and clear. Steve was saying, This is nothing to do with you. It's my baby she's carrying…

That had been the only thing he'd been able to think about all through that terrible evening. Francesca was pregnant and he'd have given everything he possessed to change places with his brother. His career, the company he'd built up with a group of friends, the fortune that had been left to him by his own mother, just to be sitting on the other side of the table with his arm draped protectively over the back of her chair, knowing that the baby she carried was his.

Total madness. He'd only just met the woman. Had exchanged barely more than a dozen words with her. The briefest touch of her cheek against his lips. The moment she'd realised who he was, the hundred watt smile had been dimmed to something more reserved. Steve had obviously given her chapter and verse on all his grievances. Real and imagined. Told her all about his older, more fortunate half-brother who had everything, including a mother who'd loved him. Especially a mother who'd loved him…

It made no difference. Even the forty-watt version lit up his soul.

'Are you going to be all right on your own?'

'I've got to get used to it, Matty. Today seems like a good day to start.'

Fran smoothed her collar, regarded her image in the hall mirror. Black suit, perfectly groomed hair. Apart from the dark shadows beneath her eyes, she looked every inch the businesswoman. Steven would have approved. He had always said that image was everything. The trick was to ignore the butterflies practising formation-flying in your stomach; if you looked confident, looked as if you knew what you were talking about, people would believe in you. Okay, so it was three years since she'd set foot in an office, but her brain hadn't atrophied just because she'd had a baby—well, not that much anyway.

Right now a load of people were sitting around in the office waiting for someone to say, It'll be all right. Let's get on with it. And there was no one but her.

'I'll get the paperwork sorted out with the lawyers first,' she said. 'And then I'm going into the office.'

'What is he doing here?'

Guy had only just arrived when a secretary announced Francesca's arrival. She came to an abrupt halt in the doorway when she saw him, but there was no stop-the-world moment this time. No out-of-control hairstyle, no clinging dress to ride up and no yard of leg. And she didn't pause to look up at him with a smile caught on her lips.

He hadn't realised just how much weight she'd lost. Her hair was paler too. More grown up than the corn gold he remembered. Maybe that hadn't been her natural colour, either, but he preferred it.

That night she had been all vibrant colour, now she was monochrome, the pallor of her skin emphasised by dark hollows beneath her eyes, at her temples. It made the quick angry flush as she saw him all the more noticeable.

'Why is he here?' she said, ignoring him completely and looking directly at Tom Palmer, the family lawyer, who'd come around his desk to welcome her.

'Guy is your...is Steven's executor, Fran. It's his responsibility to see that the will is properly executed.'

Now she turned those lovely grey eyes on him. 'So that's why you raced back from the back of beyond,' she said. 'To secure your assets.'

'I have no doubt that Steven left everything he possessed to you and Toby. It's my sole responsibility to ensure that his wishes are carried out and I will do that, no matter what they are.'

Tom, who had undoubtedly witnessed family discord on such occasions many times over a long career, intervened with a quiet, 'Please, come and sit down, Fran. Would you care for some coffee...tea, perhaps?'

'Nothing, thank you. Let's get this over with. I've a full day ahead of me.'

'Of course. The will itself is a simple enough document.' He opened a file. 'First, Guy, Steven left this letter for you.'

He pocketed it without comment.

'Aren't you going to read it?' Francesca demanded.

'Not now,' he said. If Steve, the least organised person in the world, had chosen to write him a letter when he knew he was dying, he wanted to be alone when he read it. 'Tom?'

Prompted, Tom Palmer began to read the will.

While he'd been in a position to make conditions, Guy had insisted that Steve make a will in favour of Francesca. It had not been altered, and her relief, though contained, was nevertheless evident for those with eyes to read the small signs. The briefly closed eyes, the slightest slump in her posture as the tension left her.

'Is that it?' she asked.

'It's little enough,' Tom said. 'Unfortunately, as you know, Steven surrendered his life assurance to raise some capital last year.'

'He did?' The shocked words slipped out before she could contain them. 'Yes. Of course. He discussed it with me,' she continued, swiftly covering her slip.

That had been the other condition. The life policy. So much for his best intentions.

'When I asked if that was it, I just meant, can I go now? I want to go to the office, make a start on sorting things out.'

She was incredible, he thought. She'd just received a monumental blow but she'd absorbed it and, but for those two words, no one would believe it was anything other than what she'd expected to hear.

'Not quite all,' Tom said, clearly relieved that he hadn't had to deal with hysterics. 'I just need your signature on here so that I can set about organising a valuation of the estate. It shouldn't take too long.'

'Valuation?' She looked up from the document he'd placed in front of her.

'Of the company. For tax purposes.' She looked blank. 'Inheritance tax?' he elaborated. 'I did warn Steven of the situation when he originally signed the will. At that time there was no urgency, of course, but I did suggest he talk it over with you. Maybe consider going through the motions. Just a ten minute job at the local Register Office would do.' Guy could see that Tom was beginning to founder in the face of Francesca's incomprehension. Clearly she had never had that conversation with Steven, and he wondered just how many more shocks she could take. 'Just to satisfy the legalities,' Tom ploughed on. 'Perhaps after the baby was born...'

'Inheritance tax?' she repeated, ignoring the waffle.

'Is the company likely to exceed the inheritance tax threshold?' Guy asked, giving Tom a moment to catch up. Work out for himself exactly how much in the dark she was.

'I have no idea,' the lawyer said.

They both looked at Francesca for an answer, but she dismissed their query with an impatient little gesture.

'Tell me about inheritance tax,' she said rather more sharply.

'I don't imagine it will be too much of a problem, unless the company is doing substantially better than it was at the last audit,' Tom Palmer said, clearly unsure which would be preferable. 'However, since you weren't married to Steven any legacy will be subject to inheritance tax.'

She sat and digested this for a moment, then said, 'So if we'd been married I *wouldn't* have to pay inheritance tax?'

'No, but as I said—'

'And because we didn't go through some totally meaningless ceremony I will? Have to pay it?'

'Well, yes. That's the present situation, I'm afraid.'

'But that's outrageous! We've lived together for nearly three years. We have a child...'

'If you'd lived together for twenty-three years and had ten children it would make no difference, I'm afraid.'

After the brief stunned silence she asked, 'What's the liability threshold?'

'£250,000. After that forty percent of the estate goes to the Inland Revenue.'

'But...' Guy had thought she looked pale. He had been wrong. Colour leached from her skin, leaving her ashen. 'But surely the house alone is worth ten times that?'

'You don't have to worry about the house, Fran.'

'You mean the house is free of inheritance tax?' Francesca asked.

'I mean that Steven did not own the house.'

She shook her head. 'No. That's not right. Steven bought it from Guy. Three years ago.' She turned to him. Looked up at him. 'We've lived there for three years. Tell him.'

'There seems to be some confusion, Francesca. I don't know what Steve told you, but he didn't buy the house from me. It was sold to a property company about ten years ago, along with a lot of other property.'

'But he said—you said...' He saw her trying to recall the conversation in the restaurant that night. 'He was going to come and see you. To talk about it. He asked you. That night...'

'He asked me for help with a deposit for the house, that's all. I didn't know until yesterday that you thought I had owned it. And I had no idea he hadn't gone ahead and bought it.'

'But why would he need to borrow from you? He had money...' She stopped. 'How much?'

He didn't want to go there.

'How much did you give him?' she demanded.

'Two hundred and fifty thousand pounds.'

'But he didn't buy it?' This to Tom Palmer.

The lawyer shook his head. 'As far as I know it

wasn't even on the market at the time. He has been renting it on a yearly lease.'

'But it's our home,' she said. 'Toby's home. Matty spent thousands of pounds on the studio extension, converting the place into a flat she could use. If I'd known we only had a lease I'd never have encouraged her to do that.' She caught her breath. 'They don't know about that, do they? The people who own the house?'

'I would think it's highly unlikely,' Guy said gently.

To say that she looked stunned, confused, was an understatement. It was hardly surprising. He felt as if he'd taken a body blow, but she had been under the impression that she'd inherited a house worth upwards of two million pounds. Even taking into account the taxman, that would have meant she could sell up and have a million plus change to set up home somewhere else. Suddenly she owned nothing except a company that no one seemed wildly optimistic about and a short-term lease that might not be renewed. That she probably couldn't afford to renew…

Fran discovered that reaction was beyond her. It was as if she was under water, sinking very slowly, and she was completely paralysed, unable to do anything to stop herself from drowning.

One moment it had seemed as if she could relax, shake off the nagging sense of impending disaster. Now—

'There is one other thing.'

'There's more?' She turned and looked at Tom Palmer. Until now he had been wearing the grave expression of the average family lawyer. Now he looked positively uneasy.

How much worse could it get?

'The last time I saw Steven he asked me to add a codicil to his will. I had to tell him that it was a bequest I was not prepared to add to that document. We came to a compromise. He dictated his wishes to me and I promised to read them out at this point.'

'You mean after you've told me that my son and I are homeless and penniless?'

'Francesca—'

She glared at Guy, daring him to say another word.

'I'll read it now then, shall I?' Tom waited briefly, but neither of them said a word and he took a letter from the file in front of him.

'Before I start I want to say that there is nothing in this document that is binding,' he said, clearly unhappy about something. 'These are no more than Steven's...' He stopped.

'Last wishes?' she finished for him.

'Just read it,' Guy said.

'Very well.' Tom cleared his throat. '*Well, Guy, here we are again.* It's in his own words, just as he said it,' he explained.

'Tom!'

'Sorry. Right...

> *Well, Guy, here we are again. Me messing up and you doing your big brother bit and saving my hide. Except this time my hide is well beyond saving. It's Fran and Toby who need you now.*

'Not this side of hell,' she muttered.

'First the confession. Well, you'll have worked this out for yourself by now, but I used your money for the lease on the house for some diamond earrings for Fran—since she didn't want a ring. Oh, and to pay the bill at that fancy private maternity hospital. Nothing but the best for mine. Something I learned from you. I just didn't have the cash to pay for it. But you never let me down.'

'He didn't have to do that!' Fran protested. 'I wanted to go to the local hospital. I could have lived without diamonds or any of the other stuff...'

Tom waited patiently for her to finish, but she ground to a halt, consumed with shame that Steven had taken money from his brother to give her everything her heart desired. Consumed with guilt that she had taken it without a thought. But that was Steven. He'd said money was something to be enjoyed. Spent it as if he never had to think about where it was going to come from. Maybe he never had. Maybe Guy *had* always been there...

Tom and Guy were looking at her and she lifted a hand, a silent gesture that he should go on.

'Okay, Guy, here's what I want you to do. Just about the last thing I did, before I stopped being able to do anything for myself, was to book a surprise wedding for Fran and me. A beach job in the Caribbean. It seems I was over-optimistic about my prognosis and I'm not going to be able to make it, but Toby is going to need a father and Fran will need someone to help her take care of her waifs and strays and, as always, you are it.

Tom says I can't make a codicil to the will leav-

*ing Fran and Toby to you as a bequest, but I know
you won't let me down. He's got the tickets, all you
have to do is turn up and say 'I do'. It shouldn't
be a problem for either of you.*

Steve'

CHAPTER THREE

THERE was a long, still moment after Tom stopped speaking when it seemed that everyone had forgotten to breathe.

Then Guy said, 'Is that right, Tom? You have the tickets?'

'Yes, but—'

He held out his hand and the lawyer reluctantly passed the travel folder to him. Fran watched in disbelief as he calmly opened it and checked the documents before turning to her.

'It's next week, Francesca. Is that convenient for you?' he asked. As if he was talking about dinner or a seat at the theatre and with about as much emotion. His face might have been hewn from wood for all the expression in it. His eyes chiselled from cold steel.

Confronted with so little feeling, something hot and painful clenched inside her and she recognised it for what it was.

Fear.

'This is a joke.' She looked to the lawyer for backup. 'This is Steven's idea of a practical joke...' If she'd hoped they would both laugh and admit it, she was disappointed. Tom looked down at his desk as if he wished he was anywhere else. Guy continued to look at her, waiting for her answer.

'Let me see.'

He surrendered the folder and its contents to her and she looked at them. Tickets, honeymoon suite, wedding ceremony. Everything was in order. Except that the name on the documents was Guy Dymoke.

'This is unbelievable.'

'It's a formality, Francesca. A paper marriage. Breathing space for you to sort yourself out.'

'I don't need breathing space. I certainly don't need you. I just need somewhere to live.'

'You and Toby, Matty and Connie need somewhere to live,' he corrected.

'Okay! Renew the lease if it makes you feel better.'

'I suspect that I'm going to have to do a little more than that.'

'You've done quite enough, Guy.' And she tore up the tickets. Once, twice, three times. Then she dropped the resulting confetti on the floor.

His head went back as if she'd struck him. Good. She wanted him to feel the heat of her anger. Wanted him to share the pain. Wanted him to feel...*something*.

How dared Steven leave her to his brother in his will as if she was his property?

How dared he accept the bequest as if it was his...his *duty*? Without an ounce of emotion. Everything locked down. Passionless. That was what Steven had said about him. That his brother never showed any emotion. Kept it all buttoned up. She wanted to grab him by the shoulders and shake him...

'Tell me what Steve meant when he said a marriage of convenience wouldn't be a problem for you,' he asked, 'Since you weren't prepared to marry Steve for love. Or maybe he was the one who didn't want to marry you?'

'What?'

Guy was so attuned to her, so aware of every nuance of expression, the slightest movement, that he saw the faintest start. Guy remembered the conversation he'd had with Steve that night he'd come and asked for the money. It had been such an odd thing to say; not about him—Steve had known how he felt and was having his own private game with him—but about her.

It was what he'd said... *'I've got everything you ever wanted, Guy. And I don't even have to marry her...'* Once the cheque had been safely in his pocket. It was the only time in his life Guy had ever lost control, punched his brother in the mouth.

Francesca turned on him furiously.

'Don't you dare blame Steven when he isn't here to defend himself! This is all *my* fault. When he discovered I was pregnant he wanted to marry me, begged me to marry him, but—' She stopped abruptly and glanced nervously at Tom Palmer.

'But?' Guy prompted, demanding her attention. And when she didn't answer, 'You wouldn't renege on your principles, is that it?' he persisted. His tone couldn't have made it plainer that he didn't believe her.

She looked trapped. Hunted.

'Can we talk?' she said, her voice snagging in her throat.

He recognised the turning point, the point when she stopped attacking and went on to the defence, realising that she had more to lose than gain. With anyone else he'd have gone for the kill. But he couldn't do it to her.

'I thought we were talking.'

'Guy...' Her expression softened to nervous plead-

ing. In any other woman he'd have said it was an act.
'Please...'

Oh, hell...

'Tom? Do you need us for anything else today?'

'There are some papers I need you both to sign,
but next week will do. You are going to be around
for a week or two?' He glanced at Francesca, not
voicing the question that was in his eyes.

'No more,' Guy replied.

Francesca turned to say goodbye to Tom, but Guy
wasn't in the mood for such pleasantries. As she offered her hand, he grasped her arm and, taking her
firmly by the elbow, he headed for the door, not
speaking or letting go until they were out of the building and he had his car door open.

'Get in, Francesca.'

'Where are we going?'

'Somewhere quiet,' he said, 'where you can tell me
exactly what isn't Steve's fault.'

Guy hadn't had the first clue where he was going
when he pulled out of the car park, only that he had
to get away from the claustrophobic atmosphere of
Tom's office.

'The park,' he said. 'I need some fresh air. To see
something green that isn't soaking wet. To stretch my
legs.' He glanced at her and instantly regretted his
bullying tactics. 'It takes me a while to get used to
being in a city,' he said.

'The sudden change must be difficult,' she said,
quickly seizing the chance to move out of dangerous
waters. 'Do you enjoy working out in the field?'

'Enjoy might be putting it a little strong,' he said,
letting her get away with it. 'It's a challenge.'

'What'd you do? I have this image of you scrambling over rock faces knocking lumps of them with a hammer. I imagine there must be more to it than that?'

He could imagine her at a dinner party, talking to some tongue-tied man, trying to draw him into the conversation…

She was being polite. But she didn't actually give a damn and he'd have given a lot to be high up on some rock face, with the wind tasting of nothing more than the ocean it had crossed, instead of snarled up in the fume laden air of London traffic.

'It is a bit more technical than that these days. But, with all the satellite pictures in the world, you still need people on the ground.'

'So who's doing your job while you're here?'

She sounded as if she rather hoped he might have to rush right back. The sooner the better. Maybe taking off like that had been a mistake. The longer she had to think about her plea to 'talk', the more likely she was to regret the impulse.

'No one. Which is why time is in short supply.'

'It must be wonderful to have a real career.' A wistful note had crept into her voice. 'Be respected.'

'Being a good mother is the most important job there is.' It occurred to him that maybe she hadn't made the choice. That Steve would have needed a woman who would always put him first, last… 'What did you want to do? Before you met Steve?'

'Oh, I don't know. The same as anyone with a degree in Business Studies, I suppose. To find the next big thing.' She shrugged, as if faintly embarrassed by her ambition. Then, gaining confidence, 'Be the Amaryllis Jones of my generation,' she said, referring to the legendary founder of a chain of aro-

matherapy outlets, who'd just received an award in
the Queen's birthday honours list. 'Have my picture
on the front page of the *Financial Times*.'

'Then you met Steve.'

'Then I met Steven and got pregnant,' she said.
'Not much of a reference for someone who wants to
impress the world with her organisational efficiency.'

The driver of the car behind them hooted impatiently.

'Doesn't Amaryllis Jones have children?'

'The traffic appears to be moving,' she replied,
evading an answer.

He eased the car forward. 'Doesn't she?'

'Four, I believe. Look, you want to walk and I have
to get to Steven's office. If you dropped me here I
could take the Underground. It would be much
quicker—'

She looked at her wristwatch, as if to emphasise
the immediacy of her need to be there. She was definitely regretting her impulsive appeal to get what was
bothering her off her chest. He had somehow backed
her into a corner and she'd momentarily panicked.
Now she'd had a few minutes to gather herself the
last thing she wanted to do was 'talk'.

'You're going to step into Steve's shoes and run
the company?' he asked, ignoring her suggestion.

'Someone has to be there to hold the fort while the
future is decided, to reassure the staff—and the
bank—and to deal with people like those two men
yesterday, or there won't be a company for anyone to
run. As of now, that's me.' She lifted her head a little.
'I didn't thank you for rescuing me. Yesterday.'

'I didn't think you'd noticed.'

Her tense mouth softened as she glanced at him

and fell into a natural smile. If she was trying to distract him, she was doing a good job. He'd lived with this woman in his head, in his heart, for three years. He needed to remind himself that that was all a fantasy. That he'd been in the grip of an obsession. That he didn't actually know her.

Well, all that was going to change. There was definitely something not quite right about her relationship with Steve and he was going to find out what it was.

'What, exactly, does the company do?' he asked.

'Imports the kind of stuff that no one actually needs but most of us love to buy. After his last trip he was really excited about something. He said it was just ticking over for the moment, but that once he was better he'd really show everyone.'

'Everyone' being Guy.

'Maybe he left some notes,' Guy said quickly, intent on a little distraction of his own. 'Have you been through his desk? Checked his laptop?' She looked at him blankly. What was he saying? She'd been nursing the man she loved through a terminal illness. Going through his desk for business notes would have been the last thing on her mind. 'Has anyone else?' he said.

She shook her head. 'I don't know. I suppose I should have brought his laptop with me today. Some businesswoman I'm going to make...'

'Give yourself a chance. That you're even going into the office today shows enormous strength.' Then, 'We could look at it together if that would help?'

'We? Why would you bother yourself?'

When he couldn't be bothered to visit while his

brother was alive? The unspoken question hung in the air.

'I'm Steve's executor,' he reminded her leadenly, suddenly back to square one. 'I'm going to have to take a good look at the business. Sort out the best way to go forward. I'll need your input on that. If you're going to take an interest in running it.'

'It's all I have,' she reminded him. 'If I'm going to provide a home for Toby, I don't have any choice.'

'Matty doesn't pay rent for the flat?'

'Just a nominal amount,' she said. 'To cover her share of the outgoings.' Then, with just a touch of challenge in her voice, 'I suppose sub-letting of any kind is forbidden under the lease too?'

'Don't worry about it.'

'I don't think the landlord is going to be that re-laxed about it, do you?' Then, 'We'll need some time to find somewhere else. It's not such a problem for me, but it will be more difficult for Matty. I realise she's not your concern, of course.'

'Unlike you.'

'I am not your concern, Guy.'

He glanced at her. 'Shall we discuss that once you've told me what you weren't prepared to say in front of Tom Palmer?'

Francesca had hoped that Guy might have forgotten their precipitate departure from Tom Palmer's office. Which was pretty stupid of her.

As stupid as allowing herself to lose her temper with him. She'd come so close to blurting everything out, just to shut him up. Everyone in that room knew Steven had lied to her. Well, that was what he'd been like. He had been weak. Charming, but weak. But

even when you'd known him you'd still believed him.
Even Guy had been fooled...

Guiltily, she slammed mental doors on the disloyal
thoughts. She had lived a charmed life. She'd been
pampered, cared for, envied by friends who con-
stantly worried about their partners straying at the first
temptation.

She had never doubted that she and Toby came first
in his life and now he was dead she wasn't going to
keep quiet while anyone, let alone Guy Dymoke—
especially Guy Dymoke—criticised him, judged him,
blamed him.

She had been a fool to allow Guy to take charge
and practically frogmarch her to his car. Except, of
course, if she'd resisted, walked away, he'd have kept
pace with her and all she would have been able to do
would be hope for a knight errant—in the shape of a
black cab—to swoop to the kerb and carry her away.
As if that would have shaken him off. All he needed
to do was go to Elton Street and wait for her to return.

She glanced at him. Having reminded her of the
real purpose of this journey, he was concentrating on
getting them through the traffic, taking shortcuts
through the narrow little streets that connected the
great arteries of London. His face was set, expressionless, all angles and planes that caught the light as
they zipped in and out of the traffic. A long, thin nose
that was a shade too large. The kind of cheekbones
that she'd once seen on a Roman frieze. A mouth,
full and sensuous and—

Guy brought the car to a halt, then reversed into a
parking space.

'Oh. You've brought me home.' Then she realised
why. 'You want Steven's laptop.'

'That, and it occurred to me that you'd never have managed a hundred yards in those shoes.'

'No, I suppose not.' She looked down. 'My feet are a bit small to fill Steven's shoes.'

He said nothing, did not move, did not even look at her. She swallowed, suddenly afraid. She knew that if he came inside she would have to tell him everything. That he would be angry with her. Would utterly despise her for the fool she was.

Well, that was fair. She despised herself.

'Guy?' she prompted.

He continued to grip the steering wheel. 'I want you to know that I loved Steve. He probably told you that I was an overbearing big brother, that I tried to run his life, that I had everything and he had nothing...'

A small, telltale sound escaped her throat.

'I was probably all those things, and yes, I did have an inheritance from my mother that left him feeling less loved, less important, less of everything. The unhappy truth is that he *was* less loved by his mother. That she didn't even turn up for his funeral tells you exactly what kind of mother she was. Non-existent. That woman doesn't have a maternal bone in her body, not an ounce of kindness, and I loathed her for what she did to him. I tried to make it up to him, but nothing I could do ever filled the void, the lack of self-worth, she left in his life. I hoped with you, with Toby, he might begin to find it.'

'So why did you stay away?'

'I was the one person who knew every idiotic thing he'd ever done. I'd been getting him out of scrapes since he was big enough to get into them. Always at his shoulder urging him to make something of his life like some nagging conscience.'

He finally looked at her and she felt the need to swallow again.

'And I was angry with him for not marrying you and he knew it. He said it was your choice, but I knew him…' Then, 'It's complicated.'

'Life starts out complicated and goes downhill from there,' she agreed.

'He was telling the truth for once, wasn't he?'

She didn't answer. Instead she opened the car door and swung her legs to the pavement and said, 'We'd better go in.'

She slid her key into the lock. Matty was downstairs, catching up with her work. Toby wouldn't be home from nursery school for another half an hour. She glanced at her watch and went through to the comfort zone of the kitchen, where Connie was getting ready to go and pick Toby up.

'Oh, Fran. You come home.' Then, catching sight of Guy, 'You want me to make lunch?'

'No,' she said quickly.

'I just going to fetch Toby. I take him to the park. Feed the ducks, eat ice cream.' Then, 'We could come straight home if you like?'

'No, you go right ahead, Connie. Have you got enough money?' Not waiting for an answer, she opened her bag, found a banknote and gave it to her. 'Just for emergencies,' she said. 'No need to rush back. Toby deserves a treat.' Then, feeling as if she had to explain why she was inviting a strange man into her home the day after Steven's funeral, 'This is Steven's brother, Guy, Connie. We're just going to look through some papers.' She turned to where Guy was standing in the kitchen doorway. 'Connie is our nanny, housekeeper, surrogate mother. I don't know how we'd manage without her.'

As she watched them shake hands she remembered what Matty had said. How worried she was about the future.

'Does she live in?' Guy asked when the front door had banged shut behind her.

'Yes. It's just as well the house is so big.'

She swallowed. Now they were on their own the kitchen seemed a lot less like a comfort zone.

'Would you like some coffee?' she asked to fill the lengthening silence. 'Before we start.'

'Why don't I make it while you go and fetch Steve's laptop?'

'You?' she asked, startled. Then, realising that she was as good as admitting that Steven had never crossed the kitchen threshold, she quickly went on, 'You mean you want to work in here?'

'I thought we could use the kitchen table. There's plenty of room to spread ourselves out. The study is a bit small for two people to work in comfort, I thought.'

'How do you...?' Then, 'Oh, right.' She kept forgetting that he knew the house intimately. But he was right. The tiny study tucked away on a half-landing was not big enough for two, not unless they were prepared to work very close. 'I'll go and fetch it,' she said quickly. 'The coffee is—'

'I'll find it.'

'Right,' she said again. 'I, um, won't be a minute. I'll just—' She managed to stop herself from saying, slip into something more comfortable. 'I'll just change out of this suit.'

'No rush. I'm not going anywhere.'

If he'd meant to reassure her, she thought, as she kicked off her high heels before picking them up and running upstairs, he'd failed.

Guy filled the kettle, found the coffee, and by the time Francesca had returned was pouring hot water into the cafetière. He looked up and saw that she'd exchanged her suit for a pair of softly tailored grey trousers.

Okay, she was in mourning. And she was three years older than that vibrant girl who'd grabbed his heart, but it was as if her entire personality had been toned down. Her hair, her clothes, her figure. She was just too damned restrained. Not a hair out of place, her make-up perfect. She looked nearer thirty-five than twenty-five.

Not that it was any of his business.

She busied herself with the laptop, all the time avoiding looking at him. 'The battery's flat.'

He searched the case, extracted the cable and plugged it into the nearest wall socket and switched it on.

'What's the password?' he asked, as the prompt appeared.

'Oh, good grief. I've no idea.'

He wondered if that was usual. Maybe. He'd had a couple of long-term relationships, but not the live-in kind. Not the kind where you'd exchange computer passwords. But living together for three years...

None of his business, he reminded himself again as he tried the 'forgotten your password' prompt, hoping that Steve hadn't actually taken any notice of advice to use something trickier than his son's first name. If it was numbers and symbols they'd have to hope that someone in his office knew it.

The hint offered was 'First Love'. He glanced at Francesca before he could stop himself.

She coloured slightly, but said, 'I doubt that I can claim that honour, and besides, I think my name would be a bit obvious, don't you? The first word that anyone would try.'

'Possibly. Could it be ironic? Some kind of food? There was a time when he would only eat Marmite on toast.'

'How old was he? Six?'

'Nineteen.'

Their eyes met and it was as if they'd both had the same thought. Steve, as an unshaven, scruffy student with no money.

She blinked. 'What about "Toby"?'

He shook his head. First love… And suddenly it came to him. He typed in a name…was offered the hint again. He tried it again without the capital and he was in.

'What was it?' she asked.

'It's "harry". All lower case.'

'Harry? Who's Harry?'

'He was a puppy Dad bought him for his fifth birthday. A liver and white springer spaniel. Completely brainless, but it was love at first sight.'

'He didn't… He never mentioned him.' Then her eyes dropped to the screen, as if suddenly aware that there were bigger omissions than that, and he wanted to reassure her about this one, at least.

'Steve never talked about Harry to anyone after he was killed. He just seemed to blot it out.'

'Oh,' she said, the sound small, little more than an expelled breath. 'How did it happen?'

It occurred to him that he knew things about Steve that she would like to hear. His childhood. Not just the scrapes he had got into, but the fun he'd been, too. He'd had charm, by the bucketful, even then. Talking, remembering with someone else, had to be better than bottling everything up.

'It was the summer holidays and we were at the cottage in Cornwall,' he said. Then, realising that she might think he still had it, 'Dad had to sell it, along with this house, when he had some problems a few years ago.' She nodded, obviously well briefed on how their father had almost been wiped out financially by the collapse of a bank back in the nineties. The strain had finally killed him... 'We were going down to the beach and Steve had Harry on one of those long leads that allow a dog to run without letting him go.' She nodded. 'You're supposed to lock them when you're walking on the road to keep the dog at your heels and, believe me, Harry wasn't the most disciplined dog in the world.'

'A bit like his owner, then.'

'A lot like his owner.'

And they both smiled at their memories of him.

'They were inseparable.' He paused for a moment as the sunny image of boy and dog filled his mind. Then, 'Harry made a lunge at a cat and it took off across the road in panic. He followed and went straight under the wheels of a car. The poor man driving it was devastated, but it wasn't his fault. He didn't have a chance.'

'Oh, poor Steven,' she murmured, and the hand that went to her mouth was shaking. 'Poor, poor love.' Until that moment, apart from the outburst in Tom's office, she'd had her emotions totally under control. She'd looked drawn and pale, but there had been no hint of tears. Now, as he looked sideways at her, he saw them well up, spill over and, without him knowing exactly how it happened—whether she turned to him, or he reached for her—she was in his arms, sobbing her heart out.

It was one of those bittersweet moments. To hold her against him with only the silk of her shirt between her back and his hands, to take the intoxicating hit of her scent, not in his imagination, but in reality...

Sweet, so sweet.

But to know that she was in his arms only for comfort because the man she loved was dead, that the tears soaking through his shirt and on to his skin had been provoked not so much by what had happened to Steve's puppy as knowing how much he must have suffered because it had been his own mistake.

He just held her, let her weep. He didn't say anything. What could he say? The empty comfort words... *There, there, it'll be all right...* The words people had said to him when his mother died and he hadn't understood where she'd gone, only that she wasn't coming back.

Nothing would ever be all right for her again. Or for Toby.

And he would have to live with the fact that it was his selfishness that had kept him and Steve apart for the last three years.

He'd told Francesca the truth. He had believed that Steve would do better without him around as a constant challenge, but that hadn't been all of it. His reasons had been darker. Less altruistic. He just couldn't bear to see them together. Had known that, but for the fact she'd been pregnant, he'd have done everything he could to steal her away...

'Sorry,' she mumbled into his shoulder. 'That caught me by surprise.'

'It's okay,' he said. 'Crying is okay.'

'It's embarrassing when you do it in public,' she said as she finally pulled back, not quite looking at him. 'I'm really sorry.' Whether she was referring to the tears or their unexpected closeness he couldn't say.

'I'm not "public",' he said, as she rubbed the palm of her hand across her cheek, sniffed, then looked around, as if hoping a box of tissues might magically appear. 'Steve was my brother.'

He wanted to tell her how he'd wept too, when he'd realised what he'd done. That there would never be a chance to put his arms around Steve and just hug him. He wanted to cling to her, never let her go, but he didn't resist as she pulled away, instantly releasing her and taking a clean handkerchief from his pocket. She took it, pulled a face that might have been a grin, or maybe just a grimace.

'You and Steven must be the only men in the world who still use linen handkerchiefs,' she said ruefully as she carefully wiped her eyes, blew her nose. Giving herself time to recover.

Unfortunately there was no such relief for him. He was beyond help.

'It was instilled in the nursery. Nanny was the old-fashioned variety. Starched aprons, two slices of bread and butter and all the crusts, if you wanted cake for tea. And bed by six,' he said, trying to make light of the misery of it. 'And reinforced at school. Boys always had to carry a clean handkerchief, a coin for the telephone and a safety pin.'

'Now all the kids carry mobile phones instead. What was the safety pin for?'

'I have absolutely no idea. Perhaps it was simply training for later life, although I somehow doubt any woman would welcome the offer of a two inch safety pin to rescue a snapped bra strap.'

She laughed. 'Oh, I don't know. In an emergency…' It was as if the sun had come out and cracked the ice. 'This would be boarding school, I take it?'

'It would. From eight years old until eighteen, and then it was off to university. My father came from the class of parents who knew how to keep children out of their hair.'

'It sounds ghastly. Steven put Toby down for Eton at birth, but I told him it was a waste of time. There was no way I'd let him go.'

'Well, I guess the difference is that Toby has a mother.'

'Yes, I suppose. How old were you when your mother died?'

'Four. She was thrown from a horse. Killed instantly. Steve's mother looked very much like her and I suspect she may have played up the resemblance. Dad said afterwards, when I was old enough for him to talk about it, that he thought because she looked like my mother she would be like her. He was utterly bereft, not thinking straight…'

'You had a lot in common. You and Steven.'

'You'd have thought so. Maybe if I'd been there for him, but I was already away at prep school when his mother finally left.'

'Finally?'

'She was never exactly a fixture. She'd hooked herself a millionaire with a house in London and a country estate. She didn't realise that he spent as little time in London as possible. She certainly hadn't counted on being a country housewife and mother.'

'No one seems to have been fixed in his life. A visiting god, that's what he called you. You descended on them during the holidays from Eton. Perfect. Unmatchable.'

'Maybe I should have made more of an effort to get into some serious trouble. Be suspended once or twice. He certainly found it easy enough when he followed me there.'

'Were you such a paragon?'

'No, just luckier.' Luckier all his life, until Steve met Francesca instead of him… 'I didn't get caught,' he said. Then, 'Why didn't you marry him, Francesca?'

She didn't immediately answer him. Instead, she carefully poured coffee into two mugs. 'Cream, sugar?' she offered.

'No. Thank you.'

She fetched some cream from the fridge and added a little to her mug. He sensed that she was simply spinning time out while she sorted out an answer in her head.

He didn't push. He knew she was going to tell him and he was content to wait until she was ready to talk.

She didn't sit down but picked up her mug and crossed to the kitchen door. It opened on to a small veranda created from the roof of the new extension to the lower floor. He'd need to get a surveyor over the place, make sure that it was sound. Check out the situation with planning permission. Somehow placate the owner of the house.

He picked up his own mug and followed her outside into the autumn sunshine. The veranda, a sun trap with a small table and a couple of chairs and pots overflowing with old-fashioned flowers and herbs, was a great addition, he had to admit. It was stoutly enclosed for safety and there was a gate protecting the steps that led down to the garden. The swing was new, too. And the brightly coloured garden toys for Toby to climb over and through.

'His birthday present,' she said, following his gaze. 'From Steven. We were going to have a little party...' She placed her mug on the table but didn't sit down. Instead, she leaned against the rail so that she had her back to him. 'It had to be cancelled.'

He felt he should know what to say. He'd been through this. Lived through this. All he could feel was pain that another child was going to suffer such an unimaginable loss. Vow to himself that this time he would be there. That he wouldn't let Toby down in the same way he'd let down his brother.

That was what Steve was asking him to do. Be there. And he would be.

Fran was silent for so long that he realised she wasn't going to be able to look him in the face, tell him the truth, whatever it was, and his gut twisted with the certainty that it was going to be something terrible. But Steve's features were imprinted on the boy. Unmistakable. It wasn't that. And he was at a loss to know what could be so awful.

Then she turned around to look at him and said, 'I didn't marry Steven because I was already married.'

And then he knew.

CHAPTER FOUR

AS STUNNED silences went, the one that followed her confession was epic. It went on and on, stretching the air until she thought it would snap. That Guy might never speak to her again.

Fran didn't blame him. Saying the words out loud had been as shocking to her as to him. She'd buried the truth so deep inside her that for long periods she could forget those ten minutes when she'd stood in front of a registrar, barely nineteen, burning with ideals, going through a ceremony that had seemed meaningless to her. Marriage was an outdated institution. Just another way of controlling people, so why not use it against the system?

It seemed like a lifetime ago.

It was only when, pregnant with Toby, Steven had asked her to marry him that the reality of her situation had dawned on her.

Maybe that was why she'd told Guy—to expiate herself. She was never going to be able to put it right with Steven now. But his total stillness, total silence, was so frightening that she reached out, instinctively, to hold on to the railing and brace herself for his reaction.

Guy was stunned. Steve...yes. Marriage was the kind of mess he might have got himself into when he was younger; he'd actually asked him if there was any impediment to their marriage. But Francesca...

Questions piled in on him. Who had she been married to? When? What had happened? She must have been so young...

One question, the one he least wanted to ask—the one he least wanted an answer to—pushed its way to the front and refused to be brushed aside.

'Did Steve know?'

She swallowed. He saw the nervous reaction and knew the answer, even before she shook her head.

He dragged both hands through his hair, looked up at the pale blue sky, anywhere but at her, and blew out a long breath that he must have been holding ever since she'd dropped her bombshell.

'Well,' he said, when at last he could speak through a pain that was slicing into his heart. 'He lied to you about the house. I guess you're about even.'

She didn't answer. He didn't expect her to. There really wasn't anything to say. He should walk away now. Take the easy way out and protest the needs of business. All she really needed was money, and Tom could handle that.

But he couldn't leave it. Or let it rest.

'You didn't think,' he said, twisting the knife—in her, or in himself, he'd have been hard pressed to say— 'of getting a divorce? Or are you against those on principle, too?' Then, 'Oh, no. Sorry. We've just established that you don't have any principles—'

'It wasn't a proper marriage,' she said, rallying, to cut through his vile sarcasm. But he couldn't stop himself.

'No? Maybe you'd care to explain the difference between a proper and an improper marriage to me. These are not concepts I'm familiar with.'

She flushed, but didn't crumble. If anything she stood taller... 'I meant,' she said, 'that it was in name only. I married a fellow student when I was in my first year at university. He was going to be sent back to a country where he'd have been in danger.'

'But that's—'

'I know. Illegal. But his father had been murdered, his mother was in prison. He was desperate.' She shrugged. 'At least, that was the story. It took me a while to realise that it was just a racket. Gullible students hot on human rights issues who thought they were being noble were being used by people who knew how to work the system.'

It just got worse... 'Are you saying he wasn't a student?'

'I'd seen him on the campus. He knew enough to convince me that he was reading law and I had no reason to doubt him.'

'Surely you had to live with him? At least make it look as if you did?'

'Only if Immigration decided to investigate. I don't suppose they have the resources to investigate everyone, and I never saw him again once we'd parted outside the register office. Him clutching the marriage certificate to prove his bona fides to the authorities. Me clutching my ideals to my bosom, thinking I'd done something good.'

'You didn't think to go to the police when you realised the truth?'

'It took a while for me to catch on. He'd said he would have to go to London to sort everything out. That it would probably take a few weeks. It was only when he didn't return the following term and I was concerned that he'd been deported after all that I asked someone in the law faculty to try and find out what had happened. Of course no one there had ever heard of him. I'm not stupid—' She paused, gave the smallest of shrugs, 'All right, I *am* stupid, but I knew what I'd done was against the law. That at the very least I could be thrown out of university as an example. A warning. So I just put it out of my mind. Tried to forget it had ever happened. Told myself I'd clear up the mess after I'd graduated.'

Her knuckles, white as she gripped the railing, gave the lie to her apparent insouciance.

'I didn't, of course. I was too busy with my first job, too short of money to pay anyone to find him. Not that I had the first idea where to start. And it just didn't seem that important.'

'And then you met Steve.'

'Even then... Until I realised I was pregnant and Steven was so excited, wanted to get married immediately. I went to see a solicitor then, but since I had no way of finding the man I'd married I was told I'd have to wait the full five years before I could institute divorce proceedings without his consent.'

'Why didn't you just tell Steve?'

'You wouldn't understand.'

Understand? Of course he didn't understand! 'Try me,' he urged.

'It's difficult.'

'I'll bet.'

She looked a touch desperate. 'He worshipped me, Guy. Had me on this pedestal...' She looked at him. 'It's an uncomfortable place to be.'

'Especially when you don't deserve to be there.'

She flared up. 'I told you you wouldn't understand. But then you're comfortable up there looking down on the rest of us, aren't you?'

'I'm not...' He stopped. He'd asked for that.

Deserved it. 'Is there anything I can do to help? To sort it out?'

'It's a little late for that, wouldn't you say? But no. The five years were up this year. The decree was finalised a couple of months ago.'

The relief he felt was foolish beyond words. But real none the less.

She turned away from him to look out over the garden. 'How ironic that Steven should have booked a wedding. I was going to do that. Take him to a tropical island, tell him the truth... Maybe he found the brochure I'd brought home and thought I was hinting.'

'You were that sure he'd say yes?' he demanded brutally. 'When he knew what you'd done? Or maybe you were going to gloss over that bit?' And then, when she flinched, he'd have given anything to call the words back. Of course his brother would have said yes. Maybe even come clean about his own deception...

'Unfortunately there was no way to get around that word "divorced" on the marriage certificate. Besides, I wanted to climb down to earth. Ground our relationship. Think about having a brother or sister for Toby.'

The tears were close again, but she managed to hold them back as, with a gesture that took in the house, the garden, everything, she glanced back at him.

'That's what all this was about, Guy. He was so insecure. He thought he had to give me all this to keep me with him. It was a long time before I understood that. He deserved to know, to be sure that I would never have left him...'

'And now?' The knife was definitely in his own gut.

'Now?' Francesca released the handrail as if, having unburdened herself, she no longer needed its support. 'Now I think we'd better get back to business. I'd still like to go into the office today. I've got a business to run.'

She didn't wait for him to speak, but walked resolutely towards the door, leaving him to decide whether he would join her or not. He stepped back, let her pass, and then after a moment he retrieved their untouched mugs of coffee and followed her inside. She'd brought down Steven's large briefcase, too, and she started emptying it of files, notebooks, catalogues. Keeping her head down in an attempt to hide the fact that tears were running down her cheeks.

'Why don't you check the laptop?' she suggested.

'If that suits you,' he said briskly, as if he hadn't noticed.

She dug his handkerchief out of her pocket and blew her nose. 'I don't actually have much choice in the matter, do I? And the sooner it's done, the sooner you'll be gone.'

He was saved from answering by Toby, who raced through the hall and then came to an abrupt halt just out of his reach, suddenly overcome with shyness.

'I'm sorry,' Connie said, following him at a more sedate pace. 'He lost all interest in the ducks the minute he heard that his uncle Guy was here.' Then, seeing Francesca's expression, her face fell. 'I should not say?'

'No problem,' he said quickly. Then, 'Hi, Toby.' His voice was unexpectedly thick with emotion as he smiled at the child, wanting to sweep him up, hug him, but his long absence denied him that pleasure, that joy. He would have to earn his place in his brother's family and he hadn't made a good start. 'I didn't know I'd be seeing you today or I'd have brought your ball with me.'

''s'okay.' The boy took a step nearer, his eyes wide as he looked at the laptop. 'Can I play on that?'

'Oh, right! Budding genius,' he said, grabbing his chance before his mother intervened and sent him off for a nap—anything to keep the bullying monster away from her precious boy. Held out his hand in a mute invitation to join him. Toby didn't need any further encouragement, but scrambled up on to his lap. 'Right, Mr Einstein, this is what we're going to do. Since this fine machine has a CD rewriter, we're going to copy some files so that I can take them home to look at and leave your mother in peace. Want to help?'

'Can I?' Toby looked up at him with a wide-eyed wonder that tugged at his heart. 'Really?'

'Absolutely.' He took an unused CD out of the laptop case. On the point of giving it to Toby to hold, he spotted the state of his fingers and thought better of it. Instead he said, 'Can you press that button for me?' When the drawer clicked out he laid the CD in place. 'Now push it back until it clicks—gently.'

It took Toby a couple of goes to make it click shut and he looked up for reassurance.

'Good job. Okay, now I'm going to take your finger...' He took his tiny hand in his own and laid the end of his finger over Toby's. 'And we're going to press that key. Just once. Lightly.' He tapped the key with Toby's finger and a list of files came up.

'Oh!'

'You liked that? Want to do it again?'

After doing it half a dozen times they moved on, and between them they marked the files and copied them to the CD. It took longer than if he'd done it on his own, but that didn't matter. He'd wasted too much time, staying away, doing the right thing. This was the right thing…

When they'd done he looked up and discovered that both Connie and Francesca were watching them, apparently transfixed.

'What?' he said.

'Nothing.' Francesca swallowed. 'It's just that…people don't usually let little boys play with thousands of pounds worth of computer hardware.'

'No? Believe me, this was easy. Toby speaks English. It's a lot harder when you're in some place that the world forgot—or more likely never knew existed—and the kids only speak some dialect that has never been written down.' Then, 'And I resent "playing". We weren't playing, we were working.'

'Yes. Well. I'll, um, get on. Connie, maybe Mr Einstein over there could do with a nap.'

He lifted Toby down and said, 'Off you go, partner. Next time I come I'll bring your ball.'

'Will you play f'ball with me?'

Football. He swallowed. His brother might have protected his laptop from sticky fingers, but he knew that Steve would have played football all day with his little boy: he'd never quite grown up himself, after all. And who would be there for the child now if Guy disappeared back overseas, left lawyers and money to do what his brother had expected him to do personally? Care.

'I'd like that,' he said. And, when the little boy put his arms up for a hug, it was his turn to choke back the tears.

After Guy had gone, with Toby asleep and Connie tackling a pile of ironing, Fran determinedly ignored the faint smell of scorching and took everything up to Steven's office. She longed to just put her head down on his desk and weep, but what use was that?

Instead, she set about looking through the papers. What she should have been doing instead of watching Guy with Toby.

Guy drove to his office, dealt with the condolences, then worked his way through his messages. One of them was from the pair he'd met at the funeral. There was no point in putting it off and he called back, only to discover that they didn't want money. They wanted to buy an option that Steve had negotiated to import silk goods from China. Things were looking up. He took the details and promised someone would get back to them.

Then he shut himself away in his office, leaving instructions that he was not to be disturbed. He booted up his computer and inserted the CD holding the files he'd copied from Steve's laptop. And he laid the envelope containing Steve's letter on his blotter.

If Francesca's confession had been in the nature of a hand grenade, the letter had all the allure of an unexploded bomb, and he put it, unopened, to one side. First he had to know how bad things were—and, since Steve had cashed in his life policy, it had to be bad.

He spent the afternoon picking over the financial

bones of Steve's company. It did not make for happy reading.

The business had initially been successful. Supplemented by the money that should have been used as a deposit for the house it had made enough to support the lavish lifestyle Steve had created for himself and Francesca. But in these recessionary days it was making little more than enough to pay his staff and sometimes that had been a close shave. As Guy had suspected, Steven had cashed in his life policy in a desperate bid to reduce his overdraft and hold off the bank. But he hadn't cut back on his own expenses.

And in the last six months, since he'd been sick, it had simply been ticking over with repeat orders. Basically, it was a one-man band. If he wasn't out there finding new stock, drumming up new business...

It could probably be saved, turned around. It would need some painful pruning to reduce costs and someone at the helm who knew what they were doing. Time maybe for Francesca to exercise her marketing muscles. Work for her designer dresses.

As for personal expenses, the lease, property taxes and utilities were the biggest drain and nothing could be done about them. Then there was Connie to pay, the fees for Toby's private nursery school. And keeping Francesca on her pedestal didn't come cheap.

Just as well she was keen to step down.

Finally, when he could put it off no longer, he opened Steve's letter.

It was handwritten and, as he read it, he could hear his brother's voice as clearly as if he was sitting alongside him, saying the words.

Guy, if you're reading this I guess I've cashed in my chips before I've been able to make everything right and, as always, you're the one picking up the pieces. Just as well you've had so much practice.

You already know what I'm asking you to do. You'll know why, too. I want Toby to have two parents. To be loved by someone who knows what I went through and will never allow that to happen to him. Fran may not see it that way but I've left her with nothing. Less than nothing.

We had a good first year, but you know me, I wasn't built for the long haul. I just wish I could have lived up to her. Frankly, it was something of a relief when I opened a letter from a lawyer and discovered that she'd been married before. Just to know that she wasn't perfect, you know? I did tell you it was her decision, but I don't blame you for not believing me... Not that I ever let her know that I'd found out. Read her letters. Besides, my secrets were far worse. The house, the money I owe.

Take care of her, Guy. And my boy. Duty, honour—you're so much better at that stuff than I ever was and so is she. I know she'll do what's right.

I've not been the best of partners, I'll be the first to admit it. But she was always loyal and true. I didn't deserve her and, believe me, I know that the night that condom broke was the luckiest in my entire life.

Okay, this is getting tough, and I want to finish it before she comes back. I've told that wet lawyer to lay the 'wishes of a dying man' bit on thick, but I don't suppose he will. You're going to have to do that for me. Tell her it's for Toby. That should do

*it. And, if she's still not willing, add in Matty and
Connie. Without her they're going to be in real
trouble.*

*About the money, Guy. Well, it's too late for
sorry and I'd do it again like a shot given the
chance. To be honest, I still can't believe I kidded
you so easily. You're usually sharper than that, less
trusting. I don't think I'd even have tried if I hadn't
seen the way you looked at Fran that night. You're
usually so good at hiding your feelings, but when
I walked in behind her you were lit up... I can tell
you now that it frightened the life out of me because
I knew I never deserved someone like her. Let's
face it I'm so shallow that I make a puddle look
deep, while you... Well, let's just say that I know
your worth, even if I never admitted it. I couldn't
risk you coming back, though. Finding out. That's
why I provoked that final row. You throw a mean
punch, brother, but it was worth the pain just to
keep you away.*

I can't tell you how much I missed you.
Steve

'Idiot,' Guy said, but softly. 'I missed you, too,
brother.'

He dropped the letter on his desk and stood up. He
needed to think. Needed air.

Leaving his car at the office, he headed in the direction of Green Park, but it was too small to do more
than take the edge off his driving need to do what his
brother had asked. To move mountains, divert rivers,
change the world for Francesca Lang.

That she was in trouble was clear. Whether she
knew how much trouble might not yet have dawned

on her, but she had no house, no money, no job and a company that, if it was a horse, someone would have taken out and shot.

That she would resent his interference in her life after an absence that she believed was due to his own personal pettiness was crystal clear. She loathed him and, right now, he didn't blame her. He certainly hadn't done anything to improve the situation since he'd arrived.

He could show her the letter. The temptation to be absolved…made whole in her eyes…was almost overwhelming. But that would diminish Steve. And expose his own feelings for her.

She didn't need that. What she needed was to be able to believe that he was going to marry her purely out of duty and guilt. And was going to keep his distance.

Fran poured a couple of glasses of wine from a bottle she'd found open in the fridge and handed one to Matty. 'Today is a day I never want to repeat,' she said, raising her glass. 'Here's to the back of it.'

'That tough?'

'Honestly?' she asked.

'That would probably be best,' Matty replied.

'Well, the good news is that I won't have to sell the house to pay inheritance tax on it.'

'Well, that *is* good. What's the bad news?'

'I won't have to sell it because Steven didn't own it.'

The silence was complex. Full of unspoken thoughts. Fran wished she'd kept that news to herself. At least for the time being. But she needed to talk to somebody…

'I thought you said he bought it from Guy,' Matty finally managed.

'That's what Steven told me. Apparently he was being economical with the truth. The house did once belong to the family, but was sold off by his father some years ago. It was just chance it happened to be available to let when we were looking for somewhere to live.'

Matty choked as she swallowed a mouthful of her drink and let slip an expletive. 'What did Guy have to say about that?'

'It's none of his business, Matty.'

'Look, I don't want to sound over-anxious, but you're going to need someone on your side—'

'Not him,' she snapped back.

'Is there anyone else?'

'You don't understand—'

'I understand the situation perfectly. Guy Dymoke is the devil himself. The one whose name must never be spoken. Anyone would think the pair of you had had a passionate affair or something—'

'No!' Then, because she knew she'd overreacted, 'We only met once before. When Steven and I had dinner with him when we told him that we were moving in together. And about the baby.'

'Oh, please! I wouldn't have blamed you. I thought he was absolutely dishy. I gave the eyelashes a thorough workout but, charming though he was, I could see I was wasting my time. The man was too distracted to notice.'

'Distracted? Who by?' She felt her face grow warm. 'Not that it matters,' she said quickly. 'If he chose to flirt at the funeral reception—'

'Did I say he was flirting?' She didn't answer. 'He was distracted, that's all.'

'Guilt-ridden, more like. Guy and Steven had a difficult relationship and I made it worse. He thought we should have got married and gave Steven a hard time about it. Thought he was the one who wouldn't commit.'

'Oh, I see.'

'At least I could put that right.'

'You told him? About your marriage?'

'I had to.'

'Oh, I see. You wanted *him* to feel guilty.'

'I feel guilty enough for both of us, Matty. But I have no doubt he's wishing he'd taken the time to mend fences.'

'How do you know he didn't? Steven might have had his own reasons for not wanting a family reunion. He probably owed him money.' Fran was too slow with her reassurance. 'He did, didn't he?'

She caught the edge of panic in Matty's voice as it began to dawn on her that her home was now seriously at risk. 'No. No, of course not,' she said reassuringly. 'And I'll have the company up and running at full speed again before you know. I'm looking forward to the challenge. We'll be fine.'

'Good. I like having a roof over my head.'

'I'm really sorry about the money you spent. I know—'

'Don't...' Matty reached out, took her hand. 'Don't blame yourself. I would have done it anyway. Where else would I go, for heaven's sake?'

Don't blame yourself?

That was easier said than done. She'd been sleep-walking through life. If she'd cared enough she'd have known...

'What about the lease? How long is it for? Did the lawyer say anything about that?'

Tom Palmer hadn't said anything much. If she hadn't prompted him she'd still have been in blissful ignorance about the house, and it occurred to her that even now he'd probably kept back more than he'd revealed. She'd seen the silent exchange between Tom Palmer and Guy. The 'we'll talk about this later' look, decide what to do when there isn't a hysterical female to disrupt proceedings. No wonder he'd bustled her out...

But she managed a reassuring smile for Matty. 'There's nothing to worry about. Guy said he'd deal with all the loose ends.'

All she had to do was marry him.

'He can't be that bad, then.'

'What? Oh, I don't know. One minute I'm convinced he loathes me, the next he's being so sweet with Toby...'

'Don't drive him away, Fran. Toby will need a good man to be there for him.'

'The way he was there for Steven?'

'You've only heard Steven's side of that.' She didn't add... *The man who lied to you about this house.* But then she didn't have to. 'He was Steven's brother, Fran. Toby's uncle.' She held out her glass for a refill. 'Besides, he's very ornamental. The kind of man you'd want to share a sofa with on a cold winter's night when there was nothing on the television.'

'It's a little soon to be thinking that way.'

'For you, maybe. Not for me.' Then she laughed. 'It's okay. I promise I'll be good.'

'Don't bother for me,' she managed, but her laugh was too brittle. 'If he whisked you away to a life of luxury and ease that would be enough for me.'

But it would mean seeing them together. Living with it every day...

'Enough for you, maybe. I'd want a man who was around a little more of the time. Besides, there isn't just me,' Matty pointed out. 'There's Toby. And Connie. And that stray cat Steven didn't know you kept fed on the finest cat food.'

'She visits half a dozen houses in this street. I don't think I'm prepared to sacrifice my virtue so that she can eat.'

'No. I'm sorry. That was uncalled for. I guess I'm edgier than I thought.'

'It'll be okay, Matty. I'll talk to Tom Palmer. He'll mediate with the landlord's agent if necessary. There's no reason why they should terminate the lease. I was Steven's partner, after all. I'm sure there's some legal thing about being able to hand a lease on...'

To next of kin. Or a wife. She was neither.

'Okay. But don't leave it too long to sort out the details, will you. As I said, I like to sleep at night. And in the meantime we're going to have to re-negotiate our arrangements. Just paying my expenses isn't good enough any more.'

'This is a nightmare. I can't tell you how sorry I am—'

'Enough. It isn't your fault.' And Matty waved away her apology. 'And I'm beginning to get back on my feet.' She pulled a face. 'Where work is concerned, anyway. So, how did you get on at the office this morning?' she asked, firmly changing the subject.

'I never got there. After visiting the lawyer we came back here.'

'We?'

'Guy and me.' Matty's eyebrows rose a fraction. 'We decided we'd better go through Steven's things first,' she said quickly. 'He copied some files from the laptop…'

'What's so funny?'

'Funny?'

'You were smiling.'

Fran curbed a smile that had somehow sneaked beneath her defences and said, 'Oh, nothing. He let Toby think he was helping, that's all. Then he took them home to study while I went through Steven's briefcase.' This time Matty's eyebrows shot up. 'He's Steven's executor. Not that there's much to execute.'

She groaned inwardly at the apparent callousness of her remark.

'It's me, Fran. You don't have to pretend.'

'No. No more pretence.' Then, 'But I wrote a pile of cheques last week for bills, including Toby's nursery fees. I'm going to need to know if the bank will honour them. They may be a little less relaxed about the overdraft now that Steven is dead.'

'I suggest you leave the bank to fight that one out with the lawyers.'

'No, Matty. I've been living in a dream world. Letting life happen to me instead of taking it by the scruff of the neck and taking control.' She looked up at the ceiling. 'We have a lease, but I suspect it's one on a house of cards, one that's going to collapse around my ears unless I do something to stop it.'

Matty made no attempt to reassure her, which was worrying. Instead she said, 'What did you have in mind?' Then, 'Have you got *anything* in mind?'

'Actually, I've got a three point plan. One,' she said, ticking them off on her fingers, 'I'm going into the bank on Monday to see exactly where I stand. Reduce any outgoings that aren't absolutely essential.' She managed a grin. 'I'm not going to have time to waste at the health club for a start. From now on I'll have to take the cheap keep-fit option and run in the park.'

'Whatever turns you on.'

'Then I'm going to have to find out what Steven was planning when he was taken ill. He had something in mind, but said it would wait until he was feeling better.' She hadn't pushed him. Hadn't wanted him to see that she knew he was never going to get well, although obviously he'd eventually worked it out for himself. 'I've been going through his stuff trying to find out what it was, but all I can find is some paperwork written in Chinese.'

'Why don't you try the local Chinese takeaway? Someone there might be able to help.' Then, 'Sorry. I don't suppose sarcasm helps. What's number three?'

'Hot and sour soup, isn't it?'

Matty pulled a face. 'I meant on the three point plan.'

Marry Guy Dymoke.

She pulled herself together. 'I'm going to buy a Lottery ticket.'

CHAPTER FIVE

EASY enough to announce that she was answering the wake-up call that fate had rung so loudly in her ears. It was quite another to look the world in the eye at eight o'clock in the morning—and most of it appeared to be packed into the underground train with her—and act on it.

Francesca had put in a couple of years at the coal face of marketing before she'd met Steven. It hadn't exactly been a riveting experience. What ideas she'd offered had been brushed aside before, as the most junior member of the team, she'd been despatched for coffee, sandwiches, photocopying. She hadn't needed too much persuading not to return after Toby was born. None of the wives or partners of Steven's business friends had worked, and it had been easy enough to fall into the round of gym workouts, lunches and dinner parties. To pretend to herself that she had a full and rewarding life.

Easy to pretend that she was happy. Bury the memory of a moment when the world had appeared to light up. Steven was Toby's father. They were a family and she would never do anything that would tear them apart. Even if some days she had felt as if she was being crushed by cotton wool...

No more. From now on she was going to keep both feet firmly on the ground. Make a new start. And as she stepped out of the station and into the daylight she tugged her jacket firmly into place. At least she looked the part. But then that was easy. She'd been playing the role of perfect partner, mother and hostess for so long that she could do it with her eyes closed.

But this wasn't playing house. Make believe happy families. This was the real world and she wasn't fooling herself into believing that the right suit and a confident smile was going to be enough. But it was a start.

Thankfully she wouldn't have to confront the staff immediately. She'd have an hour before anyone arrived. An hour to sort through Steven's desk and root out any more little bombshells he'd kept hidden from her. An hour to fit herself behind his desk and make it look as if she belonged there and maybe come up with a plan to fill the big empty space in her brain. If not, she thought as she unlocked the door and let herself into the small, rather scruffy office and storage area tucked away in a courtyard beside the canal, it would be a question of playing it by ear...

Easing the key from the lock she heard a drawer being opened in the little cubby hole that served Steven as his private office.

Had she walked in on a break-in?

A muttered curse released her. She'd know that voice anywhere, and just at that moment a burglar would have been more welcome, but she closed the door quietly and crossed the outer office.

Guy looked as if he'd been there all night. Dishevelled, unshaven, gaunt with fatigue and almost unbearably desirable. She'd coped with the first shock of seeing him at the funeral because, numb with the tragedy that had overtaken her and Toby, she had somehow been immune. Functioning on automatic. Beyond any real feeling. But his arrival had jolted her out of her emotional stasis and each unexpected appearance battered at her defences. Anger helped shore them up, but seeing him like this utterly demolished them. Just like the first time when she'd walked into that restaurant and lost her heart.

When it had already been too late.

She'd told herself that it was nonsense. That her hormones were in turmoil. That Steven was the father of her child. That he was kind and funny and charming and she'd have married him like a shot if it had been possible, just as Guy had urged.

Right at the moment she yearned to go to him, put her arms around him and comfort him, as he'd comforted her yesterday when she'd practically thrown herself into his arms. When he'd backed off as quickly as decency allowed, she reminded herself.

No. She'd keep all thoughts of comfort to herself. He despised her enough already without any suggestion that, in deep financial trouble, she was ready to throw herself at the nearest man with a fat wallet. Particularly not one she'd berated for his lack of feeling.

'What's the matter, Guy?' she said, as he slammed the drawer shut. 'Couldn't you find what you were looking for?'

At least she had the doubtful satisfaction of seeing him completely thrown for once. He hadn't heard her let herself in and he visibly started as he looked up and saw her standing in the doorway. Had the grace to look uncomfortable at being caught with his hands in Steven's desk.

'Steve wasn't the greatest record keeper. I suspect that it was deliberate. That he didn't want to know how far out on a limb he was.' Then, 'What time is it?' he asked, raking his fingers through his hair before dragging his hands over his face.

'Just after eight,' she told him, trying not to worry too much about the 'out on a limb' remark. 'Would you care to explain how you got in?'

Even as she said it, she saw the bunch of keys lying on the desk. She reached out and picked them up before he realised what she was going to do. Beating him to them by a heartbeat. But then he did look as if he hadn't slept all night.

She held them up, letting them dangle from her finger, looking at them as if they were a strange and foreign object. 'Where did you get these? Did Tom Palmer give them to you? I thought the company belonged to me now.'

'It does,' he replied wearily. 'Tom didn't give them to me.'

She waited, but since he didn't enlighten her she said, 'So? Did you help yourself to them from Steven's briefcase? Take a unilateral decision not to disturb the little lady's dusty brain cells? Expect her to be able to think for herself...'

'No. You don't—'

'What? Understand?'

This time he didn't even bother to try to explain.

'What, Guy? Are you telling me it's worse than that? How could it be any worse?' On second thoughts, that wasn't such a stretch either. 'Don't tell me Steven didn't own this place, either?' And, when he didn't answer, 'Oh, great. Were you underwriting his business too?'

'No. I helped him with the lease when he needed somewhere. Just to get him started.'

'So it was all talk? Not just the house, but the business too? Steven was a man of straw and you were his prop and mainstay. Why did you walk away from him?'

'He didn't need me any more, Francesca. Married or not, he had you and he didn't need me around. I told you.'

'Yes, you told me. But what about him? How did he feel about that?'

'Oh, rest assured, he was completely happy about it.'

That stopped her. She didn't ask why. Didn't want to believe that Steven had seen that split second reaction, that moment when she'd first set eyes on Guy Dymoke and seen a different future. An impossible future...

A bit wobbly around the knees, she sank on to the secretary's chair placed at an angle to the desk and for a moment or two all she could hear was the sound of her own heartbeat hammering in her ears. The silence gathering.

After what seemed like for ever, Guy finally said, 'Is that it? Have you finished?'

'What?' She shook her head. 'I'm sorry. I interrupted you. You were telling me about the keys.'

'Brian Hicks called me yesterday, asked me to come down and see him at the office.'

Steven's office manager? 'How did he know your number? Why didn't he phone me?' Then, 'Why didn't you?'

'It was late.'

'I'm allowed out after dark, Guy. I mean, it's not as if I'm a proper widow or anything—'

'I thought you'd want to be with Toby,' he said,

cutting off her sarcasm. 'I was going to talk to you
this morning.'

'It's morning. I'm here. Talk to me.'

'I met him at the reception. After the funeral. He
seemed anxious about something so I gave him my
card and told him to ring me if he needed any urgent
decisions made.'

'How cosy. Clearly it didn't occur to either of you
that I might actually want to be bothered. To know
what was going on.'

'It wasn't like that. He didn't know what to do. He
assumed you'd need some time to—'

'To what? Grieve? I mourned Steven as I watched
him die. All I can feel now is relief that he isn't suffering any more. Now I have to think of Toby and
Matty and Connie and the people who work here. All
the people who are relying on me.'

'Well, you don't have to worry about Mr Hicks.
He gave me his keys and this.' He pushed an envelope towards her. 'It's his resignation. He asked me
to tell you that he's sorry, but he's found another job.'

Shocked, she said, 'So soon?'

'He'd apparently been looking for some time.'

It was just as well she was sitting down. 'Would it
be paranoid of me to suggest that the words ''sinking
ship'' seem appropriate at this point? Not that I'm
suggesting Brian is a rat.' She realised that he was
looking at her with concern and she straightened her
back, forced herself to meet his gaze head on. 'He
has a family to consider. Did he say anything else?'

'Apparently a couple of the staff were temps. He
let them go last month. You appear to be left with
Steven's secretary—that would be the young woman
in tears at the reception—?'

'Claire. Yes, she was very upset. The poor girl had a terrible crush on Steven. She wasn't his type and I told him off once for flirting with her. That it wasn't kind…' Then, realising that she'd implied a lot more than she'd said, she quickly went on, 'He said it saved him paying her what she was actually worth.'

Which, if possible, sounded even worse, and she bit her lip. Concentrated all her attention on the keys that were cutting into her palm she was holding on to them so tightly.

'Brian Hicks,' she said, coming back to the point. 'He must be owed money. Salary, holiday entitlement. Until I've been to the bank…'

'I paid him.'

'Oh. Well, thank you. I'll reimburse you, of course,' she said, mentally crossing her fingers. She had no idea what the company finances were like.

'It's not necessary. We're going to be partners, remember.'

'No.' She didn't want Guy's disturbing presence invading her life. Him being there every time she turned around. She'd had three years of feeling guilty because every time she closed her eyes…

'It's what Steve wanted. The dying wish of a man who loved you,' he said. 'It will make everything simpler, although I do intend to be a silent partner. In all aspects of the arrangement,' he added.

'You mean you don't anticipate leaping into my bed with the same speed with which you've taken over my office?'

'I somehow doubt that's what Steve had in mind. I don't suppose he imagined that you'd feel like leaping into anyone's bed for some time.'

'No. I'm sorry. You're the one who's been lumbered with all of us. You should be getting angry, not me.'

'I think you've got reason enough to be more than a touch irritated. I, at least, have gained a family.' She looked up, surprised by something unexpected in his voice. A warmth... He was looking down at the notepad in front of him. 'It would seem your staff now consists of Claire and a young lad who appears to be on some kind of work scheme.'

'Jason,' she said and, since he was keeping it businesslike, she did the same. 'That will certainly cut the overheads.' Then, 'Tell me, in your search through Steven's office, did you come across any good news?'

'Not much. I went through everything with Brian before he left. The company is still just about ticking over on repeat orders. You need new stock, though. And to take less money out the business for it to prosper and grow. I've laid it all out for you,' he said, indicating the notepad, then sitting back in the big chair, seeming to fill it in a way that Steven never had. 'One of the problems is that the company seems to have had no real focus. Steve imported anything that caught his eye and, to be honest, he didn't always get it right. Too many times he's had to sell on at a loss just to shift the goods. I suspect the bank will be disinclined to continue extending the overdraft in the present circumstances.'

'Then I'll have to convince them otherwise. Quickly.'

'The sooner we tie up the loose ends, the better.'

She didn't ask what 'loose ends' he was referring to. Just said, 'Is there any more bad news?'

'Well, there's the lease on this place.'

Fran belatedly wished she hadn't been quite so sarcastic about the lease. One look at his face made her wish that Guy did own it.

'What about the lease?'

'It expires in two months' time. The rent increase being asked is going to be a problem unless business picks up quickly.'

She couldn't think of any response that would adequately convey the way she felt, so she said, 'Not much good news, you said. That implies there is some.'

'That depends on your point of view. You've got a store room filled with stock. Most of it has been there for years, by the look of it. It'll give you something to practice your marketing skills on.'

'You're not going to stay around and help with that, too?'

'That's your line of expertise, Francesca. I have to get back to my own business. In fact, I'm grateful you tore up the tickets to St Lucia. A trip to the local register office will be far more convenient.'

'Well, thanks. I needed that bit of good news. No house. No company premises. Just a load of old stock that Steven couldn't sell and a cheap ten-minute wedding to keep the bank happy.'

'Low-key was what I had in mind. I don't imagine it will prove to be cheap,' he replied. 'Of course, if you'd like to throw a party to celebrate the occasion I'm sure Connie can manage a few of her more exciting sandwiches.'

She flushed. 'There isn't going to be a wedding. Low-key or otherwise. I will not marry you just to keep a roof over my head!'

'No, you'll marry me to provide Toby with a roof over his head in accordance with his father's dying wishes. Not forgetting your cousin and Mrs Constantinopoulos.'

'You took the trouble to find out her name?'

'I needed it for my company payroll. In the meantime you might get Jason to start on an inventory of stock so that you can sell it before it gets seized by creditors.'

You?

Her.

He really was going to leave her to run it?

'Is there anything else?'

'Yes. Those characters who were hassling you at the funeral. They weren't after money. Apparently, Steve managed to persuade some Chinese co-operative into giving him sole rights to import all their goods for a year. Something to do with silk, I think. They've been buying it from him, but now that...' He checked himself. 'They represent another importing company who are prepared to pay you a substantial sum of money to take over the remainder of the option. I've been looking for it.'

'Oh. Well, there was something in his briefcase that might have been it. It was written in Chinese characters. With a little chop mark. I thought I should get it translated.'

'The sooner the better. Find out exactly what it's worth before you part with it.'

Silk. She liked the sound of that...

Then, realising that she was still clutching the spare set of office keys, she dropped them into her bag. 'You look exhausted, Guy. How long have you been here?'

'Too long, but my body clock is shot to hell.'

'You're fortunate that it's just your body clock

that's gone wrong,' she said sharply, her apparent lack of sympathy a desperate bid to ignore something in his voice that tugged at the very core of her being. Being angry was the only way to keep her feelings at bay.

His expression didn't change but she could feel his reaction: it was almost physical, as if he'd been slapped.

'In comparison with what happened to Steve, your own problems, it was tactless to even mention it.'

'No!' Immediately full of remorse she said, 'I'm sorry, Guy. I'm not the only one who's lost someone. I'm just...' She didn't know what she was feeling. A bit lost. Very confused. But mostly just empty, when everyone expected her to be racked with grief. It was as if her emotional core had been injected with Novocain and was completely numb. And, since the funeral, there had been so much else to worry about. 'You should get some sleep,' she said.

'What about you? How are you managing?'

'Keeping busy helps.'

'Sufficiently to counteract the threat of bankruptcy, the risk of losing your home?'

She reached out, put her hand over his. 'Go home, Guy.'

'Home?' He withdrew his hand, pinched the bridge of his nose between his fingers as if to stave off the tiredness. 'I don't have a home. I just have a barn of an apartment that I bought as an investment. Every luxury. No...warmth.' Then, 'I don't suppose you'd consider having breakfast with me?'

'At your luxurious but cold apartment?' She forced a smile. 'Are you sure you don't mean will I cook it for you?'

'I mean, will you come and have breakfast with me? As in, can I buy you breakfast? There must be somewhere nearby that can rustle up half a pint of espresso and a bacon sandwich two inches thick. For once in my life I can't face the thought of eating alone.'

She put the temptation to take him up on the invitation firmly behind her. 'The last thing you need is espresso—' the last thing he needed was to go home to an empty apartment '—and I really need to stay here and go through a few things before everyone arrives. But there's no reason for you to be alone. Go to Elton Street. If Connie's on your payroll I don't see why she shouldn't make you a bacon sandwich. As thick as you like. She can speak English, more or less, but she can't read it very well. Did Matty tell you about her?'

'She just suggested that the sandwiches might be a risk, although it's hard to imagine how she could mess up on something that simple.'

'For heaven's sake, it was just once. Anyone can make a mistake—' She stopped. He didn't want to hear about her domestic arrangements.

'Where did you find her?'

Apparently he did.

'In the park, if you must know. I'd seen her feeding the ducks there. Talked to her. She's Greek. Came here years ago to marry some café owner who used her as free labour until he left her with a mountain of bills she couldn't pay and, terrified by debt collectors, she just packed what she could carry and ran away. She just spiralled downwards until she ended up in a hostel for the homeless. I knew I ought to do something about her but I didn't know what. Then one day she just keeled over in front of me and I realised that I had known what to do all along. I'd just been putting it off.'

'You took her home?'

She could understand his astonishment. 'Once bitten?' she replied. 'This was different, Guy.'

'Yes. Of course it was. How did Steve take it?'

'He understood that I couldn't send her back to that horrible place,' she said crisply, not wanting to remember how hard he'd tried to talk her into doing just that. How angry he'd been that she'd even been talking to some bag lady. Even angrier at her letting Toby talk to her. How irritated he'd been to discover that his 'princess' had a stubborn streak. They'd almost had a row. She'd almost felt alive. But then Matty had rather slyly pointed out that it was the kind of thing 'princesses' did... 'All she needed was a home. To feel useful.'

'That's all?' he said wryly.

'Actually, she was—is—a huge help to Matty, and she's wonderful with Toby. Look, I really think you should go home before your body decides it's had enough and you bang your head on the desk as it shuts down.'

'I'm touched by your concern.'

'Bag ladies, stray dogs, jet-lagged males, they're all the same to me. I'm a walking care centre.'

'You have a rescue dog too? I seem to have missed that one.'

'No. At least not for long. Steven came out in a rash. He said he was allergic. It was a spaniel.' Damn! The bloody tears would catch her out... She might not have been in love with him, but she had loved him. She couldn't have lived with him otherwise. And he was Toby's father. 'Anyway, that's not my concern,' she said briskly, refusing to give in to them. 'What's worrying me is that if you fall asleep in that chair I won't be able to get into the desk. Did you come in your car?'

'No, I left it at my office yesterday.'

'Good. You're in no fit state to be behind the wheel.' She dug around in her bag for her front door key—which she laid on the desk in front of him—and a tissue, which she used to blow her nose. And wondered how much of his car Steven had owned. Whether she'd be able to use the money to ease finances a little. It was a company car so it would be hers. The papers must be here…

'Should you be here at all?' he asked, distracting her as he got up, came around the desk. 'This would be tough for anyone.'

His eyes were full of compassion, concern, and something else that she thought might be despair but was more likely exhaustion. She wanted to lay her hand against his cheek. To kiss his brow. To wrap her arms around him and hold him for a moment.

Instead she said, 'Of course I'll cope.' Then she looked at the tissue as if she'd just realised he thought she was crying. 'Oh, this! This is just hay fever.'

'Sure,' he said, not bothering to hide his disbelief.

'Really. It's the autumn kind. Brought on by chrysanthemums. It's quite common, apparently.' But she couldn't quite meet his gaze as she said it. Instead she picked up the key and, taking his hand, she placed it in his palm. 'Take a taxi, let yourself in. Connie will show you where you can crash out, and she'll make you your bacon sandwich while you take a shower. Help yourself to Steven's stuff if you want to shave,' she said, then added, 'Actually, you might be wiser to leave that until after you've slept. We can talk about the business later.'

He closed his fingers around the key, removing his hand from hers as he straightened so that he was towering over her.

'The will is my sole concern. The business is yours.' Then, 'Just don't do anything…' He stopped, obviously thinking better of what he'd been going to say.

'Stupid?'

'You might think I was going to say that but you're going to have to torture me before I'll admit it. You're right. I definitely need to get some sleep. I'll see you later, Francesca.'

As the outer door banged shut behind him, she flinched. What on earth was she doing, feeling sorry for him? He didn't need her compassion. He didn't need anything. He was Guy Dymoke.

Guy made it to Elton Street without falling asleep in the cab. That was because he was too busy storing up those moments when Francesca had reached out, touched his hand. As if she actually cared about him. But he had no illusions. She'd adored Steve and the only reason she'd consider marrying him was because he'd seen it as the only way to provide security for her and her army of dependants.

That's why he'd forced himself to break contact first. Before she became embarrassed by a simple gesture of kindness. Might think he'd mistake it for a gesture of intimacy.

Connie was out but it didn't matter. Breakfast had only been a pretence to stay with her. He was long past food and, realising that a shower would only wake him up, he went straight upstairs to the guest room and ran a bath. He needed to think about the best way to deal with the mess fate—and Steve—had thrown in his lap.

Clever Steve. He had known him so well. Known he'd look after his family come what may. But suggesting a marriage of convenience had meant he would now never be able to show his feelings for Francesca.

He'd marry her because it would be his joy, his honour, his dearest wish. But he could never tell her that.

She'd think he was saying it to make it easy for her. He'd never know if she was accepting him because she had no choice. Out of desperation.

Fran looked at the figures Guy had spent the night putting together for her. He was right. It wasn't good, as he'd no doubt tell her again, in words of one syllable, over dinner.

No. Not dinner. Dinner suggested intimacy.

She'd give him nursery tea in the kitchen with Toby. And she smiled again as she remembered how good he'd been with her little boy. Became solemn again as she remembered Matty's conviction that Toby would need him. Steven hadn't been the best partner in the world, but he had been a good father. The truth was that he'd still been a little boy at heart himself, with that same see-it, want-it irresponsibility.

She dragged her mind back to the job in hand. The company was hers now and, if Guy would give her a little breathing space, she would make a success of it. She took off her jacket, found a brown warehouseman's coat to protect herself against the inevitable dust and switched on the lights in the small warehouse.

She'd heard Steven say often enough that the whole premise of importing fancy goods was to shift them as quickly as possible. Sell before you had to pay. Before the public lost its taste for the latest fad. The unforgiving strip lights immediately revealed why the company was in trouble.

She heard the door bang as someone arrived. 'Claire? Jason?'

Jason appeared in the doorway. 'Hello, Mrs...Miss...'

'Miss Lang, Jason. But please just call me Fran.'

'Oh, right. We weren't expecting you.'

'Unfortunately Brian Hicks has left and so have the temps. It's just you, me—' the door banged again '—and Claire,' she said with considerable relief. 'So, we're going to have to do the best we can between us.' She indicated the cartons that stretched into the darker recesses of the storage room. Calling it a warehouse was an exaggeration even in estate agent terms. 'Have you any idea what all this stuff is?'

He shook his head. 'It was all here when I started.'

She took a deep breath. 'Okay. What I want you to do is make an inventory of all the stock and put a sample of each item on my desk.'

'Everything?'

'Yes, Jason. Everything. Along with a note of how much of each item we have.'

'You want me to count them all?' he asked, without bothering to disguise his lack of enthusiasm.

'Not individually,' she said, curbing her impatience. 'The contents will be on the outside of the boxes.' It would have to be done anyway, so that it could be valued for probate. The sooner the better.

'Shall I put the kettle on first?' he asked. 'Steve usually—'

'No. I want you to get started on the boxes. I'll bring you some coffee.' Later. 'In the meantime will you look out for anything made from silk? From China?'

'Two sugars,' he said.

She was cheerfully brisk with the still red-eyed Claire, asking her if she knew where to find the documents for the car. And when she'd found them she set her searching for the paperwork to match the stock, so that she'd have some idea of how much everything had cost. She could have left it to the valuation consultant but since she didn't know what else to do it gave her the impression she was doing something useful.

Steven's nearly new car, she discovered, was, like everything else, leased rather than owned. She called the company and arranged with them to pick it up. It would be cheaper to take taxis everywhere. And a heck of a lot cheaper to go by bus.

'What shall I say?' Claire asked. 'When people ring and want to know what's happening?'

She didn't know. There was an awful lot she didn't know, she realised. 'Leave a message on the answering machine saying that the office is closed until Monday due to a bereavement.' That would give her breathing space. Time to think. Then, 'Have there been many calls?'

'Dozens. They're all in the day book.'

'I'll take it home with me.'

Then, after glancing at the odd assortment of ob-

jects that Jason was laying out on her desk—paper
fans, pottery frogs that no one but a mother could
love, some particularly hideous lamps—she packed
up all the stuff that Guy had left for her and, leaving
them to get on with the inventory, took the public
transport alternative home. It was cheap but endless,
and she was anxious to get back to the house and take
another look at that Chinese document. Get it translated.

Although, if the rest of the stock was anything to
go by, it wasn't going to be anything to get excited
about.

She dumped her bag in the hall and ran upstairs,
stripping off her jacket, unzipping her skirt as she
went, eager to get on. She'd have to rethink her working wardrobe, she realised. Dark suits and silk shirts
were out for the time being. She didn't have to impress Jason and Claire, and she'd be much more useful wearing the kind of clothes in which she could
help shift and unpack boxes.

She stepped out of her skirt and tossed it on the
bed with her jacket and slipped the buttons on her
shirt. Then, pulling a face at the state of the cuffs
after just a few hours, she crossed to the bathroom to
dump it into the laundry bin.

At which point Chinese characters became the very
last thing on her mind.

CHAPTER SIX

FRANCESCA'S heart stopped. Guy had fallen asleep in the bath. His arm was hanging over the edge, his fingers brushing against the floor. The tension had flowed out of his face and his long, elegant limbs were totally relaxed and, for the first time since he'd come home, she caught a glimpse of the man who had looked at her across a crowded restaurant bar and made her feel as if she was the only woman in the world.

Her gaze drifted down the length of his body, then stopped, transfixed momentarily on what might just have been the movement of water caused by his breathing, or a stirring of something much more dangerous. Her heart kicked back in, racing to catch up as she forced herself to return to his face, certain that he'd be watching her, his eyes mocking...

But no, he was still fast asleep. He looked so much younger, so much more approachable with the harsh lines smoothed from his face. So much more vulnerable...

She really should wake him. If he'd come home and got straight into the bath—although why he was in her bath was a mystery—the water would be cold, but she could scarcely reach out and touch him on his tanned, broad shoulder or stroke back the hair clinging damply to his forehead...

She swallowed.

What she had to do was back out of the bathroom

right now. Very quietly collect her clothes and, once dressed and safely downstairs, she could bang a door or shout to see if Connie was about and leave it to him whether he decided to climb into bed—and presumably that would be her bed, too—or come downstairs.

Guy's first thought was that he must be dreaming. Nothing new there. He dreamed of her all the time, but never before when he'd been lying naked in the bath, with Francesca, clad only in a bra that would stop traffic and a thong that left him in no doubt that the money she spent on bikini waxing was well spent, standing near enough to touch.

Never had it been this real.

His second thought was that if this was a dream, why would the water be cold? That really wasn't fair...

Even so, it was taking every ounce of willpower to remain perfectly still, keep up the pretence that he was asleep so that she could gather her wits and retreat in good order. That way they could both pretend this had never happened. Preferably before the water began to heat back up...

She took a step back, her gaze fixed on his face, ensuring that he did not open his eyes...

Then, very carefully, she took another one. And caught her elbow an eye-watering blow on the edge of the door. At which point there was no need for further pretence.

'It's usually wiser to look where you're going,' he said.

'Is that right?' she snapped. 'Well, thanks. I'll be

sure to remember that for the next occasion I find a man in my bath.'

'I was simply trying to be helpful.'

He wanted to be more than helpful. He wanted to go to her and put his arms around her and kiss the pain away. Hold her so that she would forget everything. Know only him.

He doubted that she'd appreciate the thought, let alone the gesture. Besides, she was clutching her left elbow with her right hand and was bent almost double, a position which was doing indescribable things to her cleavage which, cold water notwithstanding, left him in a position where concealment was the only option.

'You were just pretending to be asleep, weren't you?' she demanded, glaring at him.

He thought of denying it. Decided against it.

'I thought it might save us both considerable embarrassment,' he said somewhat thickly as he attempted to summon up a memory of the months he'd once spent in the Antarctic. *Cold. Freezing cold. Frostbite cold...* 'I have to admit, I didn't expect you to take quite so long over your retreat.'

'I was just...' she forgot about her elbow long enough to make a vague gesture as she sought some kind of explanation '...taken by surprise. That's all.'

'So was I, but in my case it was excusable.'

'Excuse me? I offered you the guest room.'

'And?'

'Which is at the end of the hall,' she cut in. 'With its own small, but perfectly adequate bathroom.' Then, 'Why didn't you lock the door?'

'It never occurred to me. In the field there isn't a door. At home there isn't anyone to keep out.'

Struggling to maintain his composure in the face of extreme provocation he said, 'Look, would you pass me a towel?'

'Get it yourself!'

'Fair enough.' He'd tried. A man could only do so much... But as he sat up, water cascading from him, she latched on to the flaw in that arrangement and said, 'No, wait! I'll do it.' And she pulled a towel down from a stack on the shelf and passed it to him, looking pointedly the other way as he stood up, wrapped it firmly about his waist and stepped out of the tub.

'I still don't understand why you're in here,' she said, not letting the matter drop. The fact that she was wearing next to nothing herself had obviously slipped her mind. 'Connie wouldn't have put you in my room. And why didn't you leave your clothes all over the floor to warn me that you were here, like any normal man?'

'Because I hung them up.' He reached over her head and unhooked his clothes from the back of the door.

'You're housetrained?'

'Don't bank on it,' he said. Right at that moment, the civilised veneer of the modern man was being strained to breaking point and he was using the armful of clothes to disguise the fact. 'But I have lived in some places where clothes left lying on the floor are an open invitation to the kind of creatures you wouldn't want to share with. It gets to be a habit.'

'You'll make some woman a great husband,' she said. Then clearly wished she'd kept her mouth shut.

'I believe it takes rather more than the ability to hang up your own clothes. Being in the same country for at least fifty per cent of the time would seem to be fairly high up on the list.'

'I know a lot of women who'd be delighted with that arrangement.'

'Is that right? Then since I don't usually manage to spend more than ten per cent of my time in London you'll be the envy of your friends, won't you?'

'You don't think I'm actually going to tell anyone?' Then quickly, 'Even if I was prepared to contemplate marrying you.'

'You've married for someone else's convenience. I don't see why you'd find it so difficult to marry for your own.' Then, realising that probably wasn't the best way to convince her, he said, 'Look, I'm sorry for intruding on your space, but Connie wasn't in when I arrived and since this was the guest room the last time I stayed here I assumed it still was. Don't you use the master suite?'

'No—' Then, 'Well, yes. Of course. But—'

But it had been Steve's sickroom. She'd nursed him in there. She probably never wanted to go into that room again.

'I'm sorry. That was incredibly stupid of me. Obviously you wouldn't want to sleep in there.'

'No…' Her mouth made the shape, but no sound emerged. She cleared her throat. 'No.'

'Maybe I could have it redecorated for you? When you're ready. If that would help.'

'What's the point? It's just temporary. I'll be looking for somewhere else just as soon as I've got the business sorted out.'

He wanted to tell her to stop being so stupid. He wanted to take her by the shoulders and shake her and tell her that he'd move heaven and earth to keep

her safe in the home she loved. His body was way
ahead of his mind and he made a move towards the
door, needing to put an end to this torture. She still
didn't move.

'I imagine that's where I'll find a razor, then?' he
prompted, not prepared to get any closer. There was
altogether too much naked flesh in a confined space
to risk that. 'Across the hall?'

She frowned, as if coming back from somewhere
inside her head. 'Oh, yes. And Steven's clothes.
Please do help yourself to whatever you like…'

And that was when she realised that she was somewhat underdressed to offer that kind of invitation.
Underdressed full stop. And blushed all the way down
to her toes.

'A clean shirt. Socks,' she rushed on. 'There's a
new toothbrush in the cupboard under…'

'Thank you. I'll find it.'

'Right, I'll go and, um…' She made a vague gesture at her figure, indicating that she was going to put
some clothes on, changed her mind about drawing
further attention to herself halfway through and, practically falling over her feet, made a rapid retreat, this
time face forward to avoid further disaster.

As he waited, giving her time to clear the room, he
realised he should have asked her how her elbow was
doing. Unfortunately, the quick flash of her smooth,
golden backside as she'd finally turned and fled had
knocked it clean out of his mind.

Francesca didn't hang around to ask whether Guy was
going to continue his nap or would prefer to go downstairs and have something to eat. She just grabbed the
first clothes that came to hand and bolted. And, hav-

ing gathered up the paperwork she'd brought back from the office, she shut herself away in the study.

Her jeans were the comfortable baggy fit cut that she'd worn when Steven wasn't around to grumble that she looked untidy, the top something loose and equally figure obscuring. It felt disloyal somehow— even in the last couple of weeks, when he'd hardly been able to lift his head, he'd still wanted to see her looking like his 'princess'—but it was too late to think about changing. Too late to think about obscuring anything, too.

Guy had seen everything there was to see while she'd stood there talking to him as if they were at a cocktail party, instead of quietly retreating the minute she'd realised that the bathroom was occupied.

In retrospect it was so obvious that she should have simply turned around and walked out. She couldn't imagine what had possessed her to just stand there, gawping like a complete idiot. Or maybe she could, she just didn't want to think about it too hard. Maybe she should stop thinking about it now.

She definitely shouldn't be thinking about that moment when she'd seen the flash of anger burn in his eyes, the involuntary movement of his hand when she'd rejected his offer to redecorate the master bedroom. As if it was something he needed to do to make up for his blunder over mentioning it.

In fact her best plan would be to go out, she decided. Right now. And, grabbing Steven's briefcase— she'd put everything back in so the Chinese stuff had to be in there—she checked the landing to ensure that the way was clear and then went quietly downstairs to find Connie and tell her about their guest.

Toby was having his lunch, and she gave him a big

hug, admired the pictures he'd made at nursery
school, had a tiny bite of the fish finger he offered
her and let herself out through the back door to avoid
the risk of running into Guy in the hall. She needed
a little time to eradicate the image of him lying in the
bath, the embarrassment of her berating him in her
underwear, before she could face him again.

As she walked towards the gate, she saw Matty
working at her drawing board, undoubtedly catching
up with work put on hold while she'd spent time with
her.

Another thing to feel guilty about, she thought as
she walked down the road towards the market.

When she returned, it was Guy she wanted to talk
to.

'He go,' Connie said. 'I want to make him something nice for lunch, like you say, but he see fish
fingers and he eat them with Toby.'

'Good grief. Weren't they cold?'

Connie waggled her hand to suggest they had been
neither hot nor cold. 'He say is okay. He make himself sandwich.'

Guy Dymoke had eaten fish finger sandwiches for
his lunch? She decided she didn't want to go there.
It made him seem much too human. As if she needed
proof...

'When...' She cleared her throat. 'When did he
leave?'

'Not long. He stay and talk with Toby until nap
time, then he go. He have things to do. He say you
not to worry. He take care of everything.'

That was more like it. Managing, bossy...
Somewhere else.

'That's it?'

'He went to see Matty. Maybe he tell her where he go. Maybe he still there?'

Matty? Something very like jealousy caught in her throat as she remembered how easily the two of them had talked. How he'd smiled at her cousin when he never smiled at her. How Matty had thought him very fanciable...

She caught herself. That was vile. How could she be jealous of her cousin? She should be glad...

She *was* glad. She was just disappointed that Guy wasn't there, that was all. He'd said she'd been offered a substantial sum to surrender the sole importation rights. She wanted to know how much. Wanted his advice. Because if it was valuable enough for someone to want to pay good money for it as a matter of urgency...

On the other hand, maybe it was just as well Guy had gone home. She was already beginning to rely on him. He'd made it clear that the company was her concern and she had to start thinking things through for herself. Besides, there were more pressing concerns. If she wasn't going to marry him she needed to talk to the landlord's agents. Negotiate a new lease for the house.

Apparently using nothing but thin air.

The sooner, the better.

'Right. Well, I'm going to the study.'

Connie placed her hands on her hips. 'And when are you going to eat? Tell me that.'

She'd been saying the same thing every day for weeks. Today she had an answer. 'I had a bowl of soup while I was out.'

'Ha! My soup not good enough for you?'

'It was a business lunch, Connie.'

She'd been given a bowl of chicken soup by the owner of the local Chinese restaurant while his teen-age son translated the document she'd found. Steven had been very fond of Chinese food and they'd all been so sweet to her. So kind. She'd even managed a couple of mouthfuls of the soup.

Connie wasn't impressed by her 'business lunch', however. 'What kind of business you do dressed like that, huh? What would Mr Steven say if he saw you go out like that?'

'Steven isn't with us any more, Connie. I have to do things my way from now on.' And it was about time she made a start. 'I'll be upstairs if you need me.'

She phoned Claire to check how things were going.

'The inventory is complete and I've found most of the paperwork.'

'Okay, leave it on the desk and lock up. I'll see you both on Monday.'

'You're going to carry on?'

'That's the plan.' Then, 'Claire, tell me about the silk goods that Steven's been importing. I didn't see anything among the stuff Jason was unpacking.'

'No, the shipments went straight out the moment they arrived. The perfect deal, Steve said.'

'Haven't you got any samples? A catalogue.'

'Not a catalogue.'

'But surely he must have had something to show buyers?'

'Well, there were a few bits and pieces,' she admitted.

'And where are they now? Claire?'

'When Steven didn't... When the company... I thought it was a crime to just let them lie there in a cupboard gathering dust. And it doesn't matter does it? I mean they were a guaranteed sale. You didn't need samples—'

'Are you saying that you took them?' Then, quickly, 'Look, I don't mind. I just need to have a look at whatever you've got.'

'Well, I gave one of the wrappers to my mother, but I've got the other one. I suppose you want it back?'

'No, Claire. You can keep it, but I really need to see it. I want you to go home now and bring it to the house.'

'Now? But that will take for ever and I've got a—'

'Claire!'

'I'll be as quick as I can.'

And when she saw the shimmering beauty of the silk, the workmanship, the style, she knew why Claire had taken it home, why those two men were prepared to pay good money for the right to import it directly.

Focus. That was what Guy had said was lacking in the business. And Steven had found it. Too late for him. But not for her.

It was one thing to calmly state that she would go into the bank first thing on Monday morning and demonstrate that she was a responsible adult who was determined to take control of her finances—or lack of them—and her business. And ask for backing to finance her plan.

Quite another to have the bank forestall her with the letter that arrived on Saturday morning, informing her that there were no funds in the account to pay the standing orders, including the one for the rent on the house, and asking her to call in at 10 o'clock on Monday morning to 'discuss' her situation.

She might have wondered if a genuine 'widow' would have been summoned in quite such a peremptory fashion, but, having seen the sum involved, she was too busy wishing that she was alone so that she could have howled with unrestrained fury at yet another blow. Especially when she needed the bank on her side.

Taken by surprise as she'd worked through the post and toyed with some scrambled egg that Connie had forced on her, she'd just had to catch at her breath, bite her lip and be grateful she was sitting down.

'You okay, Fran?'

Maybe she'd caught her breath rather loudly, because Connie stopped emptying the washing machine and turned to look at her. 'Bad news,' she said, without waiting for an answer. 'I make you a nice cup of tea.'

'No. It's fine, really. Nothing,' she said, scooping up the mail and forcing herself to her feet. 'I just need to...'

What?

What could she do?

She found her throat closing with rage, frustration, the need to weep, when she knew she didn't have the time for such luxuries as self-pity. Until today her 'situation', whilst bleak, had not appeared to be so imminently close to disaster. While she couldn't work up much enthusiasm for marketing frogs or lamps she wouldn't give house room, the silk was something else. All night her mind had been running hot with ideas.

She'd been through the recycling box looking

through newspapers—it was too late for magazines—
for the names of the editors of the women's pages.
The ones with the power to put products in front of
millions of eager consumers. Christmas was coming...

She'd still been living in cloud-cuckoo-land, she
realised. Despite the revelations of the past week
she'd been wilfully blind to the size of the disaster
that had overtaken them. It was definitely time to
come down to earth. No matter how hard the landing
might be.

'I'll be upstairs,' she said.

'Okay. It do you good to lie down.'

'No...'

'Toby and I make cakes. We bring you tea when
you wake up.'

'I'll be in the study, Connie,' she said, knowing
that it was useless to argue. Connie was simply trying
to help, but it was going to take a lot more than tea
to fix the mess they were in.

Right now, a miracle would be good, she thought,
gathering up the mail and shutting herself away in the
tiny study.

Then she looked at the glowing silks lying across
the chair. They held out the possibility of a miracle,
but not one that would arrive soon enough to save
her. Save any of them.

'Oh, Steven! Why didn't you bring one of these
home for me? If I'd known...'

But she knew why. Ship the stuff in and ship it out
again before you have to pay for it. That had been
his strategy. It had worked for frogs.

This was different.

But it would have to be her long-term, comeback

strategy. Her future. And Toby's. Right now she needed hard cash, and quickly, or she was going to have to marry Guy to save her family and friends from disaster and what had once been an impossible dream, locked in the deepest recesses of her heart where she never dared go, would become the darkest of nightmares.

Not before she'd examined every other option, she swore. There had to be another way.

She picked up a legal pad, drew a line down the centre, and at the top of one side she wrote 'Assets', and on the other side, 'Liabilities'.

What assets did she have? Her jewellery, mostly. Maybe some of those designer evening gowns could be sold through a dress agency. They had some good pieces of furniture—

Then she realised with another shock that, but for a couple of pieces she'd bought herself, some pictures, she didn't even own that. The house had been furnished when Steven had 'bought' it.

Now all she needed was to find out that the diamonds he'd lavished on her when Toby was born, on their first anniversary in the house, for any excuse, it had seemed, were cubic zirconium and she'd be in the situation Connie had been in before she'd taken her in.

Broke and homeless. Except it wouldn't just be her.

And who would give a damn? Certainly not any of the people they'd socialised with. The women she'd wasted time with at the gym. And when Guy pushed himself into her thoughts, saying, 'I care…', she shoved him right back out again and began on the list of liabilities. It was a relief when the telephone rang, interrupting her.

'Francesca, it's Guy.'

Almost a relief.

For a moment her mouth opened and closed in an attempt to say something. Finally she managed, 'Yes.'

'I'm glad we're both in agreement about that. I wondered if you had any plans for today.'

'I'm sorting out Steven's study,' she said quickly. She needed time, a lot of time, before she could look him in the eye without a blush. 'There's so much to do.'

'Then you won't mind if I take Toby out.'

'Toby?'

Of course, Toby. He wanted to bond with his nephew. Why would he want to take her anywhere? He was going to have to marry...

'To the zoo, or something,' he said.

'The zoo? Oh, *please*!'

'You object? Is that on idealistic grounds? Or are you unhappy with me taking him anywhere? I'd understand, of course. You scarcely know me.'

She knew him. Had known him from the moment she'd set eyes on him. Had been hiding from the fact ever since...

'A fact that doesn't stop you from expecting me to marry you.'

'That's different. Purely business and—'

'And I've done it before. Thanks for reminding me. I hope you'll be easier to divorce.'

There was the slightest pause before he replied. 'Of course. The minute you're back on your feet. It will be a simple matter of annulment for non-consummation.'

Non-consummation.

Well. Great. Why on earth was she hesitating?

'So, what's your objection to the zoo?' he pressed.

'Nothing, I suppose. It's just that it sounds too much like something an every-other-weekend parent would do.' Then, because she'd been abrupt, and because Matty was right, Toby needed a masculine presence in his life, 'You mustn't feel you have to take him out to see him. You're welcome to come here any time.'

'Thank you. I appreciate that, but indulge me for today. I'm new at being an uncle and it was his birthday a few days ago. I understand a treat is mandatory on these occasions. Something involving burgers, ice cream and chocolate?'

'When I mentioned his birthday I didn't mean...'

'I know you didn't. I was well aware of the date. So, is there anything he'd especially like to do?'

'Well, I suppose you could take him on the London Eye. He'd love that.'

'What about you? Would you love it too?' His voice was unexpectedly gentle. 'You could come along and keep an eye on me.'

It was just as well she'd chosen the Eye so she couldn't be tempted to change her mind.

'Wouldn't that rather defeat the object of this male bonding exercise?' Then, as the doorbell chimed, 'Sorry, I've got to go; there's someone at the door. When can we expect you? I don't want to get him over-excited by telling him too soon.'

'I won't be long,' he promised.

She hung up. Sat for a moment, trying to gather herself, then, as the doorbell sounded again Connie shouted, 'You get that please, Fran?'

'No problem.' She leapt to her feet and ran downstairs, flinging back the door.

Guy was leaning against a late model Saab, talking into his cellphone and, as she watched, he put away his wallet, flicked the phone shut and reached into the car to pick up Toby's football. Then he turned and saw her. And, like her, seemed momentarily lost for words.

Then he locked the car and walked up the steps towards her. 'I was beginning to wonder if you'd seen me and made a break for it out the back way,' he said.

'No… It was…'

Toby, hurtling through from the kitchen, rescued her from the necessity of having to say anything. 'Have you come to play f'ball?' he demanded, as she caught him before he could fling himself, covered in cake mixture, into Guy's arms.

'Maybe later,' he replied, crouching down so that he was on Toby's level before handing the ball to him. 'First we're going out to have some fun. If you'd like to?'

'Is Mummy coming, too?'

'Uncle Guy is going to take you on the London Eye, Toby,' Fran said quickly, before Guy could answer him. 'Just the two of you. But not before I've cleaned you up. Come on, upstairs with you.'

'Sure you won't come with us?' Guy said, when she returned with Toby, face shining, hair neatly brushed. 'You look as if you're the one who could do with a break.'

'I may not be wearing black but that doesn't mean I'm ready to—'

'At the very least some fresh air,' he said, cutting off her excuse as if he knew it was just that. An excuse. 'You need to get rid of that sickroom pallor.'

'I can get that sitting peacefully in the garden while you're practising being an uncle. And when you've got the hang of that, take a few years to work on your compliment skills.' Then, quickly, before he was tempted to prove that he could pay a compliment along with the best of them, 'Okay. There are just three rules.' And she went through her 'no' list, ticking them off on her fingers. 'No fizzy drinks. No chocolate. No fries.'

'Are we allowed to laugh?' he asked.

'Okay. Be clever. Give him whatever you want. I just hope you think it's funny when he throws up all over you.'

'No fizzy drinks, no chocolate, no fries. You've got it. Say goodbye to Mummy, Toby,' he said, opening the door.

'Bye, Mummy,' Toby said, looking back suddenly uncertain as Guy lifted him into the back of the car. She wanted to go and snatch him back. Not let him out of her sight.

'Bye, darling,' she said, fixing a reassuring smile to her face. 'I'll see you soon.'

Guy, concentrating on the seatbelt, said, 'Oh, by the way, in case I forget, there'll be a surveyor coming to look at the house some time next week. He'll ring and make an appointment first.'

The blood drained from her face. 'A surveyor?'

He closed the car door, walked around to the driving seat. 'It's nothing to worry about. I took a look at the extension and it seems sound enough, but I'd rather have a structural survey. He'll be able to sort out the planning requirements, too. Among other things.'

'What things?' Fran who, in an effort not to appear

overprotective, had remained at the top of the steps, now wished she'd gone down with them to check the seatbelts, make a nuisance of herself fussing like any decent mother should. 'Why would you care whether the extension is sound or not?' she demanded.

'I care because I've bought the house.'

And with that he got into the car, closed the door and, by the time she'd managed to gain some control over her bottom lip and close her mouth, restart her brain, he was already halfway down the street.

CHAPTER SEVEN

THIS would have been the perfect moment to hail a passing black taxi and say, 'Follow that car!'

Guy couldn't just drop a bombshell like that and then drive away. She wanted an explanation. She wanted to know what the devil he thought he was doing and she wanted to know now!

By some miracle—and she was certainly due one—a cruising taxi appeared just when she needed one and she hailed it. The drama of the moment was somewhat spoiled, however, by the fact that women didn't walk around with wallets in their hip pockets.

Guy's car was long out of sight by the time she'd fetched her bag and she had to content herself with, 'The London Eye, please. As quickly as you can. It's an emergency.'

Even as she said it, she realised how stupid that must sound. What kind of emergency called for a ride on the London Eye? Not that she had any intention of going on it. But the driver—who'd probably heard everything in his time—just said, 'Yes, ma'am', and set off enthusiastically enough in the direction of the huge wheel that carried people high into the sky over the Thames.

Enthusiasm was no match for the slow-moving traffic, however. The meter was moving a lot faster than the taxi and, caught up in a bottleneck at Hyde Park Corner, it occurred to her that she could have

got there quicker on the Underground. That she was
wasting her time as well as her cash.

Guy and Toby would undoubtedly be five hundred
feet above London before she could get there. In fact,
the longer she lingered in traffic, the more she was
beginning to regret chasing after him. What was she
going to do? Berate him in front of the queue for a
popular tourist attraction?

And what was she going to say to him anyway?
You *can't* buy my house, I won't let you. It wasn't
her house and he could do what he damned well
pleased. He'd bought an apartment as an investment,
why not her house? It had, after all, belonged to his
family once, and if he wanted it back it was nothing
to do with her.

'This is it, miss,' the driver said.

'What? Oh…' Her desire to reach her destination
had waned with every passing click of the taxi meter.
She had to go home before she made a complete fool
of herself. Think this through calmly…

One look at the fare stopped her from telling the
driver to turn around and take her back. In the interests of economy, the return journey would have to be
made via public transport and she opened her purse.

'It's okay, I'll get it.'

And this time when she looked up, it wasn't the
totally scary 'Eye' looming over her, but Guy, taking
charge, paying her fare, opening the door as if he'd
been waiting for her. Expecting her. And 'calmly'
went right out of the window. Perhaps it was just as
well that Toby's, 'Mummy! Uncle Guy said you'd
come!' gave her a moment to catch her breath.

'He did?' She looked up. With his back against the

sun, his face was shadowed, unreadable. 'You did?' she demanded.

'It must be difficult letting Toby out of your sight just now. Especially with someone you don't know very well.'

It had been a stupid question, inviting a smug male response, but he was better than that. Kinder, to let her off so lightly. 'I, um, hoped I hadn't let it show.'

'You didn't.'

He just knew?

For a moment she felt warmed by his understanding. Then reality caught up with her. 'Are you telling me that what you said about the house was just a ruse to get me to follow you?'

She couldn't decide whether to be relieved or infuriated by that but before she could make up her mind he said, 'So what took you so long? Come on, we're ready to go.'

She glanced up at the wheel. 'Already? I thought you'd have to queue.'

'I phoned ahead and booked while you were taking your time about answering the front door.'

Toby caught at her hand and began dragging her towards the boarding area. 'Come *on*, Mummy!'

'Oh, but I don't have a ticket,' she protested, digging in her heels.

'I booked three.' *Oh, right. Now he was a smug male...* 'It'll do you good,' he assured her in the most maddening way. 'In fact, I believe you've already got a little more colour in your cheeks.'

She didn't doubt it. But it had nothing to do with fresh air.

Restrained by her son's presence, she couldn't say

the word she was thinking, but she gave Guy a look
that would have left him in no doubt. He just grinned.

And took her breath away.

He'd smiled at her before. Once, twice, maybe,
when Steven had introduced her. Restrained things
that hadn't reached his eyes. As if from the beginning
he'd disapproved.

This was something else.

'Come on,' he said impatiently, as she remained
glued to the spot. 'You know you want to ask me
about the house. Once we're aboard you'll have me
at your mercy.'

'Ple-e-e-ease, Mummy!'

The combination was lethal. How could she possibly say no?

It would be okay if she didn't look down, she told
herself, as she allowed herself to be ushered into the
capsule along with the rest of the group. So long as
she didn't stand up, kept her eyes on the distant horizon, she'd be fine. The trick was not to look down.
Not even to *think* about looking down...

Toby ran straight to the far end of the bubble so
that he could see everything. 'Oh, wow!' he said.
Then, 'Look, Uncle Guy! Look, Mummy!'

So much for sitting on the bench in the middle, as
far away from the 'view' as possible. At least she
didn't have to speak. Guy pointed out the sights as,
slowly, they began to rise, allowing her to turn her
back on it as if she was more interested in something
far in the distance on the opposite side.

Realising that Toby didn't want facts, that all he
wanted to do was look, Guy turned to her. Perhaps it
was her white face, her even whiter knuckles, that
gave him the clue that she wasn't entirely comfort-

able. Or maybe he just wanted to give her the chance
to talk.

Whatever the reason, he took her arm and said,
'Let's go and sit down.'

'But Toby…'

'He's fine.'

Intellectually she knew that. But intellect had nothing to do with a fear of heights.

'Ask me about the house,' Guy said, as he eased
out her clenched fingers and led her across to the
bench, keeping her hand between his as he sat beside
her. 'It's why you came.'

'Is it? I thought it was because I was a fretful
mother.' He didn't reply. Fair enough. They both
knew it was a delaying tactic. A putting-it-off moment
because she didn't want to know what he'd done.
Whatever it was would be wrong. 'Well, have you?'
she asked irritably. 'Bought it?'

'It's your home. Now it's safe.'

Oh, good grief, he had!

'And, I promise you, you'll hardly know I'm there.'

'There?' She caught a glimpse of the Thames dropping away from them, felt a familiar sickening lurch
in her stomach. This was more important. 'What do
you mean, *there*?'

'That's the ''among other things'' I mentioned. I'm
going to convert the attic into a small self-contained
apartment to use when I'm in London.'

About to demand to know what gave him the right
to think he could do any such thing, she checked herself. He'd bought the house. He had every right. Since
her mouth was open and she had to say something,
she said, 'Won't it be a bit of a squeeze after the
Thames-side loft conversion with every luxury?'

'I won't miss it,' he assured her.

'Miss it?' *Miss it?* 'Are you telling me that you've sold it?' she demanded. She'd assumed he was simply increasing his property portfolio. Using the opportunity to let the loft conversion at some fabulous rent. And the sinking sensation in her stomach had nothing to do with her fear of heights. 'Please don't tell me you've had to sell it to buy the house?'

'I wish I didn't have to force myself on you in this way.' He didn't look exactly distraught, but then he'd as good as admitted he hated the place. Even so... 'Fortunately, I'm not around that much.'

'Wouldn't it just be cheaper to pay the rent until I get myself sorted out? If you're that worried about Toby being homeless?'

'It isn't just Toby, though. Is it?'

'Steven wouldn't expect you to take care of Matty and Connie.'

'He asked me to take care of you and Toby. It seems to me you're all a package and it really is easier to do it this way.'

It certainly would be no simple matter rehousing Matty...

'But you could have just renewed the lease.' She didn't want him to have bought the house, she discovered. That was too...personal.

'That was my first thought,' he said. 'There's no easy way to tell you this, Francesca, but your landlord gave Steve six months notice to quit four months ago. You only had a couple of months before you'd have had to move out.'

Surprisingly, she didn't feel any huge sense of shock. The revelations of the last week had taken her beyond any place where she could feel shocked.

Steven had known he was on borrowed time, that there was nothing he could do to put things right. Her only regret was that she hadn't overridden his insistence that she shouldn't send for Guy sooner. In time.

She couldn't find it in her heart to blame him for lying to her, even when he had been dying. Keeping up the pretence. There was no point. He was gone and all she could think about was the stress he must have been under. Keeping up the front of a successful businessman. The doting husband and father. The lavish gifts. Never letting it show. For months…years…

No wonder he'd been so adamant that she need never get involved with finances. It was the last thing he had wanted.

'Poor Steven,' she said at last. 'How he must have suffered. No wonder he asked you to marry me. He obviously couldn't think of anything else to do.'

Guy blenched. The compassion in her voice sliced deep into the hope buried so deep within him that he had dared not acknowledge it.

Despite everything, she couldn't bring herself to blame his brother for the magnitude of the disaster he'd brought on her. She should be railing against what he'd done to her. Instead she felt empathy.

Any hope that one day she might recover from her loss sufficiently to see him as anything other than Steve's disapproving brother was dealt a mortal blow.

'Do you think that the stress might have been a factor in his death?' she asked. 'He went down so fast. I did ask him if I should get in touch with you, but we all thought he'd have more time. At the time I was just grateful he didn't linger, suffer more, but—'

'Francesca,' he said, desperate to stop her blaming

herself. 'There was nothing you could have done. His charm, his persuasiveness, were his greatest gifts. He fooled me more times than I can remember.' Had fooled him into parting with a 'deposit' for the house. 'Believe me, he was irresistible and he knew it.'

She almost smiled. 'There's no need to be kind.'

'Not kind. Realistic. You've nothing to blame yourself for.'

She looked at him for a moment. Then nodded. 'Thank you.' Then, 'I'm sorry you've been dragged into this mess. You really don't have to buy the house. We'll manage somehow.'

'It's—'

'And don't tell me you've bought it already. It takes weeks, months to buy and sell property.'

'Most of it spent with the papers sitting in some lawyer's pending tray. Tom Palmer has a century of papers on that house. Nothing has changed in the last ten years—'

'Except the extension.'

'Except the extension,' he agreed. 'Fortunately, the owner didn't know about that, or it might have caused you some problems. As it is I'll have to sort it out with the planning people.'

'No. It didn't need planning permission. Steven said…' She stopped. 'Oh, great.'

He reached out, lightly touched her hand. Immediately withdrew it when she jumped as if scalded. 'Forget it,' he said abruptly. The only way this would work was if she thought him completely oblivious. Just doing his duty… 'It's done. Your home is safe and you can stop worrying about what's going to happen to Matty and Connie and the stray cat. You've been through enough.'

'How did you know about the stray cat?'

'Give me some credit for imagination. You've got everything else. And, since you were denied the rescue dog, there had to be a stray cat.'

Guy didn't sound particularly impressed and she didn't blame him. Was that the way it had always been? Steven messing up. Guy bailing him out.

'You can't do this, Guy,' she said. And she wasn't just talking about the house. 'I won't let you.'

'It isn't in your power to stop me, Francesca. Besides, as I said, it's already done.'

'You can't have exchanged contracts.'

'I can and I have. All that was required was the finance and the will.'

She knew she should be grateful, but she wasn't. She was just angry. 'This is stupid. We are not your responsibility.' She looked up at him, trying to read his face. Nothing. He seemed to be able to lock down his emotions. Keep them hidden. 'What did Steven say in that letter he left you?' A lot more than was in the not-really-a-codicil to his will she was certain.

'He was concerned about Toby. That's all.'

It came out so easily that she had the feeling that, anticipating the question, he'd rehearsed his answer.

It wasn't all. She could see from his eyes that it was far from all. And from the set of his jaw that he wasn't going to tell her any more.

'You must see that it's the sensible solution for everyone,' he continued. 'I don't need a vast apartment sitting empty half the time. You need a home for Toby and everyone. And you needn't worry about the future, either. With Steve dead I had to make a new will. I've left everything to you.'

'Guy…' Her voice caught in her throat.

'I find it's the things you don't allow for that catch you out.'

Every time, she thought.

She thought she'd met Prince Charming, was having his baby, had thought that life was going to be happy ever after.

Then she'd walked through the door of a restaurant and discovered that life wasn't that simple.

It had been an illusion, of course. That moment when she'd looked at Guy Dymoke and had a momentary vision of what 'happy ever after' really meant. It had been over so quickly that she had managed to fool herself into believing that she'd imagined it. It hadn't been difficult. Seconds later she couldn't believe he was the same man. He'd been so distant, cold, living up to Steven's description so completely that she'd managed to put the moment behind her. Which was just as well. She was already on a path from which there was no turning back.

Except that Steven had lied. Lied about himself. Lied about his brother. And she had lied, too. The only part of their relationship that wasn't a lie, it seemed, was Toby. She looked at the sturdy little boy standing a few feet away from her, completely absorbed by something below them.

'Don't leave your estate to me. Leave it to Toby,' she said, when she'd recovered sufficiently to speak. 'He's your heir. At least for now.'

'You are his mother. You will take care of him. And as my wife you can inherit everything without the Chancellor taking his cut.'

'Oh, please! You're not seriously going to marry me as a tax avoidance measure?'

'If I fell under Matty's metaphorical bus, you'd

have to sell the house to pay inheritance tax. This way makes more sense.'

'It makes sense if you haven't got a heart, but since we're talking about the unexpected, let's really go for it.' She looked at him, demanding a response.

'What's on your mind?'

'This. We get married. You live upstairs in your little apartment. Me and Lame Ducks Incorporated are spread out all over the rest of your house. That's what you have in mind, right?'

'Right.'

'Okay. Now tell me this. What happens when you meet the girl of your dreams and fall in love?'

Fran had to ask the question, even though the very idea of him falling in love drove daggers through her.

'That's the one thing that isn't going to happen, Francesca.'

His conviction shook her momentarily, but she pressed on. 'Guy, I know you spend most of your life in the wilderness, chipping lumps off rock looking for oil and minerals—'

'Really it's a bit more technical than that,' he objected.

'—but you do return to civilisation occasionally. And please don't try to kid me that you're gay. That wasn't a submarine I saw in the bath…'

Oh, sugar! Blushing furiously, she found herself trying to shovel the words back in with her tongue, covering her hot face with her hands.

He didn't say a word. He didn't even make some snippy comment about getting some 'colour in her cheeks'. He said, 'It isn't going to happen, Francesca.' She frowned, forgetting her embarrassment. 'I've already met the only woman I ever wanted to marry. She was in love with someone else.'

She knew without question that he wasn't trying to make it easy for her. He was telling her the plain, unvarnished truth. And because she knew instinctively that, for him, love once given would be given for ever, she felt something, some small spark of hope, die inside her.

And all she could say was, 'I'm so sorry. I had no idea.'

'I've learned to live with it and Steve knew. That's why he asked me to marry you. It's no big deal, and this way if I do fall off a mountain or get eaten by a crocodile, you're taken care of. I can go away without having to worry about you or Toby.'

How ironic. How perfect. They were both in love with someone who could never return their love. They were the ideal couple.

'So? Can I go ahead and confirm the arrangements?'

'What?' Then, 'Oh, yes. I suppose so,' she said, finally surrendering to the inevitable. 'When did you have in mind?'

'As soon as possible.'

She took in a deep breath.

'There's no point in waiting. It's purely a business arrangement. I promise you won't find me in your bath—with or without submarine—on a regular basis.'

That's what was so terrible. If it had been unbridled passion there would be some excuse...

'Steven is scarcely cold in his grave,' she protested.

'It was his idea,' he reminded her.

'He was dying. Desperate.'

Whoever he was in love with was wise to steer well clear, she thought. This man could break your heart without even trying. To know that he loved someone else was difficult enough...

'This is madness,' she said. 'Impossible.'

'You said that about buying the house. Actually marriage is a lot easier. Nowhere near so much paperwork. Just ten minutes of your time and a couple of witnesses. But why am I telling you? You've married for convenience before and, unlike your last husband, I'm not going to disappear and cause you endless problems.'

'No, you're going to stick around and cause them.'

'Not even that.' Before she could say the words exploding on her tongue he went on, 'The registrar is free the Thursday after next. Eleven-fifteen. There's no need to dress up for the occasion.'

He had never doubted that she would say yes.

'I realise it's very short notice, but I don't have much time. I'm flying back the same evening.'

'Back?'

'I still have a job to do.'

'I understand why you're going. I was just hoping for rather more detail. As your wife I think I'm entitled to at least be given a little more information than which side of some distant continent you'll be living in, don't you?'

He told her exactly where he was going.

'But...isn't there a civil war going on there?'

'You read the newspapers. Good, I don't have to explain the risks, why I need to tie up the loose ends before I go, why I have to go myself.'

'Because everyone else has a family? What are we?' He didn't have to answer. A nuisance. An inconvenience. A burden. 'Please, Guy. Leave it. No one should be going into that situation.'

'You'd be a wealthy widow.'

'Is that what you think I want?' She stood up, quite suddenly unable to bear being so close to him. Unable to bear the way he could make a gesture that was fine and noble sound cheap. 'Go to hell, Guy!'

Unable to even look at him, she turned away, at which point she realised that only the children were watching the view. The rest of the passengers were too busy earwigging their conversation to bother about the panorama of London, the surrounding counties laid out beneath them.

Fortunately Toby, who'd been staring, silent and rapt, at the view as they'd risen slowly up into the sky suddenly shouted, 'Look, Mummy! There's a ship!'

And, desperate for any distraction, she looked.

For a moment she only saw the river curving away towards Tower Bridge and the grey bulk of *HMS Belfast* looking like a toy battleship. Then reality kicked in.

She was standing in mid-air with nothing to hold on to, and marriage, convenient or otherwise, was the last thing on her mind.

'Oh, no...' She clawed at the air, in desperation for a handhold. 'Oh, please...'

Guy was at her side in an instant, blocking out the terror with the solidity of his chest, holding her anchored safely in his arms until the panic subsided. Only then did he ease back, help her to the seat in the centre of the bubble. But he still didn't let go, holding her against his shoulder, blocking out the sickening emptiness.

'I'm sorry,' he murmured into her hair, so close that it felt like a kiss. 'I'm so sorry. Why didn't you say? Idiot…'

She didn't say anything, just stayed there, tucked up safely against Guy's chest, while her pulse gradually slowed to match the slow, steady thud of his heart.

Then Toby came and wriggled up beside them and Guy put out an arm to scoop him up close.

Holding them all safe.

'Do you have the rings?'

Rings! She hadn't thought…

But of course Guy had. He produced a pair of simple, classic matching wedding rings from his pocket and placed them on the velvet cushion in front of them. Then he picked up the smaller of the pair, took her hand and, placing it on her finger, said 'I call upon these persons here present to witness that I, Guy Edward Dymoke, take Francesca Elizabeth Lang as my lawful wedded wife…'

As she listened to Guy's low, firm voice clearly affirm his vow, Fran couldn't believe she was doing this. It had taken her five years to extricate herself from her first 'marriage of convenience'. An annoyingly inconvenient marriage, as it had turned out, but at least she'd been able to tell herself that her motives had been good.

She'd almost managed to convince herself this time, too. She wasn't marrying for her own benefit, but to protect Toby, Matty, Connie. But definitely not the stray cat. Even she wasn't that much of a fool.

Except that now, standing beside him, her hand clasped firmly in his, she knew that she was every inch a fool. She wasn't just doing this to keep a roof over her family's head, but for herself. Hoping against hope that her marriage to Guy would somehow evolve from an upmarket house share, a fiscal convenience, into something much more. Something real and true.

She realised the registrar was looking at her expectantly. 'I call upon these persons here present,' he prompted, as if he'd said it before.

Fran opened her mouth, but she couldn't speak. Couldn't go through with it. It was a lie. False. She couldn't do it again. Must not do it.

She began to breathe much too fast as panic swept over her, certain that at any minute someone would burst into the room and expose her, expose them both as frauds.

'Francesca?' Guy's face was grave, his eyes steady as a rock. And then, as if he could read her mind, he gently squeezed her hand as if saying, *It's okay. I understand. You're not doing this for yourself...*

And finally she picked up the larger ring, her heart hammering hot and fast in her chest. She felt dizzy, light-headed, her voice seeming to come from a long way off as she placed it on his finger and slowly repeated the words. Carefully weighing each one, she began, 'I call upon these persons here present...to witness that I, Francesca Elizabeth Lang...take Guy Edward Dymoke to be my lawful wedded husband...'

She'd done this before, but on that occasion only her head had been engaged. This time it was important. This time she meant it and maybe that did make it all right.

Because, even if he never knew it, she was making a true vow with her whole heart.

Then it was done and she was looking up at Guy,

forcing herself to look as if this was just another
meaningless ten-minute wedding, her expression saying nothing more than, *Okay, what next?*

It was the registrar who answered her unspoken
question as he smiled and said, 'You may kiss the
bride.'

No... Yes... There was an agonising pause that
seemed to go on for ever before Guy bent, touched
his lips to hers.

They clung momentarily to hers, scorching not just
her body but her soul until she thought she would
faint—but whether from joy or from despair she could
not have said as, with a little gasp, she drew back
before she betrayed herself.

The kiss was for the registrar, to add the mask of
reality to the pretence, nothing more. As Guy had so
regularly reminded her, she'd done this before. A kiss
was no big deal. And then, nineteen years old and
with ideals rather than love burning in her heart, it
hadn't been.

This time they felt like the most solemn, the most
important words she had ever uttered.

Unable to look at him, deal with the absence of any
emotional response, she left him to sign the register,
turning instead to the two women who'd abandoned
their computer terminals for ten minutes to act as witnesses, to thank them. Blushing like any ordinary
bride as she accepted their congratulations.

'Francesca?' Guy handed her the pen and she
added her own shaky signature to the book as he took
the certificate that made her, officially, Mrs Guy
Dymoke, tucked it away in his inside jacket pocket

and thanked the registrar as he added his good wishes for their future happiness. Then Guy took her arm and led her, almost fainting, outside to the steps of the Town Hall.

CHAPTER EIGHT

'FRANCESCA? Are you all right?'

She shook her head, unable to answer, as she took in huge gasps of air.

'Take your time.'

'I'm sorry. That was…' She didn't even attempt to finish the sentence. There wasn't a word to express the way she was feeling. To have the one thing you most wanted in the world. Yet not have it. To know that you could never have it.

'I know,' he said.

'No, Guy,' she said. 'I promise you, you don't.'

His gaze met hers and for one brief, shocking moment she saw his pain. Remembered the woman he loved but could never have because she loved someone else. And she laid her hand on his arm.

'I'm so sorry. You deserve better from me than that.'

He looked down at her hand, pale against his sleeve, and the bright new gold of the wedding ring gleamed as it caught the sun.

'I do understand how hard it must have been for you. I wish there had been more time.'

'It wouldn't have made any difference.'

'No. I suppose not,' he said, apparently missing her allusion to his own unattainable love. Then, 'I'm surprised you didn't bring Matty and Connie with you. As witnesses.'

She let it go, allowed him to take her hand, walk

her to his car, open the door for her, ease her into the passenger seat.

'I didn't tell them,' she said, as he slid behind the wheel. She was already missing his hand in hers. The warmth of it. The strength of it. 'About this. I don't want them to feel...' She stopped, unable to say the word. But he had no problems filling the void.

'Guilty?' He started the car, pulled out into the traffic.

'Responsible. All I've told them is that you've bought the house and will be moving into the top floor flat when it's been converted.'

'And they've accepted that?'

Fran recalled the look of relief on her cousin's face. Uncharacteristically, she hadn't asked what was going on. Grateful that she'd avoided a difficult interrogation, she hadn't elaborated. Matty, she realised belatedly, hadn't asked because she hadn't wanted to be told anything she didn't want to hear.

'You only went through with this for them, didn't you?' he said. 'Nothing else would have persuaded you.'

She glanced across at him. He was concentrating on the traffic and all she had was his hard, unyielding profile. She wondered what he'd do if she told him the truth. Recoil in horror, in all probability... 'What would you have done if I'd said no?'

'It was Steve's dying request. I don't think you'd have denied him anything, let alone that.' For a moment he met her gaze head-on. Then, as the traffic moved, 'And, even if you were inclined to, I wasn't about to let it happen.'

'No?' she challenged him. 'No, of course you weren't. Steven told me that you'd only backed down once before in your entire life. What was it, Guy? A charging rhino?'

'Something equally obdurate,' he assured her. 'The human heart.' She stared at him. The woman he'd loved? He'd walked away? Let her go without a fight? 'Something that isn't involved on this occasion,' he said so coldly that she shivered. Then, as they were temporarily halted at the lights, he turned to look at her. 'Which is why I wasn't prepared to take no for an answer, Mrs Dymoke.'

And she knew he'd added the 'Mrs Dymoke' just to demonstrate how obdurate he could be.

'It's Miss Lang,' she snapped back at him. 'It will always be Miss Lang...'

She looked down at the circle of polished gold around her finger. It was bright and pure, a burning a brand on her finger, and she tugged at it, desperate to be rid of it. Wrenching at it when it refused to slide over her knuckle.

After a moment he pulled up and closed his hand over hers, stopping her. 'Leave it, Francesca.' And for a moment something in his voice made her look up, made her hope... 'You'll hurt yourself,' he said, removing his hand as if stung.

And realising that she was just fooling herself, she gave the ring another tug, just to show him that she didn't care how much it hurt, she just wanted to be free of it. 'It's too damned tight,' she declared, ignoring the fact that it had slipped on as if made for her.

'It'll come off easily enough with some soap when you get home.'

'There is no way I'm going home wearing this!' His head went back, as if she'd punched him on the jaw. 'I don't want Matty or Connie to know,' she said, pleading with him to see. Wishing she hadn't said it. He was only doing what he thought was right. For the best. He had no way of knowing... 'It's so soon...after Steven. They wouldn't understand.'

'No? I believe they would. I think they have more faith in you than you have in yourself.' And for a moment it was there again. An unexpected gentleness... 'But it's your business, not mine. And, speaking of business...' He leaned across her, opened the glove box and took out a large envelope. 'These are your new credit cards. Everything you'll need.'

'But...'

'Why don't you indulge yourself in a little retail therapy? Treat yourself to lunch in Harvey Nicks or Claibournes? I'm sure their powder room will supply all the soap you need to wash away the last hour,' he said.

'Don't! Please! I can't bear it.'

When she didn't take the envelope, he said, 'You're my wife. Whatever I have is yours,' he said, brushing away a tear that had spilled on to her cheek. 'Take it.'

For a moment they seemed so close. She felt as if all she had to do was reach out to bridge the chasm, go into his arms.

'I really do have to go,' he said, dropping the envelope into her lap. And the gulf was wider than ever.

'Go?' Fran forgot all about her desperation to remove his ring, her hurt at his suggestion that she might even consider doing anything as mindless as shopping. 'Go where?' she asked. Then, realising that he meant *go*, get on a plane, fly away to the other side of the world, 'So soon? Without saying goodbye to Toby or Matty?'

'I said my goodbyes yesterday. While you were at the office.'

'They didn't tell me.' It was as well that her eyes were already full of tears. 'Toby was very quiet last night. I should have known something had upset him.'

'I promised him that I'd come back as soon as I could.'

'You'd damn well better—' She fought back the sob in her voice. There was no reason in the world for her to cry. This was a marriage of convenience. No heart involved. He'd said so. 'Small boys don't understand when people go away and don't come back,' she said. 'I've told him his Daddy is with Jesus, but I'm afraid he thinks it's just like one of his business trips. That he'll be back after a week or two.'

Guy was dying inside. He felt torn in half. In one moment he'd gained the one thing he had wanted most in the world. And lost it. He'd actually planned to take her to lunch, spin out for as long as possible the moment when she wore his ring, when he could make believe that she was his. But he couldn't do it. Not after the kiss he should have resisted had burned itself into his brain so that he could think of nothing else. He could only pray that it would replace the dream that had haunted him for so long, because it was all he'd have of her.

She'd loved Steve. Stayed with him. Had been prepared to commit herself to him for life. Even now she didn't blame him for what he'd done to her. Only pitied him, blamed herself.

His plane didn't leave until early evening, but the

sooner he put himself safely on the far side of the check-in barrier the better.

'I won't let Toby down,' he said. 'You have my word.'

She blinked, looked away, out of the window and up at the apartment block, then out across the Thames.

'Is this where you live?' she asked.

'Lived. Someone will pick up the few things I'm sending over to Elton Street. If you'll store them until the conversion is done?'

'Oh, yes, of course.'

'I just have to pick up my bags, then drop the keys in at the office. You can take the car, keep it,' he said, handing her the keys. 'It's insured for you to drive.'

'But how are you getting to the airport?' she asked. Then, not waiting for him to tell her, she opened the door and got out. 'What am I saying? I'll take you.' She forced a smile. 'That's what wives do, isn't it?'

Guy, quite unable to help himself, looked at her across the roof of the car and said, 'You might not want to go into what wives do, Francesca.' Then, taking pity on her as she blushed, he said, 'It's okay. I really don't expect you to morph into the perfect wife. There is, after all, no one either of us has to convince and I really can't see you as the kind of woman who'd get up at the crack of dawn every morning to run her man to the station every morning with her coat over her pyjamas.'

'Don't you?'

She was wearing a pale grey designer suit, sexy high-heeled shoes and her pale hair swept up in the height of sophistication. Steve had turned her into his ideal. The kind of woman who never had to wash a dish or iron his shirt. Just look good and display his success to the world. But her eyes told a different story and oh, dear God, yes he could see her all too clearly, hair mussed, no make-up, soft, warm and with the imprint of his body still on hers…

He was nearing the end of his tether.

He'd been through an emotional bombardment. Swearing death-us-do-part commitment to the woman he loved, while having to convince her that it meant nothing more to him than honouring a debt to his dead brother, had taken a painful toll because, unlike Francesca, he'd meant it. Every word. She couldn't wait to see the back of him, while he was wrecked at the thought of leaving them, leaving her, and he knew, just knew, that Steve was looking on somewhere, watching, laughing, saying 'Got you!' as he taunted him with what he most desired, all the while knowing that it was impossible for him to take it.

He'd only fully understood how difficult it would be since that moment on the 'Eye' when she'd surrendered briefly, let him hold her safe and, in the most bittersweet of moments, he'd realised that he'd both won and lost.

That she would marry him for the sake of her family, no other reason. That any chance of allowing her time to grieve, to come to see him as someone special, someone she might in time grow to love, was lost to him.

The minute money had become the prime force of their relationship, any hope of emotional commitment had to be put on hold. How could he reveal his feelings now because she wouldn't know for certain that he was being sincere. That he wasn't simply making the best of a bad job and expecting more than a paper marriage for his money?

And it worked two ways. If she surrendered, he'd never be sure if it was because she felt she had no choice.

He was going to have to sit it out. Wait. Prove himself over however long it took and maybe one day she would trust him enough. Feel enough. He could do it. He'd lived three years without hope. Now he had the faint glimmer of a possibility of a future, he was prepared to wait a lifetime...

So, instead of foisting himself upon her, he'd spent time with Toby, visited Matty, eaten the food that Connie had insisted on cooking for him—whether he had wanted it or not. Made friends, allies, of all of them. But he'd given Francesca all the room she had clearly needed. Even the most thick-skinned of men couldn't have failed to get the message that, having agreed to marry him, she was doing everything she could to avoid him.

Why else would she spend all her time in an office that wasn't doing any business? How much clearing up could there be?

But right now all this careful reasoning meant nothing. He wanted to kick something, take out his rage on some inanimate object, howl like a wounded animal. He was having to wear a civilised front, behave like a man unmoved by anything or anyone when he'd never felt so close to exploding.

The truth was that he couldn't bear another minute of her sitting beside him, her scent seeping into his skin, her hair, sleek and smooth, a blatant invitation to a man to pull at the pins, let it loose.

She did something to him that no other woman had ever managed. Robbed him of reason.

He'd believed he could do this, but he'd been right to stay away all these years. He should never have come back.

Not that he imagined it had been easy for Francesca, either. She'd just lost the man she loved— a man she'd forgiven every kind of betrayal—and he'd sensed her struggle, felt her hand trembling in his as she'd nearly failed at the last minute, barely able to get out the words. Seen her distress as, outraged at his apparent carelessness, she'd tried to tear off the ring he'd put on her finger and throw it back at him. And his heart broke for her. Broke all over again for himself.

'It really isn't necessary to take me to the airport,' he said abruptly, wishing he'd handled this differently. It had seemed so simple. Drive to the apartment, hand over the car keys, say goodbye. No emotion. No fuss. But nothing in this situation was simple, and there were no self-help guides on how to avoid the pitfalls. He was on his own and it was a steep learning curve. 'I'll take a cab to the office and someone will run me in from there.'

'Your secretary?'

'She's rather more than that,' he said. And, picking up an edge to her voice, 'Does it matter?'

'Is she pretty?'

'Catherine?' He looked at her more closely. A definite edge. She was jealous? Why? And, because he was human, he said, 'She's tall, blond and sensational.' Which was the truth. She was tall and blond— although he imagined that mainly due to the intervention of science—and she was a sensational administrator. 'You know, you're beginning to sound like a jealous wife,' he said. And, since he felt much too good about that, he punctured his own ego with, 'Were you like this with Steve?'

She looked at the ring he'd placed on her finger, then raised those sinfully long lashes and said, 'I wasn't married to him, Guy. Maybe I'd better get this off before I completely lose the plot.' And, when he didn't leap to agree, 'I imagine you do have some soap in your apartment? Or is everything packed?'

Left with little choice but to run the swipe card through the lock on the entrance, he held the door for her and summoned the lift. The doors slid open immediately and they were whisked, in silence, to the top floor.

And then, as she stood in the entrance to the vast living room, it seemed that she was the one lost for words.

Fran had never doubted that Guy was wealthy. Steven had told her often enough that he was and the fact that he could raise the finance to buy her house at a day's notice proved it beyond all doubt. But the apartment, expensively understated, elegant, beautiful beyond anything she could have imagined, rammed the point home. This wasn't the home of a man who was just wealthy. This was the home of a man who was seriously rich.

The softest leather furniture invited the weary to relax and be cosseted. Richly coloured oriental rugs were laid on pale, polished floors. Books and fine paintings adorned the walls.

Guy had told her that this was just a convenient place for him to stay during his brief visits to London. An investment. Maybe that was what it had become, but that wasn't how it had been originally perceived. This was the home of a man who'd put thought and care into it. It was a place to share with someone. And she knew, instinctively, that this had been furnished with the woman he loved in mind.

No wonder he'd been so reluctant to let her see it. If she'd known he had to surrender this to pay Steven's debts, buy the house—and he must have done or why else would he be converting her attic into a tiny little self-contained flat for himself?—she would have... What? Refused to allow it? He'd said, just minutes ago, that he wasn't going to take no for an answer.

Guy didn't join her, but remained on the far side of the wide double doors as she toured the room, touching the spine of a leather-bound book, gazing at a painting, not quite able to come to terms with the fact that he had something of such value simply hanging on his wall. Trying to get inside his head. Trying to imagine the woman who had inspired such adoration. Trying to make it all add up.

'I'll get my bags,' he said.

'No!' She turned to face him. 'What have you done, Guy?' He didn't answer. 'This is a world away from the way you described it to me. It's a home. Full of beautiful things.'

'I didn't say it was ugly. Just not what I need any more.'

'And you've sold it? Just like that? To buy my house?'

'Francesca—'

He was going to lie to her. He wasn't as good at it as Steven. One minute he was looking straight at her, the next he was more interested in one of the paintings...

'Please give me credit for some sense, Guy,' she said, before he could. Then, with a gesture at the single box, the small trunk, all he was taking with him, she said, 'The pictures are worth a fortune. That one alone would have done it.'

And she waited.

Finally he said, 'Yes, it probably would. You're right, of course. I haven't sold the flat. I've let as it stands to an American bank for one of their senior vice-presidents.'

'Let it?' she repeated. 'Let it?' She looked around. 'With all this priceless...stuff?'

'Believe me, the rental reflects the value of contents as well as the accommodation.'

'But...why?'

'I told you. I bought this as an investment and it's done well. I've tripled my capital outlay. Something that Steve could have done if he'd used the money I gave him wisely. I should have let it before, of course. It's a terrible waste of resources leaving it empty and it put the insurance premiums through the roof. The apartment in Elton Street will be much more cost effective.'

Money? Was that all this meant to him? She didn't believe it for a minute.

'I meant why did you lie to me?'

'I didn't. You assumed I had to sell and I didn't deny it.'

'Why?' she persisted.

Because he was a fool, Guy told himself. Because he wanted to be able to help her in every way, put all of his resources at her command, give her not just a home, but everything she'd ever need. Because he loved her.

None of them were reasons he could offer for what must now seem completely irrational behaviour. Whatever he said was going to make a bad situation worse, but he wasn't going to add his unwanted passion to her burden. It was too soon after Steve's death. Even if, by some miracle, she returned his feelings, she would deny it. She could do nothing else.

'Guilt is the best arm-twister I know,' he said, distancing himself from his voice, his actions. Her confused expression as she silently mouthed the word back at him.

'Guilt?'

'Steve taught me that. You're right, of course. I could easily have bought the house, given it to you, but I needed you to marry me.'

'Needed?'

'Yes,' he said, knowing that he was breaking every tiny link he'd forged with her in the last few days. Destroying her memories of those moments when they'd been close. Smashing every one of his dreams beyond any hope of repair with each word he uttered. He'd tied her to him out of his own longings, hoped that he could one day win her affection, her trust, her love. Now he was giving her the freedom to hate him for it. Releasing her from any need for gratitude.

'This might be a good moment to tell you that Tom Palmer is sorting out adoption papers for Toby. It's just a formality. I simply want to be sure that when you move on, find someone new, I'll have some family rights. That he won't just disappear from my life. Fortunately he won't have to change his name.'

'Find someone new? Are you mad? Steven has

been dead less than a month!' Then, frowning, 'Is that what was in Steven's letter?'

How easy it would be to lie. Blame Steve. 'No, he didn't think of it. But then I always did have a better grasp of reality than my brother and Toby is all the family I've got.' All the family he was ever likely to have. 'Don't even think of trying to fight me on it, Francesca. And if you do think about it remember your responsibilities and leave well alone.'

'You bastard!'

'Yes, well, Steve did tell you. You should have listened to him.'

'You can't do this,' she said, floundering in a mixture of outrage and helplessness. Every atom of his being reached out to her, yearned to reassure her, but he held his ground. 'I'll…I'll have the marriage annulled,' she declared.

'On what grounds? You're going to find it rather difficult to prove it wasn't consummated unless I cooperate. And I will, but only when I have what I want.'

'You think I'm prepared to wait? I'm going straight back to the registrar. Tell him the truth…' And she headed for the door.

All Guy wanted was to stop her looking at the pictures he'd bought because he'd known, instinctively, that she would love them as he did. Touching the books he wanted to share with her. Running her hand along the back of the huge sofa that was big enough for two people to lie in each other's arms as they watched the setting sun suffuse the sky with soft pinks and mauves.

He wanted to stop her asking questions that he couldn't answer without betraying himself.

Wanted to make her angry enough to walk out, leave him, so that he could gather himself, restore the outward calm. But not like this. He couldn't let her leave like this.'

'Francesca, wait—'

She pushed past him, refusing to stop, refusing to listen and, in desperation, he caught at her sleeve.

She was moving faster than he'd realised and, as he grabbed her, she spun around, almost losing her balance on her high heels. Would have done if he hadn't caught her, held her.

'Don't...'

She was breathing heavily, flushed, and her hair had broken free of the restraining pins. She looked distraught, as if she was hurting so deeply that nothing could make it better, and tears filled her eyes as she stood there, powerless, his unwilling captive bride. But she wasn't surrendering. She lifted her chin, lifted her hands to capture the loose strands that curled about her face, as if somehow she could restore her dignity by anchoring her hair smoothly back in place.

But as she raised her lashes to stare him down, met his gaze head on, it was as if time had slipped sideways to another place. And her eyes, which a second earlier had been as cold as steel, melted, darkened...

Neither of them spoke. She just let her hair fall and it tumbled loose about her face, her shoulders, gold in the autumn sunlight slanting in from the skylight above them. He might have been dreaming, except that when he reached up to cradle her cheek he could feel the warmth of her skin against his palm, his fingers. When he tightened his hold on her waist, her body moulded into his as if they had been made to fit. And when he lowered his mouth to hers, her lips parted, hot, honey-sweet, everything he'd ever dreamed of.

He'd lived this moment over and over in his imagination. Knew exactly how it would be. The way he'd pick her up and carry her to his bed, undress her slowly, taking his time as he explored every part of her with his hands, his mouth, his tongue, until she was crying out for him. Until he could wait no longer to claim her. In his head, his heart, he knew it would be precious and beautiful and something neither of them would ever forget, no matter what happened afterwards.

The reality was the swift, explosive and purely physical coupling of two people in desperate need. No sweet words, no forever promises, nothing gentle or giving, yet it was the most perfect act because in that moment it was exactly what they both wanted, both needed, engaging the senses in a totally spontaneous response to the emotional clamour of their bodies. It was the completion that his body had been demanding since that split-second connection in a restaurant three years earlier and he knew that nothing would ever surpass the exultation he felt as he plunged deep into her, compete with the stinging excitement of her nails biting into his shoulders, driving him on. Knowing that her passion equalled his as she clasped him against her, crying out as he brought her to release, burying her face into his shoulder, her lips into his neck as with a roar of triumph, he spilled into her. Made her his. Became hers in every way that it was possible for a man to be possessed by a woman.

He had always known that she was the one woman in the world who could make him lose his mind. She had just proved that beyond a doubt. And, while he held her, kept her close, her hair against his cheek, his lips against her hair, he thought reason well lost. While she clung to him as he wrapped her in the protective afterglow of tenderness, he could hope.

And when she finally lifted her head, her eyes huge and shining with the aftermath of love, her mouth invitingly soft, he had one sweet moment when he was certain that hope had been fulfilled.

But then he saw that the shine was not love, but tears.

He had been right. She wouldn't forget this moment in a hurry. Nor would he. But for all the wrong reasons.

He eased back, releasing her from the hard grip of the wall, supporting her as she lowered her feet, found her balance. Searching for some words, any words, as she pulled her clothes about her, straightened her skirt, all the time with an unceasing, silent stream of tears tearing at his heart. There were no words to convey his regret, his shame.

To say that he was sorry would insult her.

To tell her that he'd never intended it to happen would sound like so many empty words. She had just threatened to annul their marriage. His response could only be taken one way. And that was the charitable interpretation.

The other was that he had simply decided that, despite his fine words, his promises, he expected payment in full for his investment in an unwanted high-maintenance wife. Why else would he be planning to move into her home when, as she had just discovered, there was no need?

How could he ask her to forgive him, when he
wouldn't be able to forgive himself?

Instead he picked up her jacket, handed it to her in
silence.

'Bathroom?' she enquired, so quietly that he could
barely hear her.

'Through here.' He opened the door to his bedroom
and the untouched bed, just yards away, seemed to
mock him. 'You'll find everything you'll need.'

Soap, hot water to wash him from her body.

She ducked through the opening, leaving him to
straighten himself out. Consider a future that was suddenly bleaker than he could have imagined even a
week ago. An hour ago. Then he'd had some hope.

He began to fasten his shirt, discovered that several
of the buttons were torn from it, and dug a fresh one
out of his holdall. On the point of balling up the discarded one and tossing it into the bin, he stopped,
held it to his face, breathed in her scent for a moment,
before folding it and putting it in the bag.

Fran didn't undress or take a shower. If she undressed
she'd have to put the same clothes back on and she
wasn't going to do that ever again. They were going
into the bin the moment she got home. From the
Jasper Conran suit to the Manolo Blahnik shoes she'd
been wearing while she'd thrown herself at Guy like
a whore. Her only consolation was that he could never
call her 'cheap'.

Instead she splashed cold water on to her face.
Washed her hands. Pulled out the pins that were falling out all around her and, since she hadn't got her
bag with her, shook her hair loose. Then regarded
herself in the mirror.

Her lips were bruised and swollen, her eyes bright and dark. One of the buttons on her jacket had been torn off and she had a rip in her stockings. She looked exactly what he must think she was.

A woman who'd come close to throwing away the soft option in a fit of pique. And had used the oldest trick in the book to save herself.

It hadn't been that way. It had been as if she'd stepped back in time to the moment she'd first seen him and recognised the moment for what it was. A *coup de foudre*, a lightning strike, a split second in which she'd known that he was the only man in the world for her, the one man she could never have. Only now there was nothing to hold her back, and all that pent up yearning, desire, had been loosed in a frenzied outburst of passion. Uncontrolled. Glorious in its absolute truth. Inexplicable unless the response was mutual.

But even if she couldn't explain, she would have to face him. The sooner the better.

She found him in the kitchen, slumped over the table, his face resting on his hands as he stared into space, as if into the jaws of hell.

'Guy? Are you all right?'

'What?' He started, looked at her.

'Can I get you something?'

'Oh, no. I really do have to go, but help yourself. Take your time…'

'We've already had this argument, Guy,' she said. 'I'm taking you to the airport, so if you have to go, let's do it.'

'Fran…' She'd loved the way he always called her Francesca. Her whole name. Soft and low. Suddenly she was reduced to Fran.

'Don't! Please, Guy. Don't... Don't say a word.'
Please don't say that you're sorry. 'It happened. Let's
just forget it.' For a moment their eyes locked and
she knew he was as shocked, as overcome, as she
was. And undoubtedly hating himself for betraying
Steve's memory. 'Please.'

'If that's what you want.' Then, rising to his feet,
'Let's go.'

Which more or less put a stop to any attempt at
communication, beyond the banal. The heavy traffic.
The chance of rain. It was worse than silence, Fran
thought. She wanted to say so much. Couldn't say
any of it. He'd married her out of duty. Guilt. Because
it was the last wish of a brother he felt he'd let down.
He hadn't counted on getting some sex-starved female flinging herself at him at the first opportunity.

And when he'd pulled up in the drop zone at the
airport and she'd climbed out so that she could take
his place in the driving seat while he took his bag
from the boot, all she could say was, 'You will take
care of yourself, Guy? Don't do anything stupid, will
you?'

He glanced at her sideways. 'It's a bit late for that,
wouldn't you say?'

'That's not—'

'I know.' He dragged his fingers through his hair.
'I'm sorry.'

She shook her head. 'Guy, about Toby...'

'He's your son. Nothing can happen without your
agreement. When I said—'

'I was going to say that he'll miss you,' she said.
I'll miss you. 'Don't let what happened... Just don't
stay away because of that.'

'I'll miss him too,' he said. But not making any

promises. 'If you have any problems, need anything, just call my office or go and see Tom. He'll look after you.'

'Who'll look after you, Guy?'

'Me? I don't need anyone to take care of me.'

'No, I mean it. It's dangerous out there. Do you really have to go?'

He reached out as if to touch her cheek, then, as if remembering what had happened the last time he'd done that, he thought better of it and curled his fingers tight against his palm before picking up his bag. But her cheek remembered his touch and her body responded to the memory.

'If you need to get a message to me the office will know how to get hold of me.'

'Your sensational secretary?'

'The very same.' Then, before she could reply, he walked away and, as the automatic doors swished open, disappeared into the mêlée of the departure hall.

'Guy!' she called desperately. But too late. The doors had already closed behind him and as she made a move to follow she saw a traffic warden looking pointedly at the car.

'You can't leave that there, miss. It'll be towed away.'

'But...' But what? 'No. I'm just going.'

It was probably just as well. What would she have said to him anyway? I love you?

Not under these circumstances. After today he wouldn't want to hear her say it under any circumstances.

CHAPTER NINE

FRAN felt as if she was grieving all over again.

She'd pulled into the garage and finally given way to the dammed-up tears she hadn't been able to shed for Steven in a mind-clearing storm of guilt and loss. And when it was over she finally understood it all. That their marriage of convenience had been entirely for his expedience, not hers.

Not cheap. But then this wasn't about money. It was about control. Toby was all the family he had. His heir. The boy who carried the family name. Marriage was the simplest and most effective way of stopping her from becoming involved with someone else, giving him some other man's name.

Which answered any question she had about what was in the letter Steven had written to him. He had been a less than perfect partner, a less than perfect anything, except father. Relaxed to the point of being comatose on most things, he had been uncharacteristically firm in his insistence that Dymoke be added to Toby's name.

Too late she saw that all that stuff about inheritance tax had been so much wool being pulled over her eyes. Guy had bought the house to keep her in place, and while she was still reeling from shock, still confused enough not to be able to think things through clearly, he'd rushed her through the marriage ceremony.

There had been nothing altruistic about any of it.

He was even converting the top floor of the house into an apartment for himself. Moving himself into their lives...

And the sex? Had that been planned too?

She shook her head, trying to clear it...

She hadn't been thinking straight. The wedding had upset her and then she'd realised that his apartment wasn't the sterile environment that he'd led her to believe, lacking the emotional warmth of a home, but a carefully, lovingly prepared setting for the woman he'd hoped would share it with him. Her presence had been so strong in the room that she'd almost felt her...

At that moment she'd been hurting so much that she'd have said, done, almost anything to wound him. But then he'd looked at her...

He'd never taken a woman like that. Without thought, control, consideration of the consequences.

Never before had he experienced that kind of no-holds-barred response. It had made him feel invincible. Made him shake with need...

But the fact that she'd been an eager and willing partner, matching his own need with a breathless urgency and heat that had swept away any thought of restraint, excused nothing. He had taken on himself a duty of care. She'd been distraught, upset, vulnerable, but when she'd looked up at him all of that had been blown away. She had looked at him as if... As if...

He cut off the pitiful tricks of his subconscious. There was no excuse. What did it matter how she'd looked at him? He'd not only betrayed her, but everything he stood for.

Bad enough to lose it so completely, but he'd left

her without a word of apology, of explanation. But what else could he have done? Tell her truth? Tell her that he loved her?

She'd made it plain enough she didn't want to hear his pitiful apologies. All she'd wanted was to get him out of her life.

He had thought he'd known what it was to be alone. He hadn't begun to imagine the emptiness...

'Fran?'

It seemed like hours later when Matty's voice broke through the pain and she gathered herself, looked at her watch. She didn't know what time Guy's flight left. He'd probably already taken off. Been glad to go.

She wished she hadn't let him leave that way, had let him say what was on his mind no matter how painful the words might have been. She should have had the courage to confront him, confront her own weakness.

But regret was just a waste of time.

She had to think of the future, grasp the chance to make something of the business Steven had left her. Make something of herself. If Guy saw that she was not just some pathetic female who needed a man to look after her he might, one day, look at her like that again...

'Fran, what's happened? Where's Guy?'

'He's gone,' she said.

'But he'll be coming back?'

'Yes, he'll be coming back.' And she climbed out of the car and held out her hand with the tell-tale ring still fastened immovably to her finger.

'Oh, my dear. What have you done?'

She told her exactly what she'd done. And why. All of it. The whole truth, and when she'd finished Matty just hugged her. There was nothing else she could do or say.

Not that she had time to dwell on what had happened. She had the business to keep her occupied. And the weekly calls from the 'sensational' Catherine who, no doubt, had instructions to check that she had everything she needed—just in case the credit cards weren't enough—and that the builders were getting on with the job. To ensure that she hadn't taken his money and disappeared with her son... His heir...

And, as the weeks lengthened into months, to despatch gifts for Christmas for all of them. Even Connie was not forgotten, squealing with delight as she unwrapped the handbag that had been gift-wrapped and delivered by a top-people's store.

He'd sent her a book. A biography of the woman she'd once told him that she admired, aspired to be like. It was an obvious choice, top of the bestseller list, and she tried not to fool herself into believing he'd picked it out himself.

And, as winter retreated and the first daffodils began to appear, Catherine's calls had the added comfort of reassuring her that he was safe in the terrifying country that seemed to have swallowed him up so completely he might have disappeared off the face of the earth.

It was nearly Easter when, sitting glued to the early-evening news, watching pictures of riots, the reports of civil unrest that seemed worse with every passing week, she heard the doorbell rang. She left it for

Connie to answer, only looking up when the sitting room door opened.

A tall fair-haired woman hesitated on the threshold. 'Your housekeeper said it was all right to come through…' And when she still didn't speak, 'I can't believe we haven't met already. I feel as if I know you so well.'

'Catherine?' She recognised the voice, but the reality did not match the picture in her imagination. Tall, blonde… And old enough to be her mother.

'Can I come in?'

Realising that she was staring open-mouthed, she scrambled to her feet. 'I'm so sorry,' she said, taking the proffered hand. 'I was miles away…'

'Watching the news. It's not good, is it?'

Fran's heart gave a wild leap of fear. 'Is that why you've come? To tell me—'

'No, no. I'm sorry. I didn't mean to give you a fright. I've just come to bring you something. Well, for your little boy. I just thought that perhaps you should have the opportunity to veto it first. Is he around? Toby?'

'No, he's downstairs with Matty.'

'In that case I'll go and fetch it from the car.'

She returned a few moments later with a cardboard box that she placed on the floor and when she opened it the small silky brown and white head of a spaniel puppy appeared. Then a body wriggled free of the blanket and he looked up at her and whined to be lifted out.

She was lost for words. Guy might have left Catherine to pick out Christmas gifts, but this could only have come direct from him. Proof that he was thinking of her... She caught herself. Thinking of Toby.

'I made the woman at the kennels promise she'd take him back if you didn't want him. Men have these great ideas...'

'When? When did Guy ask you to do this?'

'Oh, months ago. In fact, I think he called from the airport... It was supposed to have been Toby's Christmas present, but since he was so particular it had to wait until the right spaniel produced the right pup.' She shrugged apologetically. 'You know Guy. He's never satisfied with less than perfection.'

'No?' Her heart lurched uncomfortably. 'No,' she agreed.

'The puppy had to be from a private breeder he'd chosen. And it had to be brown and white. And male.'

'Yes. He'd want that.' And when Catherine lifted her eyebrows. 'Steven had a puppy like this when he was a boy.'

'Oh, I see. I wondered...' Then, when she didn't— couldn't—say anything, 'Unfortunately, the mummy dog wasn't on the same schedule as Santa. Anyway, the breeder is happy to take him back if this is a less than thrilling surprise,' Catherine said, clearly assuming that her shocked reaction was horror at this unexpected arrival. 'Men have these great ideas, bless them, but they don't have to deal with the puddles. Or the walks. I speak from experience here...'

'No. He's perfect,' Fran said, kneeling down to rub the pup's head with her fingertips. 'Hello, Harry Two.' Then, when he whined to be picked up, 'Oh, no. You're not mine. Toby gets first cuddle.' And she tucked him carefully back in the basket with the blan-

ket around him before turning to Catherine. 'Want to
see a little boy's face light up?'

Half an hour later, looking on at boy and puppy
lost in mutual admiration, Catherine said, 'This is so
what Guy needs. A family to come home to. All he's
done the past few years is fieldwork but it's a young
man's game. Have the builders actually started work
on the alterations yet?'

'No, not yet,' Fran said. 'The architect is having to
sort out the retrospective planning permission for the
extension, which is slowing everything down.'

Thank goodness.

'But the interior designer came to see you? About
the redecoration of your bedroom?'

'Oh, yes. God bless him,' Fran said.

'He's that good?'

'Oh, he's great, but it isn't that. The sweet man
nearly wet himself with excitement when he saw a
hideous frog I'd brought home from the warehouse to
prop open the garage door. Made an offer for the lot
on the spot. And then bought a truckload of equally
unattractive lamps when he came to the warehouse to
collect them. I thought I was going to have to pay
someone to take them away when I moved out of
Steven's offices.'

'How's the business going? I saw that Christmas
piece in the *Courier* last November, featuring your
fabulous silk wrappers,' she said. 'Great PR, by the
way. I did all my gift shopping with one phone call.'

'I was lucky. I sent the editor a wrapper and she
came to see me, make sure I was for real, and she
fell in love with them. She's doing a feature on me
next week. You know the kind of thing. Plucky-
mother-runs-business-from-her-attic... Happily, it co-

incides with the arrival of the new summer-weight
wrappers and some totally gorgeous matching pyjamas. I couldn't afford that kind of advertising.'

'I was going to ask if you had anything new. It
always seems to be someone's birthday…'

'I went out to China in January and talked to the
cooperative who make this stuff—'

'On your own?'

Who else was there? She'd been scared witless, but
she'd had to do it. As Guy had said, there were things
you couldn't send anyone else to do. And she'd been
welcomed so warmly. Treated with such respect…

'I needed to go myself.'

'Yes, but surely in your—'

'Did you mention any of this to Guy? About the
company, I mean?'

'It's not my business, Fran. I'm just a messenger.'

Which was a tactful way of saying that he never
asked about her, Fran thought. Didn't want to know.

'Do you want me to tell him?' Catherine prompted.

'Oh, no,' she said. Then laughed as if it wasn't
important. As if she didn't want to astound him with
her brilliance when he finally got home. 'He's got
more than enough to worry about, I should think.'

'In that case I imagine you'd rather I didn't mention that you're expecting a baby.'

Guy wiped the sweat from his eyes with his sleeve,
booted up the laptop and downloaded his report via
the satellite uplink. Checked to see if there were any
messages from the office. The one from Tom Palmer
with an attachment leapt out at him. It was as if he'd
been holding his breath, waiting for it. But it wasn't

the formal application for an annulment he'd been anticipating for months.

It was an article about Francesca in the *Courier*. About the success of her fledgling mail order business. As he read it he found himself hearing her voice as he read her words. Filled with joy as he looked at her adored face, delighted with her success.

The camera had caught her as she'd swirled around in a loose silk wrapper, throwing her head back, laughing, looking wonderful.

She'd put back the weight she'd lost. Her hair was a deeper colour. She looked exactly as she had that moment he'd first...

No.

He rose to his feet, fighting for breath.

Not exactly the way she had looked then. On that occasion her pregnancy hadn't shown. This time, although disguised by the loose wrap, he could see that it was well advanced. He didn't need to guess how well advanced. He knew exactly how many months, days, hours it was since he'd held her, given her the child she was carrying.

Every day since he'd left her he'd had to fight the urge to go back. Punishing himself. But his feelings no longer mattered. He had to get back. Had to be there for her. With her. Giving her his emotional as well as his financial support. He refused to listen to the voice in his head warning him that she wouldn't want him. She needed him and he would take whatever she hurled at him by way of accusation, anger, abuse. And this time nothing would stop him from telling her the way he felt about her, the entire truth from beginning to end. Tell her and keep telling her until she believed him.

'Fran, are you watching the news?'

It was late and, deep in thought, she'd picked up the phone on automatic. 'Oh, Matty... No, I'm trying to decide whether we need to expand our range of goods.' The lightly quilted wrappers had been joined by a summer-weight companion—pyjamas, jewel-rich scarves and some little silk embroidered boxes which she knew were going to be a huge hit. 'I've been offered some rather special scented candles to match our colour range and I've really got to max-imise the cost-return on this catalogue—'

'Shut up, Fran! It's Guy, he's on the television...' She didn't hear the rest of the sentence, dropping the phone as she reached for the remote, flicking desper-ately through the channels until she found one of the rolling news channels.

'...concerns for the missing geologist's where-abouts have grown since he left camp planning to travel to the capital last week and failed to arrive. Isolated rebel groups who have recently moved into the area have seized foreign nationals hostage in the past, using them to force concessions from the gov-ernment. Neither the Foreign Office nor Mr Dymoke's company would comment on whether any such demands—'

The doorbell began to ring. A long, urgent blast that sent her flying to the door. It was Catherine.

'Tell me,' she demanded.

'I tried to get to you before the damned news...'

'Tell me, Catherine!'

'I don't know. He wasn't due to come home for

another six weeks but he sent an urgent e-mail telling me to book him a flight and apparently left camp straight afterwards. He never arrived...'

Fran sank on to the bottom of the stairs. 'I begged him not to go.'

Catherine joined her, putting her arms around her. 'It'll be all right. He's tough as old boots.'

'He's not bullet-proof.'

'He's no use to anyone dead, Fran. If the rebels have him they'll want to negotiate.'

'And how long will that take?' Months. Years. 'What the hell is he doing there risking his life?' Then, 'I wish I'd told him about the baby. I wish I'd told him that I love him.' She looked at Catherine, pleading for understanding. 'I should have told him that I love him...'

The sound of the stair-lift announced the arrival of Matty. She took one look at them and said, 'I'll go and make some tea.'

'Tea? Where's your bottle of Scotch when we need it?'

'Safely downstairs where it won't play havoc with your blood pressure. Go and put your feet up—'

'Don't treat me like an invalid!' The phone began to ring and she leapt up before Catherine could beat her to it and snatched it up. 'What?'

'Francesca...'

'Guy...'

She could scarcely hear him, his voice breaking up, too distorted to be recognised. But it had to be him. No one else called her Francesca. It was the one word that came through whole and unbroken as the poor connection stuttered and hissed so that all she caught were fragments that she had to guess at.

'Okay… Home…'

Words that tortured her and she cut them short. 'Guy, I don't know what the devil you're saying so stop wasting time talking and get back here! Right now! Do you hear me?'

And then there was nothing. Only an echoing silence. Had he hung up? She stared at the phone in horror.

'That was Guy? Is he okay?' Matty demanded. 'What did he say?'

'He rang me…'

'Who else would he ring, idiot…?' Catherine was grinning. Why was she grinning?

'I don't believe it. He rang me and I shouted at him. How could I do that? I was going to tell him that I love him…'

For two days she wouldn't go out, but remained glued to the television. Never moved out of reach of a telephone. Waiting for him to call again. Waiting for news. There was plenty of it, but most of it was confused, contradictory. He was still a prisoner. The rescue helicopter had been brought down. He had never been kidnapped but was simply lost somewhere. He'd been shot—

All she had to hang on to was his voice, her name in the ether…

'Fran?' She looked round. 'We're going now,' Connie said. 'You going to be all right?'

'Going?'

'Toby has a birthday party with his friend.'

'Oh, yes…' She forced herself away from the television. 'Yes, of course. I'd forgotten. Have you got money for the taxi? A present? You'll be good, Toby, won't you? Remember to say thank you.'

'Maybe you should go,' Connie muttered darkly. 'Baby could do with a change of scene.'

Baby needs his daddy, she thought, looking back at the television.

'We'll be home about six.'

'Have a good time,' she said. Then, 'Damn!' as the front door slammed shut.

Angry with herself, she turned off the television, got to her feet. Guy might not be rescued for months. Was she planning on spending every hour in front of the television in case there was the slightest snippet of news? It was the last thing he'd want. Catherine would let her know the minute anyone heard anything and in the meantime there were a hundred things that needed doing. She still hadn't settled on the final lay-out for the slender catalogue that was going to be mailed out to all their customers, as well put as an insert in one of the Sunday supplements.

It was going to cost a fortune. It had to be right.

She caught sight of herself in the hall mirror. What a wreck. She needed to take a shower, wash her hair, change. Get her mind back on the job. On her family...

But when she opened a drawer, searching for underwear that would stretch around her expanding belly, she found herself staring at the tiny silk box that contained the wedding ring Guy had put on her finger and she opened it.

The simple circle of gold gleamed rich and warm and she picked it up, slipped it on to her finger, felt...comforted. As if he were closer. And, instead of working on her catalogue, she went across to the newly decorated master bedroom where the few possessions he'd packed up and removed from the apartment had been placed, waiting to be unpacked.

She opened a large, old-fashioned leather trunk and began putting away his things. Shirts. Sweaters. Suits. She lifted up the sleeve of the one he'd worn at their wedding, touching it to her cheek.

Put his shoes on the racks. His socks and his underwear in drawers.

An affirmation that he would soon be home.

The box contained sealed packets of personal papers and she stored them in the lowboy. Then took out a large padded envelope that had been sent to Steven. Opened. Marked 'Return to Sender'. And nothing on earth could have stopped her from looking inside.

She stared at the silver rattle for a long time. Guy had sent Steven this family treasure for Toby. And Steven had returned it. He hadn't wanted to let his brother back into their lives.

Why?

She finally put it to one side, finished emptying the box. Took out the few books he'd brought with him, placing them beside the bed. A piece of paper fluttered out of one of them and as she bent to pick it up she recognised the writing.

Steven's letter. She sank on to the edge of the bed, holding it in both hands, knowing that it was private. Knowing that it held all the answers...

She was still staring at it when the doorbell rang. It would be Catherine. She had said she'd drop by after work. She hadn't realised it was so late and glanced at her watch. It wasn't...

And then she knew. Was running down the stairs,

fumbling with the door, but when she flung it open there was no one on the step and for a moment she was utterly confused.

Had she imagined it? She stepped outside to look up and down the street but there was no one about, only someone paying off a taxi that had stopped a few yards away. His hair was long and unkempt. His beard days old. His clothes past saving. He didn't look as if he could have afforded the price of a bus ticket, let alone a taxi. And then as he turned, looked up, she saw his face. The cut roughly stitched over his right eye, his cheek bone bruised black, his arm in a makeshift sling…

Guy.

Shock took her breath away. She struggled for air so that she could say his name. Say the words that were rushing in a torrent to get out. But as she walked slowly down the steps to meet him, his gaze dropped from her face to her burgeoning stomach, to where the baby they'd made in an explosive moment of passion lay beneath her heart.

Guy was exhausted, aching in every limb, but as he saw the woman he loved standing in the lamplight he felt a surge of something so powerful that he could have taken on the world. He felt such overwhelming gratitude that she hadn't rushed for the morning after pill. He could not have blamed her…

Choked, all he could do was smile stupidly and say, 'I really buggered up your plans for an annulment, didn't I?'

For a moment Francesca thought her heart might break. Was that all it meant to him?

She'd kept his baby when Matty had tactfully suggested the morning after pill. Protected it against the raised eyebrows of neighbours, the gossip of Steven's friends. Cherished it with her love and hope for the future and all it meant to him was that he had stopped her from ending their marriage.

Then, as she saw the tears glinting in his eyes, she realised that she had been wrong. That he was simply protecting himself from hurt, from rejection. That somehow he'd found out and rushed back to her. And she finally understood the few words of Steven's letter that she'd read before the ring on the doorbell had her racing down the stairs.

...when I walked in behind her you were lit up...

It had not been an illusion. That split second of mutual recognition when their eyes had met...

It was why he'd gone away. Why Steven had returned the rattle. If he'd shown it to her she'd have written to thank him and Steven didn't want her even that close to his brother.

It had happened again in his apartment. It was as if they had both been locked in that moment for the last three years, holding their breath, waiting for the completion of a connection that could only have one outcome.

And she reached out, took his undamaged hand in hers and placed it on the baby growing inside her, holding it there with her own so that he could feel the life they'd created kicking strongly. See his ring gleaming softly in the light spilling down from the street lamp.

'It's all right, Guy,' she said. 'It's all right. I know.'

And she reached out for him, drew him close, pressed her cheek against his. Kissed him.

His mouth was cold and for one terrible moment she thought she had it all wrong as he pulled away to stare down at her. Then, with a desperate cry that broke the silence, he called out her name and caught her to him, kissing her until she thought she would turn to liquid heat, crushing her to him so that she felt his tears mingle with her own.

'You going to stand out here in the street kissing like kids all night? Letting in the cold?'

He broke away, but his eyes never left hers as he said, 'Hello, Connie. I've missed your cooking.'

'Don't you "Hello, Connie" me. Where you been, eh? Worrying Fran half to death...'

'Were you?' he asked. 'Worried? You didn't fancy being a rich widow?' Maybe he already knew the answer because he didn't wait for it but looked down and said, 'Hello, Toby. Been to a party?'

'Mmm.' He gave Connie the balloon he was holding and offered up his goodie bag. 'I've got cake.'

'Any to spare? I'm starving...'

'Later. It's bath time,' Fran said. 'Can you take care of Toby for me, Connie?'

'I can take care of both of them if you like,' she offered. 'He's going to need help with his arm in plaster. No? You don't want Connie?' And she went inside chuckling to herself. 'Just you make sure you wash behind his ears, Fran.' Then, 'I call Matty and tell her Mr Guy is home.'

'What do you want first? Drink? Food? Bath?'

He circled her with his arm as they walked up the steps into the house. 'I've got everything I want right here, my love. Absolutely everything.'

'My love?'

'I've waited too long to tell you.'

'No. Before would have been too soon. Today is just right.'

'You believe me? I thought I'd have to keep telling you for the next ten years before I managed to convince you.'

'Oh, I'll expect you to go on telling me for longer than that. A whole lifetime more. But right now you should have a bath, and while you're soaking you can tell me exactly what happened to you.'

'Tom Palmer sent me an e-mail,' he said a few minutes later, as he lay back, relaxing in the warmth of the newly decorated bathroom. 'I thought it was about the annulment—I'd been expecting it for months. But it was an article with a photograph of an amazing young woman who was running a business out of her attic. A very pregnant young woman.'

'Oh.'

'I thought… I don't know what I thought… I just knew I had to get home. To be here for you. Help. Do anything. Everything. Except go away. Why didn't you tell me, Fran?'

'How could I tell you when I didn't know how you felt? I wanted you to come home but not out of guilt. I wanted you to come home because nothing would keep you away.'

'You think I didn't want to? Words can't describe how much I yearned to be here with you. I thought you hated me. I'd given you every reason—'

'I know. I know why you did it.' She knelt down beside the bath, took his hand, lifted it to her lips. 'I was beginning to wonder if I'd have to absolve Catherine from the promise I extracted from her…'

'Thank goodness you didn't get at Tom. I've never packed up a camp so fast, but by the time I left it was dark and raining stair-rods. Of course I was driving like a complete maniac and didn't see the road had been washed out until it was too late. Fortunately some villagers found me, took me to the nearest clinic to be patched up, but communication was a bit hit and miss.' Then, 'But I did get the message.'

'Message?'

'What was it? Something along the lines of "...get back here. Right now..." Very forceful.'

'Oh, *that* message.' She grinned for a moment. Then, more seriously, 'I didn't mean to shout at you but you were all over the news as missing, kidnapped, shot... I was so scared. So desperate. I meant to tell you then how much I love you...' Then, when she saw him grinning, 'And, by the way, you're staying home from now on. I don't care how important the project is, someone else can do it.'

A long time later, after he'd had a bath and a shave and they'd tucked Toby up in bed and they were curled up on the sofa, his arm around her, she said, 'Steven knew how you felt, didn't he?' She twisted around to look up at him. 'I found the rattle while I was unpacking your things earlier this evening. And his letter. I never had a chance to read it, but a couple of lines seemed to leap off the page at me...'

'Yes, he knew. When you burst through that door you caught me off-guard. If I'd had any idea what was coming I might have been ready...' Then, looking down at her he smiled, leaned forward to kiss her. 'No. I've been fooling myself. Nothing could have saved me...'

'You are getting better at the compliments.' Then she frowned. 'I think.'

'He had no idea that you were equally felled, if that helps. I didn't know myself.'

'He used it, didn't he? To drive you away.'

'He was afraid that he wouldn't be able to hold on to you. He was so insecure he thought that if I was there, if I wanted you...' He shook his head. 'He was wrong. I wouldn't have done anything to come between you. He didn't have to—'

'What?'

'Make me angry. I already knew I had to stay away. You were having his child. Whatever I felt, in the face of that, was completely irrelevant. And I was right. If he hadn't died, you'd have married him.'

'He loved me, Guy. He was a good father.'

'I'm glad he was happy.'

'And that he had the good sense to leave me to you. In his will. Give you a second chance.'

Guy didn't disillusion her. Instead he said, 'Oh, right. And what would you have done if I'd come home demanding to move into my non-existent attic flat?'

'You don't need a flat, Guy. I, on the other hand, had to cut overheads to the minimum when the bank refused to back me and the top floor is the perfect place. Just big enough for Claire and Jason and me.'

'Don't you need a warehouse? Thousands of people answering the phones and despatching the goods?'

'I outsourced that to a call centre and a warehouse facility. We just do the buying and the marketing.'

'It couldn't have been easy.'

'It wasn't, but then nothing worthwhile ever is.' Then, 'Anyway, forget business and forget the flat. The master suite has been redecorated just for you. I know it's not quite what you had in mind but it's very comfortable—'

'It's perfect, Francesca. But I'm done with our marriage of convenience. Unless you come with it—'

'I thought I already had,' she said, grinning up at him wickedly.

'—until death us do part,' he went on, although his voice wasn't quite so steady, 'I'd rather take my chances with pushing together two desks in the attic.'

'Guy, when I made that vow in front of the registrar and those two sweet ladies who were our witnesses, I meant it. That was why it was so difficult for me when I thought you were simply doing what you saw as your duty.'

'Is that what you thought?' And, taking her hand, he slipped the wedding ring from her finger, tilting it to show her the inscription engraved inside. There was just one word.

Forever.

Fran caught her breath. 'I didn't know,' she began. 'I didn't see…'

'I wanted it written somewhere, even if I was the only person in the world who would ever know.' Then, 'Would you like to do it again? Properly?'

'I'm sorry?'

'In church, with a big dress, a vintage Rolls and a reception in a marquee in the garden with everyone we care about around us.'

'You mean a blessing?' She couldn't keep the smile from breaking out all over her face. 'That is the most beautiful…' For a moment she thought she was going to cry again, but this time from sheer happiness. Then, 'But there's just one condition.' He waited. 'If

I'm going to wear the big occasion dress, I'd like to wait until it's only the dress that's big...'

The Saturday after the baptism of Stephanie Joy Dymoke, her mother and father made eternal vows to love, honour and keep one another in sickness and in health for all their days.

Matty, her wheelchair decorated with white and silver ribbons, held her little god-daughter throughout the service.

Toby performed valiantly as ring-bearer.

Connie wept buckets and told everyone who would listen that Francesca was the kindest, most wonderful woman on earth and Guy kissed her and told her that she was absolutely right.

The marquee was a picture in yellow and white, and after lunch and a great many toasts Guy took Francesca's hand and took the first turn around the dance floor to the applause of family and friends.

'Do you realise that this is the first time we've danced together?' she said.

'We have a whole lifetime of firsts ahead of us, my love. Our first honeymoon—'

'You can only have one proper honeymoon,' she objected.

'True, but once you've got the hang of it you can have endless improper ones.'

She giggled, then said, 'Our first family holiday—'

'By the sea. Rock pools and sandcastles and paddling.'

'Toby will love it. And so will Harry Two.' Then, 'Our first Christmas together. Trimming the tree, buying presents—'

'Toby's first day at school—'

'And before we know it he'll be our first sulky teenager—'

'Producing our first grandchild—'

She laughed. 'Okay, you win. I really don't want to go any further than that.'

He stopped. 'You do know that I love you so much that I can hardly bear it, Francesca Lang?'

She knew, and she'd told him a thousand times, shown him in a thousand ways, how much she loved him. All but one. And now was the time.

'Not Lang,' she said. 'Dymoke. I want the whole world to know that I'm your wife; "...from this day forward..." I am Mrs Guy Dymoke.' And then, just to be sure that everyone had got the message, she put her arms around his neck and kissed him.

WHEN ENEMIES MARRY...

Lindsay Armstrong

CHAPTER ONE

'JUSTIN, this is unbelievable; there's a photographer—oh, sorry, I didn't realise you were with someone.'

Lucinda Waite paused on the threshold of her husband's study, then swept in, continuing, 'But it's only you, Sasha—well, you and someone else. How do you do?' she added politely to the third party in the study. 'I'm Justin's wife Lucinda, but most people call me Lucy. Who are you?' she enquired, extending her hand graciously.

'Robert Lang,' the third party murmured, rising hastily and taking the extended hand. 'How do you do, Mrs Waite?' He was about twenty-three and looked both embarrassed and slightly dazed.

'Not very well, thank you, Mr Lang,' Lucy Waite replied with a grimace. 'My privacy is being invaded—and I can't help feeling you might be responsible for it all.'

Robert Lang blinked beneath a clear blue gaze and made a mental note that registered some surprise. They *were* the colour of deep blue velvety pansies, her eyes, and her skin had the texture of cream rosebuds while her hair, caught back carelessly, was the colour of ripe wheat. Now, now, he cautioned himself, letting his gaze drift over the rest of Lucinda Waite, it can't be all perfection. Short legs possibly, out of proportion with the rest of her, or hippy and pear-shaped, *thick*

5

legs—no, his eyes widened, talk about legs, they were sensational...

'You're staring, Mr Lang,' Sasha Pearson said all but inaudibly and not quite kindly. She was an elegant redhead in her early thirties but whether she was family hadn't been made clear.

But Robert Lang, despite his youth, was not without charm and ingenuity. 'I sure am,' he conceded boyishly. 'In point of fact, I'm quite bowled over. I don't think I've ever seen anyone as lovely as you, Mrs Waite— er—if you'll forgive me for saying so, sir!' He turned deferentially to Justin Waite still sitting behind his desk, not altogether in a further demonstration of his charm but because, to his mind, Justin Waite was not the kind of man one gave offence to and possibly least of all in the matter of his stunningly beautiful, flawless, twenty-year-old-if-she-were-a-day wife.

'You're forgiven, Mr Lang,' Justin Waite said. 'My wife has been having that effect on people since she was in her cradle.' He moved in his chair and stood up, revealing most of the over six foot, lean, muscled length of him that, coupled with rather hard grey eyes and a look of worldliness and experience, had kindled Robert Lang's wariness in the first place. 'My wife has also,' he went on coolly, 'been leading people up the garden path for almost as long.'

Lang's eyes widened and jerked to Lucinda. But, far from any expression of outrage, she merely smiled faintly, and murmured, 'What have I done now, Justin?'

'Invaded your own privacy, my dear, from what I can gather. Did you or did you not write to a certain publication and invite them up here to do a story on the place, and on you?'

'Yes, I did—so that's who you are!' Lucy said to Lang with a glorious smile. 'But you didn't let me know you were coming. I thought you must be one of those maverick journalists who turn up from time to time and make my life a misery.'

'Lucy, that happened once and has never been repeated,' Justin Waite said in the kind of voice that caused Robert Lang some trepidation, although it didn't seem to have any effect on his wife.

'And the reason you didn't know he was coming, Lucy,' Sasha Pearson—where *did* she fit in? Robert wondered—rose and picked up a letter from the desk, 'is because while Justin and I were away you didn't bother to open any mail although you assured me you would.'

'That's right,' Robert Lang said eagerly. 'I did write and suggest today if it would suit you.'

'Oh, dear,' Lucy Waite said regretfully. 'You really should have waited for a reply, Mr Lang, but now I know who you are, we might as well go ahead. I've got nothing else on. By the way, you are indispensable, Sasha, aren't you? Forgive me for ever doubting it! I'll just go and get changed.'

'You'll do no such thing, Lucy.'

'Justin,' Lucy protested. 'Why not?'

Blue eyes stared into hard grey ones and, despite only mild protest registering in Lucy Waite's expression, the atmosphere was suddenly electric and Robert Lang found himself, to his amazement, wondering what went on behind locked doors between Justin Waite and his wife. Did he beat her or did he throw her down on the bed and make punishing love to her...

'Because I say so, Lucy,' Justin Waite said with sudden detachment as he looked away from his wife thereby seeming to cut the electric current between them. 'Go back to your horses, my dear, and I will apologise for this misunderstanding.'

Lucy Waite shrugged. 'Whatever you say, Justin,' she murmured. 'Do forgive me, Mr Lang,' she added. 'I haven't been married very long, you see, so I'm not altogether familiar with the *rules*, I guess, but I—'

'Lucy—'

'Just going, Justin. Bye!' She strolled out with a wave.

'I gather,' Justin Waite said across the dinner table, to his wife, 'that today's events were more shots in the war you promised me the day you married me, Lucy.'

Lucy Waite smoothed down the skirt of the clinging, long-sleeved black dress with a heart-shaped neckline that she'd changed into for dinner and picked up her soup spoon. She'd also tucked a creamy gardenia into the hair that was lying loose and rippling on her shoulders. 'You gather right, Justin.'

'It wasn't much of a shot.'

Lucy sipped her soup then grinned. 'As a matter of fact I thought it quite got you off the bit for a moment, Justin.' She changed her expression to one of severity and mimicked, '"My wife has been leading people up the garden path from the cradle." But yes, it would have been better if it had come off,' she conceded. 'You do so hate publicity, don't you, Justin?'

'I can't believe you really enjoy it,' he commented drily.

Lucy wrinkled her nose. 'It was only a rural paper. I thought it was rather tasteful to choose a rural paper instead of a national daily. And all I'd planned to do was show them the house and some of...*our* treasures, and all your improvements to the property. It would have been quite a scoop for that young man, don't you think? Something about the Waites in a newspaper, even just a rural one. You've probably blighted his career, Justin, and he was rather sweet, really.'

'I haven't blighted his career at all, but he does understand now that my wife is off limits so you might as well forget him, Lucy. And any other young man who takes your fancy.'

Lucy laughed and pushed away her soup. 'You perceive me quaking in my shoes, Justin,' she murmured. 'Still, all may not be lost,' she mused. 'There's got to be at least one person out there now who's thinking that the Waites of Dalkeith and Riverbend have a very strange marriage.'

'On the contrary, there could be at least one person out there who is actually thinking that Lucinda Waite is a spoilt brat and deserves a good lesson.'

'From my experience of young men, Justin, they don't generally have those thoughts about me. It's only your generation—at least, you're the only one of your generation I have to go on, and I have to tell you that if you mean what I think you mean—'

'That you deserve to be put over someone's knee and ceremonially spanked?' he broke in lazily.

'How picturesque.' For the first time a little glint of anger lit Lucy's eyes. 'I have to tell you I should probably get so angry I'd even be capable of taking a potshot at *you*. Don't forget I'm an excellent shot and I would know exactly how to inconvenience you considerably without doing a lot of harm—and make it all look like an accident anyway.'

'That wasn't what I had in mind, Lucy,' he drawled, and reached for the decanter to pour himself some wine.

'How brave you are,' she retorted.

'What I had in mind—were I so minded,' he continued, holding his wine glass up to the light meditatively, 'was a lesson of another kind. Such as—' he put the glass down gently and their eyes locked '—removing your dress from your delectable body, uncovering your breasts and the rest of you and making love to you until you're—shall we say, in a much more amenable frame of mind? I have this theory on women,' he went on, idly inspecting the pulse that had started to beat rather erratically at the base of Lucy's throat. 'That without regular, satisfying sex they become fractious and troublesome, and in your case in particular, dear Lucy, that what you really need is a couple of kids to keep you out of mischief.'

It took Lucy several moments to gather enough composure to be able to speak, moments that were made worse for her because her tall, satanic husband did not relax his leisurely scrutiny of her in the slightest and then had the gall to pour her a glass of wine and push it towards her with a faintly amused twist of his lips.

In the end, as she sipped the golden liquid, it was he who spoke first. 'You don't agree?'

'I think,' Lucy said carefully, 'that it's a pity you didn't live in a different era, a bygone era for example, when women were treated like chattels and it was accepted practice to generalise about them as if they were so many...sheep. As if they had no minds, only instincts.'

'Then tell me this—you've ordered the course of this marriage so far; how happy has it made you?'

'You've gone along with it,' she said tautly.

'Were you secretly hoping I'd do something as un-couth and as—*exciting* as taking you against your will after you made your dramatic declaration on our wed-ding-night?'

Lucy gasped. 'Only minutes ago *you* were talking about…you *were* talking about…'

'Something quite different, Lucy,' he said.

'I can't see it, personally.' She looked at him defi-antly.

'I was talking about finding out what your will really is in this matter,' he said and his teeth glinted in a sud-den grin. 'Don't look so worried, I'm not going to do it. Not tonight, at least. But I do make the point that to a certain extent you've given me yourself as a hostage in this ridiculous war, Lucy, and perhaps you should bear it in mind the next time you decide to fire any shots. Would you care to dish up the casserole or shall I?'

Lucy put down her napkin and stood up. The silver casserole was on a hot plate on the sideboard. 'I will,' she said, but didn't move immediately. 'Justin, you gave me very little choice about marrying you. You made it very plain that I could lose everything I possessed, not the least my home, where I've lived all my *life*, if I didn't marry you. You put it to me that we could fight each other for years over Dalkeith and that you *would* fight for it although it was more or less all I had, while you'd inherited Riverbend and made yourself a huge for-tune on top of it—'

'That's debatable—'

'Don't interrupt,' she commanded. 'But since you have, it was never my fault that our fathers were foolish enough to own this place in partnership and then even more foolish to fall out with each other and leave us to inherit this mess—'

'Lucy, the cold, hard facts of the matter are a little different. Because Riverbend and Dalkeith are adjoining properties and because our fathers were friends, when your father got into financial difficulties, *my* father offered to inject some money into the place and accept a partnership in return—a *silent* partnership,' he said significantly. And waited while Lucy tried to look unaffected but failed. He went on, 'What broke up the friendship, despite this concession to your father's ego, despite trying to help save Dalkeith from going under the hammer, was that your father persisted in believing that Australia could ride on the back of its sheep forever and fought every suggestion my father ever made for diversification away from growing wool.'

Lucy bit her lip. 'I didn't know all that,' she said bravely, however.

'No, but that wasn't my fault,' he retorted impatiently. 'It was his fault that you didn't know, his fault that you were allowed to queen it over all and sundry as Lucinda Wainright of Dalkeith and never suspect you'd have to share this place with anyone, let alone with *me*, whom your father had given you the impression you shouldn't want to know any more anyway. Although—' his eyes glinted '—there were times when you didn't mind knowing me, Lucy.'

She coloured faintly but said with spirit, 'If you're referring to the days when I was barely out of rompers and didn't know better than to follow you around whenever you were here—'

'As a matter of fact I'm not referring to those days,' he said softly—and said no more.

She blushed properly this time, which made her angrier. 'If this is your revenge for—' She stopped abruptly.

'It isn't,' he answered equably. 'Not against you, anyway.'

'Then tell me this, Justin: what *was* your motivation for coming to see me only a fortnight after my father's funeral and telling me that the only sensible course for us to pursue was to get married?'

'Ah, well, my better nature did slip a bit then, I have to confess. You were so proud. I could also visualise the complications that might arise if someone else married you or got you pregnant before we'd sorted it all out. You have to agree, Lucy, that you left a trail of broken hearts around the district—it was really only a matter of time before you—er—fell. But of course, there was also the way you'd grown up, five foot six of sheer perfection, a bobby-dazzler in fact,' he said with a shrug. 'It occurred to me that not only would I not mind being married to you, but, since we had such a lot in common—' his eyes drifted around the beautiful room '—it would simplify matters considerably.'

'I'm only surprised you don't have another theory,' Lucy said through her teeth. 'That wives can be schooled and trained like horses. Or is that still to come?'

'Provided you get them young enough, it could be a possibility, even though you were so spoilt and indulged by your father,' he said indifferently and shrugged again. 'Lucy, how much longer do we have to wait to eat? We've had all this out before. And you were the one,' he said with sudden impatience, 'who accepted my proposal. Which to my mind, if we're really discussing moral superiority, puts us on a par. Although you mentioned earlier that I threatened you with something like poverty. In fact I offered to buy you out, and that would have been a long way from poverty, my dear.'

'But I didn't want to be bought out. I decided to fight in the only way I could think of for my birthright, Justin. My great-grandparents happen to be buried here, and my mother and now my father, I love every acre of Dalkeith and sometimes, when you love something enough, you're prepared to go to extraordinary lengths to preserve it. Besides which, it occurred to *me*,' she said softly, 'that you'd find it not considerably simpler but much more difficult to dispossess a wife, Justin.'

'A wife, yes, Lucy,' he said. 'But there are certain things you have to do to become a true wife.'

'It's only your word against mine—ah,' she said to herself. 'So that's why you haven't forced me to go to bed with you! You're keeping your options open, aren't you, Justin? But while an annulment on the grounds of non-consummation may entitle me to less of your property, it is only your word against mine.'

He lay back in his chair and watched her. 'Would you lie about something like that, Lucy?'

'Where you're concerned, I might. Don't forget, I have to put up with your mistress parading herself around my home—who knows what flights of fancy the mere fact of that might prompt in me—where is Sasha, by the way?'

'She's gone back to Riverbend and she's not my mistress.'

'Then she's dying to be your mistress.'

'She happens to be an employee, my private assistant in charge of the stud at Riverbend, as you very well know, and she's extremely good at her job, that's all;

what makes you think she has...the ambition you're accusing her of?'

Lucy turned to the sideboard at last. 'You'd probably have to be a woman to understand that. But I would have thought even you could see the sort of censorious way she treats me.'

'There are times when you lay yourself open to that, Lucy.'

Lucy heaped a fragrant portion of lemon chicken on to a plate, and some steaming, fluffy rice, and laughed. 'Perhaps I do. But she does so obviously hold this conviction that you were mad to marry me whatever else she is or isn't, you see. On the subject of mistresses, by the way...' She turned and carried his plate over to him, not unaware that his gaze was following every move she made, then went back for her own. 'At thirty, you must have had some, probably dozens. You're successful, you're good-looking when you're not being critical and superior—did none of them prompt you to think of marriage for all the right reasons?' She sat down and helped herself to salad then courteously handed the crystal bowl to him. 'Take Joanna Madden, for example,' she added pointedly. 'I'm sure a lot of people thought that was a *fait accompli*.'

'So did I—once upon a time,' she said musingly after a while when she thought he wasn't going to answer.

'What happened? Did she have nothing as enticing as the other half of Dalkeith to offer you?'

'She—had her reasons.'

'You don't seem particularly perturbed,' Lucy said witheringly.

He smiled fleetingly. 'One lives and learns, I guess. Lucy,' he said after a pause, 'considering our feelings on the subject of Dalkeith—and while I acknowledge mine aren't as unaltruistic and loving as yours, none the less it is very important to me—considering that we have its best interests at heart in other words, would it be so hard to see whether we couldn't make a go of this marriage?'

She considered for a long time then she said rather bleakly, 'That's like asking a nation to love their invaders. I don't think it's possible. I mean, for another thing, there's the problem that you don't respect me—you surely couldn't if you really believe that regular sex is all I need to keep me happy—'

'There's a difference between regular sex and satisfying sex.'

She shot him an oblique look. 'Your ego is really monumental, Justin, even for a man. All *right*, but I'm still just another giddy girl to you, aren't I?'

'I suppose it wasn't a help possessing such stunning looks on top of a father who spoilt you rotten, but you certainly don't go out of your way to dispel that image, Lucy.'

She looked across at him and there was something curiously haughty in her eyes. 'Perhaps not, but that might not be all there is to me. For example, I do know quite a lot about Dalkeith and how it runs—if young men can sow their wild oats, why can't girls have a few giddy salad days, anyway?'

He put his knife and fork together and stared at them for a long moment, before raising his eyes to hers. And then there was something curiously enigmatic in them as he said, 'I've told you, what's history can remain so. Your legion of lovers and my—multitude of mistresses. Unfortunately, you've got into the habit of sending out unmistakable signals—you're probably right about young Mr Lang and the kind of thoughts he's having about you now.'

Lucy grimaced.

'Not picking up the bait, Mrs Waite?' Justin said softly but with an undercurrent of mockery.

She tightened her mouth and subjected him to a deep blue look of considerable scorn.

He only laughed quietly. 'Just one more thing, Lucy. In case you haven't already got the message, if celibacy is becoming irksome then I am your only alternative. Remember that.'

She burst into speech. 'What about you? You don't really expect me to believe *I* am *your* only alternative.'

'Well, you are, so bear that in mind as well, my dear. But I'm afraid celibacy, inside marriage, certainly won't suit me forever.' He stood up. 'And you know, Lucy, while I give your devotion to Dalkeith full credit, there's no way a twenty-year-old girl could run it. There was no way you could have gone on without the kind of cash it needs again—and Dalkeith has become a rather expensive pastime for us Waites.' He stopped and watched her as she took the point and looked away uncertainly. Then he went on quite gently, 'But *this* way, here you are, mistress of it, and if you've got as much sense as I think you have in your more rational moments you must know it's in good hands. By the way, I'm taking a couple of weeks off and we're giving a house party this weekend. You might need to get in extra help. Goodnight.'

A couple of hours later, Lucy walked into her bedroom and closed the door.

As part of the austerity measures her father had been

forced to introduce before his death, there was no live-in house help on Dalkeith. In fact Lucy had cut short her bachelor of arts degree to come home and look after her father six months ago and after her marriage, a curious marriage to say the least, she'd decided to keep it that way. It gave her something to do, and she'd discovered that, in lieu of her deep interest in Dalkeith being taken seriously, her interest despite herself in the crops Justin planned to grow and the sheep it still ran across its thousand acres of outback western New South Wales, that only left her horses for her to occupy herself with. And two mares in foal and two gelding hacks, devoted to them though she was, didn't take up a lot of time.

She did have a cleaning lady who came in daily and a farmhand to tend the fireplaces, but it had come as some surprise to her, in those last days of her father's decline, to find that she enjoyed cooking and gardening.

She sighed suddenly, pushed herself away from the door and picked up the silver-framed photo of her father from her dressing-table. No matter the things that she'd come to suspect even before his death, such as his being eminently suited to being a gentleman of leisure but *not* a gentleman farmer, and what she'd discovered about him after his death—that he'd tried to rescue Dalkeith from the brink again by gambling on horses, despite it all, she'd loved him and, only three months later, still missed him unbearably at times. If nothing else he'd certainly loved her unstintingly, and he'd taught her all the things he held dear to his heart, among them riding, shooting and fishing. He'd also taught her about art and music, he'd taken her to faraway exotic places, he'd

helped her to fix her taste in clothes and all manner of
things and yes, spoilt her wildly. But he'd never foisted
a stepmother on her after her own mother, whom she
couldn't remember, had died. In fact, she suspected he'd
never got over her mother's death, and certain things in
life hadn't had much meaning for him after it. Including
Dalkeith.

He'd also sent her to a very expensive convent school
where the Mother Superior had been strong-minded
enough to persevere with the motherless, precocious,
mischievous and often downright naughty Lucy
Wainright despite the battles royal they'd had since Lucy
had been placed in her care at nine and a half, and she'd
continued there until she was seventeen and a half.
They'd even parted on terms of mutual respect and by
that time quite some mutual affection, although each was
loath to admit it.

But had her father, Lucy wondered, as she stared
down at his handsome likeness, never really realised
how much Dalkeith, above all else, had meant to *her*?
That even in her giddy salad days when she'd been
queening it over all and sundry—her eyes flashed
briefly—it, even more than her father, had been the rock
to come back to. Did she have more of her Scottish
great-grandparents in her than he'd ever had? A spiritual
affinity with the land that was like a physical tie? Had
he not known that, without him and without Dalkeith,
brave, bright Lucinda Wainright, darling of society, was
in fact lonely and more than a little frightened? But he
had known how much she loved Dalkeith; wasn't that
why he'd never told her he'd lost half of it to Justin's
father?

She pushed off her shoes and curled up in the pink

velvet armchair beside the fireplace, and stared into the flickering flames with a faraway look in her eyes.

It was ironic but true that she had hero-worshipped Justin Waite as a child. It was also true that Justin had, without her quite understanding it, achieved the status of a hallmark in her mind during her adolescent years. A hallmark that she had involuntarily found herself measuring other boys, then men up against, and finding most of them wanting. This had also led her, once she'd left school and on the few social occasions that they had met, to treat him with cool hauteur, yet to experience an undoubted desire to be *noticed*.

'And he noticed,' she murmured a little bitterly, her cheeks feeling warm again. 'Although the only sign he ever gave of it was that hateful little glint of amusement in his eyes—I really do hate him now!'

She sat up breathing quickly but also feeling a curious mixture of confusion and guilt. Why hadn't she pressed her father for details about his rift with the Waites, despite his extreme reluctance to say more on the subject? Well, I did try, she admitted. And of course I know now that he couldn't bring himself to tell me what was going on—the fact that Riverbend did diversify and go into breeding racehorses with spectacular success must have been an awful blow to his pride, but why couldn't I have realised it at the time? And then what he did say, about us no longer being good enough for the Waites, set my back right up. With the result, she conceded gloomily, sinking back in the chair, that I made myself ridiculous by treating Justin the way I did. But did I really offend him enough for him to take this kind of revenge? To make me marry him although he didn't love me and so he can get all of Dalkeith? she asked herself miserably.

And answered herself a little tartly—apart from amusing him, I doubt it. I mean, I never *saw* him without some beautiful woman on his arm or doing something spectacular like playing polo or crewing on some twelve-metre yacht, and of course he then proceeded to make his own fortune.

She brooded darkly for a moment on how Justin had taken a run-down saddlery business and built it into a nationwide success story—another one—and so not only did Riverbend Stud produce top-flight progeny, but Riverbend Saddlery produced saddles of the finest quality, with an international reputation and all sorts of horse products, as well as clothing—riding boots et cetera. Yes, Justin was clever and not only with horses—and there was a ten-year age gap between them, damn it!

She got up and paced about angrily. 'So what?' she murmured to herself, and picked up her silver-backed hairbrush and turned it over and over in her hands. Then she stopped and looked down at it and fingered the ornate 'W' engraved into the handle, and drew herself upright and stared at her reflection with cold eyes. 'Just remember what he said when he proposed. He said, ''We won't even have to change the monograms, will we? Surely that demonstrates what a *practical* arrangement it would be.'''

But she shivered suddenly because, in a moment of rage and panic, she *had* accepted. And then, in a moment of further panic on her wedding-night had made her 'dramatic declaration'. That she'd never willingly sleep with him. Had she in fact been seriously unbalanced by grief and everything else?

CHAPTER TWO

'I NEED you. Justin—'

'Well, well—' Justin Waite put out a lazy hand and grasped his wife's wrist '—did my little lecture set you thinking, dear Lucy?'

Lucy closed her eyes, attempted to free herself to no avail and ground her teeth. 'I need to *talk* to you. About this party.'

It was a bright, chilly morning but Justin had apparently been up well ahead of her, which was how she'd encountered him coming in through the kitchen door as she was on the way out. Normally she'd have kept on going.

'Ah.' He released her wrist. 'Then talk away while I start my breakfast.'

'What have you been doing?' she said involuntarily as she followed him reluctantly back into the kitchen where his breakfast was keeping warm on the range. He had on jeans, boots and a yellow sweater, his thick dark hair was ruffled and the cold morning air seemed to have agreed with him. In other words he looked fit, tough and capable, alert and slightly mocking, and more than a match for her. But when did he look any different these days? she wondered bitterly.

'I've been out and about,' he said idly, and carried the plate of sausages, scrambled eggs and toast to the kitchen table. There was a pot of coffee bubbling gently on the stove.

22

Lucy went over to it and poured two mugs which she carried to the kitchen table and sat down opposite him. 'You can tell me, you know. Not only is the place still half mine but I'm *interested*,' she said with extreme frustration before she could stop herself. 'Wouldn't I under normal circumstances have some sort of voting power or some *say* in what you do?'

'I've only been inspecting fences in the twelve-mile paddock, Lucy,' he said mildly. 'I made no momentous decisions other than that they need repairing.'

Lucy drew a breath and thought how much she'd have enjoyed a gallop down to the twelve-mile before breakfast instead of the lonely, aimless ride she'd been about to take. 'What about the boundary rider's hut?' she asked tonelessly. 'The last time I saw it it was a bit ramshackle. Grandad always liked to keep it provisioned and weatherproof because the twelve-mile can flood, but it's on the only high ground, so if you did get marooned out there—'

'That too. They're starting on it today.'

She lowered her lashes instead of glaring at him. 'Well,' she said even more tonelessly, 'tell me about the house party. You haven't given me much notice.'

Justin spread marmalade on his toast. 'I can get someone in to do it all if you like. I have mentioned that there's no need for you to do so much of your own work, Lucy.' He put the lid on the marmalade with some impatience.

'And I've told you, I'd go round the bend that way, Justin, not to mention feeling as if I was on the receiving end of your patronage.'

He smiled. 'I can assure you it's not patronage to provide one's wife with household help.'

'But then we've agreed I'm not much of a wife. Look, I can do it. I can get Mrs Milton and her sister to come up—as I've done before on Dalkeith.'

'Then do it,' he said curtly. 'What do you want to know?'

'When they're arriving, when they're leaving, who they are and just what kind of a weekend you have in mind!'

'Why, the kind of weekend Dalkeith is famous for, Lucy,' he said blandly. 'I'm sure I don't have to tell you. There'll be four guests and Sasha.'

She stared at him then forced herself to relax. 'Well, if they come on Friday afternoon, we'll have an informal dinner, a buffet and a simple evening—music, cards and so on. Saturday, a picnic at the creek, some sightseeing around the place, some target shooting or archery, a little gentle croquet for the ladies, then a formal dinner to which I could invite some locals.' She considered. 'Yes, I could invite the Simpsons, and Miles Graham for Sasha! That should even things up.' Her eyes glinted. 'Then on Sunday morning a late breakfast, and they can do what they like until they leave after lunch.'

'And you and Mrs Milton and her sister can cope with all that?' he queried.

Lucy shrugged. 'They've got it down to a fine art. Mrs Milton does the cooking, although a lot of it is prepared beforehand, and her sister makes the beds, tidies up, waits on table et cetera. It's all in the preparation, Justin. So long as you feed people really well, the rest seems to take care of itself.'

'It's Tuesday today, Lucy,' he warned.

'That gives me three full days, Justin,' she said wearily. 'Besides, I think I need a challenge,' she murmured, and propped her chin on her hands.

He regarded her steadily then said quietly, 'You're making things awfully hard for yourself, Lucy.'

'No, you're making them hard for me, Justin.'

'I hesitate to labour this point, but if it weren't for me you wouldn't be here.'

'Perhaps. But I might have felt I'd gone down in a fair fight—who knows?'

'How are you going to handle us in front of these people?'

She blinked, then grinned. 'I hadn't thought of that—yet.' She sat up suddenly and tossed the thick plait she'd braided her hair into over her shoulder. 'Do you mean we'll have to put on a loving show?'

'It's not unexpected in newly-weds,' he observed.

'Oh.'

'And I don't expect I'd take kindly to being made a fool of,' he added without the least emphasis, yet a curious underlay to his words that made her nerves prickle oddly. Perhaps it was something in his eyes as well, as they rested on her.

She opened her mouth, closed it then said with dignity, 'It's not a pre-requisite to...I mean, some of the people I've known who really were in love didn't...sort of flaunt it.'

'Perhaps not,' he agreed. 'What I'm trying to get at is, are you prepared to be sensible or are you going to cook up something like yesterday to advertise to the world that we're not in love?'

Lucy pursed her lips. 'I might just be normal and let them work it out for themselves,' she said thoughtfully.

'I don't think you can expect much more from me, Justin.'

'When you say normal, do you mean you'll include me in your *come hither*—?'

'I *don't* do that,' she cut in sharply.

'Perhaps you don't realise you're doing it. Perhaps it's second nature now. Didn't you notice Robert Lang going weak at the knees when you smiled at him yesterday?' He lifted a dark eyebrow at her.

Lucy set her teeth.

He waited then gathered his plate and took it over to the sink.

'I can't help how I smile!' she said in a goaded sort of voice at last.

'No, but with a bit of age and maturity you should be able to use it with discretion. Otherwise you could find yourself in a situation you might find hard to handle one day.'

Lucy tossed her head and stood up, with not the slightest idea, as he came back to the table, what he had in mind. 'Like this,' he said softly, standing right in front of her so she had to tilt her head back, and taking her in his arms as her eyes widened. 'In the position of being kissed by your sworn enemy.'

Her lips parted. 'Justin...'

But he ignored both the look in her eyes and the incredulity in her voice, and held her closer so she couldn't help being aware not only of the feel of his hard, muscled body against her own but of the faint tang of aftershave and sheer maleness about him—and finding it curiously heady, like some primitive assault on her senses. This both stunned her slightly and made her less able to cope with what followed. A searching, not particularly deep kiss to which she didn't respond particularly yet which didn't exactly repel. It was really strange, she reflected afterwards. It was as if her body had gone languid and her mind was suspended above her, recording and storing the event, monitoring her own reactions but, above all, searching for his.

And when he lifted his head at last she blinked once then stared into his eyes, with her heart in her mouth suddenly at what she might see.

What she did see was the way he narrowed his eyes immediately, and then the little laughter-lines beside them creased. 'Well, Lucy,' he said wryly, 'you have got that down to a fine art, haven't you?'

She licked her lips and said huskily, 'What do you mean?'

His hands slid down her back to her waist and he lifted her off her feet and moved her away, and steadied her but didn't take his hands away. 'The art of kissing and giving nothing away at the same time.'

A tinge of pink came to her cheeks and a pulse beat at the base of her throat, a pulse of anger as it happened. 'If that's not exactly what you did, I'll eat my hat,' she retorted, and removed herself from his grasp but sat down almost immediately.

'Then why are you so cross?' He leant against the corner of the table and folded his arms.

'Perhaps I'm tired of having it continually pointed out to me what a *femme fatale* I am.' She picked up the lid of the sugar bowl and replaced it not gently. 'And if that was a warning of the deluded sort you were issuing yesterday—'

'It was a warning to behave yourself this weekend, Lucy.'

'*Listen*, Justin!' Her eyes were a deeper, decidedly stormy blue now.

'No, you listen to me, Lucy.' He unfolded his arms and pinned one of her wrists to the table as her hand wandered towards the sugar bowl again, and he lifted her chin in his other one, also not gently as she resisted stubbornly. And his eyes were a cold, hard grey as he said, 'You can fight me all you like in private, but not in public, because if you do, I'll retaliate, believe me, in a way you wouldn't like at all, and in a way that will make your little war look like child's play. Do we understand each other?'

It was Mrs Milton who broke into Lucy's reverie. Mrs Milton came in daily and Lucy was still sitting at the kitchen table where Justin had left her, staring into space, as she arrived.

'Morning, Miss Lucy,' she said brightly and placed a parcel on the table. 'There's those sheets that needed mending.'

'Oh!' Lucy jumped. 'Oh, thank you, Mrs Milton—sorry, I was miles away. How are you?'

'Fine, love. Miles away where?' Mrs Milton poured herself a cup of coffee.

Lucy grimaced. 'Are you doing anything this weekend? You and your sister?'

'No. Got a party on?'

'Yes, and I want it to be—something special, Mrs Milton. Hang on, I'll get a pen and paper.'

Whether by design or not, Justin stayed out of her way over those next three busy days, although they did meet for breakfast on the Wednesday morning.

'You have a dirty mark on your chin, Lucy,' her husband said after a more formal greeting had got him a cool look and a barely audible murmur in reply.

This time she responded with a raised eyebrow and a shrug, causing him to narrow his eyes and appear to drop the subject. But as they passed each other later, he stopped her with a hand on her shoulder and put his forefinger on the 'mark' on her chin.

'Did I do that?'

She merely nodded.

He took his finger away and inspected the faint blue bruise. He also let his gaze wander over her mouth, innocent of any lipstick yet rose-pink and finely chiselled, the smooth lucent skin of her cheeks, the deep pansy blue of her eyes with their sweeping lashes, darker than her hair, and the escaping tendrils of wheat gold curling on her forehead. 'My apologies,' he said. 'I didn't know you bruised so easily.'

'I don't bruise so easily. Perhaps you don't know your own strength. Or perhaps you do.'

'What I haven't known,' he said with a twist of his lips, 'is anyone quite as stubborn as you. I suppose you've now added the fact that I'm a callous brute to your list of my sins.'

'Some of your threats left me in no doubt of it at all even before this,' she murmured coldly. 'May I go now? I have a lot to do.'

'How's it going?'

'It's all under control.'

'Do you need any assistance? From me,' he said gravely.

Her look spoke volumes. 'All you have to do is be here, Justin.'

'I still haven't told you who's coming—apart from Sasha.'

Lucy shrugged. 'I rang Sasha myself and got it all from her. She was a mine of information, in fact. Two couples, although one unmarried couple who will nevertheless share a bedroom—'

'Unlike some *married* couples I know. I wonder if it's a new trend? Go on,' he said politely.

'Yes, well,' Lucy said evenly, 'Sasha also told me that although it's not strictly a business weekend, they will be inspecting some yearlings at Riverbend on their way here and might be interested in buying them at the upcoming yearling sales in Sydney—she said that very significantly, Justin. In other words—don't rock the boat, Lucy, *if* you can help it! And, she also gave me some helpful suggestions which—'

'You will go out of your way to ignore,' Justin said amusedly.

'Indeed I will.' Lucy's eyes flashed briefly, recalling Sasha's helpful advice which had included the maxim that keeping things simple might be a good idea. 'How you put up with her I've no idea!'

'I've told you, she's very good at her job.'

'She's certainly got a superiority complex. Is that why you two get along so well?' she asked innocently, and went on impatiently, 'Besides, being good at your job doesn't mean you have to be treated as a friend, necessarily.'

'Well Sasha is both actually, Lucy. And since I moved to Dalkeith, so that you might remain in your ancestral home,' he said and held her eyes in a suddenly cool look, 'she is more up to date on matters relating to the stud and this crop of yearlings than I am. So she will be here in what you might call an unofficial business capacity.' He paused then added with that same cool look. 'Don't upset Sasha, Lucy. She may rub you up the wrong way but she has a brain like a computer when it comes to horses, and extremely good judgement.'

'As a matter of fact I believe you, Justin. I've even thought she has a certain horsey look about her—nothing less than a chestnut thoroughbred with wonderful lines, of course!' she finished with a grin. 'As for upsetting her,' she added, 'I wish you would tell me how to, because it doesn't seem possible.'

They stared at each other—rather, Lucy found it suddenly impossible to evade his gaze or to understand why it made her suddenly feel a bit small, but it did and she said at last, 'Oh, all right! I *won't* upset Sasha—so far as it's humanly possible for me not to!'

'Good.' He said nothing more but moved out of her way.

'Am I being dismissed now?' she demanded.

'Why not?'

'There are times, Justin Waite, when you irritate the life out of me,' she said precisely. 'And what with you and Sasha telling me what I should do and what I shouldn't do, it will be a miracle if this weekend doesn't turn out to be a disaster—' She broke off and made a disgusted sound.

'And there are times, Lucy, when it's impossible to tell you anything—I wouldn't be too happy about this weekend turning into a disaster, so if you have any doubts tell me now.'

'*I* don't—'

'I suppose the proof of that will be in the pudding,' he said drily, and studied her. 'By the way,' he said, flicking his gaze over her denim overalls, and the two pigtails she wore her hair in, 'Would you mind not wearing your hair like that over the weekend?'

She blinked. 'Why not—as if I would, anyway.'

'I could be accused of cradle-snatching, that's all. Off you go.'

'Perhaps you are!'

'Now, Lucy, we both know I'm not. Don't we?' His grey gaze bored into hers until she reddened and turned away abruptly and angrily but without words.

Fortunately for her seething state of mind, there was enough to be done to calm her and force her to concentrate—and not only that. There was the knowledge that both Justin and Sasha had doubts about her capabilities as a hostess. In her less angry moments she recognised that it was a useful spur, in her more angry moments she told herself she would certainly show them a thing or two. And by Friday midday the fruits of her labour and Mrs Milton's were very evident. The house was polished and shining and filled with flowers. The guest bedrooms were impeccable, with not a wrinkle in their bedspreads, and the cold room was filled with a selection of pies and pastries, cold meats, quiches, fruits and vegetables and three splendid, plump ducks hung there, ready to be roasted for Saturday night's dinner.

It was also not long past midday when disaster struck, in the form of a distraught phone call from Mrs Milton who'd gone to pick up her sister to take up residence in the staff quarters for the weekend.

'...Your mother? Oh, I'm so sorry, Mrs Milton,' Lucy

said into the phone and a moment later, 'Yes, of course if it's that serious, I do understand. Um...you and your sister must be worried sick and will want to be with her... Look, if there's anything I can do, please—'

'You've got enough on your plate as it is, pet,' Mrs Milton said down the line in tones quite unlike her normal cheerful ones. 'I've been racking my *brains* and all I can come up with is my niece, Shirley. How would it be if I send her up, Miss Lucy? She's a good cook, that I can guarantee, and doesn't mind what she turns her hand to. There's only one problem and that's—'

'Oh, Mrs Milton, please do,' Lucy said into the phone. 'I'd be so grateful, and between us we've done most of it, haven't we? What's the problem?'

'Well she'd have to bring her son, Adrian—'

'That's no problem!'

'Mmm, I haven't told you about Adrian, have I? Look, just...if you're *firm* with him he's fine, but his father ran off when he was two, so... And Shirley worships the ground he walks on.'

'Don't worry, I'll tie him up if...no, of course not, Mrs Milton, I wouldn't dream of it, but I'm sure we'll be able to cope with him between us. Now you just worry about your mother and give her my love—I'll be thinking of you all.'

She put the phone down and took several deep breaths, then remembered she'd forgotten to ask how old Shirley's Adrian was.

He was ten, with red hair, prominent blue eyes and buck teeth. He walked with a swagger and didn't reply when spoken to. His mother had faded blonde agitated-looking hair but otherwise was clean, neat and presentable and obviously anxious to do her very best.

'Well, Shirley,' Lucy said with a dazzling smile, half an hour before the guests were due to fly in, 'I guess the important thing is not to panic. Everything in the buffet is either cold or only needs heating up so tonight will be quite simple, and I'll nip in later to give you a hand.' And she took Shirley step by step through the evening's requirements. Then she showed them to their room and showed Adrian the television and even fetched some of her old books and games for him.

'He's not much of a reader,' his mother said with an apologetic smile, 'but it's lovely of you to bother, Miss Lucy. Now, Adrian, you will be a good boy, won't you?'

At five-thirty, the long, lovely veranda room played host to the glow of lamplight, the chink of glasses and some exuberant conversation. And despite the fact that part of her mind was elsewhere, Lucy was in the thick of it.

She wore slim scarlet trousers, matching flat shoes and a cream pullover with a wonderful red, green and cream scarf worn shawlwise. Her hair was loose and she was faintly pink from some of the extravagant compliments she'd received—most on the subject of new brides and early wedded bliss. Their guests were of course all older than she was, the two women in the same mould as Sasha, elegant late twenties or early thirties, experienced and articulate and both with careers of their own. But apart from that aspect of it, it was a milieu she was very familiar with and one her father had taught her to hold her own in some years ago. She'd been hostessing his parties since she was about eighteen, after all. And if she had fewer resources to hand than she'd ever had before, plus one Dennis the Menace on hand, she was damned if anyone was going to know it. Least of all Justin, although she'd caught him looking at her once or twice with something oddly alert in his eyes. But he's not a mind-reader, she reassured herself, and there's no earthly reason for him to go into the kitchen tonight, anyway. The longer I can keep him in the dark and still cope, the better, she reasoned—somewhat obscurely, she realised briefly, but didn't have the time to elaborate.

All the same, at six-thirty, when she suggested to everyone that they might like to freshen up although not to worry about changing, she breathed a sigh of relief when they all took themselves to their bedrooms and she repaired to the kitchen as unobtrusively as she could. To find Shirley standing in the middle of the room looking wild-eyed and tearful.

'What's wrong?' she demanded.

'He's gone!'

'Who?'

'Adrian! He could be anywhere out there! He's not a country boy, Miss Lucy; we're just spending a holiday with Auntie Vera!'

'The little...um, calm down, Shirley. I'll find him. You just keep on with the buffet. We've got an hour.'

It took her half an hour to locate Adrian in the loft above the garage. And the mild lecture she gave him brought no visible reaction from him even when she told him he'd frightened the life out of his mother. 'Now just stay put,' she admonished as she marched him back to his room. 'Tomorrow you can go out and see the horses, I'll organise a ride on a tractor for you, whatever you like—and your dinner's coming in a moment.'

'Are you all right, Lucy?'

'Fine, Justin,' she said brightly, finding him alone in the lounge. He'd added a sage-green sweater to his informal gear and his hair was brushed and tidy, his grey eyes watchful. 'No one down yet?'

'No. Have you been running somewhere?'

She laughed. 'No. Why?'

'You look a little—harassed. Are Mrs Milton and her sister coping all right?'

'Everything's fine. If you could just have some confidence in me, it would be a big help.'

'Very well, Lucy. Ah, here are the first of our guests.'

The buffet went off smoothly and with plenty of compliments and afterwards for a while they played music and all chatted together, and then the men tended to group together at one end of the room, leaving the women at the other and Sasha looking for once in her life as if she didn't quite know which group to join.

Lucy seized the opportunity and murmured in her ear that she'd be grateful if she could deputise for her for a moment, while she checked that all was well behind the scenes. Sasha looked gratified, as much, probably, Lucy reflected, that 'behind the scenes' should need checking. But she did as she was asked.

Behind the scenes, there was another story. The dining-room was cleared, the kitchen was tidy and a tea tray was set out but there was no sign of Shirley. What she was doing in fact, was swabbing out the staff bathroom and passage leading to it because Adrian had allowed the bath to overflow. He'd got so wrapped up in the television programme he'd been watching, his mother explained, he'd forgotten.

Lucy closed her eyes and counted to ten. And, on opening them, noticed Adrian watching her interestedly. Why, he's testing me out, she thought, the little wretch.

'Isn't it time he was in bed?' she said as mildly as she could.

By the time she got back she was feeling decidedly limp—it had taken the two of them a good twenty minutes of vigorous mopping to dam the flood, her feet were damp inside her shoes and she had trickles of sweat running down her back, but no one appeared to notice and the party had come together again and was dancing to the CD player.

'Oh damn,' she muttered to herself.

But two hours later her ordeal was ended, or so she thought. The party broke up at last and everyone went up to bed appearing happy and contented with their stay on Dalkeith so far.

'Let's hope I can keep it that way,' she murmured to herself as she tidied up. She'd sent Shirley to bed, reasoning that it might keep Adrian out of more mischief as well as having her bright and fresh for the next day. But when it was all done she stood in the middle of the dining-room, thinking about the three other women in the house, excluding poor Shirley.

Thinking about them in a context that surprised her a little. In other words, how much more appropriate any one of them would be as a consort for Justin than she was. How, for example, *they* would react to being told that without regular, satisfying sex they could become— what had he said—fractious and troublesome?

Well, she mused, she couldn't imagine him saying something like that in the first place. To them. So how would communication on the subject take place with someone older and wiser? A more sophisticated play on words? A simple expression of need—with Sasha he'd probably only have to crook his finger, she thought somewhat maliciously, then sighed.

But a moment later she discovered herself feeling a sense of righteous indignation—talk about her *come hither* smiles! Had he not noticed that despite two of their female guests being partnered there had been throughout the evening a discreet summing up of Justin taking place, an awareness—yes, very subtle, but *there*. Of course it was always there with Sasha and he must be blind not to notice it. Why didn't he? But not only that, her thoughts ranged on, a subtle summing up of herself had been taking place all evening, in the direct context of her suitability for Justin.

She stood in the middle of the dining-room deep in thought, wondering if it was all part of the games people with a bit of age and maturity played, wondering if he played it himself, or wondering finally if he just had this devastating effect on women and had got so used to it that he didn't notice it any more!

'*Lucy.*'

'Oh!' She turned with a start to find the object of her deep, dark musings regarding her with some amusement. 'You—I didn't hear you,' she said lamely.

'I gathered that. You seemed to be a hundred miles away.'

'Not really,' she replied ruefully. 'Well, that's all done. I think I'll go to bed now—goodnight.'

'I'm coming up myself.' He strolled beside her to the foot of the staircase. 'It was a very successful evening, by the way.'

Lucy paused with her hand on the banister and tried

to think of something to say but ended up unsuccessfully trying to smother a huge yawn. 'Sorry, I—'

'You're exhausted. Come,' he said, and without further ado he picked her up and started up the stairs.

After a moment of supreme surprise, she lay quiet and composed in his arms, her lashes fanning her cheeks, her only thought to wonder what was coming.

But all he did was to put her down on her bed and turn away to stoke up her fire. She lay quite still, watching him and feeling an odd little sense of loss, which translated upon a moment's thought to the realisation that she hadn't felt quite so lonely or strung up in his arms as she did lying alone on her bed the way she was... She bit back a husky exclamation and sat up, feeling unreasonably annoyed and stung to retaliation.

'It's a pity we couldn't have done that for the benefit of the gallery,' she said ironically. 'Justin, is it important to you the kind of impression I make on these people? I mean, are they going to judge you on me, sort of thing?'

He straightened and came over to the bed. 'Why?'

'Why what?'

'Why are you asking me that, Lucy?'

She stared up at him. 'Why shouldn't I? I'm curious, that's all.'

He looked faintly sceptical but said, 'I guess it's human nature to wonder what people see in each other and make some sort of judgement.'

'So,' she said slowly, 'were I to be judged—if they were to think for example, well, she's pretty enough and all that but mightn't she bore Justin to tears after a while?—how will that affect how they think about you?'

He frowned. 'Lucy, if I knew what was behind this I might—'

'You're the one who wanted me to make a good impression and not look as if I'd been snatched from my cradle,' she broke in tartly.

He smiled. 'Is that how you've been feeling tonight? A little out of your depth? I thought you were a bit wrought up about something.'

The accuracy and the inaccuracy of his words brought a faint blush to her cheeks and a further sense of maltreatment to her heart. 'You can't have it both ways, Justin. You did marry me, even if it was for all the wrong reasons, but they don't know that, so—'

'Lucy,' he interrupted gravely, 'let me set your mind at rest. *I* don't give a damn what people think about my private life; I never have. My concern about how you might behave this weekend was motivated by this— when you invite people to spend time with you, especially way out in the backblocks like this where they can't get up and go that easily if they want to, I think you're fairly obliged not to make them feel uncomfortable and as if they're in the midst of a domestic brawl. Don't you agree?'

She opened her mouth, closed it then said scathingly, 'Of course! That doesn't explain the cradle bit, though.'

'Well, as to that,' he said musingly, and picked up a strand of her hair, 'I wondered if it mightn't be part of your strategy, that's all.'

Lucy blinked at him. 'I don't understand.'

'Don't you? I thought since I'd made it plain that your *femme fatale* act—your words, not mine, but not inappropriate—was something I wouldn't approve of you might—change tack.'

Lucy closed her eyes. 'Funnily enough, it didn't occur to me at all,' she said bleakly.

'You wouldn't be losing your grip on this—war, would you, Lucy?' he queried, slipping her hair through his fingers then smoothing it back into place and standing back a step.

For the briefest moment Lucy wondered if she was. But she said, 'I'm rather tired, Justin, that's all.'

'Is it, Lucy?'

The way he said it, on a different note entirely made her open her eyes. 'What more could there be?'

'Unless you tell me, I don't know.' His eyes searched hers.

She looked away and found herself considering telling him that she didn't have Mrs Milton and her sister, only one flustered and anxious substitute—and Adrian, and that if the rest of the weekend went well it would be something of a miracle—he'd probably find out soon enough, anyway. But almost immediately she decided she couldn't stand his scorn, not tonight, so she said wearily, 'There's nothing,' and lay back exhaustedly.

'Perhaps you're trying too hard, Lucy.'

She stretched her throat and rubbed it. 'I really don't know what I have to do to *make* you approve of me, Justin.'

He moved so his face was in the shadows and she couldn't read his expression. 'Just the one thing you won't do.'

For the life of her she couldn't help it, couldn't stem the images that flooded her mind, of lying in his arms and being made love to, of not being lonely, at least. Images of surrender in the most complete way a woman could to a man, but... 'But then I might not approve of myself. It's a real dilemma, isn't it?' she whispered, and sat up suddenly with her hands to her face as hot tears sprang to her eyes. 'Please, just go away, Justin. I can't cope with you and all this at the same time.'

He stared down at her shaking shoulders for a long moment, then he said evenly, 'All right, I'm going. But if there is a problem you don't have to—'

'There's nothing!' She raised her tear-streaked face abruptly. 'Other than that you've now managed to undermine my self-confidence.'

'Why, Lucy, I never thought to hear you say that. Goodnight, my dear. Don't do anything stupid, will you?'

She didn't, not then, but before the weekend was over she seriously interfered with Adrian's freedom and committed a social solecism of considerable proportions.

CHAPTER THREE

IT WAS Sasha, who else, who broke the news on Sunday morning.

She came into the veranda room where everyone was lounging around comfortably just prior to getting ready to leave, still commenting on the great dinner party last night and lovely day they'd had yesterday, and she said into a lull in the conversation, 'Justin, there's a child handcuffed to a fence outside. He says Lucy did it and that she threatened to shoot him.'

Everyone sat up with wide eyes and turned to Lucy.

'Oh,' she swallowed, 'that's Adrian. He's only been there for about ten minutes. I...' She stopped and blushed bright red.

Incredibly, it was Justin who came to her rescue. 'What's he done now?' he said resignedly, and added for everyone's benefit, 'Adrian is the son of our cook, Shirley—a great cook, I'm sure you'll all agree.'

Lucy stared at him open-mouthed but he murmured gently, 'Tell us, Lucy, otherwise people will think you're some sort of a monster.'

'He...' Lucy licked her lips. 'Yesterday *he* handcuffed *me* to the towel rail in the kitchen. Um—one of his uncles is a policeman and he gave him this set. Fortunately his mother came to the rescue—eventually... And today,' she said hastily, 'he actually picked the lock of the gun cupboard—I caught him at it but of course luckily we keep the ammunition in a safe and I *didn't* threaten

43

to shoot him…but in light of the fact that he laid waste every tomato plant in the vegetable garden yesterday, lit a fire in the chicken shed and downed all the washing on the line in the duck pond, I thought some of his own medicine might be good for him… You *knew*!' she said to Justin. 'All the time you knew.'

'Not all the time. Where are the keys? I'll…let him out on parole.'

But a combination of all sorts of factors worked powerfully in Lucy and she was deaf to discretion. 'How could you?' she accused. 'Of all the low-down things! To let me go *on* pretending…oh!' She ground her teeth. 'I hate you, Justin Waite, you're the most arrogant, self-opinionated man I've ever met and that's only some of the things I hate about you.'

The silence was electric but Justin laughed, as if he was really amused. 'Well, we nearly made it,' he said obliquely. 'Sorry, friends, but Lucy has had a traumatic weekend, haven't you, my love? I'm sure you only need to apologise, though. To them, not necessarily to me,' he added, and his eyes mocked her.

Lucy glanced round, flinched visibly as no one's eyes quite met hers, then became aware of an agitated murmuring she was coming to know well behind her. She dug into the pocket of her jeans and removed a set of keys. 'Here you are, Shirley,' she said swinging round. 'He hasn't been there long and if I were you I'd confiscate those handcuffs—they're more of a temptation than some people can bear. I am sorry,' she said contritely, swinging back. 'I've been short-staffed this weekend and I have an unfortunate temper, apparently. I do hope you'll all forgive me.'

She lay on her bed with her eyes closed but knew it was Justin when she heard the door open and close. She'd heard the plane take off about half an hour earlier but she'd made her farewells—she winced as she thought of it—from the house.

What caused her to open her eyes was the sagging of the other side of her double bed, and she saw before she closed them again that, not content with sitting, he'd stretched out with his hands behind his head. He also said, 'You're not sulking, are you, Lucy?'

She sat up abruptly and crossed her legs. 'No. I'm still angry as a matter of fact, so if you've come to *lecture* me you're wasting your time.'

'The thought never crossed my mind,' he murmured.

She frowned then turned to him. 'Aren't you—angry?'

'Do I look it?'

She hesitated because in fact he looked perfectly relaxed and at home and there was only a sort of bland query in his eyes. 'I—there are times when I don't understand you, Justin,' she said at last.

'That's rather obvious.'

'I mean, I've just done the one thing you didn't want me to do: discomfited our guests in other words—yet you—'

'They *were* on their way out, but go on.'

She breathed deeply. 'All right. I displayed sentiments not exactly common to new brides, I'm sure; I probably gave them cause to wonder whether I wasn't round the bend, handcuffing children to fences! Isn't that enough?'

'And all without even trying.' He smiled unexpectedly. 'Are you so annoyed because you feel its sheer spontaneity robbed it of malice aforethought and robbed you therefore of some satisfaction?'

Lucy bit her lip.

'As for my—low actions, what actually happened was that I knew something was up so I bearded a lady I *thought* must be Mrs Milton's sister in the kitchen yesterday morning, only to have the whole sad story explained to me—although she didn't tell me what a monster young Adrian is. I then acted as if I'd in fact known and decided to resume my mantle of ignorance with you mainly because you did seem to be coping admirably and I thought it would help restore your confidence. That same confidence you accused me of undermining. I now realise I should have bucked in and helped or something like that but then that would have meant explaining to people like Sasha—'

'That I'd got myself in a bind,' Lucy said gloomily.

'I thought you might not appreciate that.'

'I wouldn't have.' She pulled a fold of the bedspread through her fingers. 'Well,' she said grudgingly after some thought, 'I suppose I'm now in the wrong on all counts.'

'Is that an olive branch?' he queried.

She shrugged. 'Of a kind. Which means we're only back to square one, so—'

'Don't get any ideas, Justin. In other words.' He said it with utter gravity but when she looked at him there was a wicked little glint in his eyes.

She turned away hastily with her heartbeat doing an odd tattoo. 'I still have to live with the thought of at least five people seriously wondering about me,' she said with a toss of her head.

'I wouldn't worry about that; one of them even suggested you could be pregnant,' he said placidly.

'Well, I'm not!' Lucy sprang off the bed agitatedly.

'You know that and I know that, but they don't.' He stretched his arms lazily.

'In a few months' time they're all going to know it. What will they think then?' she demanded.

He regarded her in silence for a moment. 'Things could change in a few months' time.'

She made an exasperated sound and stalked over to the window. 'I still can't understand why you're quite happy for everyone either to know I do hate you or to think I have such a volatile disposition you must have been mad to marry me!'

'I told you, I don't give a damn what people think. I also happen to prefer you when you're being spontaneous, even if a shade volatile, Lucy.'

She stared out of the window. It had started out as another bright, cold day but it was pouring now. She shivered. 'Remind me to be spontaneous the next time... it happens.'

There was silence, then she tensed as she heard the bed springs creak, but she refused to turn even when she heard his soft footfall across the carpet stop right behind her. She said, with her tension reflected in her voice, 'Where do we go from here?'

'I don't know. Any ideas?'

She couldn't contain herself any longer. She swung round. '*No*. I'm the hostage, don't forget.'

'You're also seriously overtired and overwrought,' he said impatiently. 'Why don't you have a bath and go to bed?'

'At three in the afternoon!' she said jerkily. 'Apart from anything else, Adrian is still on the loose—'

'He's not. I've had a chat with Adrian and I doubt if we'll have any more trouble with him. I've also told

Shirley to relax for a couple of hours and thanked her for her considerable efforts.'

'And she's no doubt got stars in her eyes now and thinks you're just marvellous,' Lucy said bitterly.

He raised a mocking eyebrow. 'Being bitchy doesn't become you, Lucy.'

'I wish I knew what did—other than gracing your bed! As a matter of fact I also thanked Shirley and apologised for what I did to Adrian,' she said with irony.

'Then you won't mind if they stay on for a few days. Shirley to help you and Adrian to perhaps benefit from some male supervision.'

Lucy's eyes widened causing him to say with genuine irritation, 'He's only a kid suffering from the lack of a father. As a kid yourself who suffered from the lack of a mother, surely—'

'Oh, shut up, Justin,' she broke in. 'Don't you think I feel guilty enough as it is? In any other circumstances I'd never have...' She grimaced. 'I was just surprised you would want to take the time, that's all. Is that really—' she hesitated '—what you feel is the root cause of all my so-called problems, as a matter of interest? The lack of a mother?'

He shrugged. 'It mightn't have helped.'

'Thank you,' she said very formally, and added, 'Do you know what? I think I will do as you suggested after all. There just doesn't seem to be any alternative.'

'There is,' he said drily. 'And one day you'll take it, Lucy. Because I'll tell you what it is. Assuming you and I were in any kind of mental unity—let's leave the physical aspect out of it for the time being.' He smiled but it didn't reach his eyes. 'Assuming we were mentally attuned, we could go downstairs and have tea in front of the fire in the library, we could discuss the plans I have for the next week, all to do with Dalkeith and the kind of things that have been begging to be done for years, you could play the piano for a while—it's that kind of afternoon and I would enjoy listening while I read the papers the plane brought in this morning—then we could have dinner, watch a video and go to bed early. You would sleep like a top and be all bright-eyed and bushy-tailed in the morning.'

Her lips had parted as he spoke and she stared into his eyes with a kind of longing dawning in her own, which he saw, but he made no movement, no gesture.

She turned away.

She took a long bath and in a sudden spirit of urgency tried to sort out her thoughts in the process and to reduce her dilemma to stark facts rather than overheated, panicky emotion.

But the results *were* stark, she decided as she added more hot water and stared dismally through the steam. She was married to a man who didn't love her, who'd stood to gain by marrying her and had virtually forced her into it. A man, she mused, who must have taken a conscious decision that a marriage of convenience suited him best and had possibly decided he could mould her into the the kind of wife he wanted. What kind of man would do that? A man with a grudge, perhaps, yet it wasn't really *his* affair, more his father's, and it seemed an extreme length to go to surely, especially when he could have had virtually any wife he chose. No, there had to be more to it, she reflected, and wondered if there'd been anything in the Justin she'd known as a child to indicate this...hardness, sort of.

'He was always—I don't know,' she murmured to herself, 'you just knew he would always get what he wanted somehow, that's true. He was self-contained and...and of course, talking about mothers, he didn't have one either after she ran off with someone. Perhaps he suffered from a lack of it more than I did.' She sat up with a frown in her eyes. 'Perhaps that's why he thinks he can treat women like this: because he never had a woman he could respect or appreciate in his formative years. I bet that's got something to do with it!'

But a moment later she sank back ruefully, as it crossed her mind that coming from *her* this character-analysis of her worldly, sophisticated husband would probably be treated as laughable. Her thoughts ranged on. Assuming she did give in, she moved uncomfortably in the water then forced herself to consider the possibility. Assuming she did, what kind of a husband would he be for the rest of her life? Always a little distant, always the boss, so to speak—what kind of a marriage would that be? Or would she really, once she was *bedded*, be so besotted it wouldn't matter, or it would all come right in some mysterious manner she just couldn't foresee.

'And I *can't*,' she said with some force, 'because if he's an enigma now, he always will be, and even if he isn't a terrible husband it will only be half a life. Of course, there's always Dalkeith...is it such a price to pay?'

She shivered suddenly, and not because the water was cold but because it was occurring to her more and more that she was going to have to pay a price for her beloved home.

She also slept for a couple of hours, something that was unheard of for her during the day but although she woke feeling less tired she also felt cold and lonely as the rain-laden dusk blotted out the landscape. She pulled on a navy-blue tracksuit and sat brushing her hair for a long time, staring at her image in the mirror because it was in her mind to take a step she hadn't believed she ever would...

Justin was reading the papers in the library as she entered and closed the door behind her. He raised his dark head and watched her thoughtfully as she stood just inside the door, her hand still on the handle as if she might change her mind and leave again.

Then he said, 'Feeling better? Dinner's nearly ready, I believe.'

'Oh. Yes. I am. Justin—' She stopped as he stood up and was nearly overcome by nerves and by something else. A sudden sense of frustration, because knowing Justin Waite was like knowing the cover of a book you'd never read and because there were some ways she knew him that were infinitely disturbing, and not things she'd taken into account during her bathtime analysis of her situation. Things, for example, that only struck her when she was in his presence—or in his arms. Things like the feel of him and the feel of his mouth on hers, the easy strength of his arms and shoulders. And the knowledge that he was a dangerously attractive man, and suddenly being in the position of having to admit to herself that she'd always known it and that no amount of taboos on him could make her completely immune to it. It had been there, of course, when she'd been measuring other men up to him, there when she'd resolutely ignored him but noted every little detail of the women he was with. There now, as he stood watching her looking big and casual in his jeans and green sweater—and the treacherous thought came to her that if she just walked across the room into his arms, if he would just hold her and perhaps smooth her hair and touch her face gently, before he did anything else, it *might* all come right...

'Justin.' She released the door-handle and took a couple more steps. 'What you said earlier,' she went on hurriedly, 'about being *mentally* attuned. Could we—talk about that a bit more?'

His lips twisted but he said after a moment, 'Sure. Would you like a pre-dinner drink to—help it along?'

'Thanks,' she murmured and sat down opposite his chair.

He poured her a brandy and soda and one for himself and came back but didn't sit. Instead he propped an elbow on the mantelpiece and sipped his drink, not looking at her. 'Go ahead.'

Lucy took a large swallow of hers. 'Would it compromise me if I said,' she paused and licked her lips, 'if I said I could give it a try?'

'Compromise you how?' he enquired.

'I mean, would it lead you to think that it's a preliminary to going to bed with you?' she said tartly.

He considered gravely. 'Probably.' He lifted his head at last and there was amusement in his grey eyes.

She tried consciously to stem the tide of pink that came to her cheeks but of course that wasn't something one could consciously control so she said evenly, 'Well, you'd be wrong.'

He moved his shoulders briefly and murmured, 'My mistake. What would it mean, Lucy?'

She hesitated then said honestly and bleakly, 'I can't think what else to do, that's all.'

'Are you proposing, in other words, that we spend the rest of our lives in only mental affinity?'

Her nostrils flared and she took a huge swallow of her brandy this time which caused her to cough and splutter a bit before she got out, 'I can't *think* that far ahead! All I'm suggesting is that—all I'm saying is that I can't go on like this. I'm...I just don't know what else to do. For the moment. And while I'm in this awful situation, which is all your fault, don't forget, life is sort of slipping away from me and I feel useless and...' She gestured helplessly.

He studied her in silence for quite some time and until her nerves started to prickle. Then he said, 'You're very young, aren't you, Lucy.'

'Are you asking me or telling me?'

He smiled faintly. 'Telling you, I guess. All right, we can give it a try. So long as you understand I won't be content with it forever.'

She raised her eyebrows ironically, 'Who knows, things might change in a few months.'

'Yes, well, you're also very articulate, my dear,' he said drily, 'for someone so curiously...naïve, sometimes.'

'That's a change—again. Has it occurred to you, Justin, that you haven't really worked out what I am?'

'On the contrary, I know exactly what you are, Lucy. I wouldn't be married to you if I didn't.'

Her eyes narrowed and another faint flush stained her cheeks and her heart started to pound uncomfortably. But he can't know, she thought. Everything he's ever said has gone along with... 'And what would that be?' she asked with a quiver in her voice.

'Oh—' he shrugged and stared into the fire for a moment '—a bit confused, a bit volatile at times—' he lifted his head and that wicked glint was back in his eyes '—stubborn but not without courage, bright as a tack, possessing a sense of style—quite a lot of admirable virtues, in fact.'

'Is that a fact?' Lucy tossed her head and grimaced. 'Then I was right—I think I mentioned it to you before. I'm trainable in your eyes, aren't I? You really feel you can mould me into a suitable wife, don't you? You must also feel I'm not too far gone down the path of *femme fatality* to be redeemed, and of course I'm also a Wainright of Dalkeith, let's not forget that. I'm just wondering what I'd get in return—assuming I ever allowed you to mould me into anything. In other words, Justin, say I had ideas about the kind of husband I'd like you to be—am I allowed to do that?'

'Why not?'

She blinked.

'What did you have in mind, Lucy?' he asked casually.

'I...' It was one thing to tell yourself in a bathtub exactly the kind of husband you'd want him to be, another to tell him to his face, she decided darkly, as the words were curiously difficult to formulate.

'I've always held the theory that honesty and openness between men and women is the best way, if that's what you mean,' he said seriously after waiting politely for a moment. 'But women, some women,' he amended, 'find it rather difficult—uh—they have a natural reticence on the subject. Are you naturally reticent about those things, Lucy?'

'What...what things?'

'How you like to be made love to, for example, how

you like to be touched and what turns you on—all things that are really at the core of a marriage wouldn't you agree?' he said softly, and added, 'I certainly think it can make or break a relationship so, yes, if you have any preferences I'd be quite happy to go along with them.'

It was a moment or so before Lucy realised that her facial muscles actually felt stiff with effort. The effort not to contort with anger. Her voice, she realised, sounded even stiffer, but there was nothing she could do about it. 'I didn't mean that. Do you ever think of anything else?'

'Frequently.' His eyes were amused again. 'In the context of a marriage it just seems to spring to mind, however.'

'But there must be more to it!' she burst out. 'There should be *love*, otherwise you grow tired of each other. There should be—there shouldn't be the kind of unequal feeling our marriage would have to have, and the gaping chasm of me knowing I'm being altered and made suitable for you—of just not understanding you, Justin, and why you've done this!'

'Or why you agreed to it,' he said significantly.

'Or why I...' She stopped and sighed.

'What if I told you I had no desire to make you feel unequal, Lucy?' he said into the silence.

'But you do.' She grimaced at the slightly forlorn note in her voice. 'And just the fact that this is a marriage of convenience for you will always make me feel unequal and I'll always feel I don't understand you.'

'Is there anything, apart from the way I married you, that you particularly dislike or distrust about me, Lucy?'

She'd turned her head to stare into the fire dispiritedly

but she looked up with a frown because there was no amusement in his voice now. And she saw that his eyes were rather intent as they rested on her.

'I...well...' She stared at him helplessly. He waited as her lips worked again but all she could say finally and foolishly was, 'Why?'

'I mean, does the thought of going to bed with me fill you with disgust and make your skin crawl, and do you seriously believe that I don't have the best interests of your beloved Dalkeith at heart?'

She stared at him fixedly and discovered she was breathing rapidly as she wondered frantically how to answer him. She licked her lips. 'I haven't *really* thought of going to bed with you; I—'

'Haven't you, Lucy?' His impenetrable grey gaze was nevertheless mercilessly compelling and her cheeks flamed right on cue.

She took a deep breath. 'Not...seriously, then.'

'What was the verdict—unseriously?' His lips twisted.

'I thought I mightn't feel so lo...' She stopped abruptly.

'So lonely?' he said very quietly.

'Yes,' she whispered.

'You wouldn't.'

'Justin,' she got up agitatedly, 'this—'

'What else did you think?' he overode her. 'Any revulsion, Lucy?'

She closed her eyes. 'No. But that's not the same thing as *wanting* to, with every fibre of your being!'

'I agree, but it's a start. How many times have you really wanted to with every fibre of your being, Lucy?'

She tightened her lips. 'That's for me to know and you to worry about, if it worries you at all.'

'All right—what about Dalkeith?'

What about Dalkeith—the words seemed to reverberate through her brain. 'Yes,' she said and the word was torn from her, 'I think you do have its best interests at heart, but—'

'Then, Lucy, I think it's time you grew up and accepted that life isn't all roses and sweet dreams, and that, when reality comes, most of us pick ourselves up and make the best of it. And the reality is, I am—and I apologise for it, but I am—to some extent a disillusioned cynic, I do want Dalkeith, for a variety of reasons, and if you want it too, and as badly as you say, then this is the price tag for it. On the other hand, I wouldn't have married you if I hadn't believed that, while it might not have been made in heaven, it could be made to work. Many, many marriages have worked on less. Nor do I expect you to be grateful or feel patronised; in fact if you made it a *commitment* I wouldn't expect a passive, unequal-feeling wife at all. I'd expect and be happy to accommodate your feelings for this place as well as your spirit and your courage—and even those times you feel justified in losing your temper with me.' He stopped and lifted his head. 'Dinner's ready, by the way. I hear the bell. Bring your drink, it's quite informal tonight.'

It was, in fact, macaroni cheese served at the kitchen table in company with Shirley and Adrian.

Lucy managed to contain her surprise—she was still a bit dazed by what Justin had said anyway—and then there was this facet to him that she'd not suspected. That he'd take seriously the plight of one fatherless boy and his mother.

It was obvious he'd already worked a small miracle with Adrian. Not that Adrian was suddenly a model of virtue but his surliness had disappeared and he caused Lucy to all but choke when he handed her his handcuffs and said, 'Mum reckons you better keep these until I'm reformed.' And she recognised that, coming from Adrian, this was equivalent to an apology.

But there were more surprises in store. Justin remarked, 'It's school holidays, Lucy. Adrian has three weeks so he's going to stay with us—'

'And Mum too,' Adrian said through a mouthful of macaroni.

'Of course, darling,' Shirley said. 'Mr Waite's asked me to help you out for the three weeks, Miss Lucy, and he's going to set Adrian some chores every morning to make up for the...damage he did.' She blushed, then brightened. 'And if he's good, he's going to take him up in the plane and teach him to ride a horse and drive a tractor. Is that all right with you?' she added anxiously.

'Fine!' Lucy said heartily. 'Yes, that'll be great, Shirley.' But she avoided Justin's eyes because of two simultaneous thoughts she had—a sudden ridiculous affinity she felt with Adrian, and the rather indignant thought that, given the right time and circumstances, she could have managed him just as well. Why the affinity? she pondered. Oh, I get it. There are times when Justin makes me feel just like a recalcitrant child and times when he uses the reward system, the old donkey-and-carrot trick, she thought bitterly, just as he's doing to Adrian. And, just like Adrian, I've got the feeling I've met my match, she reflected.

She couldn't help brooding on this, but no one seemed to notice her reticence—she winced at the thought—as Shirley responded to Justin's conversation yet didn't for a moment lose her deferential air, as if to assure him she

would never take advantage of this lapse in normal
household relations, and Adrian ate his way solidly
through three helpings.

But as Shirley was bustling about, making coffee and
clearing away, Lucy looked directly at her husband at
last and said suddenly, 'Do I have to make a decision
right now?'

'You could think it over for a few days.'

'I will.'

He smiled faintly and changed the subject—or did he?
'I thought of doing an aerial inspection tomorrow if it's
stopped raining. Care to come?'

CHAPTER FOUR

THE next week proved to be a comfortable, peaceful one—for the most part.

They did all the things Shirley had enumerated and Adrian trod the road of being "reformed" quite successfully while Lucy discovered herself delighted to be included in the goings on of the property for a change—for the most part. It did sometimes sadden her to realise how neglected it had been, and occasionally it irked her to watch Justin in the role of owner, a role he played not flamboyantly at all but with a cool, businesslike practicality, a deep knowledge of the needs of Dalkeith and the unmistakable aura of a man who was not to be trifled with.

Like the great white hunter, she thought irreverantly once, but was conscious that she couldn't help secretly admiring his stewardship of her home at the same time. Which places me in an awkward position and no doubt induces this ambivalence in me, she thought with some bitterness.

It was that same afternoon that she was in her bedroom trying to decide what to wear to a dinner party being given by their nearest neighbours, twenty-five miles away, that Justin walked in on her as she was conducting a conversation with herself.

'Why, Lucy,' he murmured, stopping on the threshold and raising an eyebrow at the colourful array of clothing that littered the bed, 'are you moving out? And I thought I heard voices.'

Lucy put her hand on her hip and surveyed him imperiously. 'I was talking to myself, something I do frequently and always have—perhaps you should take that into account if you intend to persist in being married to me. And I'm trying to decide what to wear tonight— perhaps you should *also* take into account that it can sometimes take me *days*, let alone hours, to decide what to wear.'

'Dear me,' he said gravely. 'Mind you, that's not uncommon in women.'

'It may not be,' she replied with a toss of her head, 'but I don't intend to change.'

'I'm not asking you to. On the other hand—' he strolled over to the bed and picked up a dress '—husbands can be quite useful at times likes these.' He picked up a dress. 'I don't believe I've seen you in this one.'

It was a grey flannel straight dress with long sleeves and a white, lace-trimmed collar and cuffs. 'Funnily enough,' Lucy said. 'I'd almost—' She stopped abruptly.

'Almost decided on it?' he said with a lazy lift of an eyebrow. 'I'm quite sure you're about to change your mind, then.'

Lucy bit her lip and said stiffly, 'I'm not that stupid.'

'Why don't you give me a preview, then?'

'Why should I?'

'We could both reassure ourselves it's the right dress for the occasion. This is the first time we've been invited out as a couple,' he added.

'I know that only too well,' Lucy said with irony.

'Is that why you're a bit worked up?' he queried. 'You

shouldn't be. We've both known the Gardiners for as long as we can remember.'

'Who said I was worked up?' Lucy countered coolly, because she would rather die than admit she *was*, on top of everything else, at the prospect of having to parade with Justin before a set of people she had known all her life, but as Lucy Waite now. 'Anyway, if I am it's not without cause,' she added shortly. 'I feel—' she paused '—I feel like a yearling about to go on display.'

Justin moved away from the bed and sat down in her pink velvet armchair. 'Sometimes you remind me of a long-legged yearling,' he commented. 'Why don't you try this dress on so I can give you the benefit of my wisdom on the subject?'

'Not with you sitting there—I mean...'

He scanned her jeans and jumper. 'I presume you have underwear on?'

'Of course I do, but I'm not about to even give you a glimpse of my underwear,' she said virtuously.

'Is it—particularly saucy?' he suggested with a perfectly straight face.

'It's not saucy at all; well—' Lucy hesitated '—all underwear is—'

'Suggestive?' He laid his head back and his eyes were wickedly amused although his face was still straight.

Lucy frowned. 'Justin—this conversation doesn't become you, you know,' she said scathingly then. 'In fact I find it particularly gratuitous, if you must know!'

'I don't think it is, not between a husband and wife, Lucy,' he replied politely, and stayed where he was, apparently perfectly relaxed in her favourite chair. 'But if you'd care to change in your bathroom, I wouldn't mind.'

Lucy muttered something beneath her breath then scooped up the dress and went to do just that. But once out of her jeans and jumper she looked at herself in her pretty white underwear with little red bows and felt a *frisson* run down her spine as she wondered several things. How would she look to a worldly, experienced Justin Waite in said underwear, and why was he doing this? But the most concerning of her mental processes was the undeniable little mesh she suddenly found herself caught in of being so aware of him sitting only feet away and then, like a tide growing in her and causing her to tremble foolishly, the thought that she could go out to him as she was, the thought *again* that she could stop fighting and put it all into his hands; this was a perfect opportunity to do just that...

Is that what he's trying to create? she asked herself, and observed that her eyes were wide and stunned in the mirror. The next instant she was climbing into the grey flannel dress hastily.

'There!' She glided out of the bathroom, did a couple of pirouettes and came to rest in front of the pink chair. 'I do think we're right about this dress, Justin. I'm quite sure the Gardiners would approve, anyway; they're extremely strait-laced and absolute sticklers for modesty and propriety, aren't they, fond as I am of them? And I wouldn't be at all surprised if Colonel Howard is there, and he's a real old fuddy-duddy, fond as I am of *him*, so—I will wear it.'

For a couple of moments Justin simply stared at her and Lucy was quite sure, with a piercing sense of embarrassment, that he knew exactly why she was talking

nineteen to the dozen, and knew the rest of her tangled
emotions all too well also. And she held her breath as
their gazes locked.

But at last he stood up, although he still said nothing
as he smoothed the lace-trimmed collar about her throat
and let his gaze linger down the lines of her figure beneath the grey flannel that ended just above her knees.
Then he said gently, 'Yes, dear Lucy, it is a model of
modesty and propriety. You look almost Quakerish in it.
However, you also look young and lovely and infinitely
desirable, as I'm sure even Colonel Howard and the Gardiners will recognise.'

Her eyes widened and she could feel his hand that
still rested on her shoulder as if it was burning through
the cloth, as well as being devastatingly aware of everything else about him that attracted her so much, she
thought with a jolt. The tall, lean lines of his body, the
clever eyes... So much...she thought with another jolt,
and said because she couldn't help herself, 'Do you
mean that in a general way? Of course you do, how silly
of me.' She swallowed and went on hurriedly, 'Well, I
can't think of what else to wear, I mean that would be
less—'

'Lucy.' He put a finger to her lips. 'The dress is fine,
in fact it's perfect for you, but then so would sackcloth
be, probably.' He smiled slightly, but not with his eyes.
'And yes, I did mean in a general way—but also in a
very private way, and by that I mean just between the
two of us. When you're ready to acknowledge and accept that, my dear, I promise you life will be a lot easier.'
He stepped away and said then, perfectly normally and
with a slight grimace, 'I guess it's time I got changed.'

                        *   *   *

'Well, it wasn't such an ordeal after all, was it?'

'No,' Lucy said quietly as they drove through the dark, chilly night back to Dalkeith.

'You're very quiet,' Justin said a couple of miles further on.

'Sorry.'

'Lucy, you've got me seriously worried,' he said wryly.

She moved restlessly and wondered how he would react if she told him he'd got *her* seriously worried. 'It's nothing, I'm just tired,' she said, and managed to yawn right on cue because she was a bit tired as well as everything else. 'It's quite a tiring business playing at being a wife, you know, Justin,' she added, and could immediately have kicked herself.

But he didn't make the rejoinder she expected. He drove on in silence, although he did speed up rather abruptly while she held her breath then cast a curious glance at him from beneath her lashes. But all she could see was the familiar angle of his jaw, the way his hair lay, thick and dark, and not much else as the powerful Land Rover chewed up the miles of the uneven, unmade road.

And some little devil of perversity was just about to prompt her into further, no doubt foolish observations, when there was a sudden dark shadow on the road in front of them, the Land Rover swerved wildly then skidded off the track, hit a large boulder with a sickening thump, came to rest at an angle with the engine cutting out—and Justin slumped forward over the steering-wheel.

'Oh, no! Justin! Are you all right. Oh, no!' Lucy scrambled on to her knees awkwardly on the seat and felt for a pulse in his neck. It was an all too familiar scenario on outback roads, either a kangaroo or some form of stray livestock bounding in front of a vehicle at the last moment, and then an unhandily placed boulder causing Justin to crack his forehead on the steering-wheel and knock himself out.

'That's all it is, please God,' she said to herself as she found a pulse, 'something temporary—oh, don't let him have fractured his skull or anything like that. And what do I do in the meantime?'

But after a few panicky moments she calmed down and decided all she could do was make him as comfortable as possible so, with quite some effort, she eased him back so his head was resting on the back rest. There was already a livid bruise on his temple, she saw by the interior light, and decided to apply a cold compress from the water bottle that no self-respecting vehicle travelled without, attached to its front bumper, in the bush.

So she climbed out, retrieved the thankfully undamaged water bottle, tried quickly to estimate whether the Land Rover would go again, and climbed back in because it was very cold.

It took him half an hour to come round.

Thirty minutes while the chill inside the vehicle grew, and it resisted all attempts to start the motor so she could have the heater on, and she stopped putting the compress on and concentrated simply on keeping them warm. Thirty minutes that felt like hours and acted in a strange and powerful way upon her for two reasons—the lurking, terrible fear in her heart that he might be more seriously injured but at the same time, the unaccustomed freedom of being able to look her fill upon him and not to have to hide anything from him...

Oh, dear, she thought, as she realised all this, it's no

good trying to pretend I haven't fallen deeply in love with him, is it? It doesn't even help in the slightest to remind myself of all the injustices of the situation, not now when I'm alone with him like this, holding him and wanting to be nowhere on earth but here because he intrigues me and fascinates me and attracts me and I fear for him—and I can't imagine life without him.

Indeed, she was still looking her fill with her head on his shoulder, her arms around him, when his eyes fluttered open, and although they were dazed with pain, his lips twisted into a semblance of a smile as he said, 'Lucy? Is it you?'

Her heart lurched and her breasts felt curiously heavy and her stomach tightened beneath a sudden onslaught of sheer longing for him that told its own tale. 'Yes, it's me,' she said softly, sitting up. 'I'm trying to keep you warm—you hit your head. How do you feel?'

He groaned and gathered her back against him. 'Like hell.'

'Justin,' she said urgently.

But he chuckled huskily and stilled her movement. 'No, I'll survive. I just didn't feel like letting you go.'

Lucy subsided but only briefly. 'Are you sure you haven't fractured your skull or something,' she said anxiously, but didn't move as he started to stroke her hair.

'Quite sure—well, reasonably sure. It's all coming back now. Did I do much damage to the Land Rover?'

'It won't start. We hit a big rock—'

'Are you all right, Lucy?' He pushed her away a little at last and looked into her eyes.

'I'm fine,' she reassured him.

'You look quite pale,' he said slowly, his eyes roaming over her face.

'I was…I was worried about you.'

'How long have I been out?'

'Half an hour. I was putting a cold compress on your head but then I thought I might give you hypothermia because it's so cold anyway!'

He raised a hand and touched the bruise on his temple, wincing as he did so. But he smiled ruefully at her, touched her cheek gently and said ruefully, 'Thanks. I feel like a bloody idiot,' he added drily, pushing himself up. 'I was driving far too fast—well, let's see if we can get this show on the road.'

Somehow he did get the Land Rover going again and they limped home at a very sedate pace.

'Look, are you sure you're all right?' she said anxiously again as they came into the warmth of the kitchen and he flung the keys on the table. 'You look terrible now.'

'Nothing a couple of aspirin, a cup of tea and a good night's sleep won't help. What's this?' He took a piece of fine Swiss cotton, white with little blue flowers on it, out of her hands and held it up.

'Oh. It's my half-petticoat. It was the only thing I could think of to use as a compress.'

His lips quirked. 'Very…Lucy,' he said. 'Is it part of a matching set by any chance?'

'As a matter of fact, it is,' she said slowly.

'I thought it might be—don't look like that.'

'How am I looking?' she asked uncertainly.

'As if you're not sure whether to subject me to another lecture on the impropriety of discussing your underwear or—something else.' And for once his eyes held a sober, direct enquiry.

Lucy blushed, to her chagrin, then heard herself say

gruffly, 'If you're sure there's nothing more I can do to help, I think I'll go to bed.'

'Nothing—I think that would be a good idea,' he said with a certain irony but, curiously, she couldn't tell if it was directed at her or him, and her confusion caused her to murmur goodnight and leave rather precipitately.

But as she lay in bed listening to him moving around the adjoining room—and then deep silence—the turmoil in her heart and the bereft feeling she experienced didn't make for a peaceful night.

And for the next few days the fact that he was not in a good mood at all didn't help.

'It's his head,' Adrian said philosophically when he'd received a cool, sharp set-down over something very minor.

'Yes, it's his head,' Shirley agreed with adoring overtones that caused Lucy to grimace.

'Well, I don't know why he doesn't take his head to the doctor,' she said, forgetting for the moment how concerned she'd been over Justin Waite's head.

'I'm sure it's nothing serious, Miss Lucy,' Shirley said very seriously. 'But a bump like that can give you a headache for a couple of days. I'll think up something extra nice for him for dinner!'

'Well, I think I'll keep out of his way for a while,' Adrian remarked, causing Lucy to grin this time and utter a similar sentiment, but this was something she didn't prove successful in.

Nor was the confrontation she finally had with him helped by her feelings of uncertainty and restlessness, the new awareness that she'd fallen in love with him up against the old awareness that he didn't love her...

It started when Sasha came to lunch two days after the accident. Justin was looking much better but he still had the bruise on his temple, which prompted Sasha to make enquiries, not unnaturally, Lucy supposed.

Justin explained briefly and then was called away to the phone as they sat down to a meal of soup and quiche.

'I hope you're looking after your man, Lucy,' Sasha said archly with her soup spoon poised but a highly unfriendly little glint in her green eyes at the same time.

Lucy raised an eyebrow. 'What makes you think I wouldn't?' she countered coolly.

'Why, nothing,' Sasha murmured. 'It was just one of those things one says. But, come to think of it, the last time I saw you two together you were, well, not in the greatest harmony, shall we say?'

Lucy gritted her teeth. 'That has nothing to do with you, Sasha.'

'Oops! Sorry,' the other girl murmured. 'Now I've upset you,' she added blandly.

'I'll tell you what should upset *you*,' Lucy retorted, 'is the fact that you wouldn't have the courage to say things like that if Justin were here.'

'Courage to say what?' Justin enquired coldly as he re-entered the room.

There was a short silence then Lucy said, 'Nothing.'

'If you two are squabbling,' he said sardonically, 'would you mind cutting it out? Sasha, we have quite a lot to discuss, so I'd appreciate it if you turned your mind to the business of the upcoming yearling sales.'

Sasha actually blushed, but Lucy smiled sweetly at her, turned an equally sweet smile upon her husband although she was thinking that she must be mad to feel herself in love with him, and said in a grave, hushed voice, 'We're suitably squashed, Justin. You don't feel we ought to write out a hundred lines after lunch? Do not squabble, do not squabble—that kind of thing?'

His mouth tightened and his eyes were very grey and hard as they rested on her. He also said with the kind of precision that would have cut through a steel plate, 'You're not very long out of school, are you, Lucy?'

If Sasha hadn't been there she might have poured her soup all over him, although what she did do was nearly as bad. She clanked her spoon down but said meditatively, 'I don't know why, but I seem to have lost my appetite, so why don't I leave you two to have a very adult discussion—yes, because to be honest, both of you *grown-ups* bore me to tears. Have fun!' And she got up and walked as lightly as she was capable of out of the room.

But when Justin found her in the stables ten minutes later, there were real tears streaked down her face, tears of anger and anguish as she employed a pitchfork with considerable energy to lay down new hay in an empty stall.

It was his tall shadow that fell across the floor of the stall that first alerted her to his presence and she stopped what she was doing, turned to him and said brightly but witheringly, 'Finished already? That *was* quick.'

'Lucy—' he reached over to take the pitchfork from her '—no.' And as she resisted, added curtly, 'Don't be an idiot, you'll only get hurt waving that thing about.'

Whereupon she resisted even harder, but after an undignified, quite unequal little struggle he wrested it from her and leant it against the wall. So she glared at him, stalked past him and plonked herself down on a bale of hay. 'All right, go ahead! I'm sure you've come to tell me how childish I am again.'

'I haven't, as a matter of fact, but I did warn you once, Lucy, that you could fight me all you liked in private, but in public—it would be a different matter.'

'Fight you!' she marvelled with magnificent scorn. 'You started it! And I'll tell you something, Justin Waite—I don't enjoy fighting in public either but I will *not* put up with being insulted *in* public. You're only lucky you didn't cop a bowl of soup.'

'For someone who doesn't enjoy it you seem to indulge in it fairly frequently,' he said drily.

'Only when I'm provoked,' Lucy said proudly. '"If you two are squabbling…"' she repeated. 'Who do you think you are?' she added intensely. 'If you really want a wife then you better start treating me like one.'

'And if, Lucy,' he drawled, 'I were treating you like a *wife*, this wouldn't keep happening.' Then he added with a relaxed little smile suddenly playing around his mouth, 'But I have to give you full marks for sheer spirit and courage. I'm also beginning to wonder how your father ever coped with you, not to mention your school.'

Lucy stared at him then whispered suddenly, 'I hate you, Justin. I was mad to think anything…anything—' She stopped abruptly.

'Anything…?' He raised an eyebrow.

'*Nothing*.' She got up, but found he was barring her way. She looked up at him for a long, tense moment, then her shoulders slumped suddenly and she said wearily, 'What now?'

'What *did* she say to you?'

Lucy's lips parted. 'Do you mean…?'

'I mean Sasha.' He lifted a hand and traced a tear streak down her face then kept his fingers on her chin.

Several emotions chased through Lucy's eyes but finally she said with simple dignity, 'I'm not going to tell you, Justin. I was quite capable of dealing with it on my own.'

'Until I stuck my oar in?' he suggested, looking wry.

'Yes,' she said pointedly.

'Something to do with the fact that we—don't always get on?' he hazarded.

But Lucy refused to speak, although her pansy-blue gaze did not attempt to evade his and after a long moment he laughed softly, kissed her lightly on the lips and released her chin. 'Such a proud, stubborn little wife. For what it's worth, I've sent Sasha back to Riverbend with a lecture.'

Lucy's eyes widened. 'Why?'

'Why?' He grimaced. 'You are my wife, while she is only my assistant.'

'If that's the case, why did you—?' She stopped and frowned bewilderedly up at him.

'Why did I say those fatal words in the first place? About squabbling?' He paused and shrugged. 'Well, Lucy, I have to be honest and confess to you that there are times when it's not easy—*playing* at being a husband,' he said with a significant little look up and down her figure.

A slow tide of colour started to travel up the line of her throat. 'Is that...is that why you've been in such a bad mood?' she whispered, her eyes wide. 'Not your head?'

'Well my head hasn't helped,' he said amusedly.

'I didn't...I didn't realise,' she said confusedly. 'But

now I do, I don't quite know what to do about it. I can't...just suddenly...come to bed with you,' she said agitatedly. 'Only a moment ago I was quite sure I hated you!'

'And now, a moment later?' he queried with a wicked little glint in his eyes.

'I haven't entirely forgiven you yet; I may still feel quite annoyed even to think about it for a time!'

He looked down at her with something in his eyes she couldn't read, something that made her feel very young, though, and realise the total irrationality of what she'd said, and she closed her eyes suddenly in a fever of embarrassment.

'Then why don't we approach things from a different angle for a while?'

Her lashes lifted and she frowned up at him. 'What do you mean?'

'We began this week in a kind of harmony; let's just try to get back to that,' he said seriously but his grey eyes were amused again.

'All right,' Lucy replied slowly.

'Good.' He took her hand. 'Shall we finish our lunch now? I don't know about you, but I'm starving.'

CHAPTER FIVE

So THAT was what they did, and once again their household started to shape up in a rather jolly way.

Adrian spent a few hours each day in the vegetable garden and the chicken house, repairing the damage he'd wreaked, and was rewarded for his efforts each day with a flight over the property or a tractor ride or just being allowed to accompany Justin. Lucy again took part in these expeditions and Shirley, seeing more contentment in her son than she'd ever seen, probably, cleaned and polished, washed and ironed and cooked up delicious meals. She even began to lose her agitated look.

But Lucy was hauntingly conscious that it couldn't go on like this forever, that she would have to make some decision soon, and confess to herself that, her own feelings aside, these glimpses of what harmony with Justin and Dalkeith could be like were nearly irresistible. Where did all my hostility go? she wondered once, and felt her cheeks burn as she remembered the rash thought that she could somehow make him regret marrying her, and another even rasher thought—the crazy idea that she might enslave Justin Waite—only to end up the one who was ensalved herself... What she would have done once that was accomplished was not quite clear, but that she should even have entertained it proved to her, now that she could think more clearly, that being really married to him had never been so unthinkable. Indeed, perhaps

75

at the back of her mind there had always been a fatal fascination about it.

I think I must have always been a little in love with him, she mused painfully, and all that anger was caused more by hurt pride than by anything else, because he doesn't love me the same way. What would be worse, she wondered: to be married to a man you hated or married to a man you loved who didn't love you? And even if you did decide to live with it, how did you take that final step...?

It was ironic thus that what in the end did help her should also be the cause of Justin Waite's not loving her as she believed she loved him... She had thrown Joanna Madden's name at him once—their relationship had after all been long-lasting and well-documented. Come to think of it, Joanna's was the only name Justin had been linked with like that... Then, out of the blue, Joanna had married an older man who was very wealthy and twice divorced. But what Lucy had not expected was to meet Joanna Madden in the flesh and at Riverbend.

They'd taken Adrian and Shirley to see the yearlings that so soon would be going to the sales—Shirley in quite a flutter of excitement because this was her first flight. They'd not alerted Sasha other than buzzing the stud office, which was Justin's way of saying he was arriving, and they'd arrived. There was another light plane on the runway which Justin had stared at with a frown—the Maddens'. And they'd all met up in the stud office with Sasha looking pink and confused and as if she couldn't believe this was happening to her.

'Oh, Justin,' she said as he walked over the doorstep, 'I...um...the Cawnpore filly...that is Mr Madden here...is very interested in her breeding and he called

me up on the HF and said they were flying over
Riverbend and asked if he could take a look...'

'That's no problem, Sasha,' Justin said smoothly as
his grey gaze swept the room and took in the couple
standing across it. 'Joanna, Tim, how are you? I don't
know if you've met Lucy?'

Joanna Madden, Lucy decided a bit dazedly as there
was a slight pause, was still lovely. About thirty, she
was dark, tall and graceful and she had an air that
marked her as a person of inner grace—she had had it
when Lucy had met her briefly years before but now it
had another quality that was hard to define except to say
that it was slightly haunting...

'Yes.' Joanna came forward, breaking the pause that
had begun to stretch. 'We did meet once, Lucy; I don't
know if you remember? Tim,' she turned to her husband,
who looked to be in his early fifties but was tall and
spare, 'this is Lucy Wainright from Dalkeith, Justin's
next-door neighbour.'

This time the pause was crashing. Sasha actually
closed her eyes before Justin said quietly, 'In fact Lucy
and I got married a couple of months ago, Joanna.'

Joanna's eyes jerked to his, but that was the only sign
she gave that this news might be momentous, because
the next moment she murmured, 'We've been overseas
for so long! Oh, I do wish you both every happiness. *We*
do, don't we, Tim?' And she turned to him and slipped
her hand into his.

'Justin?'

'Mmm...?'

It was that same evening and, as they'd got into the

habit of, they were sitting in the library after dinner. It was raining again.

'I think you should tell me about Joanna Madden, Justin,' Lucy said.

He stretched his legs and looked into the fire for a while. 'What do you want to know?'

'Why she didn't marry you. Why she looks...sort of sad. Why she couldn't hide for a moment what a surprise it was that we'd got married. And why, considering past history, her husband should even consider taking her to Riverbend, let alone buying the Cawnpore filly.'

He turned his gaze to her at last. 'Taking things unchronologically, Lucy, that Cawnpore filly is the best of the bunch. She shows signs of wonderful conformation, she has marvellous bloodlines on the distaff side—so much so that I've put a reserve price on her even Tim Madden might find hard to fork out.' He looked towards the fire again and his gaze was extremely meditative.

Lucy was briefly diverted. 'If that's the case, why are you even contemplating selling her?' she queried.

After a long moment he shrugged. 'I own her dam and her grandam and—' he gestured '—Cawnpore. He was a gamble but he's proving himself as a sire now, so you could say I'm on a bet to nothing. It's all still there at Riverbend, the genes. Not that everything is ever a certainty, but then again, I could keep the filly and race her and have her break down on me or a hundred other things go wrong with her—it happens. It happens all the time with horses. I've hung on to what I've thought were the best before, only to find it wasn't so.'

'But mares—well, fillies,' Lucy protested, 'even if they don't race well—'

'They can be barren, they can run into fences, they

can get colic. I think too,' he frowned, 'that while I would have liked to retain an interest in her if I didn't have her dam and grandam, I see myself essentially as a breeder. Racing horses is another game in a sense.'

Lucy stared at him. 'All right. I guess I can see the logic in that,' she said slowly. 'But why would Tim Madden want her? From you, I mean.'

Justin smiled faintly. 'Tim is a racing man above all else. Horses are a subject that transcend everything with him.'

'Even to putting his wife through—an experience like that?'

Justin didn't move but he transferred a slightly wry grey gaze to her. 'What makes you think it was such an experience? Joanna and I broke up two years ago.'

Lucy hesitated then she said simply, 'Why?'

She thought he wasn't going to answer so she then said, 'I'm not asking this because I want to poke or pry—'

'Don't you?' He raised an eyebrow at her.

'No,' she insisted a little heatedly. 'But my intuition tells me it could have something to do with why you married *me*. So why should I be kept in the dark?' She lifted her chin defiantly at him.

He smiled again, idly and as if at some inner thought. 'Very well. Joanna discovered she was unable to have children.'

Lucy felt her eyes widening and had to stop herself from staring at him open-mouthed as well. 'So she wouldn't marry you and—and married a man who already had a family. Justin! Oh—how terribly sad!'

'Now don't get all carried away, Lucy. It's not nearly as dramatic as you make it sound.'

'But it must have been! When two people really love each other—'

'That's fairy-tale stuff you're talking, Lucy,' he said drily.

'But she looked so—haunted for a moment or two!'

He said nothing, and his expression was indecipherable as he looked into the fire until Lucy said, 'And you've never forgiven her, Justin, have you?'

He looked up then and said impatiently, 'Of course I have. The sadness you see in her is probably to do with not being able to have anyone's children.'

'I—well—Justin—' Lucy looked at him confusedly '—I don't know about that but are you sure you didn't marry me because it didn't matter much to you who you married after—her?'

'Lucy,' his lips twisted and his eyes were suddenly amused, 'if that were the case, that I married simply for the sake of it, don't you think I would have found myself a much more *compliant* candidate for a wife?'

Lucy's brow creased. 'I suppose so, but don't forget they didn't have the other half of Dalkeith.'

'That's true,' he said wryly. 'So you're unique in several senses.'

She tightened her mouth. 'I also very much resent being married because it's so *practical*,' she said bitterly. 'That's what you said to me!'

'My apologies,' he replied gravely. 'If I'd put it to you that we'd once been good friends, how would that have affected you?'

'I'd have probably liked it better,' she said but grudgingly.

'Would you have admitted it, though?'

She opened her mouth, closed it and reddened. Then

she said haughtily, 'I don't know what point you're trying to make, Justin, it's quite lost on me. But the point I'm trying to make is that we're locked in a loveless marriage—and I'm beginning to see why!'

'Lucy,' he said evenly, 'I've never denied the practicalities of our marriage. But its lovelessness hasn't been put to the test yet. I've told you that from my point of view it's a commitment, not some nine-day wonder, and I mean that. When you try it, you'll see what I mean.' He stood up and stretched. 'And here endeth that lesson, but perhaps I could say one thing more. Romance and moonlight and declarations of never-ending love are all very well—indeed, I wouldn't expect you to live without them entirely.' He smiled down at her unexpectedly and added wryly, 'Not you. But there's a whole lot more to it, as many a romantically inclined girl has discovered to her cost. So don't be too scathing about practicalities; they often build into something strong and enduring *because* they have a basis to build up.'

Lucy's lips parted and she frowned. 'Why not me?'

He lifted a lazy eyebrow. 'Why not you what?'

'Why wouldn't you expect me of *all* people—you didn't say that but you might as well have—to live without—well, all those things *you* were being scathing about?'

His lips twisted. 'Are you not the Lucy Wainright about whom some bloke flew a plane over Sydney Harbour trailing a banner asking you to marry him?'

Lucy's eyes sparkled with indignation. 'I don't think it's fair to blame me for that! I'd given him absolutely no cause to imagine I would!'

He grimaced. 'Perhaps not. I do remember the papers writing you up as rather heartless because you declined.'

He grinned. 'Still, some very romantic gestures have come your way, you must admit.'

'They did,' she said with youthful dignity and a very steady gaze from her pansy-blue eyes. 'It may have escaped you that I didn't take any of them up, Justin. No one rushed me into marriage because of moonlight and roses. You were the one who did the rushing.'

'You're only twenty,' he said mildly, ignoring the rest of her speech.

'I may be, but I'm not entirely a fool.' She stood up herself. 'I'll have to think about *this* revelation now! I hope you have no objection to that?'

He took his time replying. He studied her brave stance and her outfit of grey cords and a lovely chunky grey and white sweater. His gaze lingered on her loose hair and finally her face and there was something in it that caused her to catch her breath slightly and be suddenly aware of him differently, something undoubtedly admiring in his eyes; it was as if they were a man and a woman caught in a moment of intimate curiosity. *No*, she thought, as a sensation that was becoming familiar coursed through her body, a sensation of leaping pulses and trembling anticipation. He can't do this to me. Not when he's just told me about Joanna! And she switched her gaze away confusedly.

'By all means, Lucy,' he merely said after a moment.

She turned away and walked towards the door, praying he wouldn't guess what an effort it was to appear completely normal.

Yet despite that puzzling look, over the next few days Lucy couldn't help feeling that Justin was withdrawn and preoccupied, in fact he spent a lot of time at Riverbend, much to Adrian's disgust.

And she couldn't help wondering how much that unexpected encounter with Joanna had affected him. It also occurred to her that he had never denied being in love with Joanna. And she thought to herself often, it's all falling into place, isn't it? It has to be. You don't marry someone the way he married me unless there's a reason like that behind it. So what do I do now?

It also struck her as unfair that during those few days she could settle to nothing because of a curiously bereft feeling...

What she did do was quite unexpected, as it happened, and it all boiled up one evening out of the blue...

She was sitting at the piano playing Chopin when Justin came in—she hadn't seen him for two days and he'd arrived after dinner, which Shirley had kept warm for him, and elected to eat in the kitchen where Adrian had regaled him with *his* doings of the past few days.

Lucy had stayed for a while then wandered into the library and started to play softly. She looked up now as he closed the door, and felt her heart contract. He was wearing jeans and a black sweater and there were marks of weariness on his face beneath his ruffled dark hair and something drained and moody in his eyes. He also said briefly, 'What's wrong?'

'Nothing. I...I was going to ask you the same.'

'Why?'

She played a chord quietly. 'I thought you looked—tired and disenchanted, that's all.'

He shrugged. 'I am tired. A consignment of twenty-five yearlings to break in and get ready for a sale is a tiring business.' He sat down in an armchair and lay back. 'Play some more,' he suggested after a minute or so. 'How come you play so well?'

'Mother Angelica, at school,' Lucy said with a grimace. 'She used to tie me to the piano stool—no, not really, but she was a very determined person, and eventually I grew to love it.'

'She was your music teacher?'

'She was much more than that,' Lucy said wryly. 'My headmistress, the bane of my life often, yet, looking back, rather wise and someone I'll always admire.'

He said no more, so she played, and noticed out of the corner of her eye that his hand on the arm of the chair clenched and stretched a few times, then relaxed. What she didn't notice was the way he watched her straight back, the sweep of her eyelashes as she concentrated, how she sometimes, as a lovely melody evolved beneath her fingers, bit her bottom lip.

She also found herself thinking about Mother Angelica as she played, that hard-headed but wise nun who had had very clear ideas on a whole host of subjects including the role of wifedom that would come to most of her charges...

And she must have played for nearly an hour with those thoughts on her mind, until she began to wonder if he'd fallen asleep, but, as she closed the piano softly and stood up, she saw that he had not.

'Sorry,' he said, and grimaced. 'I'm not great company tonight, am I? That was very...relaxing.'

Lucy hesitated then sat down opposite him. 'Strange to say,' she said very slowly, 'I'm sorry I can't offer you the more conventional form of relaxation wives are sup-

posed to provide—but I don't think it would help to try
to be a substitute tonight—do you?'

She saw his mouth harden briefly then thought he
might have forced himself to relax as he drawled, 'So
that's what's bothering you—Joanna again.'

'Yes,' she admitted composedly, 'but it may surprise
you to know all my thoughts on the subject.'

He lifted one black brow wryly. 'Well, go on, surprise
me.'

She looked down and smoothed the fabric of the long
tartan skirt she wore with a dark green angora cardigan
that had little pearl buttons. Her hair was tied back simply with a matching green ribbon. And she answered
obliquely, 'Do you...could you believe that I think do-
mesticity is overtaking me, Justin?'

He narrowed his eyes. 'I think you'll have to explain
a bit better than that, Lucy.'

'I...I just have it in me at the moment to believe I
could be quite a good wife, to be modest and industrious—you're probably going to laugh—'

'No,' he said slowly with a frown in his eyes. 'But
when did all this hit you?'

When you walked in tonight, she answered in her
heart, and when I thought of Mother Angelica, that's
when it all crystallised, but she said, 'Over the last few
days, I suppose.'

'Well—' He paused and watched her searchingly.
'What are you suggesting?'

'That's up to you, really. I mean—' she hesitated
'—if you still feel we could make a go of it.'

'I've never changed my mind about that. Lucy—' he
paused '—you're not about to sacrifice yourself on the

altar of your no doubt highly dramatised version of what happened with Joanna, are you?'

'Not while she's still so close to you,' she said, and thought he swore under his breath but made herself go on bravely, 'and not that, no. Just—well, you yourself told me it comes to most people, a time when they have to make the best of things, so…that.' And she lifted her chin and stared into his eyes with dignity.

He swore properly this time and said roughly, 'Do you know how old you look, Lucy? About sixteen.'

She flinched. And said honestly, 'I feel a lot older than sixteen, Justin. I know how young I must appear to you but right now I feel like a woman for the first time in my life probably.' She stopped awkwardly and licked her lips nervously as she sought to explain what was in her heart. 'And I'm beginning to understand what my options are, I guess. Go away from here, or try to build something worthwhile with you. And I suppose it came to me that if I'd had the courage to go away, I would have done it at the beginning. It's also come to me that even if you couldn't love me as you did Joanna, if you did care all the same, then you're right, there is something to work on.'

'What if,' he said very quietly, and she thought she saw a tinge of pain in his eyes, 'my…the way I love you doesn't come up to expectations?'

'You mean if I really fall in love with you but it doesn't happen the same way for you?' She stopped, but he didn't answer or make any gesture so she said, 'Then I'll have to pour it all into Dalkeith, and you'll have to give me some children, Justin. But there's one thing I've got to tell you before you make up your mind.' She hesitated, then took a deep breath. 'It's one of the reasons why making this decision has been so difficult for me—I don't know if you'll believe this but I'm not very experienced about lovemaking. In point of fact...I've never actually done it.'

'I know—'

'Now if that alters *your* decision I'd quite understand. I mean it's a bit different for two reasons at least—you *what*?' She stared at him with her lips parted and her eyes huge.

'I know that you're a virgin, Lucy.'

'But how can you possibly—know?' she whispered.

'Because your innocence in these matters—shines like a lamp,' he said with irony, self-directed irony she thought, but such was her confusion that she didn't give it more than a passing thought.

'But everything you've *said*,' she protested, and bit her lip.

His lips twisted. 'It suited me to—go along with everything *you* said with such bravado, my dear. I also—' he paused and regarded her crestfallen countenance with something unusually gentle in his eyes '—have known you for a long time and always had quite a bit of respect for you, Lucy.'

'Respect,' she murmured dazedly. 'But what about—' she licked her lips '—what about getting a proposal of marriage from a plane over Sydney Harbour? And, I did have—well, quite a few boyfriends, although—' her eyes flashed suddenly '—I certainly deny "queening" it over all and sundry!'

'My apologies. In fact you were a sight for sore eyes when you were—in full flight. Is that a better way of putting it? But still quite obviously a lovely, laughing girl who had given herself to no one.'

'Oh.' Lucy groaned and put her hands to her hot cheeks. 'This is so humiliating!'

'On the contrary, it's something to be proud of.'

'So you married me—you don't mind, in other words?'

'Why should I mind?' He smiled faintly.

'Well, I could turn out to be frigid for one thing,' she said starkly. 'And isn't it a little bit different—taking someone untouched into a marriage like this, other than someone who might have a better idea of...all sorts of things!' She eyed him indignantly.

He sat up abruptly. 'You're not frigid, Lucy.'

'That sounds so essentially male!'

'It may be,' he said with a tinge of impatience, 'but believe me, it's true.'

'Do all men know so much about women?' she asked then with turmoil and confusion showing in her eyes.

He shrugged. 'I don't know. And you're only one young woman we're talking about. I don't claim ultimate wisdom on the subject. All it means is that I'm quite a few years older and have a lot more experience.'

She stared at him for a long moment, then said, barely audibly, 'Do you know what I wish? I can't help wishing at this moment,' she whispered desolately, 'that I were planning to be a modest, industrious wife to someone who didn't necessarily have any experience but who loved me so much that it wouldn't matter.'

'Strangely enough,' he answered very quietly, 'at this moment, so do I.'

'Justin—'

But he stood up and walked over to her and held out his hand. 'Lucy—you could still take my other offer. You talked of an annulment once...' He paused as she put her hand into his uncertainly, and pulled her gently to her feet. 'If that's really what you want to do,' he finished.

She didn't realise the leap of fright that showed in her eyes, but she did make herself say, 'Because you saw Joanna again, is...is that—'

'Lucy, that's over and done with,' he said grimly. 'I—'

But she wouldn't let him go on. Speaking from a deep well of fear in her heart, she said haltingly, 'Well, perhaps if you can't have her and I can't have—an imaginary person who might never exist anyway, could we console each other, do you think?'

It was his turn to stare down into her eyes with something like real regret in his, until he said, 'We could try.'

'Well—'

She got no further, because he put a finger to her lips and murmured, 'I think we've probably said as much as one can say on the subject. I think the time has come now to—let things take their course. Like this.' And he took her into his arms and started to kiss her.

It was quite some time later when his mouth left hers and she discovered that just about everything else had left her mind, Joanna Madden included, because it seemed she was wholly focused on Justin Waite and the rapture his lips and his hands had inflicted on her body and imprinted on her soul. It was also a revelation because she hadn't expected it, yet this kiss couldn't have been more different from the only other time he'd kissed her, and that was what she'd expected—another give-nothing-away experience. And it was what she'd expected to bestow, she realised shakily. But she'd received and bestowed far more, and her breathing was

undoubtedly erratic as she stared up at him, not wanting
to be released. Heady again with the feel and the taste
of him but completely abandoned to it this time, her skin
trembling finely in anticipation as his hands wandered
down her back and found the gap between her cardigan
and skirt and lingered on her waist, then slipped beneath
the elastic waistband of the skirt and slid down to her
hips, scantily clad in a tiny pair of fine silk bikini briefs.

Her breath jolted in a little flare of shock and his eyes
narrowed as he saw it, but the shock waned almost as
quickly as it had flared, and she came unresistingly as
he pulled her even closer because there seemed to be a
current flowing between them, or from him to her, she
thought, a sort of sensual pull that both amazed her and
filled her with an inner quivering that was a mixture of
longing and excitement—and the knowledge that she
wanted to be nowhere else on earth but in Justin Waite's
arms.

It was like a compulsion such as she'd never known,
and an awareness that made her drink in everything
about him, the way his dark hair fell and those little lines
beside his eyes—they weren't creased in amusement, she
noted, in fact his eyelids were half lowered in a rather
intent way and he seemed to be watching her mouth with
interest, just her lips, which sent another tremor through
her as she remembered how his own had explored the
soft skin of her neck and a little further down when he'd
flicked open a couple of little pearl buttons...

And she made a helpless little sound because it was
also terribly unfair that he could make her feel like this,
though of course, to be perfectly honest, it had been
growing in her for a long time, hadn't it? It had probably

been there when she was fourteen and measuring up her
very first date at the school dance...

'And what is going through your mind at the moment,
Lucy,' he said very softly and kissed the corner of her
mouth chastely.

'I still think we should wait until...'

'No, now,' he said and took her back into his arms.
'This has gone on long enough, and it will be all right,
I promise you.'

'Justin,' she whispered, her colour fluctuating, her
breathing erratic, 'do you mean...?'

'Yes, now, tonight.' And stopped anything further she
might have said by kissing her.

'I feel—I feel so different,' she said later.

'Do you?' Justin drew his hand down her pale, slender
body and rested his dark head on his hand so he could
look into her eyes. There was one lamp on in her bedroom and the bed was rumpled, the fire now low. 'Tell
me.'

'I feel translated somehow.' Her voice was low and
husky. 'Does that sound odd to you?'

'Not at all.' He stroked her cheek. 'I feel a bit that
way myself. You're incredibly lovely, you know.'

'But was I any good?' she said very quietly. There
were faint blue shadows beneath her eyes, her hair was
damp and disordered and there was something young
and bewildered in her eyes, as if she couldn't quite believe what had happened, couldn't quite make the tran-
sition to having him lean and strong, dark and naked in
bed beside her.

He smiled and pushed some golden strands of hair off

her face. 'You were tender and—delicious. Didn't you notice my reaction, incidentally?'

She thought for a moment and closed her eyes at the memory of the feel of his hard body on hers and how he'd made her want everything he'd done to her, how he'd made her feel soft and smooth and told her she was like a work of art—how there'd been no pain at all, how her eyes had opened and her hands on his back had fallen slack and she'd gasped as sheer pleasure had risen in waves through her body and she'd felt the convulsion of his with a sweet sense of triumph.

'And you came yourself, didn't you?' he said as all this passed through her mind.

'I...yes, something happened to me that was quite wonderful,' she confessed.

'Then—' he pulled up the sheet and held her close '—all is well.'

But she said seriously, 'Justin, I just have this feeling I may have given myself away and I'm a little worried about it, you see.'

He moved his chin on her hair and she thought he laughed softly. 'Given yourself away how, Lucy?'

'Let you know that I do love you—'

'You don't have to worry about that.'

She grimaced. 'I suppose you knew that too all the time I was—pretending to myself. But what I'm worried about is that it might be a burden to you so—'

'No, Lucy—' he put his fingers to her lips '—it's not, it never can be, so don't say any more. Let's just relax and be happy. Go to sleep, in other words, my sweet, talkative wife,' he said wryly, and kissed her brow.

Lucy subsided, although part of her wanted to have it out with him, but the rest of her couldn't help but feel warm and safe, and it was so lovely lying against him and feeling his hand stroking her back that she ended up falling asleep before she knew it.

And morning brought her some reassurance.

She woke to find him watching her with something unmistakably tender in his eyes. He also said, 'How do you feel, Mrs Waite?'

Her lips curved. 'Fine, thank you, Mr Waite.'

'Then would you mind—if I did this?' And he drew the covers aside and touched her nipples until they started to unfurl and a sense of longing travelled down her body, and her eyes widened in such surprise that he laughed and kissed her. 'Don't look like that, it's quite normal to wake up feeling sexy. I've been doing battle with it for about half an hour.' And he eased his weight on to her gently.

They showered together afterwards and she ate a huge breakfast then went for a ride, during which, for the first time since their marriage, she told him about some of her ideas for Dalkeith and he listened attentively and with approval. But after lunch he said he had some work to do so she, somewhat to her surprise, found a book and curled up with it for the whole afternoon.

'Lucy?'

She looked up to see Justin standing over her with something wry in his eyes.

'Hi!'

'I wondered where you were—the place was so quiet.'

She stretched and yawned and closed the book then glanced at her watch and blinked in surprise. 'It's nearly dinnertime! Is this what being married does to one?' she asked with a glint of humour.

'There's no sin in it,' he replied, helping her up and kissing the top of her head.

'It seems very slothful, however,' she commented, and leant against him.

'Perhaps that's what honeymoons were designed for.'

'Oh! Perhaps you're right!' She glinted a smile up at him. 'To help new brides get over the shock of it all.'

'Shock?' he queried tilting her chin up and with something quizzical in his expression.

'What I mean is—'

'Did it come as such a shock, Lucy?'

'No, not really.' She lowered her lashes. 'But something has to account for the fact that I seem to be—' she paused '—in a state of suspended animation at the moment,' she said thoughtfully. 'I mean, after all the weeks of trauma, it's finally happened—you'd think I'd at least be analysing it, turning it over and over, trying to poke holes in it—that sort of thing, instead of peacefully reading a book all afternoon. Oh, no!' And she looked up at him with a curiously comical, wide-eyed look of horror.

'Lucy, you've got me seriously worried,' he said wryly. 'Oh, no what?'

'I've just remembered something you said to me!'

'Well, tell me.' He fingered the collar of her blouse and his lips twisted. 'Before I die of curiosity.'

'I don't think I should—you'll be able to say I told you so! And I don't think I'd appreciate that one bit...'

He grimaced. 'I can see I'm going to have to use strong-arm tactics, Mrs Waite. Shall we go up to our bedroom?'

'What do you mean?' She was genuinely wide-eyed now.

'Just that I could kiss you there until you were happy to confide in me without the possibility of Adrian or Shirley stumbling upon us, and just in case it went— further than that.' His grey eyes were entirely grave.

'That's...incredible blackmail, Justin!'

'I know but one of much the nicest forms of it you'd probably find.'

'Then I'll spike your guns here and now, sir,' she said and started to laugh. 'It's just that you did say to me once that without regular, satisfying sex I could get troublesome and fractious—'

'Actually I said *women*—'

'It was still an amazingly superior kind of thing to say, whether you were generalising or being particular, or so I thought. Now I have to wonder if you were right, which is rather demoralising actually—'

'Then perhaps this will help,' he interrupted. 'From now on, without regular, satisfying sex with you, Lucy, I'm the one who could become fractious and troublesome.'

She stared up into his eyes and was so totally intrigued and fascinated by this possibility, she forgot to say anything at all.

Until he said softly, 'What deep, dark plans are you concocting for me now, Lucy Waite?'

'Nothing!' But she blushed and got hotter as he laughed quietly and kissed her on the lips, and said, 'If it weren't for the fact that dinner *is* only ten minutes away...' But he didn't go on as they heard Shirley come into the dining-room next door; instead he raised a rueful eyebrow—and Lucy breathed a tiny sigh of relief.

It was after dinner that he brought up the subject of honeymoons again.

'You know,' he said as they sat down before the library fire, as it was raining again, 'once the yearling sales are over we should take our delayed honeymoon. Where would you like to go?'

They were sitting side by side on the settee and Lucy raised her hands above her head and said, 'Oh—the Seychelles, where I could get around in a bikini all the time and if it rains it's warm. Or—Tahiti sounds nice, Justin,' she said, parodying a television advertisement with a pert look.

'It does indeed, but seriously—'

Her expression grew serious. 'Closer to home? I don't mind—that didn't sound very modest or industrious, did it?'

He laughed quietly and pulled her onto his lap. 'The thought of you in a bikini all the time in the Seychelles is seriously electrifying, all the same. What I was going to say was, do you have a *serious* desire to see them or were you teasing me?'

She considered for a moment then all of a sudden found herself with tears in her eyes.

'What's the matter?' He frowned down at her.

'I don't know—how very embarrassing! I think being in a position *to* tease you, Justin, is something of a revelation and...and...' She couldn't go on.

'Lucy,' he said quietly and stroked her hair, 'this is only reaction—it has all been pretty traumatic but it's *over* now.'

Lucy laughed shakily, and Adrian stuck his head around the door. 'Mum's looking for you two.'

Justin stilled Lucy's sudden movement. 'Ask your mum if we can have our coffee in here, Adrian. Is something wrong?'

Adrian advanced into the room and continued his critical study of them from close quarters. 'She sick?' he asked at last.

'No. Just tired,' Justin said gravely.

'Didn't know you two felt like that about each other,' he said with the extreme unselfconsciousness of youth and because he was Adrian anyway, and extremely perceptive with it.

'As you see, we do. I hope you approve?' Justin enquired.

Adrian shrugged. 'Don't know much about it. I haven't got a father so my Mum doesn't go in for it.'

'Yes, well, that could change one day, Adrian, and if it does I'll tell you how to handle it. The best way is to ignore it and leave them in peace.'

Adrian considered. 'OK,' he said at length. 'I reckon I get the message. I'll tell Mum to knock like the clappers when she brings the coffee and not to rush it.'

'You're a bright boy, Adrian,' Justin said with not a breath of laughter. 'In fact I'll add to that, I reckon you'll go a long way.'

'Thanks,' Adrian replied off-handedly. 'By the way, I've changed my mind. Not sure about being a farmer any more. I think I'll be a pilot. See you later.' He withdrew and closed the door behind him.

But Lucy could contain herself no longer. She began to laugh uncontrollably and felt Justin's iron control give way too. 'Oh, God, he's a character, isn't he?' she gasped.

'One of the best.'

It was minutes before they were quiet again, although Lucy was still subject to the odd breathless little chuckle.

'Feeling better?' he asked.

'Mmm.' She moved her cheek against his chest and thought how warm and safe she felt and how she'd like to stay like this all night. And as the thought took possession of her mind, she raised her lashes and whispered, 'I can, can't I?'

'Can what?'

'I'm just thinking aloud; it doesn't matter.'

'Yes, it does.' He put his fingers under her chin and made her look up at him.

'I can spend the night with you—that's what I was thinking, that's all,' she said, and shrugged and coloured all at the same time. 'You're probably wondering if I've gone feeble-minded,' she added ruefully.

He laughed quietly—and then swore as the phone rang.

It was Sasha with the news that the Cawnpore filly had severe colic.

'I'll have to go—Lucy, I'm sorry,' Justin said intensely.

'But it's dark and it's raining, Justin, and you—'

He sat down and took her hands. 'It's stopped raining and it's clear over Riverbend, and I have an instrument rating for night flying—Lucy, that filly could bring a hell of a lot of money at the sales if we can save her and I don't have to tell you that colic can be fatal in a horse. I have to go, much as I hate to.'

Her hands quivered in his but she said, 'Of course. Good luck with her. Will you ring me when you arrive?'

'Yes.' He leant forward and kissed her. 'Sleep well, Mrs Waite.'

'I'll try...'

She was actually in bed although not asleep when the phone rang, but it was Sasha to say that Justin had arrived safely, and that they looked as if they had a difficult night ahead of them and not to expect him home until tomorrow.

Lucy replaced the receiver and regarded it balefully for a moment. 'I don't know why I put up with that woman,' she also murmured. 'Only she could, in the space of a few short sentences, contrive to make me feel quite useless while she's being so strong and competent,' she marvelled.

She put the lamp out with a snap and slid down to curl up beneath the covers in her pink and white polka-dot silk pyjamas. Then it occurred to her to wonder what Sasha and the rest of the world would make of the latest development in the Waite marriage, assuming they'd been privy to what had gone before—which they hadn't, she reminded herself, but might have sensed or guessed it.

But her overriding emotion, she discovered, was a hauntingly new feeling of vulnerability. Because I'm alone? she asked herself. I didn't feel like this earlier today, I felt serene and—well, *happy*. She grimaced suddenly and tried to think back over what had happened and how it had happened but, as she'd found all day, it all seemed dreamlike and not susceptible to analysis...

It was as if all she could think of now was how much she loved Justin Waite, and how, oddly, that had opened up a whole new field of vulnerability for her.

She fell asleep with it on her mind.

CHAPTER SIX

LUCY woke up to a warm, clear morning the next day and a call from Justin this time, to say that the filly was responding to treatment but still not out of danger, and he'd have to stay with her until she was.

'Of course,' Lucy said down the line. 'I quite understand.'

'What will you do?'

'As a very new wife who's lost her husband on the second day of her—well, what should be her honeymoon?' she said with a chuckle. 'I'm not altogether sure, Justin.'

'Lucy—'

'No—I'm only teasing, I really am fine,' she said wryly, and they chatted for a few minutes more. And when she put the phone down she discovered she did feel a lot better, with none of the shadows of the night before lurking in her mind, and after helping Shirley during the morning she had lunch then saddled her horse and went for a ride.

It was such a pleasure, after all the rain they'd had, to be out in warmth and sunshine, that she actually found herself singing as she rode along. She also thought wryly that she was exhibiting classic symptoms of being in love—and that just a few words from Justin this morning had achieved a minor miracle.

It was quite unwittingly that she rode towards the twelve-mile paddock, which true to form could be more

100

accurately described as a bog in parts. Any more rain and it would flood as it often did, she thought and paused to breathe in the air and the sky and take off a jumper as she let her horse pick its way. And since she'd got this far, she decided to check the repairs to the old boundary riders' hut.

The hut could not even by a long stretch of imagination be described as anything but rough and ready but the roof and door had been repaired, a supply of firewood laid in for the stove as well as some basic provisions and there were new mattresses on the two bunks and some heavy duty blankets that resembled horse blankets in texture. She grimaced as she felt them then raised her head suddenly as she realised that in the half-hour or so she'd been poking around the afternoon had gone curiously still. And the fine hairs on her body stood up in the eerie silence which was broken, as she swung open the door, by a sheet of lightning that filled the sky and an enormous clap of thunder that caused her to jump about a foot in the air. What was worse was the fright her horse got, which caused it to rear and whinny and break its lead, and, on discovering itself free, show her a clean pair of heels as it headed for home.

'Oh, no!' The words were torn from her as the sun went out in a manner of speaking and the first raindrops fell like bullets from an enormous thunderhead and more thunder and lightning split the sky.

But it was 'oh, yes'; she was marooned, the twelve-mile was bound to flood with this storm; she should have realised the unusual warmth in the air could lead to storms and she'd told nobody where she was going...

'Well, I'm quite safe,' she told herself as she closed the hut door against the uproar outside, 'it's just that nobody knows it. And it did come up so fast; anyone could have been caught napping—well, anyone with other things to think of. Could I be blamed for this? Not really,' she reassured herself, resolutely stilling the slight niggle of her conscience by adding, 'All's well that ends well, don't they say?'

It was nine o'clock before it finally stopped raining, but there was still thunder in the air, and, when she peered out, an obliging flash of lightning illuminated an eerie scene—water lying everywhere below the high ground the hut was built on, more water than she'd ever seen in the twelve-mile, probably waist-deep in some parts, she guessed, and she shivered as she remembered her grandfather telling her about a flash-flood that had swept through the paddock once and lapped the door of the hut. So she closed the door and concentrated on the fact that she was dry and safe. In fact it was quite cheerful inside the little hut. She had a roaring fire going in the stove, she'd eaten a dinner of baked beans and biscuits and there was a pot of coffee bubbling away. She'd also pulled the two mattresses off the bunks and put them on the floor in front of the stove—it was now very cold, and a wind was getting up which would probably blow the storms away—good news really, although the danger of flash-flooding still depended on how much water was draining into the paddock.

It was probably due to the rising wind and the crackle of the fire that she heard nothing as she sat huddled on a mattress under one of those hairy blankets and sipped her coffee. In fact her first intimation that she was not alone came when the hut door opened precipitately, nearly blew off its hinges and a tall, dripping figure stood there.

She nearly died at the unexpectedness of it, spilt her coffee and yelped with pain then gasped as she put her cup down. 'Justin! You frightened the life out of me! Couldn't you have knocked—?'

But with a swift lunging movement her muddy, torn and tattered husband hauled her to her feet and grated through his teeth, 'What the *hell* are you doing here, Lucy? Have you no sense at all? Just how long are you going to be a giddy, thoughtless, brainless eternal schoolgirl?'

If he'd just not said those last words, the short fuse to her own temper might not have lit, but it did in a blinding flash because she knew she was no longer a schoolgirl or giddy or thoughtless and brainless, in fact she knew she was a woman in just about every sense of the word with a lot of the heartache that seemed to go with the condition—and all at his hands. So she wrestled an arm free, spat at him, 'I *hate* you, Justin Waite! I wouldn't *be* here if it weren't for you.' And she hit him hard and accurately on his cheekbone.

His grey eyes blazed beneath his dark, dripping hair, and his mouth twisted in a frighteningly savage way, then he jerked her into his arms, stared briefly into her widening eyes, darkening with fright as her face paled, and started to kiss her ruthlessly.

She sagged to her knees when he let her go at last, her heart pounding, her mouth bruised and her whole body shaking.

He stared down at her for a moment, their eyes locking, then he said grimly, 'Don't you realise that every able man on the place is out searching for you, that we've even called in the State Emergency Services helicopter?'

She gasped. 'I...but there was no way I could let you know I was all right. My horse b-bolted, you see—' her teeth chattered '—it was the thunder, then it started to pour—it was really all just...one of those things,' she finished helplessly in a bare little whisper, and dropped her head into her hands.

'No, it wasn't,' he said precisely. 'It was a case of plain thoughtlessness, Lucy, and in future don't you ever go galloping off into the blue without telling someone *where* you're going. Do you understand?'

'Yes. Look, I'm sorry—'

But he cut her off. 'And for someone who knows as much as you do, or claims you do, to come *here* when you know the history of this bloody paddock was sheer lunacy. Look at me, Lucy,' he commanded.

She did, and could have cried because of course he was right. If only she hadn't been so happily preoccupied! But she refused to allow herself the luxury of tears. 'You're right,' she said in a stiff little voice. 'I was extremely stupid. I won't do it again. How did you get here?'

His mouth set in a hard line then he pulled off his oilskin. 'I drove as far as I could then I walked and finally I swam.' His eyes glinted with mockery and she winced. 'I just hope,' he continued, pulling a two-way radio wrapped in more oilskin out from under his shirt, 'this survived the experience.'

It had, and she breathed a sigh of relief as he called off the search, thanked everybody, and it was decided they'd be safe for the rest of the night and a rescue attempt would be made in the morning.

'We'll bring a boat this time,' the voice on the other

end promised with more good-naturedness than one would have expected.

But it didn't appear to improve Justin's humour. He put the radio down, glanced at her coldly then started to remove the rest of his wrecked, sodden clothes.

Lucy took a breath, wondered incredulously if she was being sent to Coventry, but some impulse made her guard against putting it to the test immediately. And she turned away and busied herself.

'Here,' she said after a while, and handed him a cup of steaming packet soup. There was a pot of canned braised beef simmering on the stove and she'd hung his clothes over the bunks. He'd stripped to his underpants and was wrapped in a blanket. She'd earlier found a coarse old towel and he'd rubbed himself down with it and the muscles of his shoulders and thighs had rippled under his fire-bronzed skin.

He took the soup and drank it in silence then started on the beef, and all he said was, 'Aren't you having any?'

'I'm not hungry—I had something earlier.'

He didn't reply and she busied herself at the rudimentary sink which was a bucket on a table, and wondered how long it would be before she was considered suitably chastened and worthy of talking to.

He finished the coffee she poured for him and lay back with his hands behind his head. She hesitated, then sat down cross-legged on the other mattress half turned away from him and sipped her own.

And she nearly spilt another lot of coffee as he said suddenly, 'Would you care to explain, Lucy, why you wouldn't be here if it weren't for me?'

'I—what I meant was,' she said carefully, 'that I had

some things on my mind. And so I wasn't quite as—um—'

'On the ball as you should have been,' he completed for her drily. 'That's no excuse.'

'Well—'

'Lucy,' he said dangerously.

She grimaced and sipped some coffee. 'Perhaps you're right.'

'Perhaps?'

'All right,' she said quietly. 'I've admitted it was stupid, *I* am stupid—'

'All the more so if those things you had on your mind,' he said sardonically, 'are to do with us.'

She took a breath. 'I can't quite agree with you there, Justin.'

He swore beneath his breath and turned to look at her, resting his head on one hand and then for reasons she couldn't fathom, he swore again but added in less abrasive tones, 'For what it's worth, I don't usually go around kissing little girls quite as brutally as that.'

Involuntarily, Lucy raised a hand to her mouth, and she said a little foolishly because she couldn't think of anything else to say, 'I'm glad. It's a bit—well—' She paused, then hastened to say, 'I don't usually go around slapping people's faces either, but I did think you'd done me an injustice, you see. I still do.' She paused and looked at him resolutely, then she said, 'What I didn't take into account at the time was all you'd been through. Could we both have been just a bit at fault?'

Justin Waite stared at her expressionlessly and she was entirely unaware that the firelight enhanced the gold of her hair, deepened the blue of her eyes, had brought a delicate flush to her cheeks so that she looked troubled but almost ethereally lovely. Nor did she understand why he closed his eyes briefly and sighed as he said, 'What injustice, Lucy?'

'Well I'm not just a little girl, I'm your wife for one thing and what I meant about—not being here if it wasn't for you—was the simple but awkward fact that…that I was in a bit of a love-struck daze and *that's* why I wasn't completely on the ball,' she said in a rush. 'But now I can't help wondering when you're really going to start treating me like a wife, Justin. Maybe one who makes mistakes occasionally but who doesn't deserve to be treated like a child.'

His expression hadn't altered during her speech and all he said at the end of it was, 'Come here, Lucy.'

Her eyes widened. 'Why?'

He raised a wry eyebrow. 'So I can start treating you like a wife—why else?'

But a defiant little spark lit her eyes. 'If you think that's all it's going to take—'

'Yes, I do,' he interupted. 'It's a time-honoured custom between men and women—'

'But I think it should be *said*,' she objected.

'As a matter of fact, this will probably say a lot more than either of us could say in words—let me show you.' And he knelt up and reached for her and when she made a convulsive movement he sighed quietly but didn't release her and said abruptly, 'Trust me for once, Lucy.'

She looked up into his eyes and blinked away the tears she was still determined not to shed. And the faintest smile touched his mouth as he observed the tilt of her chin and he said, 'All right, I apologise. But when you've been wondering whether the body of your wife is going to float past you, it tends to—well, as you saw.

Do you think you could see your way clear to allowing yourself to be undressed now?'

She licked her lips and her pulses started to beat erratically. 'Well—only if you'll allow me to say that I seriously regret hitting you.'

'Thank you,' he said gravely and pulled her sweater over her head then removed her blouse, and with her help, her jeans so that all she wore in the glow of the fire was a navy blue bra with little white flowers on it and matching briefs.

'Very—fetching,' he murmured.

'They're French,' she confided, sitting on her heels, her hands on her thighs.

'There's one thing I can think of that would be prettier than you in them—and that's you out of them.'

She laughed then sobered as she gazed at him. 'You're—I have to tell you I think you're quite magnificent, you know,' she said huskily. 'Just in case you thought I wasn't affected or something like that. Indeed, the truth is, I'm quite seriously affected.'

'Lucy—' he reached behind her and released her bra '—any more words along those lines and I'm liable to become uncontrollable.'

'Well, that I can't imagine,' she said, and caught her breath as he touched her naked breasts, and she lifted her hand, not sure what she wanted to do, but he caught it and raised it to his lips and kissed the palm.

'Firelight becomes you,' he murmured, turning his attention back to her nipples until they unfurled. And he stroked all the soft, silky places of her body—her armpits, the back of her neck, the curve of her waist, but each time returning to weigh her full, high breasts that quivered on the slender stem of her body like luscious fruit. Until she could stand it no more and she leant forward and slipped her arms around his neck and laid her brow on his shoulder and said his name pleadingly.

She woke slowly to a dim grey light filtering into the hut. And she made a contented little sound and closed her eyes again, but then her lashes flew up and she was staring at close range into Justin's eyes. She blinked and other things intruded upon her consciousness, that she was nestled in his arms, that they were covered by two scratchy horse blankets—and it all came back to her and her eyes widened.

'It's all right,' he said softly, and raised a hand to brush her hair off her cheek.

Lucy relaxed and said with a little sigh, 'This is terribly nice, you know. Even here.'

'I'm glad,' he replied, his lips twisting slightly. 'It is for me too. I take it I'm quite forgiven?'

'Of course,' she said. 'I thought I'd made that obvious last night.'

'Well, you did let me make love to you last night,' he said thoughtfully.

Lucy's eyes widened. 'Wasn't that enough? I also apologised for hitting you...'

'So you did. I was only wondering whether I had sufficiently apologised for kissing you the way I did.'

Lucy took a breath and looked at him earnestly but with a trace of shyness. 'To be honest I'd forgotten all about it, and if that didn't show—well, don't forget I haven't done this often.'

He smiled rather quizzically down at her. 'All the same you do it with a lot of style.'

She forgot to feel shy. 'Do I really? In what way?'

He moved the blankets aside leisurely and his grey gaze skimmed her body. 'Well, there's the way you move, the things you say—and sometimes the things you don't say, but I can read them in your eyes all the same.'

She grimaced. 'I had the feeling I was a dead give-away.'

'There's nothing to regret in that. It's very appealing. And there's the way you're lying here discussing this so gravely with me, with not a stitch of clothing on—believe me, that's intensely appealing, speaking as a man,' he said seriously but with laughter lurking in his eyes.

Lucy blushed but laughed a little herself. 'Speaking as a woman, you're tremendously appealing, I have to say, Justin.' And she put her hands on his shoulders tentatively.

'Go on.'

Her lips quivered and she moved her hands across his shoulders. 'Well, you're tall, dark and handsome for one thing—I did tell you that last night. You can be very nice at times, for another. I must say it's also very re-assuring to have you around, yes, even when you're cross with me,' she said airily. 'Let me see,' she contin-ued, 'you—'

'Lucy,' he interupted, 'you're teasing me.'

She opened her eyes very wide. 'I wouldn't dare!'

'Oh, yes, you would. But I have to tell you I have the perfect solution for pert girls.'

'You do?' She frowned. 'Let me guess.' And she leant forward so her breasts brushed against his chest and kissed him lightly on the lips. 'Something along these lines?' she asked with her eyes dancing wickedly.

'Precisely. You're learning very fast, my dear.'

She laughed and rested against him. 'I think I couldn't have a better teacher. Justin—are you asking me to make love to you again? Because, if so, it would be a pleasure...what's the matter? Is something wrong?' she queried anxiously as he moved suddenly then swore.

'Depends on which way you look at it.' He grimaced. 'But I think I can hear our rescuers approaching. Does that sound like an outboard motor to you?'

She listened then sat up abruptly. 'Yes!'

His lips twisted. 'Well, it's not cause for alarm but they're bloody early.'

Lucy scrambled up. 'You better put some clothes on.' And she gathered an armful of his clothes, felt them anxiously then handed them to him. 'They're pretty dry.'

He sat up more leisurely. 'So they are. There is no stigma attached to being caught in bed with your husband, Lucy.'

She cast him a rueful look as she started to dress hurriedly herself. 'I know, but...'

'You think there is?' He drew on his shirt and pushed the other blanket aside. Then he stood up with his shirt still unbuttoned and the hut seemed to shrink.

'No stigma, no,' she said, 'of course not—'

'The lady doth protest too much, methinks,' he said wryly, and caught her hand. 'Tell me, Lucy.'

She stared up at him and for a moment forgot entirely what she was going to say as she studied the blue shadows on his jaw, his dishevelled hair and decided he looked younger this way, and that she rather liked it...

'Lucy?'

'Oh.' She bit her lip and coloured. 'Sorry—what was I saying?'

'Nothing,' he replied amusedly, 'but you were look-ing—perturbed about being caught in bed with me.'

'Ah, that—um…' she said, dragging her mind away from her thoughts with difficulty. 'Even married couples probably don't relish being caught in bed.'

'True,' he agreed gravely, buttoning his shirt and reaching for his mud-stiffened trousers. 'But there are probably a lot of people out there who were wondering when we were going to take up our marital bed.'

Several expressions chased through her eyes before a look of indignation took hold. 'I know, but it has nothing whatsoever to do with them!'

'True again,' he murmured, and looked with disfavour at the thick jumper he'd worn under his oilskin. 'That doesn't usually stop people wondering.'

'I'm quite sure Sasha for one,' Lucy said with con-siderable hauteur. 'If you must know, Justin, it will give me a lot of pleasure to…demonstrate otherwise to her.'

He grinned and pulled the jumper over his head. 'That doesn't seem terribly consistent with your desire to get up out of our bed a few minutes ago, Lucy.'

She thought for a moment then tossed her head and smiled mischievously up at him, 'Well, you see, Justin, there's a difference. Being caught in bed, even with my legally wedded spouse, by a boatload of grinning, know-ing men would quite possibly have rendered me all blushing and coy. Whereas dropping the odd subtle hint to Sasha would not.'

'Lucy.' He laughed and caught her again as she went to go past him and took her chin in his hand,

'Yes, Justin?' she said demurely.

'Don't change, will you?' he said after a moment but

she got the oddest feeling he'd been about to say something else. He also added wryly, 'They're here.'

They were, and the news they brought with them was not good. Not only was the twelve-mile flooded, but the whole property was in danger of inundation.

'Please, Justin, let me help!'

'Lucy—'

'You can keep an eye on me. You can give me orders as you do to the others. I promise you I'll obey them to the letter!'

He raised a wry eyebrow. 'That would be a new experience but all the same, Lucy—'

'Justin.' She put a tentative hand on his sleeve and tried to mask the hurt in her eyes. 'Don't leave me out. I love Dalkeith, and to sit by and watch this happening, to know that stock are drowning and so on, is more than I can bear. You said yourself you need all the help you can get—and I can ride as well as any of them!'

'Lucy.' He paused and stared down into her eyes. 'I know that. But there are some things you won't want to see, some things you won't be able to do.'

'Perhaps,' she conceded, 'but there must be some things I *can* do. Please.'

He hesitated. 'All right—but I have to say this: if you become a liability at all, if we have to divert someone to look after *you*—well we just can't afford the manpower.'

'You won't,' she said quietly.

She was as good as her word and for the next week, as the floodwaters peaked then started to recede, she spent every daylight hour in the saddle, herding wet, bedraggled sheep from one soggy paddock to another.

And she fell into bed every night exhausted. She noted though that she was never allowed to work on her own and, as Justin had predicted, there were sights she wished she hadn't to see. But she never flinched other than inwardly or turned away.

Once, during the week, Justin who had not only Dalkeith but Riverbend to worry about and divided his time between the two, although by a freak of nature Riverbend wasn't as badly affected, stopped her as she was about to set out at the crack of dawn, and inspected her face intently. 'How are you?' he queried.

'Fine!'

'Don't overdo it, Lucy,' he warned.

'I'm not. You must be worried sick about the yearlings and the foals.'

'I've got all the yearlings out. And so far we haven't lost a mare or a foal but it's touch and go. Look, are you sure—'

'Quite sure,' she said quietly but firmly.

He narrowed his eyes then smiled unexpectedly. 'They tell me you've been as good as any bloke on the job.'

It was what kept her going, those words of praise. But finally the day came when the crisis was past and she walked into the kitchen late in the afternoon, knowing she wouldn't be needed the next day.

Shirley fluttered about her anxiously as she sat down at the kitchen table. 'Oh, look at you, Miss Lucy, you've been doing too much! You're only a slip of a girl—'

'No, I haven't,' Lucy protested, and stood up again, but her knees buckled unexpectedly and if Justin hadn't come through the door, she'd have fallen.

'Lucy,' he said grimly through his teeth as he picked her up. 'I warned you!'

'But I helped, didn't I?' she whispered, and closed her eyes.

His expression softened slightly. 'You were a bloody marvel,' he said. 'But one day you're going to learn to really do as you're told.'

'You were the marvel,' she said huskily. 'If you hadn't been here to co-ordinate it all...' She shivered and didn't seem able to stop, and buried her face in his sweater.

'Shirley,' he said over his shoulder, 'in about an hour, could you bring our dinner upstairs?' And he shouldered his way out of the kitchen with Lucy in his arms.

'I'm fine really,' Lucy said as he set her on her feet.

'So I see,' he commented as he started stripping her clothes off. 'Lift up your arms.'

Lucy obeyed, and he removed her pink vest, which left her standing in her bra and jeans, the fact of which she seemed unaware as her brow creased. 'It hasn't been a total disaster, has it? I know we lost some but we saved plenty too...Justin,' she said on a sudden jolt of breath, as she realised he was releasing her bra, 'no...'

Their eyes locked for an instant and her cheeks started to burn but he continued what he was doing saying quietly, 'This is a bit strange, Lucy. Not that I can blame you for wondering when we're ever going to be at leisure to consummate our marriage properly but—I have done it before. And all I intend to do at the moment is inspect you from top to toe. Seven days in the saddle is tough on most people.'

'You're right, I don't know what got into me,

she said breathlessly. 'Is there any chance of the Seychelles?'

He laughed and kissed the top of her head. 'Unfortunately the blasted Yearling Sales are almost upon us.'

An hour later she was ensconced in bed in her pink and white polka-dot pyjamas, and Shirley had brought up dinner for them both, and was unfurling napkins and fussing around them.

'We'll be fine, thanks, Shirley,' Justin said eventually.

'Well, if you need anything just give me a call!'

Justin looked expressively at Lucy as she left but he said, 'I've had a thought. How would you feel about taking Shirley on permanently?'

Lucy blinked. 'I think it would be great, but would she want to stay?'

He laughed. 'Would she ever? Not only does she worship the ground you walk on, but the son of her heart is a reformed person. I'm sure she would. She'd be close to her aunts as well and Adrian could enrol in the School of the Air with the rest of the property kids. I get the feeling it might be hard to tear Adrian away, anyway.'

'I think he worships the ground you walk on,' Lucy commented.

He shrugged and said. 'Eat up, Lucy. We don't want you wasting away.'

She picked up her knife and fork. 'I don't think there's the least danger of that—'

'You certainly felt a few pounds lighter.'

Lucy ate some roast beef in silence.

'What's wrong?' he said after a minute or so.

'I don't know,' she replied, her brow creasing as she put her knife and fork together. 'Well, yes, I do, although it's a little hard to put into words.'

'I think you'd better try,' he said with a smile in his eyes.

'Would you...would you come to bed with me? Now? Not to...well, whatever you like, but I'm just feeling a little shell-shocked, sort of, and I think I need some help.'

Ten minutes later, when he'd got rid of their dinner plates and she was lying in his arms, he said, 'Feeling better?'

'Oh...yes,' she whispered with a relieved sigh. 'Sorry.'

'Don't be. You did far too much but, be that as it may, will you come to Sydney with me for the sales?'

'I'd love to,' she said huskily. 'Would I be in the way, though?'

'Of course not. You might even be a considerable asset. There's an enormous amount of socialising that goes on. You could also, much enamoured as I am of your French underwear, collect yourself a trousseau, meet old friends—have a break, in other words.'

But Lucy, much to her embarrassment when he reminded her of it the next morning, was fast asleep.

'Right. I have a few things to do—why don't you hit the shops, Lucy?'

'I will, in a while,' she replied over her shoulder as she completed a tour of the downstairs area of Justin's townhouse in a fashionable inner suburb of Sydney. 'I love it!' she added enthusiastically, looking out over the tiny courtyard. The living area was furnished mainly in subtle beiges and sandy pinks with sandstone walls, wooden-framed windows and multi-paned French doors with brass knobs. There were big comfortable chairs covered in ivory fabric and the dining table was clear glass and forged iron tinted a soft, old green.

'I'm glad,' he said gravely. 'It's yours to command.'

'Oh, I won't change a thing!'

His lips twisted. But he said, 'By the way, we've been invited to a cocktail party this evening. It's a pre-sales do. Would you care to accompany me, Mrs Waite?'

'I'd be delighted to, Mr Waite,' she said grandly.

He smiled but his eyes were faintly probing as they rested on her face. 'You're very chipper, Lucy.'

'Why shouldn't I be?' She eyed him innocently.

'You've just been through a rather harrowing experience, my dear,' he said after a moment.

'I recover quickly,' she said ruefully. 'You really don't have to worry about me.'

'Sometimes the effect of these things can be—more insidious than one realises. And I can't help thinking you have a look about you of the kind of high spirits that give way to tears before bedtime.'

She swallowed suddenly and hoped he didn't notice. Because of course he was right in a way. Her high spirits were a front for a little spring of tension that had hit her rather suddenly because on the flight from Dalkeith, it had begun to dawn on her that she and her marriage to Justin Waite were going to be very much on show over the next few days. But she was curiously loath to let him divine this. So she said with a laughing look, 'I got over that kind of thing when I was about ten, Justin,' she said with a laughing look. 'I'm just a naturally ebullient kind of person.'

'I see. All right.' He looked her over narrowly once more then shrugged. 'I'll be back at five, we're due at the party at six. In the meantime, these are for you.' He drew his hand out of his pocket and held it out to her. In it was a key-ring, a wad of money and a bank card.

Her eyes widened and she licked her lips. 'I...Justin, you don't have to—'

He picked up her hand and closed it over the contents of his. 'Of course I do,' he said lightly. 'You can't shop without money, you need transport and you need the keys of the house. Go ahead and enjoy it.' And he kissed her briefly on the top of her head and walked out.

She got back to the townhouse at three o'clock, parked the racy little sports car that was apparently hers in the double garage, and carried quite a few packages into the house. But only one of them contained clothes, the rest holding food. A quick tour of the pantry before she'd left had shown her that it was bare. She'd also bought a percolator, the one bit of equipment the kitchen didn't seem to have, and before long the aroma of coffee was drifting through the house. And she took her mug with her as she made a more detailed inspection. There were three bedrooms upstairs, the main one done out in white and yellow and overlooking the courtyard. She opened the linen closet and discovered it packed with thick, thirsty towels and matching linen sheets and pillow cases, some of them not even out of their wrappers.

And the impression that this house wasn't used a lot was reinforced when she checked the china cupboards and discovered glasses and cutlery still in their boxes. She grimaced and wondered who had bought it all. Perhaps he'd got an interior decorating firm in, she surmised, and they'd supplied it. Or perhaps... But she closed the door of her mind on that thought at the same time as she closed cupboard doors, and thought instead, resolutely, well, whoever did it, it's *nice*.

She was dressed and almost ready when she heard the front door open and close, and she looked over the banister and called out that she'd be down in a tick.

'No hurry,' he called back. 'I've got to get changed yet—is that coffee I smell?'

'Yes, it's on the stove.'

They met as she was halfway down the stairs and he was starting to come up.

'Hi!' she said gaily as he stopped with his foot on the bottom step. 'How was your day?'

'Lucy...'

'Are you lost for words? I do hope not in a *disapproving* way.'

He moved away and said wryly, 'Come right down and I'll be able to give you a proper evaluation.'

She hesitated briefly, although she wasn't sure why, then continued down and went to stand in the middle of the room.

'Turn round,' he said.

She did so obediently, then looked up at him gravely. 'Short skirts are in, Justin.'

He said nothing as his gaze flickered over her again. She wore a midnight-blue Thai silk suit. The jacket was short and fitted into her waist with a wide collar that exposed her throat and the tops of her shoulders and the sleeves were elbow-length. The straight little skirt came to six inches above the knee and she wore very pale frosted stockings and high-heeled blue shoes that matched the outfit. Her hair was piled on top of her head with some curly strands framing her face.

'What do you think?' she asked at last, unable to stand the suspense and quite unable to read his expression.

'I think,' he said expressionlessly then smiled faintly

as her eyes grew anxious, 'that you look simply stunning, my dear. And that I shall have to watch out in case any susceptible blokes out there take to flying banners over the harbour again.'

Lucy relaxed and had to laugh. 'I quite thought you didn't like it!'

'Why wouldn't I?'

She gestured. 'I wasn't sure it was a terribly—modest, wifely outfit, somehow.'

'But you chose to wear it all the same?'

'Don't you think it is?' She looked at him seriously.

'Not at all. I didn't say that. And wives are allowed to look stunning. Husbands are usually quite keen on that, in fact.'

'Then why do I get the feeling you don't entirely approve?' she said slowly.

'I don't know—why do you?' he countered.

'Well,' she frowned up at him, 'you did—sort of stop when you first saw me.'

'Ah. So I did. But that's easy to explain. I was simply bowled over, particularly by your legs.'

Lucy's eyes widened and then her lips curved into a smile. 'Thanks,' she said huskily. 'I needed that.'

'Lucy,' his lips twisted, 'it's true—you would be able to bowl a block of wood over. Hell—' he looked at his watch '—I'd better get moving. By the way, I see you did the grocery shopping. Thanks. I always forget.'

'You don't have to thank me; that's what wives are for, especially industrious ones,' she said, but distractedly. 'Aren't they?'

A wicked little smile lit his grey eyes. 'Among other things. I'll be about ten minutes.'

Lucy drew a deep breath and Justin looked down at her with a faint frown. 'Something wrong?'

They were just about to enter the cocktail party venue, she could hear the buzz of voices and clink of glasses, but she paused and realised she had a vaguely uneasy feeling at the pit of her stomach.

'Lucy?'

'Um—I'm fine, Justin,' she said with a glance at him. But that made things worse, she discovered. He wore a grey suit with a pale blue shirt and navy blue tie and he looked both worldly and enigmatic, tall, broad-shouldered and incredibly attractive—and way out of my league? she enquired of herself with a little sigh.

'Are you feeling sick or something?' he asked with a frown in his eyes.

'No,' she said uncertainly. 'Well, not really. But it's just occurred to me that there could be four people here who know about me handcuffing kids to fences, let alone telling you I hate you. And that the whole of Sydney might now know of it! And, much as I hate to admit it, my stomach is doing strange things right now and I'm not terribly sure that I can...do this.'

'Lucy—'

'*Justin*—'

'No, Lucy, listen to me.' He took her hand and turned her away from the double doors, at the same time as he gestured to a passing waiter carrying a tray of glasses, and after a short enquiry relieved him of one that contained neat brandy. 'Here, have a sip of this.' He handed her the glass but didn't release her other hand.

'It might make me sick...'

'No, it won't,' he said positively. 'It'll settle your nerves.'

She looked up at him out of huge eyes and with her lips trembling, but he pressed her fingers gently, and she raised the glass to her lips and took a sip, and then several more. Then she shuddered, but as the fiery warmth made its way down to her stomach she felt herself steadying. 'You're right,' she said blinking several times.

'I'm quite often right,' he replied wryly.

'All the same—' a frown creased her brow and she looked anxiously past him '—it—'

'Lucy—I've told you this before but it's true—I don't give a damn about what other people think and neither should you. This is between us and it's all over anyway. But in point of fact, you do know what most people will be thinking? That if I couldn't make you happy, I must be out of my mind. In other words—' his lips twisted '—it's me they'll be wondering about, not you.'

Her lips parted. 'If they do,' she whispered, 'they also must be wondering if you're still in love with Joanna Madden—don't you see?'

'No, that's over and done with,' he said firmly, his grey gaze as steady as a rock. 'Now, we can do one of two things. We can go home if you still don't feel up to this and it won't worry me in the slightest. Or we can go in there—and give them something else to talk about.' He smiled unexpectedly.

'Wh-what?' she stammered.

'Well, should you choose never to leave my side— that kind of thing—they might very well say to themselves that Justin Waite is doing it right at last.' He stared down into her bemused eyes and grimaced slightly, but he added, 'Why don't we try it?'

CHAPTER SEVEN

WHICH was how it came about that for the first time in her life Lucy Waite née Wainright had an attentive escort who was also her husband. And it was a revelation. She wasn't quite sure how he did it but he somehow contrived to make her feel special, as if he were as interested in her as if not more so than anyone else they met. Nor did he give her the opportunity to stray from his side even if she'd wanted to. And she couldn't help noticing that they were the centre of quite some attention.

It's incredibly heady, she thought a little dizzily at one stage, as she stood beside him and glanced up to see him watching her with a faint smile on his lips and a look in his eyes that was exclusively for her, a look that contrived to make her feel ravishing and *interesting* and of singular importance to him. Also to see the envy in other women's eyes as they looked at him, particularly Sasha, who had come forward to meet them as soon as they'd entered, and stayed glued to their side ever since.

Yes, well, Lucy thought privately, as Sasha, who was dressed in mint-green that went well with her red hair, moved restlessly, perhaps you won't be quite so superior with me now?

And she had almost decided to let herself just be happy—she'd certainly got over her bout of nerves and was laughing at something someone was saying to her—when she looked across the room and straight into

124

Joanna Madden's lovely, haunting eyes. And that was when it all collapsed like a pricked balloon. It was no coincidence that their eyes had caught, she knew that in her bones. Joanna had been looking at her for some moments, she was sure, and didn't seem to be able to look away either, so that it was Lucy who did. And, as she did, it crossed her mind to wonder whether what Justin had said about ''giving them something else to talk about'' might have been directed more at one particular person?

'Lucy?'

'Oh, sorry, Justin,' she said a few minutes later. 'Did I miss something?'

He looked her over thoughtfully. 'No. But enough is enough, I think. Shall we go home?'

She could only nod gratefully.

'Why don't you change into something more comfortable while I make us a snack?'

'I'm not hungry, Justin, but thanks all the same.'

'Lucy—' he caught her hand as she went to walk past him '—do it.'

A spark of rebellion lit her eyes. 'Why should I?'

'Because you'll make yourself sick if you don't eat,' he murmured with nothing other than a slight tinge of amusement in his eyes. 'I only had a sandwich in mind, and coffee.'

Her shoulders slumped. 'OK.'

He let her hand go but his gaze held hers. Then he smiled absently and turned away.

She changed into a creamy satin nightgown and a white towelling robe and sighed as she let her hair down, brushed it then tied it back in a simple pony-tail. For reasons she didn't think had much to do with her exertions at Dalkeith, she felt really tired and dispirited—in fact she knew the reason all too well, she chided herself, Joanna Madden—is she going to haunt me forever? she wondered. Why can't I just take what I've got and make the best of it? I shouldn't have come, she thought finally, I'm OK at Dalkeith but this is like being on a roller-coaster ride... How am I going to be now, for instance?

When she got downstairs, Justin had laid out his supper on an occasional table and drawn it up to a settee. There were open toasted cheese sandwiches, a bowl of fruit and a fresh pot of coffee.

'Mmm. Smells nice,' she said very mundanely. 'I didn't know you were a cook.'

He grimaced. He'd taken off his jacket and loosened his tie. 'A very ordinary cook. Sit down.' He indicated the settee. 'Would you like to listen to some music?'

'Yes, please.' Lucy sat down and watched him glance through a pile of compact discs. Then moments later some lovely guitar music flooded the room. He turned it down and came to sit next to her.

'Help yourself,' he murmured. 'It's cheese or cheese.'

'I like toasted cheese,' Lucy heard herself say, and wondered why she should be feeling unwittingly soothed. The music? The fact that Justin had gone to the trouble of making this snack? She grimaced.

'Something wrong?'

'No!' she denied hastily, and concentrated on eating her sandwich. When she'd finished he peeled and quartered an apple for her and poured the coffee.

'Tell me what else you bought today?'

She cradled her mug in her hands and tucked her feet under her. 'I bought an outfit to wear tomorrow to the sales, a dress for the ball you mentioned tomorrow night, and that's all.'

He raised an eyebrow. 'Is that all you intend to buy?'

'I don't know. One has to be in the mood.'

'How does one get into the mood?'

'I don't think one can consciously do that—you either are or you aren't.'

'So events outside you are the telling factor,' he commented.

She wrinkled her nose. 'Probably.'

'Is that to say if you were feeling happy and confident you would go out and splurge?'

Lucy considered with a faint smile. 'It could be the other way around; sometimes people do things like that when they're down in the dumps and need cheering up.'

He drank some coffee then sat back with his arm along the back of the settee. 'What I'm trying to get at,' he said after a while, 'is which of those states you might be in.'

She turned her head to look at him and whispered one word. 'Why?'

'Why do I want to know? Why shouldn't I?'

'Sometimes I'm happy and confident, sometimes I'm not—' She stopped abruptly and put a hand to her mouth.

'For a little while this evening you were both.'

'Justin,' she said huskily, and to her consternation she felt tears in her eyes, 'I...it's not easy to...' She broke off frustratedly.

'There's one thing that makes it all much easier. Don't cry,' he said with a faint smile quirking his lips and he took her coffee cup from her. 'This.' And he took her into his arms.

'Justin!' she protested on a suddenly panicky note.

'There's nothing to be afraid of.'

'It's not that I'm *afraid* of anything.'

'Good,' he said wryly, and lifted her onto his lap. 'Then you should be able to relax.' And he did nothing more than hold her lightly and after a while it seemed only natural to rest her head against his shoulder rather than sit tensely upright against his arm.

Although she did say, challengingly, 'I am rather tired.'

'So am I. Cocktail parties can be an exhausting form of socialising and I'm not at all sure why people inflict them upon themselves.'

She smiled against his shirt. 'That's what my father used to say. Why stand around doing a juggling act with drinks and bits of food stuck on toothpicks when you have to shake hands with people all the time? He used to say it was a cheap form of entertaining.'

Justin laughed.

'How are the yearlings? Is that what you did today?'

'Yes. They all seemed to have settled in well.'

'Will they go under the hammer tomorrow?'

'Six tomorrow, the rest the next day.'

'I suppose Sasha has everything in hand?'

'Sasha has,' he agreed. 'With her usual superb efficiency. She is in fact being quite painful at the moment.'

'Justin!' Lucy beamed a marvelling blue gaze up at him. 'I never thought to hear you say that.'

He grimaced. 'I don't know why, but lately it's occurred to me that Sasha doesn't have a sense of humour.'

Lucy giggled. 'Poor Sasha.'

He looked down at her ruefully. 'You don't say that with a lot of feeling.'

'No, I don't,' Lucy replied unrepentantly. 'She makes me want to bite sometimes.'

He grinned. 'She probably envies you terribly.'

'I'm sure she does, but only over you... I mean...' She stopped and moved restlessly.

He stilled her movement and put his fingers under her chin so that she had to look into his eyes. '*I* meant,' he said quietly, 'that she envies how young and fresh you are, how lovely, how natural, how vibrant your personality is—those things.'

'Little to know if so,' Lucy whispered, 'what a trial some of those things are to me.'

Something flickered in his eyes. 'They shouldn't be. They aren't to me.'

Her lips parted and her eyes widened.

'In fact they're often the opposite,' he went on, releasing her chin and pushing some strands of hair off her face. And he bent his head and started to kiss her.

'Oh,' Lucy said breathlessly some minutes later. 'Oh.'

'May I take that as approval?' he murmured.

She swallowed and moved her cheek on his shirt and was unable to reply because the fact of the matter was, she was still unbearably affected by his kisses and she couldn't help thinking how ridiculous it had been to try to pretend to him that she was too tired for his love-making when she seriously doubted that would ever be the case...

'Lucy Waite?' he said gravely.

'Justin—' it came out rather cracked '—I can't talk. I know that sounds ridiculous and I'm sure you're aware that I'm talking right at this moment, but—'

'I am. Aware of it.'

'Well, it's not the same thing.'

His lips twisted. 'It's not?'

'No.'

'All right. Then let's devise a system of non-talking for those things that can't be talked about. If you would like me to kiss you again, you have only to nod your head.'

'I...'

But he waited no longer and it was the same wonderful experience, although this time he slipped his hand beneath her robe and slipped down the narrow strap of her nightgown. And, far from resisting, Lucy sighed with delight as she felt his fingers resting very gently on her breast.

'Nice?' he queried against the corner of her mouth.

'Lovely,' she breathed. 'I didn't know it could be so...'

'Didn't you?'

'Not until you did it to me—I feel a bit of a fool,' she said ruefully, but he took no notice and continued to touch her.

'Justin?' she said, because in spite of her delight she felt slightly chagrined, she found, and *young* as well as foolish. 'Is this doing anything for you, Justin?'

He'd been looking down at her in a curiously heavy-lidded way, but all of a sudden he stopped what he was doing and that heavy-lidded look changed to one of open amusement. 'Of course it is. I wouldn't be doing it otherwise,' he said wryly, and added, 'What is going through your mind at the moment, Lucy?' as he kissed the corner of her mouth chastely.

But she didn't want to be kissed chastely, she thought rebelliously; it was too late for that now, when her breasts were feeling tight and tingly and she was dying to slide her hands over his skin—all of which added to her inner turmoil and sense of injustice. 'I was wondering if you can turn this on and off like a tap—men can, can't they?' she said tartly.

He raised an eyebrow. 'That's a rather cynical remark. As a matter of fact there is a point of no return to which men are very vulnerable.'

Lucy said scathingly, 'I know that! It wasn't what I meant.'

'What did you mean?'

'I wondered why you—stopped. I mean to say,' she said, 'one minute you were kissing me, then you were laughing at me. It's not a very elevating experience, to be perfectly honest—'

'And probably entirely new to you? I'm so sorry,' he said seriously, 'but I wasn't actually laughing at *you*. Because as anyone with you in their arms would know—'

Lucy sat up abruptly. 'I hate the thought of that, Justin, so don't say another word!' she commanded.

He grimaced. 'It was meant as a compliment.'

'No, it was not! It was just like saying, give a man a girl who is reasonably attractive and—bingo. Which is something I resent very much.' Her eyes smouldered.

'Lucy,' he said thoughtfully, watching as she pulled her nightgown up, 'if you think it only takes a pretty girl who is eager—' their eyes clashed '—I grew out of that quite a few years back. Moreover, I was actually laughing at myself.'

She blinked. 'Why?'

'Because I was approaching that point of no return rather quickly,' he said with a faint, dry smile, twisting his lips.

'In spite of me trying to pretend I was too tired?'

'Are you?'

Lucy paused then said hollowly, 'I get the feeling I might never be.'

'Well, now,' he said gravely but with his grey eyes perfectly wicked, 'that's entirely appropriate for a wife.'

'But not essentially modest,' she whispered with a reluctant smile tugging at her lips.

'Wives are allowed to be sexy with their husbands. So long as it stops there.'

'But—'

'In fact so far as being a wife goes,' he overrode her, 'there's only one serious flaw I've found in you, Lucy.'

'I...' her lips dimpled at the corner '...talk too much?' she hazarded.

'Much too much. Will you come willingly and happily to bed with me now?'

She opened her mouth to say something along the lines of, Did he know why she'd been unwilling and unhappy earlier? But in the end she said simply, 'Yes, please.'

'Lucy—can't you drive any faster? The first yearling is due to go under the hammer in half an hour.'

'We won't be late, Sasha, trust me, but I don't want to get caught speeding,' Lucy said reasonably.

'I know, but all the same—I should have been there hours ago,' Sasha said fretfully. 'Not only for the horses but there's the hospitality tent to be set up and the Riverbend Saddlery display—why, oh, why did I have to break down in the middle of the most terrible peak-hour traffic?'

'These things can't be helped,' Lucy said soothingly

but with an unholy inner wriggle of amusement. For once in her life Sasha was looking less than her usual soignée self. Her hair was ruffled, her face was hot, there was a streak of grease down her beautiful tight-fitting designer jeans, her handmade leather boots were scuffed and her expression was strained. What had happened was, when her car had broken down on the way to the sales complex, she'd rung them from a phone booth and Justin had said he'd go to the complex immediately and that Lucy should bring Sasha once she'd extricated herself from her difficulties. 'I'm sure Justin can cope,' she added, and couldn't help the faintest tinge of irony that accompanied her words.

'You don't like me, do you, Lucy?' Sasha replied as she scrubbed the grease mark then cast an almost vengeful look at Lucy's attire, which consisted of a simple but striking coffee linen, A-line button-through dress with a longish skirt, flat bronze suede shoes and a marvellous straw hat with the brim upturned. Her hair was loose beneath it and gleamed like silk, her skin was clear, flawless and glowing, her lips were painted a frosted bronzy pink and the lightest touch of Miss Dior lay on the air as she moved.

Lucy couldn't help but be conscious of this scrutiny, and she drew a deep breath and said as mildly as she was able, 'You make it rather hard for me sometimes, Sasha.'

'*You*...' But Sasha stopped, perhaps fortunately, and went on in an entirely different strain as Lucy swore beneath her breath and slowed down and stopped as she was flagged so to do by a policeman, 'You must have been speeding after all!'

'I was about two kilometres over the speed limit,'

Lucy said tartly, 'And only because *you* were so—oh, well, if this isn't a sucker spot, I've never seen one, anyway. Which I will tell him!'

Sasha groaned. 'We'll be later than ever! He's liable to throw you into gaol if you argue with him!'

'Argue with him?' Lucy smiled sweetly. 'I wouldn't dream of it—Officer,' she said to the large young policeman at her window, 'before you write a thing down on that ticket, may I say a few words in my defence? In fact, if you let me get out, I could say them even better!'

'Of all the...' Sasha appeared lost for words as they drove off, unticketed, several minutes later.

'What was wrong with it?' Lucy queried, grinning. 'I merely explained why we were in a bit of a rush, pointed out to him, quite deferentially I thought, that he really should be policing *dangerous* traffic situations and not sitting behind a bush picking off lone cars only exceeding the limit by a couple of kilometres, and I offered to donate the fine to his favourite charity if he would reconsider his position. Which he did.'

'Because he was drooling at the mouth,' Sasha said bitterly. 'But don't think Justin will be taken in by these schoolgirlish ways forever, Lucy. Oh, you may think you have him enslaved at the moment but it won't last. You're too young for him. And there's always Joanna... She did up the Sydney house, by the way; did you know it was all her doing? And I can't help wondering if Justin's flaunting you at her because he's still punishing her for marrying Tim Madden.'

Lucy clenched the steering-wheel until her knuckles went white but surprised herself as she said quite steadily, even gently, 'Sasha, I'll try to forget you ever said that to me. We're here,' she added flatly.

Try to forget, Lucy marvelled, as she sat in the stand reserved for vendors later and watched Sasha, none other, lead the Cawnpore filly into the ring to an excited buzz of the crowd.

Somehow or other Sasha had got rid of the grease stain, she saw, and was wearing a navy blazer with 'RIVERBEND' on the back, and she handled the filly lightly but expertly. And she was a magnificent filly, you couldn't deny it, with powerful quarters, a splendid deep chestnut coat with a small white blaze and one white foot, and an alert, intelligent eye as she surveyed the crowd with her ears pricked. And for a moment Lucy forgot all else as she watched.

Then Justin slid into the seat beside her and said wryly, 'She's handling it all like an old stager.'

'She's magnificent,' Lucy said with an odd lump in her throat.

'We could be in for a magnificent bidding duel too,' he said significantly as the auctioneer read through the filly's blood-lines. 'Apparently there's a South African syndicate here rather interested, as well as a sheikh from Saudi Arabia.'

'Oh! Where is he?'

'I doubt if he's here in person but that's his trainer over there.' He pointed.

'And the Maddens,' Lucy murmured. She'd spotted Joanna and Tim almost immediately—Joanna was dressed in eye-catching yellow that went superbly with her dark hair.

'Uh-huh. Here goes.'

But the bidding opened quietly and after a few minutes Lucy turned a concerned face to Justin—to see that he was quite relaxed. 'They're playing cat and mouse,' he said.

And indeed they were, because, as the tension mounted, the bids crept up then started to leap up and the buzz from the floor grew and flashbulbs popped while television crews crept among the crowd as they passed the quarter of a million mark, then you could have heard a pin drop as Tim Madden appeared to drop out and the South Africans competed with the Saudi sheikh's trainer until they too dropped off. And Lucy clutched Justin's hand, thinking it was over as the auctioneer called...*for the final and last time*! But before he could drop his hammer, Tim Madden's hand went up. There was pandemonium briefly then silence again, and finally a huge roar that sent the Cawnpore filly dancing across the ring with Sasha clinging grimly to her rearing bit, as she was knocked down to Tim Madden for a sales record.

And it was all recorded for posterity in the next day's newspapers as well as being on television that night— Lucy holding Justin's hand tightly and concentrating fiercely during the bidding, Justin hugging Lucy as the final hammer went down. Tim Madden, smiling quietly into his wife's eyes—both the Maddens and the Waites posing with the filly, Sasha posing with the filly—it went on for the rest of the day and half the night. People congratulating them, people interviewing them and in between the other five of the Riverbend consignment allotted to that day being sold most successfully to buyers who also wanted to be photographed with the breeders.

So that by the time they got home Lucy was genuinely

exhausted. 'What a day!' she said as Justin closed the door behind them.

'I know—want anything?'

'Only bed.'

He picked her up, carried her upstairs and laid her down on the bed. 'You were wonderful.'

Lucy grimaced. 'I didn't do much! Cawnpore's daughter did it all.'

'I mean—' he started to unbutton her dress '—you were wonderful with the Press, with the proud new owners of six Riverbend progeny, everything a wife should be in those circumstances,' he said with a smile at the back of his eyes. 'A considerable asset.'

'I'm glad,' she said huskily. 'But you bred her, you saved her life when she got colic.'

'All in a day's work,' he said lightly. 'Sit up.'

Lucy did so obediently and he continued to undress her like a child, then slid her cream nightgown down her body. She suffered these ministrations gratefully then said thoughtfully, 'Justin?'

'Uh-huh?' He'd got up to change himself and looked over his shoulder at her.

'Tim Madden must have an *awful* lot of money.'

'He does.'

'More than the sheikh, do you think?'

'I doubt it—but enough. Why?'

'I just wondered.'

'Go to sleep, Lucy,' he said but gently, and sat down beside her again. 'No,' he put his fingers to her lips, 'not one more word—well, unless you'd like to explain to me why Sasha arrived today muttering about you corrupting the due processes of the law?'

Lucy sat up indignantly. 'Is that what she *said*? Why,

if it hadn't been for her, I wouldn't have had to talk myself out of a speeding ticket in the first place. She really—'

'Talk yourself out of a speeding ticket, Lucy? I didn't think that was possible.'

'Well, it is. Provided you get them before they've written anything.'

He looked quizzically into her eyes. 'You've had a bit of experience in these things?'

'No, that's the first time—all it takes is a bit of eye-lash-batting—oh, no,' she said on a descending scale. 'Justin, I wasn't being a *femme fatale* if that's what you're thinking, I never was, not really and anyway, there isn't a part of me now that's not wholly taken up with you and—' But she stopped abruptly and bit her lip.

'Then that's fine,' he said gravely. 'I approve whole-heartedly of what you just said. So don't look,' he said softly, 'as if you feel you ought to retract it. And now, my dear, it's definitely lights out and silence. But only if you'll let me get in with you and only if you'll allow me to hold you, because, as you once told me, that's very relaxing.'

Which was how Lucy came to fall asleep in his arms, still unable to deal with all the impressions of an exciting yet turbulent day—what Sasha had said, how Joanna had looked, how Tim and Justin had, for one brief but pierc-ing moment before shaking hands, registered a cool yet battle-laden tension between them.

CHAPTER EIGHT

'LUCY, why don't you go home?' Justin said at about three o'clock the next afternoon. 'There's the Breeder's Ball tonight, don't forget, and you've been yawning for the past hour.'

'Sorry,' Lucy said, and promptly yawned again. 'OK.' She smiled up at him and he bent his head and kissed her lightly.

And once home, she changed, lay down on the settee to relax and bring her mind to bear on everything that had happened over the past few days, but fell asleep for a couple of hours. What is wrong with me—why am I so sleepy, why can't I come to grips with anything? she wondered as she woke up feeling terrible.

It proved nothing that a soak in the bath didn't cure, and she started to do her hair and her make-up but she was still conscious of a failing to come to grips with things. Perhaps, she lowered her brush, and stared at herself in the mirror, I shouldn't even try. What can I do to change things, anyway? How can I alter that deep hostility between Justin and Tim Madden? How can I help Joanna, and so far as Sasha's concerned, I can only hope to God she's wrong and perhaps it's about time I was a bit more charitable...

'Lucy?'

Her eyes widened as she registered Justin's image in the mirror. 'I didn't hear you come home!'

'I know, you were miles away,' he said wryly. 'What I'm wondering is, where?'

'So *much* has happened lately,' she said hastily. 'It must be that. I slept for a couple of hours and woke up feeling like a log of wood!'

'You don't look anything like a log of wood at the moment.' His grey gaze drifted down her.

She smoothed her towelling robe, took an inward breath and turned to him with a mischievous little glint in her eye as she said softly, 'You ain't seen nothin' yet, brother!'

He laughed and looked rueful at the same time. 'I only hope I can bear it.'

Her ballgown was rather modest in design, a long flowing skirt with a matching sleeveless gilet that buttoned to the throat and came to her knees. What made it quite stunning, however, was that the lined silk chiffon it was created from matched the deep pansy-blue of her eyes and the buttons down the front of the gilet were beautiful little prancing pearl, amethyst and diamante horses...

'There,' she said, standing before Justin at last. She'd put her hair up again, and dotted in it were tiny flowers fashioned from the same silk chiffon as the outfit. Her purse and shoes were silver.

He started to smile as he surveyed her. 'Where did you find it?'

Her mouth dimpled at the corners. 'I've got the feeling it found me. As soon as I saw it, I thought, now how could I wear anything else to a Breeder's Ball!'

'How indeed.'

'It's also very comfortable.' She twirled before him to demonstrate. 'Very suitable for dancing, and I know there'll be nobody in another one because it's unique and—cost an awful lot of your money, Justin.' She came to rest in front of him again and put a hand to her mouth just a little awkwardly. 'Not that these are real—' she touched a button '—but I hope you don't mind.'

'Why should I mind?' he queried.

'Well, even my father,' she said soberly, 'used to get a bit shocked about the price of these kinds of clothes. Oh, dear, I'm beginning to wish I'd never said those words about being a careful, prudent wife. I've got the feeling they're going to haunt me.'

'Lucy—' he touched the point of her chin '—I, on the other hand, am quite happy to fork out a small fortune to see you looking so happy and stunning. Just remember that.'

'That's...lovely,' she said with an odd attack of shyness, 'but it won't take that, I promise. You know,' she went on before he could reply, 'you look rather devastating yourself.' And indeed he did in a black dinner suit, pleated white shirt and hand-tied bow-tie. 'I might have to keep a sharp eye out for any ladies on the loose!'

In the car, she said suddenly, 'I suppose they'll all be there.'

'I guess so.'

They were.

The Maddens, Sasha although with an escort, a tall, good-looking man, the South Africans, the sheikh's trainer—and courtesy of the Breeder's Association they were all at the same table...

I can handle this, Lucy told herself after taking a deep breath, and went forward with her head tilted regally.

It was Sasha she had to handle first, Sasha who came to sit next to her after dinner had been cleared and a general loosening up of the company occurred as the band struck up.

Sasha said stiffly as she slipped into a vacant chair next to Lucy, 'I would like to apologise.'

Surprise made Lucy's eyes widen as she surveyed the other girl, who was wearing a black strapless gown and a troubled expression in her green eyes. 'Well, thank you,' she said slowly. 'Perhaps I've been—a bit at fault too.'

But Sasha brushed that aside. 'I should never have said what I did. It was only...sheer jealousy that made me do it. You see, after he broke up with Joanna, who incidentally is a friend of mine, I,' Sasha stopped and looked unbelievably uncomfortable. 'Well, I thought there might be some hope for me—only to have that idea crushed by a slip of a girl—by you, I mean, and it... rather brought out the worst in me, I'm afraid.'

Lucy blinked and sought a little frantically for the means to cope with this. 'Uh...I, well I wondered about that; I mean to say—'

'You don't have to say anything, Lucy,' Sasha said drily. 'I was never a contender; I just couldn't bring myself to believe it.'

'What did...I mean, why now?' Lucy asked involuntarily.

Sasha looked away, looked oddly flustered then her eyes came to rest on her escort and she said perfunctorily, 'I've met someone else.'

Lucy stared at her averted profile and wondered why this didn't ring true.

Then Sasha spoke again, 'I'm leaving Justin, by the way.'

Lucy sat up. 'Oh, dear! Do you have to? I mean, I—'

'Yes, I have to, Lucy—I should have done it years ago. I'll tell him tonight.' She looked up as a shadow fell across them but it was Joanna Madden and she said gaily. 'May I join you? All the men of the party are talking bloodlines!' She grimaced expressively. 'So I swapped my seat with one of them.'

'Of course,' both Lucy and Sasha said, but perhaps for the only time in their acquaintance they were united in the oddly very brief but wary glance they exchanged as Joanna sat down. And Lucy, looking across the table, discovered Justin watching them before he switched his grey eyes away as someone spoke to him. How strange, she thought. Three women either in love with him or having loved him. What is he thinking? What is everyone else thinking? Probably, she thought with an inner tremor, they're wondering how Lucy Waite will cope with an old mistress and a would-be mistress, so I'll just have to show them...

'Have you thought of a name for the Cawnpore filly yet, Joanna?' she said brightly.

'I've thought of sixty,' Joanna replied whimsically, 'but none of them is quite right. Did you have any thoughts on the subject, Lucy? Or Sasha?'

'Well, I always give them pet names,' Sasha said wryly. 'I used to call her Flopsy because as a baby she used to flop all over the place, but I did think of—well, he *did* save her life and I wondered about—Justine.'

Sasha, Lucy thought. How could you put your foot in it like that? As if Tim Madden is going to have any horse named after someone who lived with and loved his wife...

But Joanna handled it superbly. She said, 'Tell me how he saved her life!'

And Sasha launched into graphic account of the colic and how Justin had kept the filly on her feet and walked and walked her, how he was the only one she trusted enough to help her through her pain and misery.

'Were you there too, Lucy?' Joanna said in a bid, probably, to stem the tide.

'Well, no; Lucy,' Sasha said, 'chose to get herself lost that day—'

'It was the next day, actually,' Lucy inserted gently, 'and I didn't choose to do it, it happened quite out of the blue—oh!' She looked up as she felt a hand on her shoulder and was intensely grateful to see it was Justin.

'May I have this dance, Lucy?'

'I'd be *delighted*,' she said and stood up with a flourish, adding under her breath, 'I really need to get away!'

But it wasn't until they'd joined the growing throng on the floor and he took her in his arms that he said with a smile lurking in his eyes but also something rather querying, 'Care to tell me why you needed rescuing so urgently?'

'Well, to be quite candid,' she replied, 'I was about to... It was Sasha,' she said ruefully. 'She has about as much tact as a tank!'

'What's she said now?'

Did that odd question mark in his eyes subside, she wondered then suddenly remembered Sasha's apology and the fact that she was leaving Justin. 'Oh, it was nothing,' she said.

'Lucy—'

'No, Justin, I'd rather not be trite and petty,' she said

determinedly, then grinned up at him. 'Have you any idea how good a dancer I am?'

'You could always show me.'

She did, and she really let her hair down and soon the whole party caught her enthusiasm.

But what came as stunning little surprise to someone who could and had quite frequently danced the night away was how, just before midnight, she suddenly discovered she didn't want to be doing it any more and there was only one thing she did want to be doing but Justin was dancing with someone else, and she could only sit and stare helplessly at him as she thought of the way he made love to her or just held her in his arms when they went to bed.

And when he came back she responded mechanically to the conversation for a little while until he frowned slightly and stood up and made their farewells.

Of course there were the usual friendly remarks passed about 'the night being young but then so was their marriage', and more friendly raillery, when Lucy suddenly blushed brightly.

They didn't speak until they were home.

Then he led her into the bedroom and turned her to face him in the middle of the floor.

'Lucy?'

She winced.

He put a finger beneath her chin and made her look up. 'What's wrong?'

'Nothing...'

He raised his other hand and started to undo the little prancing horses. 'You could have fooled me.' He slid the gilet off.

'I just—didn't want to be there any more.'

'That was increasingly obvious.'

She grimaced, wondering if she'd caused another set of people to wonder seriously about her.

'On the other hand, if you wanted to be here, like this—' he reached for the zip of her skirt and it slipped to the floor '—there's nothing wrong in that.'

'You knew,' she accused, blushing again, and her body trembled.

His gaze was slightly amused as it roamed over her, wearing nothing now but a bra, a lacy suspender belt and equally lacy undies and sheer nylons, all blue, as she stepped over her skirt.

'I suspected,' he murmured.

'So did everyone else,' she said rather wretchedly and put her hands to her cheeks. 'How embarrassing.'

'There still nothing wrong in it. In fact, I'll go further.' He released her bra and drew it off her breasts. 'Don't change.'

'But I'll have to—I can't go around being so transparent!'

He laughed softly and put his hands round her waist. 'So long as I don't mind, that's all there is to worry about, my beautiful ch...' He stopped.

'Child?' she whispered. 'You must really think I am one now.'

He stared down at her naked breasts and the lovely curve of her hips, the delicate satiny softness of her skin. 'No, you're not, Lucy,' he said at last, 'and don't let me ever make you feel like one; you're just...you. Rather perfect, in fact.'

She wanted to ask him if he just meant her body or if it was the kind of perfection he could love, really love, as he'd loved Joanna. She desperately, she suddenly real-

ised, wanted to ask him to be honest about Joanna
Madden and ask him why he was subjecting her to this
close contact, although, she supposed, the alternative
would have been to leave her at Dalkeith and realisti-
cally she couldn't expect to avoid them forever. But
something held her back, she couldn't really say what,
other than the feeling that the ball was in her court
now—she loved him, she was married to him and it was
up to her to make the best of it, in other words. And at
least one problem had resolved itself—Sasha. And yet,
had it? Why was there this question mark in her mind
about Sasha?

She sighed inwardly but said in a deep, husky little
voice, 'Well, so are you.'

He smiled absently. 'No. Far from it, unfortunately,
but—'

'Justin—' she reached out and placed her fingertips to
his lips '—do you know why else I wanted to get away?'

'No.'

'I—seriously want to be alone with you for a while.
Just us. We only seem to be together in a passing sort
of way, don't we?'

'We don't exactly do this in passing, though. But I
know what you mean—Lucy, I'm sorry about all this,'
he said abruptly. 'And that includes Sasha,
Joanna—'

'Did Sasha tell you?' Lucy asked, her eyes widening.

'Yes—'

'*I'm* sorry about that. I didn't—it really wasn't anything I did.' She hesitated, then added honestly, 'Other
than being married to you.'

'I know.' He smiled, but it didn't reach his eyes and
he moved his hands on her waist then pulled her into

his arms. '*I* really didn't mean for it to be such a trau-matic experience, marriage to me. And unfortunately, with Sasha leaving like this, I won't be able to do any-thing about the Seychelles for a little while, but as *soon* as possible, we will. In the meantime, though, at least we'll be at home alone together. How about that?'

She didn't have to tell him what she thought. It must have shown in her eyes.

But first thing in the morning came the news via the newspaper that Tim Madden had suffered a massive heart attack at the Breeder's Ball and was critically ill.

'Justin!' Lucy whispered, her face paling. They were in bed together and he'd made some tea and brought the paper up without unrolling it. And for a long moment they simply stared at the newsprint picture—the one of themselves and the Maddens with the Cawnpore filly. 'It must have happened after we left.'

Justin lifted his face and in spite of herself Lucy was shocked at the deep lines of tension scored into it. But before she could say any more the phone rang—it was Sasha, but it was difficult from his monosyllable replies to make much sense of it. And when he put the phone down he got out of bed immediately and started to pull some clothes on almost at random—jeans and a black T-shirt.

'What did she say?' Lucy asked.

He came to sit beside her and took her hands in his. 'She was there when it happened, Lucy. Apparently he's had a history of heart disease although very few people knew about it. Joanna is devastated and has no one to turn to. His family always resented him marrying some-one so much younger, and she has no family of her own. Sasha has been with her all night but there's quite a bit of unpleasantness floating around. One of his sons actually accused Joanna of driving him to an early grave and tried to keep her from his bedside. He also made the accusation that spending so much money on the Cawnpore filly as a thrust in his private duel with me over her, was the *coup de grâce*. Lucy...'

'You have to go to her,' she whispered.

'Will you come with me?'

'I...no, Justin. Not this time.'

'Lucy—' He broke off and looked tortured for a moment. Then he said very quietly, 'It's *over* between us, just remember that.'

'I will, I promise,' she whispered. And he kissed her and held her hard. He also said, 'I love you, Lucy Waite.' And was gone.

She lay back and thought that it was probably true, in a way. She also lay and wondered what good his presence in the midst of the Madden family crisis would do. And she couldn't stop herself from wondering what would happen if Tim Madden died...

That day was the longest of Lucy's life as Tim Madden's life hung in the balance. Justin rang a couple of times but in between those times all she could do was think. And find herself going over everything in her mind, round and round in circles, and coming up with some surprises... Sasha, for example, who she had not known was an old friend of Joanna's and who had proved to be a good enough friend to support her during the awful night that had just passed. Sasha, who had admitted it was only after Joanna and Justin had broken up that she'd allowed herself to hope there could be a place for *her* in Justin's life. Sasha, Lucy thought, who so suddenly and surprisingly ended her little war with me but couldn't truthfully tell me why. Because she knows now, if she ever doubted it, that it's *still* Joanna she would have to fight for Justin in his heart if nothing else, not me?

She was sitting in the lounge staring into space when Justin came home. It was a dark overcast afternoon and she wore jeans and a long-sleeved cream silk blouse with her hair tied back in a blue ribbon. And her eyes were shadowed and wary as she stood up slowly when the door opened.

He came wearily into the lounge and she was shocked again to see the lines of tension in his face. Nor could she find any way to frame the query that was uppermost in her mind.

And his grey eyes ranged over, standing so still before he said quietly, 'He's going to be all right. The crisis is past but it will be a long, slow recovery.'

'Oh, thank God,' Lucy whispered, and sank down as her legs seemed to fold up beneath her.

He came to sit beside her on the settee, took her hand laid his head back wearily. And they simply sat like that for some minutes in silence. Until Lucy made herself say, 'How is Joanna?'

'All right now.'

'And the...his family?'

He sat up and pressed her hand before releasing it. 'They've come back to earth a bit; a lot of what was said was said under awful pressure.' He rubbed the blue shadows on his jaw wearily. 'Lucy—'

'Justin,' she said before he could go on and because she couldn't help herself, 'didn't they think it strange you should be there?'

He grimaced. 'It didn't exactly help at first, but I think I made them realise I was only there as an—intermediary. Joanna, you see—'

But Lucy stood up suddenly. 'You must be—would you like something to eat? You probably haven't had anything all day. I'll make us something now. How about a drink in the meantime? Stay there, I'll get it,' she said brightly, but to herself she was saying, I'm sorry, I know I brought it up but I can't talk about Joanna Madden any more, Justin, I just can't!

'Lucy—' He stood up, caught her wrist and for a moment towered over her, dark and powerful, and she trembled inwardly but didn't know that she looked both frightened and rebellious.

'Don't,' she stammered, not quite sure what she meant but suddenly sure it was all too much for her.

He paused, his eyes narrowed. 'Don't what, Lucy?' he said evenly after a long moment.

'I...I—let's just leave it, please, Justin.' Her voice shook but there was the sudden light of determination in her eyes. 'Let's just...pretend it's all over.'

'Lucy, it *is*, and—'

'Well, good! Now if you'll let me go I'll get us something to eat—really, Justin,' she tried to laugh, 'you're hurting me.'

He released her wrist abruptly then picked it up again and inspected the white marks of his fingers on it. Then he looked into her eyes and said drily, 'I'm only trying to reassure you, Lucy—'

'Oh, I'm reassured,' she broke in again. 'Is there any hope that we could go home now, by the way, Justin?'

He said after a tense moment, 'Tomorrow morning if

you like—Lucy, will you come to Riverbend with me for a while?'

Her eyes widened. 'Why?'

'Because that's where I'll have to be for most of the time until I find a replacement for Sasha.'

'Well...' She hesitated, because in her heart she was dying to get back to Dalkeith.

'We could bring Shirley and Adrian from Dalkeith.'

'All right,' she said slowly.

'After all, it is your second home now and,' he grimaced, 'it certainly needs someone to take an interest in it.'

But although that was what they did, things were different.

CHAPTER NINE

I KNEW this wasn't a good idea, coming to Riverbend, Lucy thought a week later. Which was not to say there was anything lacking at Riverbend other than a little tender loving care, which Shirley was more than happy to provide. It was a more modern house than Dalkeith but still a pleasant, gracious home. But its relative unfamiliarity was unsettling in her mood of the moment, which alternated between a kind of numbness and a kind of grief that contrived to make her stiff and awkward with Justin, withdrawn and then trying too hard and altogether right off balance.

She would also look around the rooms at times, and wonder if Joanna had designed them... There are no ghosts at Dalkeith, she thought more than once, that's why I'd be better off there. But, there was no doubt Justin couldn't have been at Dalkeith at this time; it was the peak of the foaling season and without Sasha there was undoubtedly a mountain of work entailed in running the stud, not to mention the personal interest Justin took in the horses.

For not only did Riverbend run its own mares but it stood four stallions, each of which had a list of outside mares booked to it, and nearly all of these mares arrived to be served with a foal at foot and they had to be accommodated in pastures, they had to be served and kept on the property until they tested positive to the service and their foals had to be looked after as well.

She said once to Justin, 'It's like a production line! No sooner have they dropped their foals than they're put *in* foal again; it doesn't seem terribly fair to me.'

'But it can't be news to you either, Lucy,' he replied with a faint look of amusement.

'Well, no, it's not,' she confessed, 'but on *this* scale...I mean, we're all but swamped with mares and foals and...' She gestured helplessly. 'It's a logistical nightmare if nothing else.'

'I can only agree, at times,' he commented wryly. 'That's why Sasha was so good; she had the kind of brain and horse-sense that excelled in these circumstances.'

'Have you...have you heard what she's doing now?'

'Yes I have. She's got a job with the Magic Millions organisation.'

'Oh! You mean the Queensland sales where all the yearlings sold are eligible for the Magic Millions race?'

'None other. It should suit her eminently.'

'How are you going finding a replacement for her?' Lucy asked after a moment.

'I've had a flood of applicants. It will take a bit of whittling down.'

'Could I help in the meantime?' Lucy said suddenly. 'I...I need something to do.'

They were breakfasting together but Justin had been up all night with a foal that had got entangled in a fence. The fact of this, that they had so little time to spend together, was something Lucy didn't know whether she was glad about or not. Because, in truth, whatever had snapped within her that last afternoon in Sydney had stayed snapped, and she knew she was subtly holding Justin at arm's length, knew he knew, but perhaps the most heartbreaking aspect of it all was that he'd made no real effort to break down her defences.

Well, look, he's been incredibly busy and I can understand why, she told herself a little drearily several times. All the same...

Which was not to say she hadn't shared his bed since that day, nor that he hadn't made love to her. But what she couldn't say in all honesty was that the thought that they might be interrupted by an emergency call from the stables, as did happen once when a very valuable mare got into difficulties foaling late one evening, was the real reason for her subdued, slightly tense response, although she'd offered it when she'd sensed he was about to say something. Offered it with a strained little smile then tried, too hard, to be bright and perky while she was feeling like dying within, and more so when he'd let it go...

'If you want to, Lucy,' he said at last, his grey eyes lingering on her.

'Yes, I do.' She realised immediately that she sounded defiant and stubborn, for no good reason probably, was cross with herself then tossed her head in a further gesture of defiance.

He said nothing as their gazes caught and clashed. Then, with an oddly dry inflection, he said abruptly, 'What's wrong, Lucy?'

'Nothing. Nothing in the world!' she answered brightly, and forced the tears that were so close to stay away. 'Where shall I start and what shall I do?'

She held her breath as she thought he was going to contest her statement, but although his mouth set in a rather hard line, he said unemotionally, 'There is something you could do. When the outside mares are deliv-

ered or picked up by their owners, it would be handy to
have someone in the stud office who could give them a
bit of a tour of the place, spend a bit of time with them—
that kind of thing. It makes them feel wanted.'

Lucy's eyes widened with genuine interest. 'I think
I'd like that,' she said slowly.

'I think you'd probably be good at it,' he commented.

'That would be a change,' she murmured, and bit her
lip.

'Lucy—'

'No, Justin,' she sprang up and managed to grin at
him, 'don't take any notice of me. I *do* know I'm very
good at talking the hind leg off a donkey! Can I start
today?'

'By all means,' he said, but after another lingering,
narrowed look. Then he shrugged and stood up himself.
'I'm going to grab a few hours' sleep. I don't suppose
you'd care to—join me?'

Her lips parted, her eyes widened and her heart started
to beat erratically. But she said, 'I've not been...up that
long, Justin. I mean...' She trailed off awkwardly.

He looked down at her enigmatically for an age then
he touched the point of her chin gently and said, 'I know
what you mean, Lucy. Never mind. Why don't you wander off to the stud office and—get started?' But there
was a look of irony in his grey eyes that pierced her
heart.

She hesitated then turned and walked away, her emotions in turmoil. What does he expect? she asked herself
miserably. Surely he must *know* I can't help wondering
what would have happened if Tim Madden had died, that
I just can't stop thinking about it as well as everything
else...

And for the next few weeks she threw herself into her newly created job as the flow of mares went both ways, incoming and outgoing. She also unexpectedly met an old friend, a young man who'd just qualified as a vet and was assisting their regular vet. He was a couple of years older but he'd been born in the district and they'd moved in the same crowd after she'd left school but only as friends. He was apparently delighted to meet her again and they had a few chats, recalling old times and laughing a lot. He was a tall, well-built, open-faced young man with a shock of blond curly hair and with one serious passion in his life, horses—Lucy gathered he had no romantic attachment at the moment. But in the uncomplicated pleasure she found in his company, she failed to notice that he looked at her occasionally with new eyes. It didn't occur to her for two reasons: because she wasn't looking for it and because she didn't imagine, now she was a married woman, that men would seriously think of her in those terms.

Nor would she ever have been aware of it if she hadn't one day been laughing over her shoulder at something he said as she walked past then looked ahead to see Justin watching them, standing curiously still.

She took an unexpected breath as she walked towards him, her eyes widening as he still made no move, but his grey gaze seemed to pierce hers for a blinding moment. Then at last he moved and said with a wry twist of his lips, 'Hi, Lucy. Having fun?'

'Yes—no, I mean…Justin?' She frowned at him. 'Is something wrong?'

'No, of course not, Lucy,' he said easily. But it was that evening he told her that he had to go to Sydney for several days…

'Lucy?'

'Oh! Justin.' She looked up with a smile from the brown study she'd been in since returning from the stables. 'I didn't hear you come in. Finished for the day?'

'Yes.' He threw down his hat and stretched. 'You're looking very pensive,' he remarked.

'I was feeling a bit pensive,' she confessed but added as she stood up, 'Dinner is actually ready but I'll tell Shirley to hold it for half an hour so you can have a shower. Would you like a drink?'

For a moment, his grey gaze roamed over her narrowly and she thought he was going to ask her what she'd been pensive about, but then a faint smile touched his lips and he turned away saying, 'I'd love one. I'll be back in ten minutes.'

And they had their dinner then took their coffee on to the terrace where a crescent moon laid a silvery glow over the landscape.

'Summer's really here,' Lucy murmured, and once again he let his gaze drift over her, taking in her sleeveless white blouse and white cotton skirt splashed with yellow daisies.

'Mmm. It will be Christmas before we know where we are. Lucy, now that things have calmed down a bit, I have to go away for a few days—a week at the most. Sydney mainly, and all business. I've narrowed the applicants for Sasha's job down to two and I'll be seeing them but if you'd like to come—'

'No, thank you,' she said hastily, then forced herself to relax. 'There are still a few mares coming and going. I can keep on with my job here if you like.'

'It's what *you* would like,' he said, and there was something curiously watchful and narrowed in his eyes.

She frowned faintly. 'I know you keep asking me this but it seems to be my turn now—is something wrong? I've—' she paused '—known Rob Redding for years and years, if that...' She stopped and stared at him.

But he only, once again, said wryly, 'So have I. It makes me feel quite old. Good to see him qualified. I think he'll make a top vet from what I've seen so far. No, nothing's wrong, Lucy—as you keep telling me.'

She sat back and grimaced. 'I wondered if you thought I was being a *femme fatale* again.'

'No.' He was silent for a long while then he stretched and yawned. 'I don't know about you but I'm knackered, and I've got a crack-of-dawn start tomorrow.'

'Oh,' Lucy said with some concern. 'I promised Adrian I'd help him with a composition he's got to have in for the School of the Air tomorrow. He has to read it out over the radio.'

'Never mind,' Justin said, curiously gently, as he stood up. Then he bent over and kissed her briefly on the forehead. 'Goodnight, my dear. I'll try not to wake you in the morning and I'll ring you from Sydney.'

'Goodnight,' Lucy said in a strange little voice, and watched him walk away unhurriedly with a stabbing sense of grief in her heart.

It didn't go away over the next couple of days, that sense of grief, nor did her job, or Rob Redding, or even Adrian's getting an A for his composition mitigate it. All she could think of was lying stiff and silent beside Justin that night when she did go to bed, longing for him to wake up and take her in his arms, willing herself to reach out and touch him but not being able to do it as she wondered whether he would be seeing Joanna in Sydney...

Then came the proof that he had in the form of a picture in a two-day-old newspaper she normally wouldn't have bothered reading if Shirley, who was still avid for her hometown news however late it might be, hadn't left it on the kitchen table.

She stared down at it and drew in a long, shaky breath. Ever since they'd left Sydney, she realised, she'd longed to ask Justin for news of the Maddens, but it had seemed like tempting fate as well as establishing whether he'd been in touch—if he had, would she mind? And yet it was not unreasonable for him to do so, but... Well, he has now, she thought unhappily, and wiped away a foolish tear. For the picture that had captured her attention was one of Justin and Joanna, with his hand on her elbow, leaving the Sydney hospital where Tim Madden was still recovering, and it was dated the day after he had arrived back in Sydney two days ago. It also bore a simple but cryptic caption to the effect that the Waite-Madden feud appeared to have been halted in its tracks.

Why didn't he tell me? she wondered miserably. That it wasn't *all* business.

To make matters worse, she was out riding when he rang that day—he'd rung daily—so what she got was a message that he'd call early the next morning, and would she please make sure she was in the house? To explain? she wondered dully. He's left it a bit late, or perhaps he thinks the odds against my seeing it are pretty long. And why doesn't he ring back this evening when I'm *sure* to be here? Is he with...her? I don't know how much longer I can stand this uncertainty and torment.

And the next morning Justin explained nothing, nor

did he mention the Maddens, but he did say he would be home the following day late in the afternoon, that he'd appointed Sasha's replacement, and asked her how she was.

'Fine. Fine!' she reassured him.

'Good. No other problems?'

'Not that I know of!'

'OK—see you tomorrow, Lucy.' And he rang off.

It was a moment before she put the phone down, and she said to it before she did so, I'm not terribly sure about that, Justin. Because, you see, I just don't think I can go on living with the thought of you and Joanna... any longer.

And two days later she sat in Mother Angelica's study at her old school, a room she was very familiar with and which was quite unchanged since she'd first come to know it at nine, and said jerkily, 'I need some advice— thank you for seeing me at such short notice, by the way, but I'm afraid I've got myself into a bit of a bind.'

Mother Angelica's hair was grey now beneath the short veil and there were new lines and wrinkles in her skin, but her tall, spare figure was the same and her keen blue eyes especially were as uncomfortably all-seeing as they'd ever been. 'So it would appear, Lucy,' she said thoughtfully. 'And talking of by-the-ways, I would have liked to know about your marriage at least; it would have been a courtesy if nothing else.'

Lucy sighed. 'No, it wouldn't. Because, you see, I married my worst enemy—or so I thought at the time. I married for all the wrong reasons, not to say *crazy* reasons only—then I fell in love with him and realised I'd probably *always* been a little in love with him but he loves someone else, someone he can't have, except that her husband nearly died a few weeks ago and if he had...well, I just can't stop thinking about it. You see, *if* he had, they could have been together again—if it weren't for me.'

'My dear child—' Mother Angelica began, but Lucy interrupted her.

'I'm *not* a child any more,' she said intensely, her eyes suddenly flashing blue fire in her white, weary face. 'That's how *he* thinks of me but I'm a living, breathing woman now. In all respects save one: I haven't had a child myself yet.'

'And you think that's what it takes?' Mother Angelica said quietly.

Lucy stared at her. 'What do you mean?' she said hollowly after a moment.

'Well, neither have I. But it's to me you've brought your problems, Lucy.'

Lucy grimaced. 'That's because you more or less brought me up, thankless task though it may have been, but—'

'On the contrary, Lucy. I always felt I was working with the finest material.'

'*What*?' Lucy whispered, her eyes now astounded.

'But what was more,' the nun went on in that same thoughtful, quiet way, 'despite our frequent conflicts, I always hoped that you acquired enough respect for me to benefit from my upbringing—however old-fashioned it may have seemed at the time.'

Lucy blinked several times then said hoarsely, 'Yes, I did. And yes, that's why I'm here, but—'

'Very well. Let's take this step by step, my dear—and I apologise for calling you a child.'

So that was what they did. And at the end Mother Angelica sat silent for a time then she said, 'I'm surprised at you, Lucy. I thought you had more spirit.'

Which was not what Lucy was expecting, and her eyes widened. 'Do you mean...?'

'I mean, if you really love this man, why aren't you fighting for him?'

Lucy actually laughed, although it was a pale imitation. 'You know,' she said, 'I came here all prepared for you to talk about the sanctity of marriage, but not this.'

'It's not a lot different,' Mother Angelica commented.

Lucy was silent for a moment, then she said painfully, 'But he does make me feel like a child sometimes and there are...' She stopped, then said awkwardly, 'And there are things between men and, well, women that are hard to explain—'

'Especially to a woman who has no experience of men in that way? I believe you,' Mother Angelica said, 'but I don't believe it should change one's morals or the things *you* believe in or be a cause to run away—does he know where you are?'

'No,' Lucy said distractedly. 'What did you mean about the things *I* believe in?'

'That you're a woman not a child, that you love him, have given yourself to him and are entitled to do all those things. But I wouldn't be saying this, Lucy,' Mother Angelica narrowed her eyes, 'if it didn't seem to me that you also respect him. Or if I felt he was some sort of bounder who had taken terrible advantage of a rather innocent young woman—which is how it would appear to a lot of people on the face of things.'

'I know, but that's not quite... It wasn't quite like that.

As a matter of fact, I respect him as much as I do you,' Lucy said shakenly.

'Then you've forgiven him for marrying you the way he did?' There was an even more acute than normal little glint in those blue eyes now.

Lucy paused. 'I did have another option; I couldn't bring myself to take it, as I told you,' she said at last. 'What I didn't realise at the time was how difficult it would be to live with the thought of him loving someone else.'

'You haven't done it for very long.'

'No.'

'And apart from this feeling that he doesn't love you the way you love him, how has he treated you?'

'Very well—look, I'm not denying that he might love me in a way,' Lucy said desperately. 'Or that he would ever stop taking care of me and all that. I don't even think he would dishonour me intentionally, although…' She stopped. 'It's just this awful feeling that I'm not his…soulmate, and she is.'

'Why don't you give him the benefit of the doubt? Men,' Mother Angelica said, 'can change their minds. We all can.'

Lucy sat in confused silence for about two minutes, then she said, 'Could I stay here just for a while?'

'Of course, but I do think you should get in touch with him in a day or two if you've run away and he doesn't know where you are.'

'You do?'

'Wouldn't it feel cowardly to hide away from him for any longer?'

'Well I suppose so…'

In the event she wasn't given the opportunity to do so for any longer by Justin either, but it was quite by accident that she overheard what he and Mother Angelica had to say to each other when Justin arrived at the convent to look for her quite early the next morning. She *had* been with the junior boarders playing an early game of rounders; that was where Mother had left her when she was called away, following her obvious intention of not allowing Lucy to mope or brood in the plain, rather cell-like guest-room. The previous afternoon Lucy had been called upon to umpire a couple of tennis matches and in the evening she'd been roped in to play the piano at an end-of-year concert rehearsal, then have a late supper with that year's senior girls.

But in the middle of the rounders she'd been struck by a mixture of regret that things were no longer so simple for her and the urgent thought that she had to sit down somewhere peaceful and private and *think*. She chose the little walled garden that was off limits to the girls and thus was new to her, without stopping to think that it was also directly below Mother Angelica's first floor study.

There was a bench, a patch of lawn, a bird bath, creepers along the grey stone walls and a riot of roses. There was also, as she sat down and leant back in the early sunlight and closed her eyes, the sound of voices suddenly from above, quite distinct and very familiar...

'How do you do, Mother Angelica? I'm Justin Waite and I've come to enquire whether you've seen or heard anything about my wife who would have been known to you as Lucy Wainright of Dalkeith.'

Lucy swallowed and sat upright abruptly.

'Ah, Mr Waite! I have as a matter of fact been looking

forward to having a few words with you. Please sit down.' There was a slight pause and the sound of a chair on wood. 'Now,' Mother Angelica continued in a voice Lucy recognised only too well, and her eyes widened, 'would you please be so good as to tell me *why* you took a girl as naïve and vulnerable as Lucy and forced her into a marriage of convenience? I can think of a very unpleasant name for the likes of you, you know.'

Lucy gasped.

'Is that what she told you, Mother Angelica?' There was the faintest suggestion of a drawl in Justin's voice, but it was mainly as hard and cold as the nun's.

'No, it is not what she told me. She apparently admires and respects you and indeed, thinks she *loves* you. So much so that she is prepared to leave you so that you and some other woman can be together again and be— soulmates,' Mother Angelica said with utter, icy contempt, then, 'I'm waiting, Mr Waite.'

'Madam,' Justin said softly but equally as icily, 'I have no intention of being soulmates with anyone other than Lucy, so—'

'Then how come she's not aware of this?' Mother Angelica broke in imperiously. 'How come this lovely child who was so radiant, so spirited even when she was so lonely at times, who made it a better day in most people's life even when she was being wayward, a child who is nevertheless completely *wholesome*—is like a broken flower now? Tell me that, Mr Waite?'

Lucy dropped her head into her hands and could have died.

'Look, Mother Angelica, just tell me where she is,' Justin said harshly. 'It may come as some surprise to

you but I care as much about Lucy and her welfare as
you do.'

'Then you have a strange way of showing it, Mr
Waite.'

'Would you rather I'd abandoned her after her father
died, ma'am?'

There was a little pause and the tension of it seemed
to float down to where Lucy sat so that she raised her
head—and waited.

'Why did you marry her, then—will you tell me that?'
Mother Angelica said in a very slightly, less hostile
voice.

'I'll tell you this—I have no thought of *corrupting* her
if that's what you fear; I have only her best interests at
heart. I too, you see,' he said with considerable irony,
'was aware from the start of not only her innocence but
her vulnerability when her father died, her loneliness,
the terrible burden of debt and so on she'd been left with.
And if I may bring this to your notice, Mother Angelica,
I've known her for even longer than you have, so I
too know all about the quite—special person Lucy
Wainright is.'

'Will you at least admit you haven't been able to
make her happy, Mr Waite?'

Lucy twisted her hands until her fingers went white.

'So it would seem so far,' Justin said drily. 'That
doesn't mean to say I'll stop trying. Is she still here?'

A pause then Mother Angelica said, 'Yes,' and went
on in a different, thoughtful voice, 'If I've misjudged
you in some ways, Mr Waite, I apologise. But I still
must admonish you to banish all thoughts of this other
woman from your mind, because I hold you entirely responsible for Lucy—do I make myself clear?'

'Eminently, Mother Angelica. It so happens I hold *myself* entirely responsible for her, so we are—in some agreement...'

Lucy heard no more, because she sprang up suddenly and ran to her room, where she started to pack hastily. But she wasn't quick enough, because there was a brief knock on the door—and Mother Angelica opened it with Justin just behind her.

'Lucy...what are you doing?'

Lucy cast one look at Justin from beneath her lashes and was shocked to see how pale and tired he looked before she rushed into speech. 'Packing. Hello, Justin. I...I didn't expect to see you. Oh what's the use?' she said under her breath and sank down on to the bed, 'Look, quite by accident I happened to overhear your conversation so I have to say some things—thank you for defending me the way you did, Mother, but I'm not quite such a broken flower as you imagine and—'

'*Lucy!*'

'It wasn't my fault, I just happened to be sitting in the garden below your window; I wanted to be some-where quiet where I could think,' Lucy said tiredly, and turned to look at Justin properly for the first time. 'And thank you for feeling so responsible for me, but I prob-ably know better than most how...impossible it is to banish someone from your thoughts unless there's no hope, and even then perhaps, so—'

'Mother Angelica,' Justin said quietly but quite com-pellingly, 'would you allow me to handle this on my own?'

The nun hesitated, then she went out and closed the door behind her.

'Justin,' Lucy said, 'don't think—'

'I'm not.'

'You don't know what I was going to say!' she objected after a moment.

'Was it along the lines of—don't think I'm coming back to you after what I overheard this morning?'

Lucy took a breath then sat down on the bed. 'Well, yes,' she said baldly, and added, 'If you must know, I was highly embarrassed this morning. How did you find me so quickly anyway?' she said exasperatedly.

'I remembered what you said about Mother Angelica once. I thought you might have—turned to her. But why embarrassed?' he queried.

'Because...because I felt as if I'd never left school, for one thing!' She subjected him to an indignant pansy-blue gaze.

'Some of the things you heard this morning are true, though, Lucy.'

She turned away, picked up a blouse and started to fold it on her lap. 'I know, I do know,' she said suddenly. 'I...it was one of the reasons I married you. I didn't know where else to turn, I didn't have the maturity to stand on my own, and now look at me: back here,' she said, barely audibly and with a rueful look around.

He smiled drily. 'With two people who love you nearly coming to blows over you this morning.'

Her eyes widened. 'She *wouldn't*!'

'She certainly looked as if she would have dearly loved to flatten me when I introduced myself.'

'Well—but that doesn't change things.'

'It does for me,' he said. 'That—and finding that you'd left me.'

'What do you mean?' Lucy whispered, and her heart started to beat erratically. 'Look, I have to tell you, I saw you and Joanna in the paper, holding hands! But in any case, since he nearly died—Tim—things have been different, and they were never quite right in the *first* place so—I couldn't help knowing you were thinking of what might have been. After all, you were the one she turned to. Then—' her voice cracked '—then this morning I had to listen to all those things you said about responsibility and vulnerability and innocence as if I were your *ward*, not your wife. How can you expect me to believe I'm really anything else to you, Justin?'

'I don't,' he said, 'not yet. But I'd like the opportunity to explain. Will you let me try to do that, Lucy?'

'H-how?' she stammered.

He grimaced. 'For one thing, not here. Will you come away with me now?'

'What if it doesn't—' she stopped to brush away a tear '—make sense to me?'

'Then I'll do whatever you want me to do—bring you back here, if you like.'

She hesitated. 'Well I have to warn you I'm no longer a pushover, Justin. Nor am I a broken flower.'

He was silent, just watching her as she sat straight-backed on the bed, her chin tilted although her eyes were still wet, and there were tired faint blue shadows beneath them. Then he moved as if to ease some mental burden and said, 'You never were, Lucy. Should we perhaps—get some breakfast? It's about that time.'

'Not if you live here; I've had breakfast *and* a round of rounders,' she said with a sudden faint smile, though sobering almost immediately.

'Coffee, then?' he suggested.

'All...all right, but...' She gestured almost futilely.

'I'd better make it good,' he said with a sudden touch of humour.

Lucy caught her breath, but said bravely, 'Yes.'

CHAPTER TEN

JUSTIN drove her to the Rocks and chose a restaurant overlooking Circular Quay with an open veranda where they had the Sydney Harbour Bridge almost overhead, the sails of the Opera House rising across the Quay and the waters of the harbour dancing before them in the morning sunlight. And he went inside to place their order, taking quite a few minutes.

Not that Lucy minded; she was trying desperately to get herself together and even wished he'd been away longer when he and the waiter arrived together with orange juice, a pot of coffee and two waffles spread with syrup and heaped with ice-cream.

And she said quite spontaneously, 'Oh, dear! I don't know if I can fit it in.'

'Try,' Justin murmured, sitting down opposite her. 'Look upon it as brunch; that's what I'm doing.'

And they ate in silence for a while until he pushed his plate away and poured the coffee. 'Lucy—'

'Justin…'

They spoke together, and he smiled slightly and said, 'Go ahead.'

'No.' She pushed her plate away and wiped her mouth. 'I'm not sure what I was going to say anyway.' She shrugged desolately.

'All right. Lucy, you were right about Joanna—once. When she left me and married Tim, a kind of blackness came over me and I swore I would never forgive her, or

172

him.' He paused and watched her searchingly, 'And, while it *wouldn't* have been true to say it didn't matter whom I married after that, it was not a true marriage that I offered you.'

Lucy closed her eyes then made herself take a sip of coffee. 'Go on,' she said in a gruff little voice.

'But it *was* nevertheless a gesture prompted by all those things that Mother Angelica and I catalogued so embarrassingly for you this morning. In other words, I did care very much about what became of you, not only Dalkeith, and I did know how much Dalkeith meant to you and I did mean to...always have your best interests at heart. Unfortunately—' he paused and stared into the middle distance for a moment then returned his grey gaze to her with something bleak and sombre in it '—certain things happened unexpectedly, as you know, and while I would never have gone out of my way to flourish you at Joanna, when it happened I couldn't help feeling—a certain sense of revenge.'

'Go on,' she whispered.

'But—' He stopped and looked at her white face. 'When I realised that, it very quickly changed to a feeling of remorse and I came very close, when you offered to make our marriage a real one, to letting you go.'

'I wish you had,' she whispered, then her eyes widened. 'Well, you did try, didn't you? That night. I wouldn't take you up, though...oh...'

'Lucy, don't blame yourself for that, blame me,' he said harshly. 'I could have done it if I'd set my mind to it.'

'Why...why didn't you?' she stammered.

His grey eyes held hers. 'Because I found I didn't really want to.'

'So you could go on avenging yourself?'

'No. So I could really have you.'

'But...but why?' She stared at him bewilderedly.

'It had become a matter of growing urgency for me, that's why, Lucy.'

She sat in stunned silence for a moment then said, 'Because you're a man and not a monk sort of thing?'

His lips twisted into a dry little smile. 'You've accused me of that once before. No. Because of *you*. An enchanting, sometimes wayward source of increasing fascination for me in every way, including the most intimate way—that's why I did it.'

'Are you trying to tell me you started to fall in love with me, Justin?' she said with difficulty.

'You've hit the nail on the head, Lucy,' he agreed.

'I don't know if I can believe you...'

'I think you should try.'

'But look here—' she sat up agitatedly '—it didn't stop you treating me like a child sometimes—don't you remember what happened that night in the twelve-mile?'

'Very well, as a matter of fact. May I point out that it didn't stop me from treating you like a woman either?'

Lucy sat back and felt the colour rising from the base of her throat but with an effort, tried to compose her thoughts. 'Well, it didn't blot Joanna out entirely, though, did it?' she said huskily. 'I know because,' she paused, 'for one thing I saw how you and Tim looked at each other after the sale of the Cawnpore filly, and there could be only one reason for you two to feel so hostile towards each other, couldn't there? Joanna,' she said miserably.

'No, it didn't blot out Joanna *immediately*, Lucy,' he said and unexpectedly reached across the table and put his hand over hers. 'But that was partly habit, I suspect, and mostly a sense of remorse towards *her* by then. You see, seeing us together, sensing my frame of mind that day they flew into Riverbend to look at the filly, opened it all up for Joanna again. And I began to wonder if I was some sort of monster, letting her see that flash of revenge so that it all came back to her at the same time as I was falling in love with you.'

'Did she tell you this?' Lucy queried very quietly. 'That it had all opened up for her again?'

'Yes, but not until the day after Tim nearly died.'

'But you knew it was happening to her all the same?'

'Yes, I guessed,' he said and both his voice and eyes were completely sombre. 'The kind of thing that in my black days I'd dreamt of planning, only to find a growing horror when it happened quite unplanned. And I guess most of the hostility I felt towards Tim Madden then was motivated by something you put into words once. How could he put Joanna through it, all over a horse? Which was why I was glad he had to pay so much for it in the end.'

'Oh,' Lucy said on a breath. 'But that still leaves—I mean, you still *cared* about her otherwise...not that I mind, I mean...I don't know what I really mean except that Joanna Madden is very hard to hate,' she said frustratedly. 'And she did turn to you—'

'She didn't,' he said drily. 'Sasha did that without Joanna even knowing, which was just the kind of thoughtless thing Sasha was so prone to doing. Joanna was actually horrified when I turned up at the hospital, horrified and terribly guilty. Because she blamed herself for Tim's heart attack, you see.'

'Why? And if so, why did you stay with her nearly all day?' Lucy whispered.

He moved his fingers on hers. 'I stayed because she *didn't* have anyone else to turn to and once the damage was done, I couldn't stand by and not try to bring some sanity to the situation.' He paused. 'Why did she feel guilty? Because Tim knew what she was going through too, perhaps he'd even deliberately brought her to Riverbend to find out if she'd got over me—I don't know, but I'm quite sure it was his perhaps subconscious shot in *our* war, buying the Cawnpore filly for such a high price. I think he was trying to prove something to Joanna.'

'I see...oh, yes, I see,' Lucy said, her eyes widening. 'So they were right, his children, after all?' She stared at him with her lips parted.

'Partly right,' Justin agreed grimly. 'What they didn't know was that by then what I felt for Joanna was an affection I probably will always hold but that I was no longer in love with her, and never had been in love with her the way I love you. The other thing they didn't know was that the shock of seeing Tim at death's door had opened Joanna's eyes to her love for him.'

Lucy sat staring at him, absolutely arrested. Then she said shakily, 'Do you really believe that?'

'Yes, I do. In fact, that picture you saw, which I wasn't even aware had been taken until Shirley showed it to me because she'd seen you looking at it with tears in your eyes—that picture was the final chapter. I went to see Tim with Joanna and together we told him all this, but I *only* did it because he'd had a relapse just after I arrived back in Sydney and she was desperate enough to contact me and beg me to do it. I think we got through to him. And I wasn't holding her hand as such; she'd tripped on an uneven tile and I stopped her falling, that's all. We parted outside the hospital.'

'But why—Justin, did you know how Joanna felt the day after Tim's heart attack?'

'Yes.'

'Why didn't you tell me?' Lucy whispered. 'How could you tell Tim and not me?'

'Lucy, when I came back from the hospital the day after Tim's heart attack I wanted nothing more than to do so. But—' he paused and looked deep into her stricken eyes '—you went away from me. You made it quite clear you didn't want to hear any more on the subject. You even looked...repelled by it all. And I thought it was too late, that I'd lost you and I didn't deserve any better because I'd been such a bloody fool for so long. I thought, why would you want to go on being involved with me after all I'd done? I felt, to put it mildly, as guilty as hell as I watched you withdraw further and further from me. Then I saw you and Rob Redding, I saw you laughing again, becoming in his company your old, natural, lovely—it's hard to put it into words—self. And I saw the way he looked at you and I thought...how much better it would be for you to be loved by someone with no dark past, someone young and uncomplicated—'

'Justin,' Lucy broke in urgently, 'yes, I did go away from you, although not because I was repelled but because I couldn't stop thinking about what might have happened if Tim had died, and wanting to die myself out of sheer misery. You see,' she dashed at the tears brimming in her eyes, 'you don't know this but Sasha...Sasha seemed to confirm my worst fears just the night before at the dance.' She told him what Sasha had said and how it had all seemed to add up to the fact that Sasha genuinely believed it wasn't over between him and Joanna. 'Then, when it was Sasha who rang up...' She stopped and the tears fell unchecked now.

'I might have known,' he said grimly, and closed his eyes briefly. 'You were right, why I put up with her I'll never know. But she was wrong.'

'She did apologise for all the things she'd said before,' Lucy said involuntarily.

He looked at her piercingly, 'Such as?'

'Oh, Justin,' Lucy looked away, 'I don't think there's much point—Sasha...was Sasha, I guess.'

'Do you—believe what I've told you this morning, Lucy?'

'I...' She bit her lip and swallowed, wondering if she dared to believe it.

'But there's more,' he said very quietly. 'When I got back to Riverbend and you were gone, when I confronted Mother Angelica and came close to hating a nun of all people because she thought she loved you and understood you more than I did, I knew then I could never let you go, Lucy, even if I believed you'd be better off with someone like Rob Redding. I just—in the end, couldn't do it.'

Lucy stirred. 'This morning you said you'd take me back to the convent if I wanted it.'

'Do you?' he queried quietly. 'I was hoping to persuade you to give me a second chance. I was hoping if I told you all this and told you how you've grown into my heart and life so that I'll be lost and lonely for the rest of it without you, you wouldn't want to. I was hoping to be able to prove to you that we are soulmates.'

But although he looked deep into her eyes, Lucy twisted her hands and said disjointedly, 'I want...Justin, I want to believe you with all my heart but...'

She stopped and became aware of a droning noise overhead, then aware of some of the waiters and some passers-by stopping and looking upwards and starting to smile and gesticulate, so she looked up herself and saw a light plane flying over the harbour bridge flying a banner. A banner that said in high, rather hastily painted letters by the look of it but quite clearly all the same, 'I LOVE YOU, LUCY. JUSTIN'.

She choked, looked upwards incredulously again then turned to him and whispered urgently, 'Justin, is it really true?'

'If you let me, I'll spend the rest of my life proving it to you, my darling Lucy,' he answered, and then she was in his arms and everyone's attention turned to them as it became clear to all and sundry who Justin and Lucy were, and people started to cheer and applaud.

'I think we ought to get out of here,' he said into her hair.

'Oh, yes, please,' she said. 'Oh, no! Do you think it will get into the papers again?'

'I hope it does,' he replied, and added with a grin. 'It would also make my day if Mother Angelica were to see it. Let's go.'

'How did you arrange it?' she asked laughingly as they were ushered into a suite at the Regent very close by.

'When I went to order the waffles. I rang a friend of mine who owns the plane. He gives flying lessons and trails banners and was just about to take-off, fortunately—although I'm afraid he thought I'd gone mad.'

'I should get in touch with Mother Angelica,' Lucy said sobering. 'Actually, I got the surprise of my life when she verbally attacked you this morning, because her advice to me had been to fight for you if I really loved you, you know, Justin.'

'Was it?'

'Yes—that's strange, isn't it?'

'Not so strange if she'd perceived that you do really love me.'

Lucy grimaced. 'I don't think anyone ever doubted that—Justin,' she breathed as he suddenly held her very hard.

'Sorry. I don't know how I could have been such a bloody fool, that's all.'

'Should we...should we go to bed, then?' she suggested. 'It might stop you feeling like that.'

He lifted his head and she caught her breath at the blaze of love she saw in his grey eyes as well as the laughter.

'Did I say something wrong?'

'No. Oh, no. Lucy, another thing you said once was that you'd rather you were married to someone with no experience but who loved you so much it didn't matter— that's how I feel right at the moment. Delighted, devoted, renewed—and dying to go to bed with you.'

'That's lovely,' she said softly, and moved in his arms.

They made love twice before lunch and spent the afternoon in bed recuperating, as Justin put it. They watched a movie on television holding hands but at about four o'clock he went into the adjoining sitting-room and made a couple of phone calls, telling her just to be patient when she asked about it. Half an hour later there was a knock at the door and he brought into the bedroom a large box and a slim envelope.

'What's this?' Lucy asked.

'Open it, the box first.'

So she did and discovered two dozen bikinis inside. 'But—' she stared at the colourful throng dazedly then lifted her eyes to his '—if this is what I think it is, I only need a couple.'

'What do you think it is?'

'The Seychelles?' she hazarded.

'More or less. Open the envelope.'

So she did and this time her eyes nearly fell out of her head. '*Justin*...'

'What do you think? We've missed the QEII here but we pick her up in Singapore then cruise to the Seychelles, Mombasa, Durban, Capetown, so you could well need more than two bikinis—hey,' he said softly, 'don't cry.' And drew her into his arms.

'I'm not. I mean, I am, but only from happiness. Do you remember saying something to *me* about romantic gestures—well, yours are the very best!'

'Well, my first one wasn't the most original, but perhaps I'm learning,' he commented, and kissed her leisurely. Whereupon they made love once more and then he had dinner and a bottle of champagne sent up.

'I still don't need two dozen,' Lucy remarked with an impish little smile, later.

'I know. I had an ulterior motive there, I'm afraid,' he drawled. 'I ordered them on approval so you could try them all on and select the ones you liked. With my help,' he added gravely.

'Ah,' Lucy murmured then laughed.

He raised a wry eyebrow at her. 'That amuses you?'

'No, it delights me actually, and very shortly I shall do just that, try them all on, but first of all I think I'll do this.' And she leant over and kissed him fleetingly on the mouth. 'Thank you. For everything,' she said a little shyly.

'Lucy—' he caught her wrist then pulled her on to his lap '—God knows I feel guilty enough about you as it is—'

'Justin, don't say that,' she whispered. 'It will make me start to wonder again if—'

'Then let me tell you this,' he said quietly, holding her against him gently. 'I have a vision of my life now that's inextricably linked with yours. I'll always have the memories of the beautiful girl who became a woman in my bed and told me she felt...translated, and I know I'll want to keep on translating her for the rest of my life. As well as living in love and laughter with her, as well as fathering her children, as well caring for her—and receiving the special sort of sunlight you bring to me, Lucy.' He tilted her chin and stared deep into her eyes. 'There is only one way to say it. I love you, I love your body and your soul and I can't live without you; it's as simple as that...'

If she had any last doubts they were dispelled the next morning when they went to see Mother Angelica together.

'Ah,' that wise nun said as they stood before her together in the study that hadn't changed for so many years, 'you've resolved it. Mr Waite, I *was* rather hard on you yesterday but one thing in the end convinced me that you loved Lucy and that was the look of inexpressible relief that came into your eyes when I told you she was still here safe with me. God bless you, my dears, and don't you dare have any christenings without me!'

And to Lucy's joy things like that kept happening, little touches of proof. Such as the occasion on their delayed honeymoon aboard the pride of the Cunard Line somewhere in the Indian Ocean between the Seychelles and Mombasa. It was a formal evening and she'd dressed in a strapless midnight-blue evening gown that moulded her figure and had a slit up the front, and put her hair up.

But she had to return to their state room when her tights laddered and it took about twenty minutes to change them and assure herself she was perfectly presented again. When she returned, Justin, looking magnificent in a black dinner suit, was standing with a group of people all superbly groomed, indeed he was flanked by two stunning women who seemed to be vying for his attention. And Lucy's heart missed a beat as she saw, as she approached, the distant, shuttered look on his face, something that had been missing these past few weeks. And when he looked up into her eyes, for a moment his own were moody and disenchanted.

Then they changed and he excused himself briefly and came towards her almost as if he was heading her off.

'Is something wrong?' she whispered.

'Yes. Come outside.' He put a hand on her elbow and steered her out onto the deck, and kept steering her until they reached a secluded area with no one around. 'This.' And he took her in his arms.

'But...but why?' she asked minutes later when she'd been thoroughly and urgently kissed. 'Not that I'm complaining...'

'I missed you,' he said simply. 'I couldn't work out why you were taking so long, particularly as everyone was asking me where my gorgeous, sensational wife was. I wondered if you'd fallen overboard—or found another man.'

'Justin!' she breathed her eyes wide and stunned.

'Moreover, Lucy,' he continued and while his eyes were amused there was something else lurking in their grey depths. 'I need to be reassured.'

Her lips parted. 'How...do you mean right now?'

'Indeed I do, Mrs Waite.'

'Like this?' she said not much later but in the seclusion of their state room, and reached for the zip of her dress.

But he stilled her hand as he stood before her, his dark head inclined, and murmured, 'Just so. May I?'

And he released her hair first and ran his fingers through its golden length and then undressed her item by item until there were only her new tights over brief silk panties. He laid her on the bed and drew them off slowly letting his fingers lie cool and firm on the inside of her thighs until she moved with desire and said his name in a grave, husky little voice.

Then he ripped his own clothes off and lay down beside her and took her with a lack of finesse that he apologised unevenly for, but an unmistakable hunger that told its own tale and took her to heights she'd never reached before.

And in the sweet, drowsy aftermath of their love, she cradled his head to her breasts, and felt herself to be Justin Waite's true partner in all things.

'I don't know what got into me,' he said after a while with her now lying in his arms, as he stroked her hair.

'But when I looked up and saw you coming back at last, so…utterly lovely, I just knew I had to do this very shortly.'

'I'm glad you did,' she said and drew her fingertips down his face. 'If I thought I'd been—translated before, it was nothing to this.'

He laughed quietly and hugged her gently. 'We've missed dinner.'

'It's well lost. I love you.'

'Even after—wrecking you like that?' he said wryly.

'More so, and—' Lucy paused, then sat up and looked down at him wickedly, '—you're also the man who flew a banner over Sydney harbour telling me you loved me, don't forget.'

'The second man—is it any wonder I could get a bit paranoid at times?' he replied lazily, his eyes on her pink-tipped breasts.

'The only man. For me,' she said firmly, and lay down again.

'So you do…believe me now, Lucy?' he said in a different voice as he took her into his arms again.

She turned her face to his and laid her cheek on his chest. 'Yes, Justin. Is it…is it so important to you?'

'The most important thing in the world,' he said very quietly.

'Well, you're the most important thing in the world to me, so it's worked out astonishingly well, in fact.'

'Yes, it has. Thank God, it has.'

THE ROYAL HOUSE OF KAREDES

Two crowns, two islands, one legacy

Volume One
BILLIONAIRE PRINCE, PREGNANT MISTRESS
by Sandra Marton

Wanted for her body – and her baby!

Aspiring New York jewellery designer Maria Santo
has come to Aristo to win a royal commission.

Cold, calculating and ruthless, Prince Xander
Karedes beds Maria, thinking she's only sleeping
with him to save her business.

So when Xander discovers Maria's pregnant,
he assumes it's on purpose. What will it take for this
billionaire prince to realise he's falling in love
with his pregnant mistress…?

Available 17th April 2009

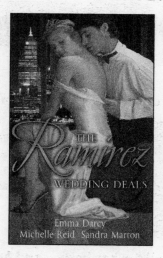

His passions were as tempestuous as his temper...

Even though Kate Whittman was young and inexperienced, she wanted moody Texas rancher Jason Donovan more than anything. But he offered her only brotherly protection.

So Kate pursued another fantasy – becoming a successful New York fashion designer. But just when it seemed that her fairy tale was coming true, fate brought her back to Texas. And to Jason.

Available 1st May 2009

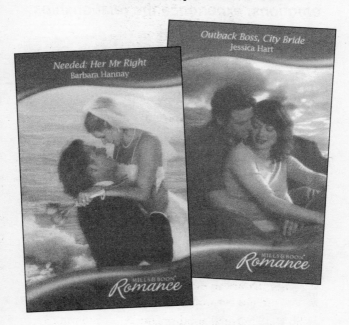

Welcome to Cedar Cove – a small town with a big heart!

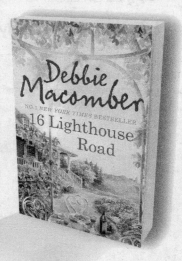

When family court judge Olivia Lockheart causes a scandal by denying a couple's divorce, the whole town starts talking about it.

Meanwhile, her daughter Justine must decide if she should stop waiting for love and accept a marriage of convenience.

And Olivia's best friend, Grace, wonders if her own husband is having an affair.

In Cedar Cove, nothing stays secret for long.

www.mirabooks.co.uk